THE THINGS
MEN DO

Published by Brolga Publishing Pty Ltd
ABN 46 063 962 443
PO Box 12544
A'Beckett St
Melbourne,VIC, 8006
Australia

email: markzocchi@brolgapublishing.com.au

National Library of Australia Cataloguing-in-Publication entry
Author: Raicu, Stefan.
Title: The things men do / Stefan Raicu.
ISBN: 9781922175144 (paperback)

Dewey Number: A823.4
Printed in China
Cover design by David Khan
Typeset by Wanissa Somsuphangsri

BE PUBLISHED

Publish Through a Successful Publisher. National Distribution, Macmillan & International
Distribution to the United Kingdom, North America. Sales Representation to South East Asia
Email: markzocchi@brolgapublishing.com.au

THE THINGS MEN DO

Stefan Raicu

PROLOGUE

1 July 2011. Sydney, Australia.

The day was grey and miserable in the *greatest city in the world*. Well, that was that my personal view of Sydney, anyway. The fresh southerly winds were sending a strong front of frosty air from that unfriendly continent surrounding the South Pole. With cold, icy whispers, winter was reminding us she was still the undisputed boss.

But not everyone was getting the message, and certainly not the Australian Prime Minister, who kept pushing on with the introduction of a so-called carbon tax, or a tax on carbon dioxide emissions. Her argument, fiercely supported by her *green* allies, was that we had to do something to fight *global warming*. There is undisputed scientific evidence that the planet is warming up, she kept saying over a glass of whisky, from her warm and comfortable Lodge, while many of her less fortunate subjects were shivering with cold.

The Lodge was the Prime Minister's official residence in Canberra – the country's capital and a very cold city in itself during the months of winter. That didn't seem to bother the Prime Minister. The whisky, the warm air conditioning and her spoiling boyfriend made the PM feel *very* comfortable with everything she did, including the backstabbing the year before of Kevin Rude, the former PM, to whom she'd been the deputy.

A female friend once told me that the PM's boyfriend, as a professional barber, also looked after her head. Well, it wasn't much to look after, was it? Another friend said the barber did the PM's *dreadlocks* and gave her a *trim* from time to time as well. Or, maybe she meant a *clip*. As for dreadlocks, as I had no idea what they were, I assumed she meant *dreadful looks*. Anyway, her name was Julia Lizard. That was the Prime Minister, not my friends.

Sitting on a bench facing the lake, my mood was in concert with the weather. I was in a natural reserve along the Henry Lawson Drive in south-western Sydney, reflecting on what had happened to me over the past few weeks.

My miserable thoughts were interrupted by an outbreak of joyous bird chirping. I looked in the direction of the sounds and smiled. Watching that small cute creature, I marvelled how charming he looked. I somehow knew it was a male, the size of a small pigeon and coloured like a magpie, in black and white. But it wasn't a magpie. It was smaller, with his little head round and pretty, unlike a magpie. It looked and sounded rather like a robin, and, though not as vividly coloured, he certainly could sing. I felt I'd seen him before, somewhere on a farm in Sydney's outskirts … and then I named him Robin.

Standing on the wooden barrier at the edge of the pontoon by the lake, Robin was ruffled and looked somewhat irritated. Maybe he was a little annoyed that, right at that moment, he didn't look at his very best. Perhaps he'd just been in a fight, or better, in a *lady robin's bedroom*. But his bad mood didn't last too long. After about a minute of apparent irritability, he began to polish and groom himself, stopping from time to time to release more passionate chirping.

What moved me about tiny Robin was that he looked so happy and content, while all he had in this world was very little. But that's according to human standards. As far as *he* was concerned, besides his life, he had the whole sky and with that, his freedom. It made me wonder: why aren't we, human beings, happy with just that?

1

Thursday, 26 May 2011. Sydney.

My fall down the hill began when I first saw the damsel while browsing at Dowes – a men's clothing store in Sydney's south-west. My presence at Dowes wasn't accidental. The evening before, I'd received on my mobile phone a mysterious text message saying, "Go to Dowes at Westfield Liverpool to meet Kate tomorrow morning. I'm sure you two will hit it off."

I am saying the text message was mysterious because I had no idea who'd sent it. The number shown on the screen did not belong to anyone on my contact list.

In the morning, I had to drive my boss to the airport and after that, though I didn't take the text message seriously, curiosity got the better of me. I decided to go to Dowes, but I arrived a little late. At lunchtime, the store was quite crowded, mostly with male shoppers. While hesitating whether to buy a leather jacket, which I thought was good value at that price, something much prettier caught my eye.

Slim, brunette and quite tall, she looked about twenty-five years old. Had she been in some other place, one would have assumed she was a librarian, or an executive assistant, or even a teacher or a lecturer. She had that intellectual air, partly given by her rimless spectacles and partly by her serious and intelligent-looking face but she was nevertheless very pretty: light complexion, high forehead and cheekbones, full, red lips and large, blue eyes.

Her dark-brown hair was cut extremely short: just two-and-a-half inches, if that. She was conservatively dressed in a white blouse and blue skirt which revealed a nicely shaped pair of legs but only from her knees down.

As she wasn't in a library, or in a classroom or in an amphitheatre, it didn't take me long to decide that her job was that of a salesperson. The fact that she was tidying up and arranging garments on racks in a clothing store, had given me a pretty good indication of her occupation.

Staring at her, I had a distinct feeling that for some reason she was trying to look plain and conceal her natural sex appeal, at which she didn't quite succeed. At the same time, imagining her with high-heeled shoes, make-up and lipstick, I had no doubt she'd look extremely sophisticated and sexy.

It made me wonder: why wasn't she willing to show off her full splendour when the majority of women went to extreme lengths to emphasize whatever *assets* they may possess to make them look more attractive to the other gender? Perhaps she was just shy, I decided.

As for me, I wasn't usually timid, and certainly not with women. That's because there have been over the years quite a number of females conveying to me that I possessed a natural talent of turning them on, even when I didn't mean to.

With dark hair and blue eyes, many said I looked a carbon copy of actor Alain Delon in his youth. They sure had a point, though I'd have preferred to be confused with a superstar from *my* generation. Not that Alain Delon wasn't handsome. He was, but being born in 1935, who would remember him these days? But … there wasn't much I could do about that. Anyway, compared with the French superstar also known as the male Brigitte Bardot, I was quite a few sizes bigger.

Built like a heavyweight and with an Alain Delon look-alike face, I had good reasons to be confident with women. I could probably go on and on describing my good looks, but to cut the long story short, I'll just say I was sexy and I knew it. And modest as well.

So, being naturally confident with women, I moved a little closer to the young lady to have a better look and help me decide my next move.

Watching that doll arranging garments on racks, I'd nearly forgotten why I was there, when a big bloke approached the object of my attention with a wide grin on his face. He was probably in his early forties and, dressed in a business suit, he had a large frame and looked very well fed and quite full of himself.

'How are we this arvo and what's your name, cutie?' he addressed the young woman.

She turned to him and frowned, pointing her index finger at the tag pinned to her blouse, just above her left breast.

I stepped a little closer, read her tag name and flinched. It said *Kate*.

The pampered-looking bloke gaped at her breasts and laughed loudly. 'I know what *those* are. They look pretty well developed, if you ask me. But I was asking what your name is.'

She gave him an unfriendly look. 'Why don't you read my name tag?'

I liked her voice; it was soft, but firm.

He laughed again. 'Sorry, I just can't see it properly, with you in a vertical position. You need to lie down for me, so I can read it from above.'

She checked her wristwatch and twisted around a hundred and eighty degrees, turning her back to him.

He seemed to dislike her move. 'Hey, I was talking to you,' he reminded her.

She returned to arranging garments on a rack, paying him no attention.

The big guy got angry. He looked at me. 'That's crap … that's not customer service,' he articulated his annoyance.

'It depends on what service you're after,' I replied.

He ignored my comment and yelled at the young woman. 'Do you have this wrinkle-free white shirt in my size?'

She turned again, facing him. 'What size?'

His good mood returned instantaneously. 'Jumbo size. It's actually, *super*-jumbo. You'd love it, cutie.'

I could see she was tempted to retaliate, but refrained, just reading her wristwatch again and biting her lower lip.

At that moment, I decided to help her, picking up a garment randomly from the table near me and calling her. 'Excuse me, Kate, could you show me where the fitting room is, please?'

From the way she looked at me, I think she appreciated the distraction. 'Sure, just follow me,' she said and moved towards the rear of the store.

Unlike Kate, the big bloke didn't seem to appreciate the disruption. 'Follow me to the fucking-room,' he said in a high-pitched voice, trying to mimic Kate's.

By then, I'd already had enough of his smart comments. As it happens to me from time to time, I snapped. 'Hey, fatso, be careful with that jumbo-size mouth of yours,' I warned him.

He seemed surprised and angry. We were facing each other, less than two metres apart, only separated by a table with clothes spread on it. A few shoppers were already watching the unfolding scene. Kate had halted as well and was staring at us.

The big guy gaped at me for several seconds as if trying to make up his mind about what to do next. He probably didn't like what he saw. I was a little over a hundred and ninety centimetres tall, or six foot three and weighed a hundred and twelve kilos, with very little fat on me.

Compared to me, he was a little shorter and probably weighed a few kilos more, but there was quite a lot of flab all over his body.

'Be a fucking moron and I'll give you a fat lip,' he said in a menacing manner.

'More likely, I'll kick your fat arse,' I retorted.

More moments of tension followed, as he kept staring at me.

'Scumbag … you're not worth the trouble,' he concluded and walked away.

There was a sound of disappointment from a few shoppers who'd been watching the altercation. They'd probably expected a physical confrontation.

'You didn't really want to use the fitting-room, did you?' Kate asked as the small group of shoppers dispersed.

'No, I didn't,' I admitted.

Gazing at her, I felt waves of magnetism pulsing between us. Whoever had sent that text message, knew what they were talking about, I decided.

'You just wanted to help me, though I didn't need any help.

There are some rude customers, every now and then. We … I mean the girls, just have to put up with it. You know, they say that the customer is always right, even when they are offensive. But … thank you, anyway.'

'I hope I didn't make any trouble,' I said apologetically.

She looked thoughtfully at me. 'I don't know. I think you might have, but … we'll see.'

'I'm sorry, Kate. Causing you hassles was the last thing on my mind,' I said and I meant it.

She nodded. 'I believe you. But there are times when we do things without meaning it.'

When Kate checked her wristwatch for the third time, I thought it was quite safe to assume that she was due for her lunchbreak. The time was just on half-past-twelve. 'If you don't mind, I'd be happy to join you for lunch,' I suggested.

She gave me another long look, seemingly hesitating.

'That's only if you don't have other better plans and if you don't find my proposition too daring,' I added.

'There would be a few other options, but probably not better. I usually have half-an-hour for lunch. But I'll take one hour today,' she announced.

I suggested a sort of bistro or steak house, very close to the Liverpool's Westfield shopping town, where Kate worked. The place was spacious, clean and tidy, filled about three-quarters, mostly with white-collar workers having an early lunch, or maybe a short-day. It was a Thursday and pay day.

We sat at the only available table for two, glancing from time to time at each other and saying nothing for a couple of minutes. I must admit, I felt nervous and even emotional in front of that very delicate-looking young woman.

She gazed at me and turned her eyes down, smiling in a shy manner, when I looked at her. We were acting like teenagers meeting on their first date.

'I'll buy you a drink. What will you have?' I finally asked.

'I shouldn't drink. I'd better have just a mineral water,' she said, unconvincingly.

'I don't usually drink at this time of the day either. But today …' I left the rest in suspense.

'Okay, I'll have a glass of dry white,' she accepted.

I went to the bar and returned with a bottle of sauvignon blanc and two glasses. We tasted the wine and both nodded at the same time, which seemed to amuse Kate. Or maybe she smiled for some other reason.

'Let's see what's on the menu,' I suggested.

While perusing the sheet of laminated paper with food listed on both sides, I noted that Kate looked uncomfortable. There were all sorts of barbequed specialities on the menu and the smell of grilled meats was very tempting.

'I've been here quite a lot. I know the rib-eye steak is very nice and tender,' I said to Kate.

She puckered her lips and I had to admit, she looked very cute when doing it. 'I think I'll have a chicken hamburger.'

There was something telling me that Kate *was* tempted by the smell coming from the grill but had her own reasons to refrain herself. Perhaps she was short of cash, I assumed.

'It's my shout. I am celebrating today,' I insisted.

She smiled. 'I don't even know your name.'

'Sorry, Kate. I probably wouldn't know your name either if not for your name tag. Anyway, I'm Cornel Toma. I am twenty-eight and I landed in Australia … about three and a half years ago.'

Kate gave me a long look, as she was trying to place me. 'Let me guess. Going by the name, I'd say you probably came from … I think, from Spain.'

'Why Spain? If I'm not mistaken, my eyes are blue, which is rather unusual for Spaniards.'

'There are always exceptions. But I'd say, Toma probably comes from tomatoes and as far as I know, tomatoes were discovered in South America by Spanish conquistadores. I assume, in Europe, tomatoes were first grown in Spain as *tomate*. Your ancestors were probably in the business of growing tomatoes, so they were nick-named Tomati, which was then shortened to Toma and became a proper family name. That's why I think you came from Spain,' Kate concluded.

'Your logic is perfect,' I admitted. 'There is only one problem with it.'

Sipping from her glass, Kate frowned, seemingly surprised. 'Which is?'

'I'm not Spanish. Never-ever been in Spain.'

She appeared disappointed. 'Ah … Maybe you came from Gi-braltar.'

She lost me with that one. 'Why would you think that I came from Gibraltar?'

She paused, seemingly focusing. 'Well, if you're not a tomato, maybe the name Toma comes from a tomcat, which is a male cat. If a tomcat is neutered, then it is called a gib. So, a gib, which is a neutered tomcat, is also short from Gibraltar. So, you must have come from Gibraltar.'

'What do you mean by a *neutered* tomcat?' I inquired.

Kate laughed. 'Well … I didn't mean that *you* are neutered. I mean … you might be, but I don't know if that's the case. So, please don't be offended.'

'I'm not offended,' I protested. 'But I still don't know what *neutered* means.'

Kate laughed again and paused, probably trying to find the right words. 'Well … a neutered tomcat is neither a male cat, nor a female cat.'

'You mean a confused cat, like a hermaphrodite?'

She sipped more wine. 'Let's just say a castrated cat.'

Though her comments were not particularly flattering to me, I had to admit, the manner in which she talked and her body language made Kate particularly charming.

And apparently I wasn't the only one finding Kate charming. I noticed at a table nearby, a couple of blokes couldn't keep their eyes off her.

'I can see your logic. But you're placing me back at Spain and I already denied any connection with Spain,' I reminded her.

'But you haven't denied an English association,' Kate said.

She'd lost me again. 'But what's Gibraltar got to do with England?'

'It's true that the small peninsula known as Gibraltar is located at the southern end of Spain, but it is actually a British overseas territory,' she explained.

I never knew that. 'Is it? But … since when is Gibraltar British?'

Kate paused for a few seconds while emptying her glass. 'Gibraltar was actually ceded to England, when the War of the Spanish Succession ended.'

I'd never heard of that either. 'The war of succession? Succession to what?' I asked.

'Succession to the throne,' she said.

I refilled our glasses. 'I see what you mean. Succession to the throne can be a problem if there is only one bathroom in the house. I mean, one bathroom and more than one person can generate a conflict. But going to war because of that …'

Kate gave me an astonished look. She moved her lips to say something, but didn't. She paused for a few seconds and asked, 'So, where are you from?'

'I actually came from Romania. But there *is* a connection between my country and Spain.'

'Both Romanian and Spanish belong to the Latin family of languages,' Kate added.

Is there anything this very sweet-looking woman doesn't know? I asked myself. 'Like Italian and French,' I added, trying to impress Kate with my vast general knowledge.

'And also, Portuguese, Catalane, Provencale, Retoromana and Sarda,' Kate continued.

'Sure … those as well,' I mumbled.

'But I can't really detect a foreign accent in your speech. You speak like you were born here,' Kate complimented me.

My English wasn't perfect by far, and actually, my accent couldn't be confused with that of a person born in an English-speaking country. She was just being nice. 'I don't know about that. But it is true that I learned English at home for many years.'

'You studied English at school?' asked Kate.

I nodded. 'Years five to twelve and then I did a special course after high school. And you?'

She sipped from her glass again. 'I am mostly Uruguayan.'

'That explains it,' I said, knowing that South American women were particularly attractive.

Kate smiled and drank a little more wine. I think she knew what I meant.

'But I have a feeling you're trying to obscure your good looks,' I continued.

She shrugged. 'I've been taught that when women emphasise their good looks, they're asking for trouble. And that's a fact, proven to me again and again.'

'I could see that earlier at the shop,' I admitted.

Kate nodded. 'So, what are you celebrating today?' she digressed.

'I'm on holidays from today.'

'It's an unusual time of the year to take holidays,' Kate noted and she was right. In the month of May, it was the end of autumn and getting chilly in Sydney.

'Unless you go skiing,' she added.

I shook my head. 'It so happens that my boss just flew to Europe.'

'And he didn't need your company.'

'*She*,' I corrected.

'Ah …'

'I'll order the rib-eye steaks,' I offered.

Kate emptied her glass. 'Okay. With salad and French dressing for me, please.'

The rib-eye steak was excellent — deliciously tasty, juicy and tender. We ate and chatted and enjoyed each other's company so much that I bought another bottle of sauvignon. By the time we emptied the third bottle, it was already close to three o'clock.

'I'm late,' Kate suddenly exclaimed, checking the time.

'You mean you might be pregnant?' I asked candidly. I probably wouldn't have asked that rather cheeky question, if not for the wine I'd consumed. Between the two of us, we drank a little more than twenty standard drinks.

'I doubt that one can get pregnant just by drinking sauvignon,' Kate pointed out. Going by the manner she spoke, I knew she was more plastered than me. No wonder: compared to her, I must have weighed some fifty kilos more.

'It depends what one does *after* drinking sauvignon,' I retorted.

'She goes back to work,' replied Kate, standing up.

'I'll take her back to work, just in case that ugly fatso decides to return,' I offered.

'Well, in fact she has the option to finish her shift at four o'clock. If … if you're on holidays, maybe you can see her again at just after four. That's of course, assuming that *she* wants to see you,' Kate added.

'And … does she?'

Kate shrugged. 'Be in front of Dowes at four o'clock and you'll find out.'

I nodded. 'I am expecting her to be late.'

'Before, or after?' asked Kate and strode hurriedly away.

As it turned out, when I arrived at Dowes, a couple of minutes before four o'clock, *Kate* was the one waiting for me in front of the shop.

'I'm sorry, but I thought you said four o'clock,' I apologised.

'It only took a few minutes to Melissa to get rid of me,' Kate explained.

'Who's Melissa?'

'The shop's manager.'

'You mean you've been fired?'

She nodded.

'But so sudden and so quickly? I mean … why?'

'The perfect trifecta,' Kate replied. 'Being late, stinking of grog, and inappropriate conduct towards customers.'

'So, the ugly fatso made a complaint?'

Kate shook her head. 'He didn't. It was just bad luck. Melissa said she was observing the staff to see how skilled they were when dealing with customers. And it just happened that right then I had a difficult client.'

Learning that news, I felt pretty awful, recalling my silly *macho-man* attempt to protect Kate earlier that day, which actually back-fired and contributed to her dismissal. 'I'm really sorry, Kate,' was all I was able to mumble.

'It's not your fault,' she said, rather unconvincingly.

I felt she was just trying to be nice to me. 'Well, *it is* my fault. I shouldn't have interfered.'

'You weren't to know the consequences of your gallant intervention. You thought it was the right thing to do under the circumstances, which it was,' she said.

'Well, it still doesn't make me feel any better.'

What Kate said next left me utterly perplexed. 'I don't feel too good either. But if there is one thing which helps me a lot when I'm stressed … that's a multiple orgasm.'

A few hours later, with Kate naked and looking contented while resting in my arms, I felt confused. Sure, the sexual experience with her had been something way out of the ordinary, but my confusion came from the fact that I hadn't expected that extremely charming and at the same time, serious and intellectual-looking woman to go to bed with me so quickly.

I'd had many similar encounters before, with very attractive dames of various ages and backgrounds, which I'd just taken for granted, without feeling any guilt or remorse. But with Kate, it was different. I was certainly attracted to her and couldn't possibly have said no when she'd hinted of her desire to make love. But after consummating the desire, I felt like I'd committed a sacrilege.

'What are you thinking about?' Kate interrupted my thoughts.

'I don't know. I think … I am confused,' I said, which was true.

'Maybe you're wondering why I was doing a sales person's job at Dowes.'

'That as well,' I admitted.

Kate paused for a little while, then went on: 'I have a degree in medicine, but I didn't want to be a doctor.'

I was surprised. 'What sort of doctor?'

'I specialised in sexual medicine.'

That, I'd expected even less. It took me a while to digest it. Having thought about it for a full minute, I then exclaimed to Kate. 'Ah … that explains it.'

'You mean it explains my … talents in bed?'

Kate's comment made me realise that I'd just made a little gaffe. 'Well, I suppose they didn't teach you how to make love at university.'

Her reply embarrassed me even further. 'So, the assumption is that I learned these skills in some other place.'

I didn't know what to say to that. 'Well, you must have learned about Freud and … all that stuff when you did your medicine degree.'

'Freud is not all about sex.'

Though I never read Freud, as far as I knew, he was a sort of philosopher whose main interest was in sexual affairs. And that's what I said to Kate, or something to that effect. 'I thought Freud wrote a lot of boring stuff at first and when he realised that no one was interested in his philosophical crap, he started to compose pornography.'

Kate burst into laughter. 'That's the best summation of Freud's writings I've ever heard.'

I didn't know if that was supposed to be a compliment. I mean, her words were flattering, but I wasn't sure about the laughter.

'Well … maybe philosophy is not my strong point,' I admitted.

'Maybe you've heard of Kant as well,' she said, still laughing.

'Sure I know of cunt,' I replied with conviction.

'I mean Immanuel Kant, the philosopher,' she added.

'Ah … I was thinking of the other gender …'

'And what else do you know about Freud?' Kate asked, laughing again.

'I'm pretty sure he invented aphrodisiacs,' I said.

'He did not,' she disagreed.

'I think he did. Aren't these … sexual performance enhancers named after Freud?'

'No, they are named after Aphrodite – the goddess of love,' Kate clarified.

'Well, they sound similar. But what else did Freud achieve in life if he wasn't even good enough to invent something like Viagra?'

'Freud founded the discipline of psychoanalysis. That's what he's best known for, not for pornography,' Kate explained.

But I wasn't going to give in so easily. 'I'm sure his sexy-analysis, or whatever you call it, was focussed on … you know … on stuff which we just did.'

Her response was a soft kiss on my lips. 'I don't recall what we just did. Please remind me.'

Half an hour later, I was again reflecting of how deceiving looks could be. I couldn't possibly have imagined when I first saw Kate several hours earlier that such a delicate and conservative-looking woman could possibly be so wild and uninhibited in bed. And another thing bothered me as well: I wasn't sure if Kate's extremely naughty conduct in intimacy was a flaw or a quality. I certainly regarded it as a quality, when rating women generally, but maybe not quite so in Kate's case.

At close to ten o'clock at night, Kate jumped unexpectedly from the bed and began to get dressed in a hurry. Observing her, I thought she looked sensational.

'What's the sudden rush about?'

'I'm late,' she answered.

'You already know you're late?' I asked jokingly.

'I'm not kidding. I should get there by ten and I've got less than five minutes.'

'You should get *there*? What's there?' I asked.

'There is *there*, as opposed to *here*,' she retorted, seemingly annoyed.

'Why go *there*, if you're enjoying being *here*?' I argued.

'Because I'm starting my night shift,' she said, rolling up her black pantyhose.

'You're starting your night shift? Where?'

She hesitated. 'At the hospital.'

'What are you talking about? What hospital?'

'Liverpool Hospital,' she replied irritably as if wondering why I wasn't aware of what hospital she was referring to.

'But … don't you work at Dowes?' I asked.

She gave me a pitiful look. 'I *used* to work at Dowes. Forgotten already?'

I hadn't forgotten that. 'But what's Dowes got to do with the Liverpool Hospital?'

'This is my other job,' she clarified while putting her shoes on.

'So you're working the night shift?'

She nodded. 'I have to run now.'

'But wait. We *are* in Liverpool, just a few minutes' drive to the hospital. I'll get dressed and give you a lift.'

'It's alright. You're too slow. And it's late night shopping tonight. There should be a few taxis near the shops,' she said, rushing towards the door.

'Hey, you forgot your undies,' I yelled after her, noticing a pair of miniscule black knickers on the floor. I knew those panties didn't belong to me and I never had other female visitors before. Not that I wasn't seeing other women – I was, but not in my apartment. My boss and landlord was very particular about that and she'd set the ground rules from the first day I moved into the flat. That day, I'd only dared to take Kate to my apartment because Helen was away and even so, I felt quite uncomfortable about my indiscretion.

'Don't worry about little things. Think Freud, Kant and the big picture!' Kate yelled back, while bolting out of the room.

Indeed, those panties were a very tiny thing. As for Freud, I found the picture *too big* to contemplate. I put on a pair of shorts and walked to the front door, which Kate had left ajar. I pushed the door wide open and looked down the stairs hoping to catch a glimpse of her. Except for a vague trail of perfume, the stairway was empty.

2

Friday, 27 May 2011

After a restless night, I woke up late on Friday morning. I'd fallen asleep very late, with Kate on my mind. No wonder her impression had remained with me all night. As far as I could remember, all my dreams that night and morning had been about Kate. Not a good sign, I reflected, fully aware that I had never remained infatuated with a woman after just a one-night stand.

Since I was an infant, I had developed a strong attraction towards the other gender. As I grew up, taking advantage of my good looks, I've had innumerable casual affairs, mostly with beautiful women. To say that I loved beautiful women would be an understatement. I was obsessed with them. I was a womaniser.

There were two other things not quite right with me. One, I overindulged in drinking on a regular basis and I sometimes did stupid things when plastered. And two, a couple of doctors had assessed me as mentally unstable. Not that I was crazy; only sometimes I had bouts of confusion, anger and even hallucinations and delusion.

That Friday was really my first full vacation day since arriving in Sydney. Though I had told Kate the day before that I was on holidays already, I actually had to take my boss to the airport on Thursday morning. She had to fly to Europe for an interview with the French president and was due back in Sydney in just five days.

Taking advantage of her absence, I had planned to have a ball during the next five days. I had made up a wish-list with things to do while on holidays and had been quite excited about it … but only until this morning. I glanced at my list, but the tennis, fishing, the weekend trip to see my friend Florin and the other activities pencilled on it failed to excite me.

I showered and shaved and had a late, frugal breakfast, still thinking of Kate.

I lived at the time in a very large apartment on the second floor of a block of flats close to the Westfield shopping centre. The three-bedroom, one-hundred-and-sixty square metre flat was architecturally designed, with an open plan and extensive use of natural light.

The whole level above, the top of the building, was taken by an enormous penthouse, about three times the size of my flat. Its only occupant was my boss – the famous Helen Longshanks.

The penthouse and the flat where I lived were connected through an internal stair which led from my laundry into a private hall on the upper level. There was also a private lift servicing the penthouse and my flat.

Helen, who owned the whole building, was happy to let me live rent-free in the fully furnished flat as part of the very gener-

ous salary package she offered me. Earning a six-figure base salary a week plus bonuses and endorsement income for advertising
and attending various functions, Helen could afford to live an
extravagant lifestyle and she certainly did.

She was the most popular radio broadcaster in the country
and a regular columnist in various newspapers and magazines and
employed me as her personal assistant, gym trainer, and chauffeur.
I also did some other personal services that Helen requested from
time to time.

★

I had scored this job with Helen even before arriving in Australia.
I was in the right place at the right time, when Helen visited my
country, back in the summer of 2006. That was almost seventeen
years after Nicolae Ceausescu and his Communist government
had been overthrown, in the gory December 1989 revolution.

Helen had come to Romania as a private tourist. She spotted
me, while enjoying herself on the beach in the luxurious vacation resort of Neptun, on the Black Sea littoral. I had just arrived
in Neptun, planning to notch up a lifeguard job that would have
paid all my expenses for the summer season, which had only
begun a couple of weeks before. It was the middle of June. I was
also intending to pick up a sexy blonde, or a sultry brunette, or
even a redhead vamp, preferably from abroad and have a good
time with her, as I had done a few times before.

I had worked in lifeguard-type positions since I was in high
school and, as an accomplished swimmer and very gifted physically, I knew I had all the skills required for the job. I was twenty-three at the time and had just completed a training course
with the Romanian post-revolution agency equivalent of the

Communist secret police, also known as the infamous Securitate. I was due to commence my new job as a police officer in September, so I had taken the opportunity to have a last extended holiday on the Black Sea. I intended to make memorable and memorable it was.

That afternoon of June, I returned to my towel after a good eight-hundred-metre swim offshore and back and noticed a not very young woman staring persistently at me from a towel a few metres away. I glanced at her and smiled. A few details about her had caught my attention. Her swimsuit and sun glasses, and her towel and handbag – they all smelled of money. It was a high probability that she was a foreigner.

It was common knowledge at the time that foreign females were in the habit of coming alone in droves and enjoyed themselves immensely on the Romanian littoral, though not necessarily on the beach.

This one, staring at me was a redhead, with a reasonably pretty face, upturned nose and a slightly plumpish body. Though she looked some fifteen years older than me, I decided she could very well be the type who needed a toy boy. I spent the next couple of minutes laying on the towel and not looking in her direction, while trying to make up my mind whether to make a move or not. But I was apparently too slow, or maybe she was very fast.

'Do you speak English?' a female voice said next to me, out of the blue.

I looked to my right and up and there she was, standing next to me: the redhead that I had just noticed before. She actually looked more appealing standing up and I took my time studying her. She was petite and, what struck me while gaping at her, were her very long legs compared with her height. She was probably about an inch under a hundred and sixty centimetres tall and had alluring curves in all the right places. She held a towel in one hand and her handbag in the other. I guessed her intention was to move in with me – I mean into my personal space – which I knew was an indication of intimacy.

'Do you speak English at all?' she prompted me, smiling.

'I do, but not as well as you.'

In addition to eight years at school, I had studied advanced English during the four-year police training course, similar to a Police Academy. I also watched plenty of movies spoken in English and listened to British and American music. I was, so to speak, fluent in English, though my accent gave away the fact that my mother tongue was another language.

'Your English sounds pretty good, but how about I give you a little test. Should you pass the test, I might have a business proposition for you,' the redhead said.

Though surprised by her very direct approach, a business proposition was always of interest to me. I became alert. 'A little test? What sort of test?' I inquired.

'An English test, at first.'

She laid her towel on the sand and sat on it, next to me.

'My name is Helen Longshanks,' she introduced herself.

'I'm Cornel Toma,' I replied.

'So, are you ready?' Helen asked.

'Yes, test me please.'

She nodded. 'Okay, let's see how quickly and accurately you can compose a little essay.'

'An essay? An essay on what?'

Helen thought for a moment. 'An essay on a given subject, which I will choose. Let's hear, for example, your description or impression of me. Just say it to me in your own words. I mean, orally.'

'I am not so gifted, orally,' I said.

Helen giggled. 'That's a very different test altogether. Anyway, go on and tell me what your description of me is.'

I had to think about that, which I did for maybe half a minute or so. 'I need you to stand up, so I can see you better,' I decided.

Helen chuckled and stood up in front of me in a posing position. 'Go on, quickly,' she prompted me. 'I don't want to risk developing varicose veins on my legs.'

'Okay, you are a female aged in her … thirties, about a hundred and … fifty-seven centimetres tall and weighing … maybe sixty kilos …'

'That's spot on,' Helen exclaimed. 'Particularly that part about being a female. Go on.'

'You don't seem to be a local, because you apparently don't speak the language. But your English is pretty good.'

She nodded, smiling. 'That's not too bad either. Go on.'

'You have dark red hair, a round, pretty face, full lips and light-brown eyes,' I continued, gazing inquiringly at her.

She nodded, which was a sign of encouragement for me.

'You have a nice body, with very long legs, high hips and round, large breasts,' I added.

Having said that, I paused.

'Is that all?' Helen demanded.

'I think you are a good woman,' I concluded.

It was her turn to pause for a few seconds. 'And I think you just passed the English test,' she announced.

Her verdict pleased me. 'And, what's next?' I inquired.

'The business proposition,' she replied.

'No more tests?' I asked.

'Not right now. I took the liberty to observe you before, when you came back from the sea. That's why I was staring at you – to get an idea of your physical attributes. So, if you thought I was perving at you, it wasn't the case. Anyway, I think you're fit for the job I'm going to offer you.'

'What job?'

'My personal trainer and bodyguard. And maybe more,' Helen stated.

I was excited about her offer. 'And … where's the job?'

'It's very far from here. It's actually right at the end of the earth, one could say.'

I laughed. 'Like … Patagonia?'

'It's further north and further east. It's the city of Sydney, in Australia.'

That piece of news excited me further. 'My best friend, Florin, is in Australia!'

She raised her eyebrows. 'Is he? What's he doing in Australia?'

'He lives there for good. I wanted to go to Australia to see him a couple of years back, but they rejected my application.'

'So, how did your friend manage to stay in Australia for good?' Helen asked.

'His parents did a runner when Florin was little. They went on a trip to Turkey and lost their way back, when Ceausescu was still in charge here.'

'And who looked after Florin afterwards?' Helen inquired.

'He stayed with his grandparents. He loved them so much that he refused to join his parents in Australia, when Communism collapsed here. He chose to stay with his grannies. But when he turned eighteen, he changed his mind.'

'Are you saying that, when he turned eighteen, he suddenly didn't love his grandparents any longer?' Helen asked.

'No, of course he did, but things were going from bad to worse here – like it happens now. And his grandparents actually encouraged him to go.'

'And did you envy him when he left?' Helen asked.

I had to think about that one. 'I don't know. Maybe I did ... a little. But I was definitely sorry to see him go. We lived on the same street and had been the best of friends since we were toddlers right until we finished high school, five years ago.'

'Well, you might see Florin sooner than you'd ever thought,' Helen concluded.

Needless to say, I didn't have to take a casual lifeguard job that summer any longer. The very day I met my prospective employer, we dined out together and later on that night, she tested me again on other subjects which were of interest to her. It's true that those topics appealed to me as well, though I found the rest of my vacation in Helen's company a little awkward.

We had a hell of a good time together, but with everything paid for by Helen. I moved in with her to the holiday town of Mamaia and stayed in the most luxurious resort on the Black Sea littoral, known as the Palm Beach of the East. We ate at the best restaurants and enjoyed the most expensive treats. In summary, I found Helen's lifestyle quite extravagant, to say the least. As for me, I felt quite embarrassed, knowing I was acting like a gigolo who accepted her overgenerous gifts, with nothing to offer in return, except my body. It's true on the other hand that she was very demanding and knew how to get the best out of me, making me work very hard to keep her content and fulfilled.

Anyway, that's how I gave that secret police officer job a miss, landing in the city of Sydney instead; within one-and-a-half years from my first encounter with Helen. With Helen sponsoring me, I was granted two consecutive eighteen-month temporary working visas in Australia. Pulling the strings and making use of her contacts in high places, Helen had then obtained a further six months visa extension, which, at the time when I met Kate, had just expired.

From my first day in Sydney I only worked for Helen and didn't have many reasons to complain about her. Everyone knew and even her enemies admitted that Helen was highly intelligent, extremely sharp and very assertive, usually without being aggressive. At the same time, when circumstances required, she could turn belligerent and quite caustic.

As far as I was concerned, I found Helen to be a good boss: the type who looked after her staff but demanded full commitment and loyalty in return. The only thing that bothered me somewhat was that I had the impression she viewed me as her private and personal property.

Friday, 27 May 2011, Sydney

The day after my encounter with Kate, I walked to the Westfield Shopping Centre, just as I'd done the day before, having dropped off Helen at the Sydney Airport. A stroll to the shops was something that I didn't usually do, as my normal daily schedule was very busy.

Though Helen's show only started at 9 am Monday to Friday, I would usually drive her to the city at around half-past-five in the morning and get there about one hour later. While Helen would go through the morning's newspapers and watch the latest headline news on television, I'd check her electronic mail received overnight, reply to some under her name and bring a few to her attention. She trusted that I had sufficient judgment and common sense to carry out that task, which pleased me, as it made me feel important.

I would also sort her e-mail messages which arrived during the show, reply to some and mark others for her attention. She would usually spend at least a couple of hours in the studio after completing her program at midday, preparing some topics for the next day and I would help her with research and whatever she needed.

I would then drive her back to Liverpool, get changed and take her to the gym. We would swim after the workout, shower and have a very late lunch, or rather tea at the local cafeteria. Back at home, I would usually be on stand-by, waiting for Helen to decide whether she needed me in the evening as well. In summary, though her original offer had been a bodyguard job, I was actually her driver, personal assistant, and gym trainer.

Rhonda Everton, Helen's best friend, was in the habit of visiting her a few times each week and I suppose that's why some rumours about Helen being a lesbian were circulating. Rhonda, nine years younger than Helen, was a highly successful fashion designer. She was blonde and a very presentable woman, standing at nearly six foot tall and weighing about eighty kilos. Everything about Rhonda was big, including an oversized pair of breasts.

One of the things Rhonda and Helen had in common was their very long legs. I knew Rhonda was quite an apparition wherever she went, and especially attractive in a sexual way, in spite of her size. Or, perhaps it was her full, appetising figure that gave her a remarkable sort of sex appeal, but whether Helen was interested in her, I wouldn't know.

I actually knew that, even if Helen fancied women in *that* sense, she also enjoyed the intimacy of men. I suppose that was a good quality, as she did not discriminate based on age, nationality, or … sex, which made her an equal employment opportunity employer.

At Westfield, I wandered aimlessly on the street level and then took the moving stairs to the next floor, stopping and browsing at stores like Roger David, Reuben Scarf, Target and Best and Less and trying to resist the temptation to pop in at Dowes. Though I knew Kate had been fired, there was something that attracted me to that place.

I finally gave in to temptation and walked into Dowes at a few minutes before half-past-twelve. Coincidentally, I'd seen Kate at exactly the same time the previous day. I browsed again at the same racks of garments and found the leather jacket which had caught my eye before. It failed to impress me this time. I guess I was disillusioned. Though I knew Kate couldn't possibly be there, I'd still expected a miracle. It didn't happen.

I exited Westfield and strolled to the Liverpool Plaza arcade, trying to make sense of what was happening to me. I had to admit, the symptoms I had were those of a man falling in love. Reflecting on it, I realised it wasn't only those symptoms that worried me: it was the fact that I'd been so absent-minded, or perhaps, so mesmerised by Kate's presence, that I didn't ask her contact details the previous day.

Then a bright idea struck me: she'd said she had another job at the Liverpool Hospital. What job, I didn't know. She'd mentioned she was a qualified doctor, but said she didn't practice medicine. I tried to think what other job she could have in the night shift if not something to do with patients care. As I couldn't come up with anything, I decided to use my investigative skills to find out. I had completed a police training course, after all.

I strode to the hospital feeling more optimistic. On reaching the Reception Desk some ten minutes later, I got deflated again. I hadn't expected the receptionist to be a bloke. I got along much better with dames and had imagined a sexy blonde sitting at the reception desk.

But the receptionist was nothing like that. I actually found him a little less pleasant than the legendary Cerberus – the multi-headed hound guarding the gates of the Underworld. To be fair, he only had one head on his shoulders, though even so he didn't look much better than the legendary hound. Slim, dark, with large, yellow teeth, he was mean-looking; the type of guy one wouldn't want to see before having their lunch.

I lost my appetite as well. Maybe the health officials employed this type of staff on purpose, I reflected. With the shortage of beds in public hospitals and the whole health system in disarray, they probably went to extreme measures to turn patients away. It would have worked for me as well, had I been a patient only and not so desperate to track down Kate.

'Good afternoon,' I said with a wide, friendly smile.

My good manners didn't seem to impress the bloke on the other side of the reception desk.

'What can I do for you?' he eyeballed at me.

I smiled again. 'My name is Cornel. I'm after some information.'

'What sort of information?' he asked, as friendly as before.

'I'm trying to find Kate. I know she works here.'

Cerberus gave me a bored look. 'Is this Kate a woman, or just a piece of information?'

'She's definitely a woman, and a very pretty one,' I winked, trying to relax him. 'Brunette, five foot ten, nice body, short hair, pretty face …'

'And what's this pretty Kate to you?' he interrupted.

I thought for a moment and found his question intriguing. I didn't really know what Kate was to me and couldn't tell him she was my one-off lover, or sexual partner. 'She's a friend,' I muttered unconvincingly.

He yawned. 'And what would you like to know about Kate?'

'Her phone number would be a good start.'

He looked sternly at me. 'If you're indeed her friend, as you pretend to be, I would expect you to have her phone number.'

I knew he had a point there, but I wasn't going to give up. 'Sure I had her number, but it so happened that I just lost my mobile …'

'And you'd like me to look for your lost mobile?'

Was he perhaps being sarcastic? 'Well, I would appreciate if you could find it, but I doubt it.'

'I doubt it too.' He looked down at a piece of paper on his desk, signalling that he wanted to be left alone.

This isn't going very well, I thought and tried another angle. 'I'm actually concerned that Kate is waiting for me to call, but obviously I can't, if I don't have her number.'

He looked up at me as if he was surprised I was still there. 'Does this imaginary Kate have your number?'

Well, he's as smart as he is good-looking, I thought. 'She sure has, but if she rings me, my mobile phone is missing.'

'And I can see that not only your mobile phone is missing,' he barked.

I didn't know what he meant by that. 'But please, you must help me find Kate. It is important that I talk to her before she starts her shift,' I insisted.

'What shift?' Cerberus bawled again.

'I'm not sure. I know she worked the night shift last night, but I don't know about tonight.'

He nodded. 'I see … And what clinic?'

He got me with that one. 'I think she's been moved to another clinic.'

'She's been moved to another clinic from what clinic?' He sounded really bored.

'From the clinic she was working before being moved to the other clinic,' I explained, praying in my mind he won't ask what her surname was.

'Right … Do you happen to know the family name of this *very good* friend of yours?'

I didn't have a chance to answer. The rock band Visage began singing "Fade to Grey" in my jacket pocket. That was the ringing tone I'd stored on my mobile phone.

'Your mobile is back. That's probably Kate ringing,' Cerberus said grinning.

I made a pirouette and made it towards the exit swearing softly under my breath, without bothering to answer the phone.

I strolled back through the Bigge Park, sat on a bench and thought of another scheme to find Kate. Sure, there was the option of trying my luck at Dowes, but I was reluctant to go back there. Knowing that she'd been sacked from that shop just the day before and being partly responsible for her dismissal, I felt an aversion to the idea.

There was another angle that worried me as well. Though I'd just met Kate, I had a feeling that my sudden interest in her wasn't going to do my mundane existence any good as far as my private life, my employment and my stay in the southern land was concerned.

My working visa had just expired and Helen hadn't done anything to obtain a further extension. It was true that she'd been ill for a while, in addition to being extremely busy, but even so, I had reasons to believe that Helen was in two minds whether to keep me in Australia or not.

I knew she regarded me as her pet, or toy boy and I also knew she suspected that I was seeing other women, of which she did not approve. Though our personal relationship was casual and purely physical, I felt she had developed deeper feelings towards me. But, as she was twelve years my senior, I had a feeling she was prepared to let me go, to avoid useless complications.

3

Helen usually didn't talk about it, but she had mentioned a couple of times that as far as she was concerned, grooming me for another woman was not on her agenda. Though I thought she was sane enough not to nurture long-term romantic dreams about me, I knew she was the possessive type who wouldn't react too kindly if she knew I was infatuated with another, much younger woman.

She had actually made her thoughts and plans on the subject very clear, just one week before flying to Europe, though her announcement was not what I would have expected.

We had dinner in Helen's penthouse that evening, which was a very irregular occurrence. When not participating in various events and functions, Helen usually dined in with Rhonda, and I knew that Rhonda was the one who cooked. However, that evening, Helen had insisted on cooking, which took me by surprise. She didn't really strike me, or anyone else for that matter, as the domestic type who found fulfilment or satisfaction in cleaning, washing, or cooking.

We ate and had a few drinks, talking about trivial things. I felt a little uneasy, wondering if Helen's intention was to create an intimate, romantic ambience. Although at times we went to bed together, it was like I was her servant – a relationship the master seemed happy to preserve.

I knew she loved my body and looks, but she'd only shown her full affection when we'd first met, on the Black Sea littoral. Her behaviour had visibly changed since my arrival in Sydney. Here, she was more distant and business-like and, except when we were in bed, I felt there was a sort of barrier between us, which so far I hadn't been able to cross. Being a prestigious personality, well-known in the high society circles, she was I guess somewhat embarrassed by her crush on a less sophisticated and much younger hunk.

That evening, she wore only a tight satin dressing-gown, which emphasised her curvy figure. Her attire reminded me of Nigella Lawson, the British superstar cook, which made me wonder if Helen was wearing that garment on purpose, because she *wanted* to look like Nigella. As she knew that I fancied Nigella, it may well have been the case.

Another reason that made me uncomfortable was that Helen had overcooked the very expensive beef cut and I hated well-done steaks. She probably didn't like it either, as she made a wry face after having eaten less than a quarter of it.

'I should stick with what I know. Cooking is definitely not for me,' she stated.

'The steak is yummy,' I lied. I liked my steak tender and moist, just as I liked my women. This one was rather dry and rubbery. I mean the steak, not the woman.

'You know what they say about the twenty-first-century woman?' she asked.

I shook my head. 'No.'

'She's well-educated, well-dressed, has a good job, is financially independent, drives a BMW and thinks that cooking and fucking are cities in China.'

'That's not true. I mean … maybe cooking, but not … the other thing. And you're not a twenty-first century woman anyway. I mean, you were born in the last century,' I said, and immediately realised I had made a blunder.

'I wasn't referring to me − I was just talking in general,' Helen clarified. 'So, I'm one century old. Is that supposed to be a compliment?'

I didn't know what to say to that. 'Yes. I mean … no. I mean … I didn't mean …'

She chuckled. 'I got the idea. Anyway, you're probably wondering why I asked you to come over to dinner this evening.'

By then, I'd decided it was safer to adopt a defensive position and deny everything. 'No.'

'It's time to have a chat about your future in Australia,' she went on.

Her words reminded me that my working visa had just expired, which meant that I was now an illegal migrant in the country. 'I'd like to stay here for another summer,' I said.

'That wouldn't be good enough. You need to think of something more permanent. That's of course, only if you want to stay here for good.'

'I like it here. I love Australia,' I said with genuine conviction.

She looked at me in a different way. It was that look that usually told me she was in the mood to make love. She had a remarkable talent of turning me on just by looking at me in a particular way: just as she was doing then. But, if her eyes conveyed a sexual desire, her words said something different. 'Why?'

There was still a lot I didn't know about women, I reflected and shrugged. 'Why? It's because I like it. I mean, I have a good job, a good boss, I am well paid, I live well, in a cosy flat … and … I have nothing to complain about.'

'Is that sufficient?' she asked.

Honestly, it wasn't, but I wasn't going to tell Helen that. 'Yes.'

'You are not being sincere,' she observed. And as I didn't try to protest, she continued: 'You're only twenty-eight and … very handsome. As far as I know, you don't have a girlfriend.'

'But, I … I mean … we … I mean, I don't need a girlfriend.'

She smiled. 'If a girlfriend's only useful purpose is sex … yes – maybe you don't need one. But, are you fulfilled with what you've got?'

She was asking the same question rephrased, so, to be consistent, I had to give her the same answer, even if it was a lie. 'Yes.'

She gave me a doubtful look. 'Okay, let's leave that one for the time being. Tell me Cornel, what are you going to do to stay in Australia for good?'

Good question, I thought, but why is she asking me? '*Me*? I'd thought …'

'I know. You've thought that's *my* job, haven't you?'

I nodded. 'Well, since you've brought me here and looked after me …'

'You know, it so happens that there are certain things which not even I can do. Particularly after the Immigration Minister took offence because of some comments I made on the radio …'

'But, everyone knows he's an imbecile,' I pointed out.

'Not everyone. I mean, the Minister himself doesn't have a clue and nor do the majority of the other ministers. It's a well-kept secret within the government's ranks. So, back to your problem, what do you expect me to do to keep you here?'

I shrugged. 'I don't know. I thought you had it all under control.'

'Well, I actually haven't. You wouldn't be in this rather precarious position if I had.'

'What precarious position?' I asked.

'You know as well as I do that your stay here is now illegal. You could be arrested and deported any minute now. Though I haven't done anything yet, I do have a plan.'

That's better, I thought. 'You do? And what's the plan?'

'You must marry an Australian and do it quick smart,' Helen announced.

'You mean I should marry an Australian woman?' I asked.

'Would you rather marry an Australian man?'

She wants me to marry her, I thought. 'And you?'

Helen refilled her glass and sipped from it. 'I'm not getting married.'

'You're not? I thought you meant …'

'No, I didn't mean you should marry me. Were I about ten years younger … I might consider it.' She'd said it with a note of regret, I observed.

I hadn't expected that. I'd have thought Helen would despise the idea of me hooking up with another woman. 'So, you want me to find an Aussie girlfriend and propose to her?'

'I have one ready for you,' Helen declared.

'You do? And who is she? Do I know her?'

She nodded. 'It's Rhonda Everton.'

She was full of surprises that evening. 'Rhonda? But isn't she your … '

Helen shrugged. 'Why would that concern you?'

What a question, I thought. But, being aware of Helen's libertine ideas, I decided not to follow that line. 'But, how old is Rhonda?' I asked.

'She's nine years younger than me.'

I did the calculations in my mind and determined that Rhonda was three years older than me. I was tempted to point it out to Helen, but I didn't. I knew that talking about age was not one of Helen's favourite subjects.

I thought of Rhonda trying to picture her as my wife. There were two big pluses that came immediately to mind about her. One was her remarkable sex appeal. The other was her passion for good food and cooking. Though the *modern woman* type, she had those *outdated i*deas that *fat was flavour* and she cooked accordingly. The best piece of the chicken roast was the crispy skin, the yummiest bit of the baked pork was the crackling, she said, and even when cooking seafood, she insisted that the higher the ratio of the skin compared to the flesh, the tastier the fish was. Being a gourmand myself, I supported those outdated ideas with plenty of enthusiasm.

'In summary, I took the initiative and found you a *permanent* girlfriend – that's a wife. This will also achieve your permanent residency status in Australia,' Helen continued.

I was simply speechless, but managed a couple of words. 'And you?'

'I happen to be a permanent resident, so I don't need any similar arrangements.'

'I know that, but how about you? I mean … I'd thought that …'

'Considering the circumstances, I can't afford to be selfish. I obviously can't marry you, so I offer you the best alternative option. After all, Rhonda is my best friend.'

Though I'd thought it was better not to pursue that angle, I couldn't help myself, saying, 'But, I'd thought you and Rhonda were … You know what people say …'

'I know and it doesn't bother me. Let them talk. So, are you on?'

I needed time to think about it, so I remained silent, but Helen didn't.

'I take your silence as a yes,' she decided. 'And frankly, you haven't got much choice.'

Generally speaking, Helen was right, but I'd never thought of a fake marriage. 'So, this is what's called a marriage of convenience,' I said.

'What makes you think that?' Helen demanded.

She left me stunned again. 'Well, the whole thing. I mean, I hardly know Rhonda and I'm certainly not in love with her. I suppose she's not in love with me either. Marrying Rhonda would be the last thing on my mind and I certainly wouldn't do it if not for the very reason of staying in Australia, which makes this act a marriage of convenience, or a sham, as they say.'

Helen gave me a stern look. 'This will be a *real* marriage, Cornel. You must understand this basic underlying fact and act in accordance. This marriage must be real to make it look real. You and Rhonda will make the announcement very soon, when I return from Europe. And, for the record, you're lovers already.'

'What do you mean *we're lovers already*?'

'This must be the official version. You and Rhonda have met in my penthouse, shortly after you arrived here. You fell for her as did she.'

'But you know as well as I do that they check these things, to catch people trying to make such arrangements,' I pointed out.

'Let them check. If you and Rhonda tell the same story and I confirm it, what can they do? No one knows what's going on inside my house. And since you've been in the flat downstairs, which happens to be coupled with mine, Rhonda has visited me hundreds of times. Who can deny that Rhonda only pretended to be keen on seeing me, when she was actually after you?'

'And what if Rhonda won't agree with this … play?' I asked.

'It's not a *play*,' Helen said. 'And Rhonda has already agreed. She's said *I do* already and she can't wait to go to the altar. Everything has been dealt with. The only thing you need to do is to propose to her. And sure, from now on, you must not see other women. There must be no playing around under any circumstances.'

'You know that, even if I wanted to, I just don't have the time for that,' I said timidly.

'If there is another woman I don't know about, you must kiss her goodbye,' Helen went on, ignoring my comment. 'This is a must, and is non-negotiable. I am giving you one week to resolve any such personal issues, if there are any issues of this kind. By the time I fly to Europe you must be free and unattached, or a very desirable young bachelor, as they say. I'm leaving on Thursday next week and I expect you to be *cosy* with Rhonda by the time I come back. Rhonda promised she'd be in touch with you before the next weekend.'

I understood what Helen was asking me to do, though I didn't particularly like her plan. It was true that I didn't have another prospective wife lined up, but I did enjoy from time to time the company of a young, sexy lady, when Helen didn't need my services.

The young, sexy lady was a twenty-three-year-old very pretty Czech. Her name was Katarina. Some friends called her Kate. With large, blue eyes, high cheekbones, a very cute face and her hair cut very short, she looked very much like the current affairs celebrity journalist from the 90's and 80's, Jana Wendt.

Now, when I thought about it, I find that Katarina, like Jana, had quite a lot in common with Kate as well. I found all three of them distinctive and very charismatic.

Though I hadn't developed a passion for Katarina, I was very fond of her and the thought of not seeing her again depressed me. I didn't know at the time that in just a week or so, if one Kate in my existence wasn't enough, another one would emerge from nowhere and change my life forever. For falling in love, it was perhaps the right place, but the wrong time and the wrong Kate.

Sitting on a bench in Bigge Park and reflecting on what had happened in the last couple of days, I hadn't noticed the weather turning nasty. The cold, southerly breeze had picked up rapidly bringing with it an ocean of murky clouds.

I walked back towards Westfield thinking of Kate. The fact that, for the first time in my life, my need to be with a woman was not motivated by lust intrigued me.

Dreaming of Kate, I entered the mall without meaning it. I loitered about for a while until I found myself bypassing Dowes. I suddenly recalled that when I was in bed with Kate, her mobile phone had beeped a few times. When she checked her messages, she'd only made one comment. 'Solveig is very insistent, but she'll have to wait.'

'Who's Solveig?' I asked.

'She's my best friend. I'll give her a beep tomorrow. I'm not inclined to waste any minute right now,' Kate had added.

Recalling her words, I wondered if Solveig worked at Dowes as well. That thought gave me an idea. I returned to Dowes and browsed around the shop for a while, making sure I read all the saleswomen's name tags during the process. None of them was named Solveig.

I purchased a wrinkle-free business shirt and headed to the

bistro where I'd been with Kate yesterday. What if Kate was waiting for me over there?

The place was even more crowded than the day before. No wonder – it was Friday afternoon. There were maybe two hundred patrons filling the venue. Kate wasn't one of them.

I tried to replay our entire encounter; I had a rare rib eye steak and a bottle of sauvignon blanc. Neither the steak nor the wine tasted as good. Then another thought struck me.

I bolted from the bistro and rushed home. Perhaps, just as I was searching for her, Kate was trying to find me. And if she did, her task would be much easier than mine. She knew my full name and she knew where I lived. Maybe she was knocking on my door right then!

Sadly, this turned out to be wishful thinking.

I spent the evening watching television, drinking wine and thinking of Kate, but not exactly in that order. I'd drunk too much wine and thought of Kate for too long, when my phone rang. I picked it up, full of hope. 'Cornel Toma speaking.'

There was a pause, then: 'Thank God, I was afraid they'd sent you back to Romania. Why don't you answer your mobile phone?' a female voice said.

I knew the voice, but I didn't think it was Kate's, or rather, I wasn't sure. 'Who's this?' I asked cautiously.

'It's Kate, who else,' the voice said.

'It's Kate?' I asked incredulously. 'Is it really Kate?'

'What's wrong with you today?' The voice seemed amused.

'I've been looking for you everywhere,' I replied.

Another pause. 'Yes? But I haven't got any messages or missed calls.'

'That's because I don't have your phone number,' I was quick to point out.

This time, the pause was longer. 'Why are you talking funny this evening?'

The penny dropped. I should have recognised the voice. The accent was East-European and pretty strong. And her English still needed quite a bit of polishing.

When I realised whom I was talking to, I also became aware that I'd drunk a lot more than I'd intended to. 'Good evening, Kate,' I said in a merry voice and high-pitched tone.

'Where have you been?' she asked.

'Why are you calling yourself Kate?' I answered.

'Because it's short for Katarina. Yes?'

'But you usually call yourself just Katarina,' I pointed out.

'You're funny this evening. Why not call myself Kate? If I call myself … Barbara, or Linda for example, that would be strange, but not Kate. Yes?'

'Yes,' I admitted. 'But you've confused me.'

'Do you know many girls named Kate?' Katarina asked.

'Just two,' I said without thinking.

'Yes? Who is the other one?'

'I don't really know,' I answered candidly.

She laughed. 'What are you doing this evening?'

'Just drinking and … dreaming.'

'Dreaming of Kate?' she asked, laughing again.

'Yes. Dreaming of Kate.'

'You want to see me?' she suggested.

'I do, but … I had too many drinks. Driving is out of the question this evening.'

Katarina lived in a one-bedroom flat in Harris Park, about fifteen kilometres away and I visited her at her place whenever I could. Now, that Helen was away, she could have come to me, but she didn't have a car, or a drivers licence.

'You could take a taxi,' she said.

I didn't say anything, while trying to think of an excuse.

'Yes?' she prompted me.

'No. I'm very tired. I won't be much fun this evening.'

'That's what women say when they don't want sex. You know … *I am very tired and I have a bad migraine*,' she said in a comical voice.

'Yes,' I said.

'You are very tired and you have a bad migraine?' she asked.

'No, that's what women say when they don't want to have sex.'

'But you are not frigid,' she retorted.

'This evening, I am not *rigid* either.'

'I think you don't love me anymore. Yes?'

'Love is not only about sex. You know, like Freud. People think that Freud only wrote about sex,' I explained, trying to show off some of the things I'd learned from Kate.

'But you said before that you never read Freud,' she reminded me.

'True, but I read a lot yesterday.'

'I think you are pulling my leg. I know you like me with my legs up,' Katarina added laughing.

'Legs up and heads down. We are all like that in this southern land,' I said, philosophically.

'Yes. And … what are you doing tomorrow?'

'Tomorrow is Saturday,' I said.

'And you're on a short holiday, while the cat is away,' she reminded me.

'The cat?' I said.

'Yes – the pussy,' Katarina clarified. 'You know, we have a saying in my country. When the pussy is away, the mice climb on the table and play.'

'I think you mean the pussy cat,' I corrected.

'Yes, the pussy, or the cat. It's the same thing,' Katarina explained.

Maybe her English was better than I'd thought. I didn't know that cat and pussy were one and the same thing.

'Don't you like little pussy?' Katarina went on.

'I do, but I'm a gib,' I confessed.

'You're a what?'

'A gib,' I repeated and spelled gib for her.

'So, what is a gib?'

Good question, I thought. Now I only recalled quite vaguely what Kate had told me a gib was. It was something to do with a tomcat, or a tomato. 'A gib is a ... a castrated tomato,' I said.

There was a long pause, then. 'I'll talk to you tomorrow. Now, Hannah is ringing me,' Katarina said and hung up.

Thank God for that, I said to myself after the line went dead.

I drank three more glasses of wine and thought of Katarina and Kate, wondering what Kate's full first name was. Maybe she was a Catherine, or Ecaterina, or Catrina, or Kathryn, or Catriona, or ... maybe just Kate. But what if she was named Katarina? The thought confused me even further.

I took my clothes off and put on the wrinkle-free business shirt. I watched myself in the mirror. The guy looking back at me seemed as confused and pretty well plastered. I crashed into bed with too many Kates on my mind.

4

Saturday, 28 May

On Saturday morning, I folded the wrinkle-free business shirt, put it in a Dowes plastic bag together with the receipt and returned to the store about half an hour after it had opened. At that time of the morning, there were only a handful of shoppers in the store.

This time I was lucky. While pretending to study the same leather jacket which I'd seen twice already, a very pretty blonde offered her assistance. I stared at her for a long while. I liked her a lot better than the leather jacket, I decided.

I read her name-tag and gave her a well-rehearsed charming leer, which I knew made quite an impression on the other gender. I thought she liked it too, as she returned a languorous smile. Her name-tag said *Solveig*. I read it and said. 'Solveig? It must be my lucky day.'

The blonde raised her eyebrows. I noted she was as tall as Kate and, unlike Kate, she had on plenty of lipstick and mascara. On face value, this dame was more sexually appealing than Kate, I noted and my naughty thoughts didn't stop there. Imagine having a sexual encounter with Kate and this blonde together! They'd be a sensational pair.

'If your lucky day means a discount … you're not very lucky. These leather jackets have been reduced already – twice as a matter of fact,' Solveig said.

'Maybe you can help me with this,' I said, pointing at the bag.

She glanced at the bag and asked, 'You're after a refund or exchange?'

I shook my head. 'Neither. By the way, I am Cornel. Kate sold me this wrinkle-free shirt the other day. She promised the shirt was wrinkle-free, no matter what I did with it, which I doubted at the time. We had a bet on it and she agreed to go out with me if I won. Now, having worn it for a full day, the shirt is quite wrinkled, so it looks that I did win.'

The blonde looked sceptically at me.

I didn't tell her that I'd slept with that shirt on about seven hours. That little detail wasn't relevant, I thought. 'But the trouble is that I can't claim my winnings, as I've lost Kate's mobile number. Actually, my mobile phone has gone missing in the meantime,' I continued.

Solveig gave me another suspicious look. 'And how would you suggest I could help?'

Well, blondes deserve their reputation, I reflected. It's quite obvious what I want from you, isn't it? I was inclined to say, but I decided to be diplomatic. 'Since it's a Saturday, I thought it would be a good time to take Kate out. It looks that she's not working today, which makes it perfect. That's if I could talk to her, which

I can't, unless you help me.'

This time, I thought she looked amused. 'It puzzles me that Kate agreed to go out with you.'

'Maybe she was very confident that she'd win the bet,' I suggested.

I had a clear feeling the blonde was amused. 'You're sure you've got your facts right?'

'But ... why not? Isn't that what young, beautiful ladies and handsome lads do?'

'Not Kate,' Solveig said with conviction. 'Her husband is insanely jealous.'

Kate hadn't mentioned anything about a husband and didn't wear a wedding ring either. 'Ah ... I didn't know she was married. We actually had lunch on Thursday, but she didn't mention that.'

'What *did* she mention?' Solveig inquired.

'She said you were her best friend. That's why I thought you'd help me.'

She paused, seemingly hesitating.

I looked imploringly at her, which probably helped my cause.

'I shouldn't do this, but ... You have the receipt?' Solveig asked.

'I do, but as I've said, I'm not asking for a refund.' I was reluctant to show her the receipt, knowing that if she read it, she'd see that I'd purchased the shirt the day before, which was *after* Kate had been sacked from the store.

'Just give it to me,' Solveig demanded.

'Well ... I'm keeping the shirt. Why would you need the docket?'

'You want Kate's mobile number, or not?' Solveig asked.

'I do, but I only need her number, not a refund,' I stressed again.

She gave me an annoyed look. 'I'll write the number on the back of the docket.'

I sighed with relief. 'Ah … that's a clever idea. I'd never have thought of that. There it is.' I handed the docket to her, praying in my mind she wouldn't read the details.

She glanced at the receipt and wrote a number on the back. 'Good luck,' she said, handing the docket back to me.

'Thanks a lot. I've been lucky enough, so far. I mean, I've won the bet.'

'You'll need more luck than that,' Solveig said. 'For some reason, Kate isn't answering her mobile. I've tried to talk to her and left a few messages, but she hasn't returned my calls, which is very unusual.'

'She's probably too busy trying to find me,' I replied jokingly.

'I hope so,' Solveig said, but not with a lot of conviction.

I noted her eyes held worry.

Back at home, I called the number which Solveig had given me quite a few times. All I got back was a recorded message. Well, at least I knew the number was correct, as the welcome message said so and also disclosed her full name: Ecaterina Morales. It sounded of Spanish origin, which made sense. Kate had said she was *mostly* Uruguayan.

Having learned from Solveig that Kate was married, I knew very well I should mind my own business and leave her alone. Moreover, the date that Helen expected me to have with Rhonda Everton was very much on the back of my mind. I knew I should act sensibly and keep my promise to Helen. She'd asked me to cut all ties with other women and date Rhonda that very weekend, as a prelude to marrying her. But acting sensibly was not high on my priority list.

I checked the phone directory and found about seventy Morales. Two of them had the initial E and just one was a K. I wrote those three addresses on the back of one of Helen's business cards and jumped into my Mazda CX-9 to have a look at them. It was early Saturday afternoon and the weather had turned glorious.

The first address was in a block of flats in Macquarie Park. It took me nearly an hour in that very busy Saturday traffic to reach the address, but this time, luck was on my side. I had a good look at the very large building, trying to decide in my mind how many flats were on each floor. The one of interest to me was number 38. There were three levels in the building, including the ground floor and I estimated there would be some 15 flats on each level. Then I realised that the letterboxes on the front of the building would give me that exact information. There were 48 letterboxes, plus one for the Strata Title Manager. There was some correspondence hanging out from several of them, including number 38. I took a letter out from box 38 and read the name of the recipient. It said Mrs Esmeralda Morales. And that was that. Though Morales was Morales, Esmeralda couldn't be Ecaterina. She wasn't my Kate.

I read the remaining two addresses trying to decide where to go next. My mobile phone rang during the process. That distraction didn't help me with making up my mind. I guess I was the type of guy who couldn't handle multitasking very well.

'Cornel Toma speaking,' I said unimpressed.

'What time do you want to see me this afternoon?' a female voice asked.

I knew the voice, but couldn't place it right then. 'What time?' I repeated her question.

She paused a little. 'It's nearly three o'clock. How about five at your place?'

'My place? Do you know my place?'

She giggled. 'Even in these new circumstances, Helen is still my best friend and she doesn't mind. You know she's actually instigated all this. You'll be alright for … five?'

I finally clicked. It was Rhonda Everton – my future significant other. 'Sure, see you at about five, if Helen doesn't mind,' I said absently.

'I can't wait,' she added.

'That makes two of us,' I said robotically.

She hung up.

I sighed with frustration. I didn't really feel like seeing Rhonda that Saturday.

I drove to Concord West, where, according to the White Pages, the second E Morales resided. Concord West was one of the more affluent inner-western suburbs, located next to the waterfront village of Canada Bay. The street of interest to me was between Concord Road and a public open space, very close to a very popular golf course. It was a verdant and very lush-looking area.

I drove slowly along the narrow street until I spotted the address. I stopped the car in front of the house and remained seated with the engine running. Having had a good look at the house, I doubted that Kate lived there.

The two-storey mansion was big enough to easily accommodate a large Greek family. And I reflected, even if Kate had kids, which, I didn't think made sense, at her age, it was unlikely she had more than two. Still, there was a remote possibility that she might have eight kids, if she'd had two sets of quadruplets.

Maybe her husband was very rich and could afford such a mansion. Or, perhaps Kate was very rich herself, but then, if that was the case, why was she working two jobs? After a bit more intense thinking, I decided it was likely that I was at the wrong address.

I peered at the letterbox, but had no luck this time. There wasn't any piece of correspondence hanging out from it. I walked up the few steps to the porch leading to the main entrance and congratulated myself for doing it. Luck had struck me again. There was a polished metal plaque affixed to the front door, which read: Mr Luigi Maslini and Mrs Ecaterina Morales.

For some reason, I was certain this was my Kate, which made me pretty happy. And I assumed that Luigi Maslini was Kate's husband, which I didn't like that much.

I stood in front of the door and did some more thinking, but not a lot. The doorbell was within a metre of my reach and the temptation too big. I pushed the button and listened to its echo inside. I waited half a minute. Nothing happened. I pushed it again and kept it pressed for several seconds. Still nothing happened.

I climbed down the stairs to the side gate and read the sign on it. It said: *Private Property. Keep Out.* That gave me enough motivation to enter the premises. I pushed one side of the gate. It wasn't locked. I wondered why they bothered to display a sign on it. I shrugged and entered the private property, my thinking being that, if the owners were serious about keeping intruders out, they should lock the gate.

I walked down on the driveway leading to a double garage not attached to the house. With the back of the house facing west, the afternoon winter sun was shining softly on the mansion's windows. It was nearly four o'clock.

There were quite a few windows gleaming in the sun and also a couple of doors downstairs, on that side of the house. All windows and doors were protected by heavy-duty security screens – just like the front of the house. I tried to open the first security door, but it was locked. The second one, in the middle, wasn't. It made me wonder again what the point of all those precautions was when they didn't even bother to lock the gate and all the doors.

I stepped into a large sun-room furnished with a couple of soft-looking leather sofas and four armchairs of the same material. There were also a couple of bookshelves aligned on both the left and right walls from the entrance and a timber coffee table in the middle.

On the right of the sunroom was a laundry and full bathroom. Another door, opposite the entrance, was wide open. It went into a dining room, connected with an eat-in kitchen to the right. On the left was a family-room leading into another living area which occupied the front of the house, divided into two by a hallway and the staircase in the middle.

I had a look around the living areas, but couldn't find what I was after. As in most houses, I expected some photos on display, but there weren't any, which frustrated me. Though pretty sure I was in the right house, I needed some definite identification to confirm my assumption. Trying to put my mind to rest, I searched several drawers in the living areas. I found plenty of postcards, business and private letters and I glanced at a few, randomly.

A private health insurance statement told me that Ecaterina was twenty-seven and Luigi fourteen years her senior. That made Kate one year younger than me and Luigi one year older than my boss, Helen. It was natural for me to conclude that Kate would be a better match for me, as Helen would be for Luigi.

I also examined a few drawers in the kitchen and discovered something which made me think that this Luigi Maslini could be quite a dangerous character. The item that caught my attention was a .32 Colt automatic pistol. There were also several magazines of ammunition. I reflected on it for a good couple of minutes and decided that perhaps Luigi possessed a firearm permit, which didn't make him a dangerous character, though a man armed with a handgun was always dangerous, whether he possessed a firearm permit or not. I hesitated and left the pistol in the drawer.

I continued my search in the sun-room at the back of the house, but still, I found no photos. Though Ecaterina's age had given me another good indication that she was indeed *my Kate*, I wasn't completely satisfied. I put my cabbage to work again and determined as a consequence that I needed to have a look upstairs as well.

I climbed the staircase to the upper level and found a number of closed doors all around: I counted eight of them. It made me wonder again: why would the owner of such a large home need to work two jobs? Perhaps this Ecaterina wasn't my Kate after all. As I didn't like that conclusion, I decided to continue my search.

I stepped into one of the rooms. It was a very generously sized bedroom, with a walk-in wardrobe and ensuite. Probably a guestroom, as it was very clean and tidy and looked like no one was sleeping there. I checked the drawers in the room but found nothing of particular interest: just fresh Manchester sets, toiletries and cosmetics.

I walked back into the hallway and stopped suddenly. There was a noise coming from downstairs. I dropped flat onto the soft carpet and listened. Someone was unlocking the front door. The next minute, there were voices: several male voices, talking very loudly. Even so, except a few words, like *casa, birra, cazzo* and a few others, I couldn't understand what they were saying. They were speaking Italian.

As they advanced inside I saw one of them through the gaps in the wooden balustrade. The others had remained in that part of the house where I couldn't see them. The one in my view was a very massive bloke, dark, with high sideburns and a gang-ster-like looking face and wearing a leather jacket, similar to the one I'd seen at Dowes. He reminded me of that actor Al Letieri, the Italian dude who was the scary hoodlum in *The Godfather*.

I wondered for a moment if this Al Letieri look-alike pur-chased *my* leather jacket and the thought filled me with envy. I then thought he might be Kate's husband and my envy turned into a silent rage. As I kept staring at him, my heart skipped a beat. I realised that, as I was watching him, he could spot me as well, if he looked in my direction. Luckily, with the blinds closed, the upper level of the mansion was only dimly lit. The view downstairs was much better, but the massive bloke quickly vanished from my sight.

The men continued to talk loudly. Rather they were yelling at each other, but I knew that wasn't unusual among Italians. After a couple of minutes, the same bloke that I'd seen before walked towards the back of the house, whistling a tuneless song. He returned carrying a few bottles. I guessed it was beer, which made me realise I was thirsty too and craving for a cold beer.

The fact that Al Letieri was carrying the beer made me assume that he was the host, or in other words, Luigi Maslini. I heard bottles being clinked and voices saying *cin-cin* and *salute*. They were toasting – but what? I wondered. Next, they were yelling again, but not for long. Suddenly there was silence.

I grabbed my mobile phone from one of my pockets as quickly as I could and pressed the *off* button, but of course, I couldn't have done it fast enough. My black, little gadget had beeped very loudly. Someone had just sent me a text message.

I rolled onto the carpet away from the balustrade. It seemed that the silence on the ground floor lasted for ages. Actually, the house had been silent for a few seconds only. Then I heard footsteps downstairs. The footsteps stopped at the base of the stairway. A voice shouted in English, 'Is anyone there?'

I nearly let out a *no*, but refrained just in time, realising that in this particular case, *no* would actually mean *yes*. Why are you so stupid? I asked myself angrily in my mind. Why don't you learn from past mistakes? I continued, recalling yesterday's episode with Cerberus, when my mobile had rung in my pocket just after I had pretended I didn't have a mobile phone.

There was more silence downstairs, then another voice asked something which I didn't understand. This time, I wasn't tempted to answer. Nor was I sure what the question was. I guessed someone had repeated the same question in Italian. So, I remained quiet, questioning my intelligence again. I had to admit, my brains weren't functioning too well that day. It was perhaps because of too much wine from last night.

While these thoughts crossed my mind, a phone rang downstairs. It was actually a voice that started singing, startling me. Another voice then said 'Alberto Gazzara' and I thanked God for that. For a second, I thought it was my phone, though I knew I'd turned it off. It also transpired to me that my name wasn't Gazzara and not even Alberto.

But the day was full of surprises. The guy who answered his phone began to talk in English – a one-way conversation, or a monologue, as they say. And it suddenly occurred to me that I'd heard that voice before. Why is he talking to himself? I wondered. Well, maybe I wasn't the only nut, I thought and I felt a little better. It took me a little while to realise he was talking on the phone and I couldn't hear what the other part was saying. That's why, it sounded like a sort of monologue. Wow, I worked that out pretty smartly, I congratulated myself.

I listened to what the familiar voice was saying downstairs, without understanding the meaning of it. 'The goods are leaving next week.' Then there was a pause, and, 'We don't know for sure,' and another pause. Then he said, 'If I can get all the papers in time.' Another pause, then, 'Yes, they're all top class – the cream of the cream. I'm sure Don will be very pleased.' There was a longer pause, and, 'No, Luigi is being held here. He's got some personal stuff to sort out.' He paused again and said, 'Yes, I'll pass it on to him. Sure, but Adolfo is certainly coming.' Another minute passed, and then the voice said. 'Sure, we'll talk again tomorrow.'

I guessed he'd hung up, as the yelling began again – still in Italian and a little louder than before. I heard steps going to the back of the house and returning – it was probably Luigi with more beer. It occurred to me those blokes were having a very good time drinking beer and shouting at each other, which meant they wouldn't leave in a rush.

After one hour of listening to them, I was getting pretty bored. Maybe the fact that I didn't understand what they were saying had something to do with it. At the same time, I knew very well that I was in a quite precarious position, practically trapped in that mansion. I was pretty sure by then there were four blokes downstairs, including Luigi. Four blokes usually didn't scare me, but this time, I knew there was at least one handgun in the house. And, as strong and fit as I was, a gun always frightened me.

I thought I'd better start to move a little, as my limbs were getting numb. I decided to explore. It wasn't just curiosity; I had to find a way I could get out of the house. Sure, I could have just walked casually downstairs, say hello and stroll out through the front door, but somehow I doubted that the Italians would just greet me and wish me a good evening without taking a personal interest in my affairs.

Taking great care and moving like a shadow, I had a look in

every room on level one and got quite depressed. There were *Crimsafe* security screens fitted on all windows. I knew these security screens were the best and toughest one could get anywhere in the country and practically impossible to break without specialised equipment.

It was past five o'clock already, which reminded me of my planned date with Rhonda. I had serious doubts I was going to make it. I did some more thinking and analysed my current situation. I was trapped in a house with four blokes whom I didn't know, unlikely to be friendly.

I thought of sending a text message to Rhonda, but I was afraid to switch my mobile phone on. My mobile was very noisy when I turned it on – nearly as noisy as Katarina when she was turned on. I wondered how noisy Rhonda was.

By six o'clock, I was thirsty and cranky and very tired. I stepped into a bedroom which didn't seem to be used – as most were in that house – locked the door from inside and left the key in the lock. I drank tap water from the ensuite and lay on the bed and thought of stuff.

I thought of my mother, who was barely five years older than Helen and that made me feel very old. I thought of Dad, who ditched Mum and hooked up with a sexy vamp just one year older than me. With my stepmother being just twenty-nine, it made me feel an infant. I then thought of Helen. I decided that under the circumstances, she must be a paedophile.

I thought of Rhonda and Katarina and Kate and fell asleep. That probably says something about how superficial I am. Or, maybe I was just very tired. I was dreaming that Al Letieri had smashed the bedroom's door and was coming at me with a knife, when I suddenly woke up. There was a noise on the upper level of the mansion.

It took me several seconds to come to my senses. I saw light coming from under the door and I heard a door being slammed and then a door being opened. After half a minute or so, a door was slammed again and then a door opened very close to the bedroom where I was.

I got up and stepped to the door. I listened at the door for maybe twenty seconds. Once more, I heard a door being slammed. A few seconds later, I heard my bedroom's door handle being turned. Someone was trying to get in, but the door was locked. There was silence afterwards.

The silence lasted a couple of minutes. I noted that the whole house was very quiet, not only the upper level. I guessed that Luigi's noisy friends had left and whoever had tried to enter my room was Luigi himself. I read my phosphorescent wrist watch. It showed twenty-two minutes past eight.

I tried to think if I should get out of the bedroom, but couldn't make up my mind fast enough. The door handle was being turned again. Then, a key was pushed into the lock. The key didn't go through. It couldn't, as I'd left another key in the lock.

There was more silence, then a voice – Luigi's voice. 'Open the door, Kate. I know you're in there. Don't try to make trouble again. You know you'll be sorry if you do.'

The voice was quite calm, but somewhat different than earlier that evening. I assumed it had been quite a bit of alcohol that made it different – thicker and a little slurred. I also guessed Luigi didn't have any idea that it was an intruder hiding in that bedroom. He believed Kate was in there. That suited me, I thought. I wasn't going to tell him it was me and not Kate.

'Open the door, Kate,' he said again, in a more threatening tone.

I didn't open the door, one reason being that he'd asked Kate to open it and I wasn't Kate.

Several seconds passed, then Luigi went on. 'Don't be a silly cow. You know you're not doing yourself any favours if you're being stubborn again.'

He only paused for a few seconds and continued. 'Listen bitch, I'm losing all my patience with you. You've made a fool of me in front of my buddies, already. I knew you were hiding in there all the time, playing with your fucking mobile. We'll find out later who you were chatting to. We'll also find out where you slept in the last couple of nights and with whom. You had no idea I only pretended to hit the road on Thursday morning, you stupid whore. We'll sort this out, quick smart. Now just open the door and let's have a little talk.'

Ten more seconds passed till Luigi spoke again. 'Listen, cow, I'll give you one minute to get out. If not, I'll get you out anyway and I'll give you a belting as well.'

He sounded pretty angry, but I was getting pissed off too. Being Kate's husband, he hadn't been in my good books to start with. And now, by threatening her with *a belting*, he'd made it even worse. And, why was he calling Kate a cow, anyway? To me, she looked nothing like a cow.

Once a minute and a half passed, there was a dreadfully loud thump on the bedroom's door. Luigi must have given it a very hard shoulder hit. The door, made of solid timber, stood. That door needed a rhinoceros charge to crack it. I guessed Luigi wouldn't have attempted to break it that way if not for the drinks he'd consumed.

Next, I heard Luigi swearing and screaming very obscene words. His shoulder must have hurt pretty badly. I did some rapid thinking. Considering the state of rage he was in, he was capable to grab an axe and break the door. Or worse, I thought, he could fetch that pistol from the kitchen and make use of it. It was time for me to act.

Quickly, but as quietly as possible, I unlocked the door and opened it a fraction, then posted myself a metre from it, tight to the wall. He stormed in like a charging bull, the door flung open and bashed against the wall and Luigi tumbled with momentum to the floor halfway across the room.

I watched him rise to his feet, swearing.

I could see him pretty well, but it took him several seconds to adjust his eyes to the semi-darkness. The lamp in the room was turned off, but there was some light coming from the hallway which gave me a good view of my visitor.

It was definitely the same bloke I'd noticed downstairs a few hours before. From close range he looked even bigger and more menacing. Maybe the rage added to his scary image. He wasn't armed, which pleased me. It made things much simpler for me, but not for him, I thought.

'Turn on the light, you whore,' he screamed.

I pushed the electric switch and watched him, waiting for him to make a move.

His facial expression changed from rage to bewilderment and back to rage again. He gaped at me with hatred in his eyes. 'So, it's you, who's having it off with my wife,' he sneered. 'Who the fuck are you and where's the whore?'

I shrugged. 'Are you telling me this is a whorehouse?'

He didn't like that. 'Being a fucking smart-arse? Where's Kate?'

'But I don't know where Kate is. I'd like to know where she is too. That's why I'm here. I was looking for Kate, but I couldn't find her.'

'You're lying,' he sneered again. 'Where's the slut?'

'There's no one here. Have a look and please yourself,' I offered.

He rushed to the ensuite, came back and looked under the bed, then opened the wardrobe and peered inside. 'She's not here,' he said, still bewildered.

'That's what I've just said,' I reminded him.

He blinked his eyes, staring angrily at me. 'I can see she's not here, but where is she? There is no way she could have got out of here. What have you done to her, you fucking moron? And who are you, anyway?'

'So, Kate hasn't come home in the last couple of nights?' I asked, ignoring his questions.

The rage got the better of him, again. 'I bet she was fucking you, that's why she didn't turn up at home. You've fucked her, haven't you?'

Luigi's admission that Kate hadn't come home in the last two nights pleased me. It was good news, as far as I was concerned. It meant that, after her encounter with me, Kate had decided she'd had enough of this beast and dumped him because of me, I assumed.

'You've fucked her, haven't you?' Luigi shouted again.

I didn't know what to say to that. If I said I hadn't, that would be lying. If I admitted the truth, he wouldn't react too kindly, I suspected. So, I gave him a sort of *politician's answer*. 'That's a private matter between Kate and me.'

'*Private matter?*' he said and I detected a tremor in his voice. It told me his temper had reached boiling point. He stepped closer to me. 'It's time I teach you a *private lesson*, you moron.'

He threw a wild punch at my head with all his weight behind it. That was some one hundred and twenty kilos. That blow would have flattened me, had I been a split second slower. Though I'd anticipated such a move, it took me by surprise. I hadn't expected him to be so fast.

I shifted sideway, enough for him to lose his balance. He fell forward to his knees. I turned around and thrust my left foot onto his backside giving him a shove which sent him flat, his face hitting the floor very hard. Even with the floor being carpeted, the contact must have done quite a bit of damage to his visage, which didn't look very flash anyway.

'What about that belting you were boasting before?' I reminded him.

He didn't answer; just released a noise like a horse's snort.

'You should have said you were a goose,' I continued to menace him. 'I'd have been more careful not to rumple your mug.'

He swore at me, moving his limbs in a weak attempt to get up.

It would have been easy for me to kick in his guts or his face, but I'd been taught to always stick to the fair-play rule, unless I was in a deadly situation. At the same time, I felt a sort of guilt towards him, because of that *private matter* between Kate and myself. He didn't need a bashing as well, I decided.

As he was stumbling to get to his feet, a better idea came to me. I snatched the key from its lock, stepped out of the room and locked the door from outside. While climbing down the stairs, I heard him screaming and slamming the door with his fists. I bolted out of the house and strode to my car without looking back.

5

It was nearly ten o'clock when I got back home. I gave the private lift a miss and climbed the stairs up to my flat. At the front door I could hear music coming from inside. It was nice dance music. I wondered for a moment if Helen had returned from Europe early. Maybe she felt intimidated at the prospect of meeting the French President and had given Paris a miss. I quickly discarded that idea – there was no one in this world that would intimidate Helen.

Then another thought came to me. Perhaps it was Kate. Maybe she somehow found her way inside my flat and was waiting for me. It was possible that she nicked one of my duplicate keys without my seeing her. That's maybe why she left her panties on the floor – in exchange for the key. The thought made my heart skip a beat.

I turned the doorknob and pushed the door very gently. It was open. I stepped inside the hallway and into the living room.

A mouth-watering smell of pork roast welcomed me. The other thing that welcomed me was an extremely pretty twenty-three-old female Czech. She turned the CD player off, threw herself at me and kissed me on the lips.

'At last, you decided to come home,' she said.

I noted she wore a black, short slip and was bare-footed. Indeed, she looked very pretty. What threw me off a little was that she looked quite a bit like Kate.

'How did you get in?' I asked.

She just pointed to the door.

'That seems quite reasonable, but I'm pretty sure I locked the door when I left.'

She shrugged. 'Yes? Maybe you did, but your housekeeper let me in. She's very nice.'

'She's very nice? Which one?' I asked.

'You have more than one housekeeper?' Katarina inquired.

I did some thinking, realising that I'd turned my mobile phone off and hadn't checked it for missed calls or messages in several hours. I remembered Rhonda and the date we were supposed to have that evening. I didn't think she was impressed being stood up. I thought some more and presumed that Rhonda had arrived at my flat and got in through Helen's penthouse, to which I knew she had a spare key. That was a little intrusive, I thought.

'So, she told you she was my housekeeper?' I asked cautiously.

'I think she's your cook as well. Yes? She cooked a very nice pork roast for you.'

Indeed, the smell was very tempting. And I was very confused.

'So, what time did you arrive here?' I asked, wanting to find out exactly what had happened and the chronology of events.

'It was after seven,' Katarina said. 'I'd rung your mobile and left a message, but you didn't reply. I thought you were very busy and

I knew the pussy was away …'

'The pussy?' I asked.

'Yes. Remember that saying which I told you last night? When the pussy is away, the mice climb on the table and play. Yes?'

I did remember something, but vaguely. 'Yes. So, when you came here, the pussy … I mean, my … housekeeper was inside and she let you in.'

'Yes, but I knocked on the door first,' Katarina explained.

'And … did she ask you who you were?'

'She said *you must be Cornel's girlfriend* and I said *yes*.'

Recalling Helen's demand to cut all ties with any other woman and dedicate myself entirely to Rhonda, I felt a headache coming. 'You said yes?' I asked.

Katarina nodded. 'Yes.'

'And what did she say?' I continued.

'She said her name was … something and I said I was Kate. She was very nice. She said that I was a pretty girl and Cornel and I were a good pair together. She was very nice, too.'

'You mean she looked nice, or she was a nice person?'

'She was a very nice person but she looked very nice too.'

'Blonde and very tall and well-built?' I probed.

Katarina gave me a puzzled look. 'I thought you knew how your housekeeper looks. But if you're asking me, yes. I think she's the type of woman that naughty boys have fantasies about. You know, like the French maid play. Dressed like a maid, with black stockings, suspenders and high heels, she'd be very irresistible. Yes?'

I imagined Rhonda in black stockings, suspenders and high heels and nodded. 'She could very well be the man-eating type, I reckon.'

'Yes, she's a very good cook, as well,' Katarina said.

I guessed she probably didn't know the meaning of the man-eating adjective.

'She cooked a very nice pork belly for you,' she added.

I shook my head. The whole scenario was incomprehensible to me. 'So, she welcomed you inside, had a small chat with you …'

'We had a drink together,' Katarina said.

'And once she finished cooking the pork belly … she just left?'

'No, she didn't finish the pork roast. She told me to let it cook at a hundred and fifty degrees for another couple of hours and going by the smell of it, I think it's ready now. Yes?' Katarina giggled, looking very merry. 'Are you hungry yet?'

I was. I hadn't eaten anything in more than twelve hours and paradoxically, though I believed I was in love with Kate, this pretty little Czech thing named Katarina had stirred in me the same sexual desire which I always felt in her presence.

It puzzled me that, after my encounter with Kate, I still felt passionate about Katarina; at least physically. Was I perhaps *superficial*? I asked myself. I thought about it and found many other adjectives which sounded more complimentary to me, like flexible, altruistic, adaptable, philanthropic and multitalented. And one more came to mind – *collectively user-friendly*. The basic assumption here was that all users were sexy females and I was the *object* being used.

Sunday, 29 May

A strong smell of Turkish coffee awoke me after a very active night session – a sort of mixed game played mostly in the bedroom. I sat on the edge of the bed and recalled what had happened in the last twenty-four hours. I felt guilty towards Kate and even towards Rhonda.

I pondered the situation in the ensuite while brushing my teeth, showering and shaving. I thought of Kate and Luigi and Rhonda. I guessed Rhonda wasn't too happy with me not showing up the day before and Katarina arriving at my flat instead and I didn't blame her.

But why had she been so nice to Katarina? I wondered. Was it perhaps because Rhonda fancied young, pretty females as well? Having met Katarina, maybe she'd changed her plans and thought of marrying her, instead of me. Like me, Katarina was here on a temporary student visa and in need of a similar arrangement to stay in Australia for good. Unlike me, Katarina was in a better position: her visa hadn't expired yet.

It was nearly half-past-eleven when I stepped into the kitchen. Katarina, lightly dressed, was sitting at the kitchen table reading a magazine and sipping from her coffee. Unlike me, she looked relaxed and content, which I appreciated. I had exerted myself very hard during the night to make her look that way.

'Have a coffee? Yes?' She welcomed me with a lovely, affectionate smile. She didn't wait for an answer; just jumped from her chair and poured me a cup of hot coffee.

I pulled a chair and sat at the table opposite her.

She kept gazing at me and it was obvious there was an ocean of deep affection beyond that look. I knew she loved me and, in a way, I loved her too.

I'd felt guilty over Kate and Rhonda earlier that morning; now I felt guilty over Katarina. Sure she was in love with me and she believed that I loved her too, which wasn't fair, as far as this charming young woman was concerned.

I had, in the last few days, rehearsed in my mind how to tell Katarina of Helen's plan. I hated the anticipated reaction. I knew she'd be devastated at the prospect of not seeing me any longer.

Now it was a good occasion to have a talk with her, but, having stood up Rhonda, I doubted the sexy blonde was still keen to marry me. So, I decided not to say anything to Katarina. Taking the easy option always suited me, when I had the choice.

'How about I cook you breakfast? Yes?' Katarina interrupted my reflections.

Though I'd consumed a heap of calories during the night, I wasn't that hungry. I said, 'I'll go to the shop and buy some bread.'

She looked surprised. 'Buy bread? There is plenty of bread from last night.'

'It's stale. I'll buy fresh bread.'

She gave me a reproachful look. 'You are wasting money. When I lived in Prague, we never wasted anything. If the bread was a few days old, we spilled water on it and put it in the oven for twenty minutes. It was then as good as freshly baked.'

I nodded. 'I know, but we're not in Prague here.'

She shrugged. 'Well … please yourself. I'll have a shower in the meantime.' She stood up, kissed me and walked to the bathroom.

I strolled to a park nearby, sat on a bench and switched on my mobile. I hadn't checked it since I turned it off in Kate's mansion. There were a few missed calls and a voice message from Katarina. There was also a text message from a good friend named Gabriel. *How about we play tennis on Sunday morning?* he'd written. There was nothing from Rhonda, which I found baffling.

I replied to Gabriel saying I couldn't make it, but would call him later and then dialled Rhonda's number to apologise. The call went straight to the message bank. Well, at least she'd know I called, I thought. I then dialled Kate's mobile number. The call didn't go anywhere. I listened to the buzz at the other end about a dozen times and then hung up.

I strolled to the shops and stopped at Dowes. Solveig wasn't there.

Back at home, Katarina welcomed me with even less gear on than she had worn earlier that morning. This time she wore … well, she wore a pair of earrings and a necklace. She embraced me, then gazed at me and smiled. Something she'd seen in my eyes must have made her smile. She glanced down at my crotch and asked. 'Where is the bread?'

It was only then I realised I had forgotten about the bread.

Late in the afternoon, I gave Katarina a lift back to her flat. She had an assignment to submit the next day and needed several hours to complete it, she said. I returned home and rang Rhonda and Kate on their mobile phones again, with the same result. I then rang Kate's home number.

'Luigi Maslini speaking,' Kate's husband answered in his thick, gangster-like voice.

I hesitated. I wasn't in the mood to chat with him, but couldn't resist the temptation to wish him a nice evening. 'Fuck off, you rotten olive,' I said and hung up.

I probably lost him when calling him a rotten olive. I'd done it automatically, as Maslini meant olives in Romanian. I didn't know if it meant anything in Italian, besides a family name.

He'd sounded well plastered again, which gave me an idea. I opened a bottle of red wine and a second one within twenty minutes. I drank more wine without feeling any better. I thought of Kate and what she'd said of Freud. Three-quarters through the second bottle of wine, I went up to Helen's penthouse and searched through her bookshelves.

I found two books about Sigmund Freud. I flicked through them and took one downstairs. I indulged myself with more wine and read of Freud's concept of character. Of the character types described by Freud, I identified myself as the *oral-receptive* one – the person who expects to be fed materially, emotionally and intellectually. He expects that, whatever he needs, will be given to him, because he deserves it, for being so good. Said Freud, this type of person expected that all satisfaction would be offered to him without any reciprocity.

It made me wonder – if I was the oral-receptive character type, why did Helen expect any reciprocity from me? I tried to analyse myself and concluded that, indeed, being prone to food and drink given to me orally, I must be the oral-receptive type. I fell asleep while reading Freud, which made me … well, an intellectual. Or perhaps, just an educated pervert.

Monday, 30 May

To my relief, just as I entered the Dowes on Monday morning, I spotted Solveig helping a customer. I browsed in the store until she finished with her client and then I approached her. She was arranging some garments on a rack and hadn't seen me. I noted she looked a little paler and had some dark circles below her eyes. Perhaps she hadn't slept too well during the weekend, or not enough, I assumed.

'Hello Solveig, I'm back,' I announced with a smile.

She glanced at me, apparently unimpressed. 'I can see you are. I was actually thinking of you, but … don't get the wrong idea. I only thought of you because of your interest in Kate.'

'Have you found her?' I asked.

Solveig shook her head. 'No luck. How about you?'

'I haven't, but I saw Luigi instead.'

She arched her eyebrows. 'I can see you're pretty big and well stacked-up, but I'd say it's some sort of a miracle that you're still in one piece.'

'Is he so ferocious?' I asked.

Solveig shrugged. 'You just said you've met him. Haven't you figured it out for yourself?'

I hesitated. 'I haven't met him - I only saw him. And I wanted to talk to you about it.'

She paused and looked around. The shop was unusually crowded for a Monday morning. 'Come back at midday,' she said. 'I'm having my lunchbreak at noon and we can talk then.'

I returned to Westfield at twelve o'clock sharp and waited a few minutes until Solveig came out from the store. Wearing high heels, a tight velvet jacket over a light-grey blouse and a blue skirt nicely moulded on her hips, she looked six-foot tall and a very sexy doll. I noted she only had a small purse in her hand, which told me she hadn't brought a lunch box from home.

That revelation gave me the opportunity to take the initiative. 'How about we have lunch at the Steak House?' I offered.

Solveig thought for a few seconds and pouted her lips. 'Thanks, but I'm on a diet. And I have to return to work quite quickly.'

'That's what Kate said the other day and we ended up having a three-hour lunch and three bottles of wine,' I bragged.

'I wonder what else you ended up doing *after* three bottles of wine,' the blonde replied, while strolling towards the Elisabeth Street exit.

'I might tell you after the third bottle of wine,' I said, walking by her side.

'How about *showing* me, rather than *telling* me?' Solveig suggested.

'Half an hour wouldn't be enough,' I replied.

'I should hope so,' Solveig said, rather tartly and changed the subject. 'What did you want to talk to me about?'

'Anything you can tell me about Kate,' I said.

'What do you know of her already?' she asked.

'Not much. We met last Thursday at Dowes, had lunch and spent … about ten hours together.'

We exited the mall and crossed Elisabeth Street into the Macquarie Street piazzetta. The late autumn afternoon was sunny and quite warm. There were lots of people around, some sitting on benches and playing chess; others just lazing in the sun or overseeing toddlers and kids having a good time in the green plush-covered playground.

'Let's sit in the sun,' Solveig said, stopping by a wooden bench.

We sat on the bench, facing the mall, saying nothing for a little while. The pleasant heat from the northerly sun made me feel warm and a little sleepy. I couldn't help myself wondering if the sensual blonde sitting next to me was in the mood to sleep as well.

'So, you've picked her up at the shop and spent about ten hours together, which was enough for you to fall in love,' Solveig interrupted my fantasies.

'I think I fell in love about ten minutes after we met,' I replied.

'You shouldn't have,' she retorted.

'And why is that?' I inquired.

'Because Kate is married, her husband is very jealous and your infatuation with her can only cause trouble, if it hasn't already,' Solveig said.

I didn't like that. 'What do you mean? Are you suggesting that Kate's fleeing might have something to do with her spending last Thursday with me?'

She nodded. 'I actually wonder if Luigi has confiscated her mobile phone and locked her in a room to punish her. It wouldn't be the first time.'

Solveig's presumed account of events angered me. I thought about Luigi and decided he *was* the type who could do such an archaic thing, though I knew this time Kate wasn't held a prisoner by her jealous husband. That's what I said to Solveig. 'No, he hasn't.'

'How do you know?' Solveig asked.

I hesitated and then decided that, if I wanted Solveig to open up to me, I had to be frank with her as well. I told her of my intrusion in Kate's mansion last Saturday. While stating how I got into the house, I changed my mind and left some things out. I told her how Luigi had arrived home when I was there and of his search for Kate while I was hiding. I finished my recount saying that I'd sneaked out from the house without him seeing me.

'So, it wasn't Luigi this time,' Solveig said after I finished my abbreviated story.

'Are you two very close?' I asked.

She nodded. 'Kate is sometimes vert absent-minded. I guess she's probably lost her mobile phone again. She's done it before - quite a few times, actually.'

'You have any idea where she might be?' I asked.

She remained quiet for a while, thinking. 'I don't think she went to her parents. I'm sure Luigi's been there already. There is some other place she could hide, but so far, I haven't been able to check if she's there.'

'But why is she so scared of this Luigi character?' I asked.

'Because he's bad and Kate doesn't want any trouble.'

'If he's so bad and maltreats her, why is she staying with him?' I said.

Solveig shrugged. 'It looks like she's decided to do something about it. It looks like she's done a runner.'

'But why did she have to do a runner? Why isn't she asking for a divorce?'

'Because she's scared of Luigi.'

'Is he brutal with her?' I asked.

She nodded.

'And how about the police?' I said. 'Why isn't she reporting him to the police?'

'It's not as simple as that,' Solveig said.

I could sense she was reluctant to say more and it frustrated me.

'I can see you aren't keen to talk and if you too are scared of Luigi, I'm sorry for you,' I said. 'But I can tell you that a jerk like him doesn't scare me. So, I'll go back to his place and have a *friendly* chat with him. I'll find out what's going on, straight from the horse's mouth.'

'Don't do that, please,' Solveig pleaded. 'You'd only stir up more trouble.'

'I'm sorry, but it's the only way of finding out what's going on.'

'Are you married?' Solveig asked, totally out of context, I thought.

I put on an offended look. 'Of course I'm not.'

'Why *of course*? Are you implying that you wouldn't have had a ... casual affair with Kate if you were married? In other words, are you saying that Kate is of a bad character, because she had a fling with you while being married?'

I thought of what I remembered of Freud's analysis of characters which I read the night before and decided it was a good opportunity to do some showing off quoting a few terms that I'd memorised from that book. 'From my brief encounter with Kate, I can only think of her character in an artistic, rather than scientific way. I should perhaps add that, even so, I was able to capture in her a relative permanent structure of passion,' I said.

Wow! I congratulated myself, having successfully reproduced all that garbage. I thought it sounded really impressive and couldn't wait to see the blonde's reaction.

Solveig smiled and I thought that what she said next didn't fit the anecdotal labelling of blondes. 'You wouldn't strike me as the type who reads Freud.'

'Are you a doctor too?' I asked.

She nodded. 'Kate and I did medicine together.'

I hadn't expected that. 'Ah … I see. What I don't understand is …'

'I know what you don't understand,' Solveig interrupted. 'Like Kate, I wasn't keen to practice medicine. That's why we both took these jobs at Dowes.'

I was tempted to say that those jobs wouldn't pay a lot, but I refrained, thinking that such a comment would be too invasive. 'So, you two met at uni?' I asked instead.

'We actually went to school together and became best friends at about ten. We had the same interests and spent most of the time together, doing the same things. We were like sisters.'

Here we are – she's started to talk, I noted and prompted her: 'So, which of you got married first?'

She showed me her hands. 'Can you see a wedding ring?'

I couldn't. 'No, but some women take it off when it suits them.'

She smiled mischievously. 'I see. You thought I was planning to seduce you.'

'No,' I protested. 'But what I don't get is why Kate married this Luigi creature.'

'She was forced into it,' Solveig replied.

'She was forced into it? Who forced her?'

Solveig sighed and thought a little. 'Well, I might as well tell you the full story. Has Kate mentioned her brother to you?'

I thought for a few seconds and decided to take a punt. 'She'd mentioned some trouble about her brother.'

She nodded. 'Diego is five years older than Kate. Their mother spoiled him when he was a kid. When he was a teenager, he mixed with the wrong mob. He was expelled from school in Year Ten and has been in trouble with the police several times.'

'You mean drugs and things like that?'

'All sorts of trouble – drugs, firearms, affray, assault, illegal racing … Anyway, their parents always paid the best lawyers and kept him out of jail. Still, Diego, having a rowdy temperament, went from bad to worse. He never had a job but always needed money, so he blackmailed his father into giving him money.'

'He blackmailed his father?' I asked incredulously.

'Well … it was sentimental blackmail, so to speak. So, the money kept coming to him, but it was never enough for Diego.'

'What did he spend the money on?'

She hesitated. 'Diego loves to live *big*. His life style is quite … extravagant. Like Kate, he was gifted by Mother Nature, or rather by his mother – who was a beauty queen in her youth – with extraordinarily good looks. So, there have been a countless number of sexy women throwing themselves at him.'

'From what you're telling me, I'd think he isn't too shy to take money from chicks.'

Solveig's face reddened – in anger, I thought. 'That's true,' she said. 'But you know how these things happen. He got money from some, but had to spend more on others. Anyway, smart as he is, one day he dreamed up a permanent solution to his financial problems. So, he started gambling.'

'What sort of gambling?'

'Poker. That's how he met Luigi, who, among other things, organised illegal poker games with some of his Mafioso mates.'

'Is Luigi involved with the Mafia?!'

Solveig pushed her index finger to my lips. 'Keep your voice down. You never know who can overhear.'

'Sorry – it came as a shock.'

'Well, I don't think it's Mafia as such, but some sort of a similar racket. So, back to Diego, it was no surprise that he started losing money … lots of money, mostly to Luigi.'

'But, was Luigi playing fairly?' I asked.

Solveig shrugged. 'Most likely not, but whatever tricks he did, I don't know. Anyway, as it usually happens, Diego kept playing on credit, in a futile attempt to recover his losses. And, as it usually happens, he kept losing. One day though, Luigi demanded payment and Diego failed to pay. So, Luigi, who knew Diego's father was making good money as a very successful doctor, went to Diego's house to talk to Mister Morales senior. There, he saw Kate and set his eyes on her. Relying on Diego's promise that he'd stop gambling, Kate's father agreed to pay part of the debt, but Diego didn't keep his promise. He lost more money and you can imagine what happened.'

I nodded. 'Luigi erased Diego's debt in exchange for Kate.'

'Exactly. Her parents persuaded Kate that marrying Luigi was the honourable thing to do and that's how she became Mrs Maslini.'

'But she kept her maiden name,' I observed.

'Kate knew that Luigi was a very dubious character and insisted that she keep her maiden name. Luigi rejected her condition at first, but he changed his mind later.'

'So, when did this happen?'

'Kate married Luigi two years ago, when she was twenty-five.'

'And it didn't work out, I gather,' I said.

'That's the understatement of the year. The marriage was

doomed even before they went through with the formalities. When Luigi demanded Kate to prove her *credentials* to him before they went to the church, she bluntly refused. He eventually accepted the situation, but when the time came, Kate was nothing but a block of ice to him. I mean, in intimacy. No wonder, as she despised him and she's the type who couldn't mask her feelings. He took revenge insulting and beating her, whenever he felt like it, which was just about every week.'

Recalling how passionate Kate had been in bed with me last Thursday, I had great difficulty trying to imagine her like a block of ice. At the same time, I could understand Luigi's frustration – but thinking of what he did to Kate pushed my blood pressure up. 'What I don't understand is, once Kate married Luigi and Diego was freed of debt, why hasn't Kate asked for a divorce,' I said.

Solveig smiled – a bitter smile. 'This Luigi Maslini is quite evil. He lured Diego back into gambling even before he and Kate were pronounced husband and wife. That's how he still maintains a stronghold on Kate and her parents.'

'But that's blackmail, which is a criminal offence,' I remarked.

Solveig checked the time and stood up. 'You may call it whatever you like, but that's how it is and it works for Luigi. I'm afraid I have to go back to work now.'

'I'll walk with you back to Dowes,' I offered.

While strolling towards Elizabeth Street, I said, 'What are we going to do about it? We can't just sit around doing nothing and let Kate deal with that brute by herself.'

'I wonder if Kate has already done something about it. But if she hasn't and we do something, it's a big risk we're taking.'

'You mean Luigi will beat her up?'

'Not only that. Kate wouldn't stay with him if not for the threats he's made to her family.'

'But what could he do to them? He couldn't sue Diego for not paying his gambling debts, as the whole thing is illegal.'

'Don't forget his criminal contacts,' Solveig said in a low voice.

'Why don't the Morales go to the police and dob him in?'

Solveig gave me a scared look. 'You don't mess with folks like Luigi.'

'But still, we can't just pretend that nothing has happened. We should report her to the police, as a missing person. I actually wonder why Luigi hasn't alerted the cops himself.'

'Maybe he's got something to do with it,' Solveig said.

'No, he hasn't. I told you I was in his house last Saturday, when he started searching for Kate after his mates had left.'

While crossing the street to the mall, Solveig said. 'Don't forget he's Italian and a very proud male – as most Italians are. He'd never publicise the fact that his wife has ditched him and fled from home. It would be too humiliating for him.'

'I don't care about him,' I argued. 'But I'm worried sick about Kate. I'd thought at first that her disappearance was just a … maybe an escapade and, I must admit, it made me jealous. But, after talking to you, I'm afraid it could be something more sinister and I can't wait to see what happens next and do nothing in the meantime.'

Solveig remained silent for a little while; then she went on. 'There is something else I haven't told you, but it looks like I have to, to make you understand why this case is not as simple as it might look and why reporting Kate missing to the police could cause more trouble.'

'Tell me, please,' I urged her.

'I'm sorry to break this news to you, because I can see you're … sort of … hooked on Kate. But this is not the first time that Kate has done a runner. '

She shocked me with that. 'So, she's in the habit of picking up blokes, playing around and then she feels guilty and seeks repentance in a nunnery.'

Solveig nodded. 'You're not too far off the mark. She's got a lover.'

That hit me where it hurts. 'Ah … I'm sorry to hear that.' I didn't know what else to say.

Some twenty metres from Dowes, Solveig halted. 'We'll keep in touch,' she said.

I stopped by her and nodded. 'I'll give you my mobile number.'

Glancing past her, I spotted a face in the crowd which looked familiar. A massively built man was pacing back and forth in front of Dowes. He was looking towards Dowes, in the opposite direction from where we were.

'I've seen that bloke at Dowes before,' I said to Solveig.

It was the fatso who'd made trouble to Kate the day when we met at Dowes.

Seeing him, Solveig appeared startled. She frowned, but didn't say anything.

'He was a smart-arse with me the other day. I'd better have a chat with him,' I said.

'Don't be a kid. You've caused enough trouble already,' Solveig reminded me.

I opened my mouth to protest, but didn't have the chance.

Solveig turned around and strode hurriedly in the opposite direction from Dowes.

I watched her moving away until her silhouette faded in the crowd. I shrugged admitting to myself there was a lot I didn't understand. I had an acute feeling that something wasn't right, but I didn't know what it was. I took the elevator to the upper level still thinking about it.

6

Wandering absently on Macquarie Street, I found myself in front of an Italian delicatessen where I'd been quite a few times before. They served freshly made sandwiches, prepared *while you wait*. I hadn't had any breakfast that morning and was very hungry. I stepped inside the shop. An enormously large lady whom I hadn't seen before welcomed me with a *buon giorno signore*.

'*Buon giorno, signorina,*' I replied with a grin, displaying my vast knowledge of her language. That was actually the most complex sentence I was able to put together in Italian.

She must have liked that, for her professional smile turned somewhat mischievous. It didn't go very well with her plus fifty-six size figure, I observed.

She must have confused me with one of her countrymen as she began talking in Italian, passionately and very fast, as most of them do. I nodded, pretending to be absorbed by her tirade. I didn't understand a single word. 'Two large sandwiches,' I ordered.

She seemed a little deflated by my English request, but began preparing my meal, taking her time. 'There it is,' she finally announced. 'It's low fat prosciutto with mozzarella, lettuce, tomatoes, stuffed olives and homemade mayonnaise on pane di casa. That will be twenty-four dollars, signore.'

That was quite a lot, I thought, but being low-fat and healthy … perhaps it was worth it.

'You eat this sort of stuff yourself?' I asked timidly.

'Sure I do, just like you – a couple every morning, signore,' she replied with pride.

I'd been afraid she'd say that, but … it was too late now. I handed her twenty-five dollars and said *molto grazie.*

'*Grazie e buon appetito,*' she replied.

I hesitated, waiting for the one dollar change which she owed me. She gazed at me inquiringly, as if wondering why I was still there. She then shrugged and dismissed me with a *ciao, ciao signore.* She seemed in a hurry to get rid of me.

I strolled back towards Westfield and sat on the same bench where Solveig and I had talked before. I ate one sandwich, but not very enthusiastically. The prosciutto piece, as thin as a sheet of writing paper, tasted like it had been sliced last Christmas. The rest of it appeared a mixture of greasy mayonnaise and other very oily sauces. I also noted that the olives were only *stuffed* with their own pits. I didn't feel like eating the second one.

A scruffy looking bloke, probably in his thirties approached me, saying, 'Can you spare a couple of dollars mate? I didn't eat nothing in weeks.'

Well, if he hadn't eaten anything in weeks, he'd certainly had a lot of alcohol, quite recently, I noted. There was a strong smell of grog coming from him and his speech was slurred.

I offered him the other sandwich, which I hadn't touched.

'Have this, mate. It's low fat and very healthy, guaranteed.'

He gave me a contemptuous look. 'Fuck you, smart-arse.' He wandered away.

I shrugged, unwrapped the second sandwich and placed it on the paved ground in the piazzetta. A couple of pigeons got stuck into it, but not with a lot of conviction.

I sauntered towards Moore Street mulling over what I'd learned from Solveig. I had to admit, the whole story intrigued me – particularly Kate's extramarital affair and her brother, Diego. I itched to have a chat to him, but how was I going to find him?

I glanced around and saw a Telstra phone booth, which gave me an idea. I checked the apparatus. It worked. One volume of the Yellow Pages phone directory book caught my eye. It was the one I needed. I looked up at the Doctors – Medical Practitioners section. There was only one Morales doctor located in CBD on Pitt Street.

I dialled the number and said to the lady at the other end that I needed to see the doctor urgently. I couldn't believe my luck. Without asking the reason for my urgent request, she took my name and said that Doctor Morales could see me at three o'clock that afternoon. She explained that another patient had just postponed her appointment.

I thanked her and marched to the train station. It was a few minutes before two. At that time of the day, driving in peak hour some thirty-five kilometres to the city wasn't a smart idea. Plus, parking in the CBD cost a small fortune, if you were *lucky* enough to find a parking spot.

Having caught a fast train to the city, I got off at Town Hall and entered the surgery on time for my appointment. A young, petite Asian doll welcomed me from the reception desk. 'You must be Cornel Tom,' she said and her accent told me she wasn't the lady to whom I'd spoken earlier. She must have replaced the other one in the afternoon shift, I guessed.

Behind the reception desk was a large inscription on a shiny metal plaque saying Doctor Juan Morales and listing half-a-dozen of his qualifications. Below was another name, which startled me. It said Doctor Ecaterina Morales. I wondered why Kate did that lowly paid job at Dowes when she could earn much better money at the surgery.

'You're right – I am Cornel, but I'm not Tom,' I replied, smiling at the receptionist. Though I had Kate, Helen, Rhonda and Katarina on my mind, I couldn't resist the temptation of flirting with another pretty woman. It was in my blood, I guess.

The Asian doll gave me an inquiring stare and looked down at the booking list. 'It says so here. There is also a note saying you haven't been here before.'

'The second part is correct,' I confirmed.

She looked puzzled. 'So, who are you, if you're not Tom?'

'I'm Cornel,' I continued teasing her, while having a better look and enjoying what I saw. She was a curvy, sexy brunette with protruding breasts and a large, sensual mouth.

'I know that, but what is your family name?'

'I don't have a family. I'm an orphan,' I said in a sad tone.

She hesitated then handed me an A4-size form. 'Please fill this in. You need to complete all sections, *including* your family name,' she emphasised.

I thanked her and took a seat. There was only one other patient waiting. I filled in the form and had a look around. A man came out from the doctor's office and the person waiting went in.

The waiting room was large but far from luxurious, which told me that perhaps Doctor Morales wasn't doing so well. Apart from the reception desk, the antechamber was equipped with a fridge, two small tables with old magazines piled on them and ten chairs. I thought that by far the best piece of work in the room was the receptionist herself.

There were also quite a number of large, framed photos on the walls, with typed explanations below each of them. There was Doctor Morales on the Kokoda Track, Doctor Morales in the Andes, in the Pyrenees, in Tibet, in Greenland, in Alaska … and so on.

I studied the man in the photos, trying to find a resemblance with Kate. I didn't. The doctor looked about fifty-something, short and slim and quite an ordinary appearance, with small, dark eyes, thick lips and black, abundant hair – too dark, too much of it and too thick for his age. I wondered if he was a Jew.

A much younger, sultry brunette was with him in some of the photos. If she was Mrs Morales, she rather looked his daughter, but except for Kate and Diego, Solveig hadn't mentioned any other siblings. So, I assumed she was Mrs. Morales.

I carefully examined the woman and I did find a lot of re-semblance with Kate. Well, she was a hot dame, but too young to be Kate's mother. Perhaps she had Kate when she was about … twelve or so, or maybe those photos weren't so recent.

I returned to the reception desk and handed the completed form to the Asian woman. I read the metal plaque behind her desk again and asked. 'Would Doctor Ecaterina Morales be in this afternoon?'

'Sorry, Doctor Ecaterina is not in,' she replied, while glancing at the form.

'When will she be in?' I insisted.

She shrugged. 'I really don't know. It could be quite a while, I'm afraid.'

'So, it wouldn't be a good idea to wait for her,' I continued.

She shook her head. 'No, I don't think so.'

'Have you been long in this job?' I asked.

She thought a little, rolling her eyes. 'Not really. Only about … six months, I think.'

'And … has Doctor Ecaterina been at the surgery at all in these six months?'

She shook her head, looked at the form again and changed the subject. 'So, your name is Toma, not Tom. It's probably the feminine form of Tom.'

'Do I look like a feminine form?' I asked.

She studied me with blatant interest for several seconds and giggled. 'No, I don't think so.'

Her answer pleased me. I'd have been quite pissed off, had she said yes.

The petite receptionist sent me in to see the doctor at twenty-two minutes past three. As I entered his office, I wondered if I was in the right place. The man behind the desk was nothing like the one I'd seen in the framed photos. Skinny, darker and smaller than in the photos, he also looked some twenty years older. And, except some thin traces of grey locks around his temples, that thick, abundant hair that had struck me in the photos was all gone. Perhaps it had been a wig.

The doctor murmured a 'Sit down, please' without bothering to even glance at me. His dull, monotonous voice sounded bored and tired.

I sat on the chair in front of his desk and gazed at his face. His face was just like his voice.   He read my form and said with the same degree of enthusiasm, 'Well, how can I help?'

The manner in which he asked the question made me think that he had serious doubts he could be of any help.

'I have a problem,' I said.

He nodded. 'You wouldn't be here if you didn't.'

'Maybe I would, if I were one of those elderly ladies who visit the doctor to have a cup of tea with biscuits and socialise in the waiting room.'

'Not here. It's too expensive and we don't bulk bill,' he explained.

'You said *we*, but you're the only doctor here.'

He looked at me for a couple of seconds and shifted his stare to the wall clock. 'Are you here with a medical problem, or you just like spending money and getting nothing in return?'

'You mean ... like gambling?' I asked.

His expression saddened a notch further, which I didn't think was possible and he looked a little older. 'Is this about Diego?'

I felt sorry for him, but I wasn't there to offer him a shoulder to cry on. I'd decided on the train about how I was to approach the doctor and now I stuck to my plan. 'It's Diego as well.'

Now he looked not only old, sad, tired and bored but resigned as well. 'If he owes you money ... I'm sorry, but I can't help you.'

'You did much more than saying sorry when Diego owed money to Luigi,' I remarked.

He made a helpless gesture with his hands. 'There is no more money in the till.'

'And there is no more Kate,' I added.

His facial expression didn't change. I guess it couldn't have gone any sadder. 'What exactly do you mean by that?'

'As far as I know, you only have one daughter, which means there is nothing else to put on the market. And even if you could trade Kate again, she's gone missing now.'

There was a flutter of interest in his eyes. 'Kate has gone missing?'

Having watched his reaction very closely, I decided his surprise was genuine, but I answered with another probing question.

'You mean you didn't know?'

'We don't talk very often,' he explained.

'No wonder. I wouldn't be very keen to talk to you either, if I were Kate,' I replied.

He let that go. 'How long has Kate been missing?'

'Since Thursday, last week. Do you know where she might be?'

He thought a little. 'If she's not answering her phone, it doesn't mean she's gone missing. She could be at home and not in the mood to talk to anyone. It wouldn't be the first time.'

'Or perhaps, Luigi has taken her mobile from her and locked her in a room. It wouldn't be the first time either,' I continued.

He thought some more and asked. 'What exactly is your association with Kate? From what I gather from you, it could be *your* fault if she has marital troubles.'

'From what *I* gather, it is certainly Diego's stupidity and addiction and *your* greed and egoism that have caused all her marital troubles with Luigi. If not for you, she wouldn't have married that scumbag in the first place.'

'What's your point?' he asked, still in a laconic manner.

'My point is, if you don't locate Kate within twenty-four hours, I am going to the police and report the whole sordid story to them. I'll tell them of your beloved son's addiction to drugs and to illegal gambling and I will tell them how the much-respected Doctor Juan Morales has literally sold his own daughter to a ruthless criminal.'

We both remained quiet for a couple of minutes. Just when I started to wonder if he'd fallen asleep, the doctor said in a very low voice. 'I can't promise anything, but I'll see what I can do. Come back on Wednesday morning and we'll have another talk. Tell Amy to book you first thing on Wednesday morning. And there is no charge for this … consultation.'

He turned his chair to a hundred and eighty degrees, fetched a glass and a bottle from a cabinet behind him and, with shaking hands, poured a shot of the drink in the glass and downed it in one gulp. I couldn't see the bottle, but I was willing to bet it wasn't apple juice or milk. He then remained motionless with his back turned to me. That wasn't a very polite tactic of getting rid of me, I thought, but I wasn't ready to leave him alone yet.

'Where can I find Diego?' I asked.

This time, he answered like a rocket. 'You can't find Diego. No one can.'

'What do you mean by that?'

He helped himself to one more shot and turned his chair back in its original position. He was facing me again. I noted his eyes were fixed and glassy. 'You can find a man named Diego Morales living in a sort of granny flat in my back yard. You've probably checked the address already. It's in Ashfield. But that man is not my Diego anymore. That's what I mean, if you can understand.'

I thought about it and concluded that I did understand. I also understood that, at that particular point in time, Doctor Juan Morales was of no further use to me. I didn't think he was of much use to anyone. I left his office without him noticing.

I rambled down towards the Central train station with a lot on my mind. It wasn't just the mystery surrounding Kate's whereabouts; it was the fact that I'd stood up Rhonda as well and all my subsequent attempts to get in contact with her had failed. She must be a little annoyed, I assumed and it bothered me. It wasn't so much Rhonda herself who bothered me. I was more uncomfortable about Helen, who was due to land back in Sydney next morning.

Sure, Rhonda would complain about my indiscretion to Helen

and I had a feeling that she wouldn't appreciate my conduct during her absence. In spite of my intimate relationship with her, I knew Helen was the type who separated business from pleasure and expected me to comply with her requests, which this time I hadn't.

It was getting very close to the eleventh hour for me and I had to do something very quickly to keep myself out of trouble. I tried Rhonda's mobile again, but she didn't answer.

On my way to Central Station, I was distracted by a flashing sign in front of a popular pub on Goulburn Street, which said *Happy Hour*. That usually meant beer at half-price and free frankfurters. I went in, sat at a table and did some more thinking and quite a bit of drinking, my excuse being that grog helped my brain to function smoother.

While enjoying a fifth bottle of Cascade beer, my mobile rang. I read the name displayed on the screen and could hardly believe it. It said Rhonda Everton.

'Hello Miss Everest, what a nice surprise,' I said with pretended excitement and adopting a formal, polite approach. Immediately I realised that I'd just addressed her as Miss Everest instead of Everton.

Rhonda didn't seem to have noticed that detail. 'Where are you?' she asked.

I hesitated a few seconds. 'I'm at the doctor.'

She paused for a couple of seconds too; then observed, 'I wonder what sort of doctor he is, with all that loud music and noise in the background. Or, is it a she?'

I laughed loudly. 'Ah no, not me. I don't fancy females. I mean, I don't fancy female doctors. I mean I've been at the doctor, but now I'm on my way back to the station.'

'So, you're in city?'

It took me a while to answer. I was actually bowled over by her friendly tone and small talk. I'd expected her to say something nasty about last Saturday, which so far she hadn't. 'That's right, I'm in Goulburn Street,' I confirmed.

'I see … Are you at that place where certain professional dames give free sex to lucky perverts on the stage?'

'No … Where is that?' I asked with noticeable attention.

There was another pause, then Rhonda went on. 'Listen, it's nearly five. How about I see you at your place at around six?'

That sounded like a peaceful , unexpected reconciliation to me. 'Sure, I'll see you at six.'

'I hope this time you won't delegate the host role again,' Rhonda added.

'Ah no,' I protested. 'Last time … something unexpected happened.'

Rhonda didn't make any comment to that. She just hung up.

So far, so good, I thought, encouraged by her amicable approach. I downed another couple of beers and strode to Central Station. I boarded a slow, all stops train, but even so, I estimated I should arrive home just on time for my six o'clock date with Rhonda.

The rock band Visage woke me up with its 'Fade to Grey' hit – the ringing tone of my mobile phone. I pressed the green button and answered robotically, not knowing who I was, or where I was. 'Cornel Toma speaking.'

There was a giggle at the other end. 'Why are you so formal this evening?' Katarina asked.

I slowly realised I'd fallen asleep on the train. I read the time – it was twenty minutes past six and the train was moving. Where was I? I wondered, fearing that I'd passed my destination point and I was late for my date.

'Fuck!' I said.

There was another giggle at the other end. 'Is that the first thing that comes to your mind when you hear a female voice?'

'No, but I think I've gone too far,' I tried to explain.

'Yes? But I like it when you go too far.'

'Not this time. I think I've gone passed Liverpool and I don't know where I am.'

'Ah … that's *very* far …'

'Just wait a minute, Katarina,' I said and asked the lady sitting in front of me where we were.

'We'll be at Campbelltown in a minute or so,' the woman replied.

Campbelltown was some twenty kilometres further south from Liverpool. 'I can't believe I'm doing it again!' I exclaimed.

'What are you doing again?' Katarina asked. 'I can hear a woman speaking to you. Is she pretty? Was it her you said fuck before?'

I sprung from my seat preparing to get off at Campbelltown. 'I asked her where we were,' I said to Katarina.

'And where were you? Where you very far?'

'Yes. I fell asleep …'

'You fell asleep while having sex with the lady?' Katarina asked.

'I wasn't having sex with the lady,' I protested.

'Ah … I see. You were having sex alone …'

She was exasperating me. 'Katarina, please. I'm late and I'm very stressed …'

'So, you were … relieving your stress, so to speak,' she went on.

'Look, the train has stopped. I have to get out quickly.'

'Or they will catch you and charge you for … exposing your-self. They must have filmed you on the security cameras. Yes? I bet you'll be on the news tomorrow,' Katarina continued.

'I'll talk to you later,' I said and pressed the red button. I leaped from the train and rushed to the other platform to catch a train back to Liverpool.

It was nearly seven when I got out of the Liverpool train station. The forty minute nap on the train had had a refreshing effect on me – I mean, not so much mentally, but physically.

Well aware that I was one hour late for my date, I thought there wasn't much point in going home, so I walked to the Liverpool Hospital instead. Though in a precarious position with Rhonda and potentially with Helen, the idea that Kate had a lover remained on the back of my mind. I felt cheated and betrayed. And I felt I had to do something to locate the woman that was consuming me.

I walked up the stairs to the main entrance of the hospital praying in my mind it wouldn't be Cerberus *welcoming* me at the reception. Someone up there must have listened to my prayers. Behind the reception desk was a woman; not too young and not very pretty, but infinitely better than Cerberus.

Now, that I also knew Kate's family name, I felt self-assured and optimistic. I flashed the receptionist a smile and she beamed back at me.

'Could you tell me if Kate Morales will be doing the night shift this evening?' I asked, displaying loads of confidence.

The woman frowned. 'You said Kate Morales?'

I noted she had an East-European accent and nodded. 'That's right. Like in *morale* with an s at the end.' I spelled Morales for her.

She puckered her lips. 'I don't recall the name, but maybe she's new. Is she a doctor, or a nurse?'

Don't start asking stupid questions like Cerberus, I prayed in my mind. 'She's actually a doctor *and* a nurse.'

The woman gave me a confused gaze. 'I'll have a look on the computer.'

I couldn't see the computer screen, but I could see her face. It showed doubt and confusion.

'Sorry,' she said after a couple of minutes. 'There is no Kate Morales shown on the staff list.'

It was my turn to show perplexity. 'You're sure?'

She shrugged apologetically. 'I don't recall the name and is not listed on the computer.'

I did some quick thinking and asked. 'How about Maslini?'

'How about Maslini?' she repeated my question.

'Maybe she's shown as Maslini, instead of Morales. That's her other married name. I mean, Morales is her maiden name,' I explained.

She giggled. 'In my language Maslini means olives. I thought you were offering me some olives to eat.'

'Well, we're talking the same language then,' I said in Romanian.

Her smile widened by an inch and she switched to Romanian as well. 'It's a small world. My name is Mioara.'

I gave her another wide grin. 'I'm Cornel and I'm very pleased to meet you.'

'Me too, but I'm sorry I can't help you with finding Kate,' she apologised.

'Well, I'm sorry too. But I'm glad to meet such a pretty countrywoman.'

Mioara blushed visibly impressed with the attention. 'That's very nice of you.'

'I hope I'll take you to a movie one day,' I added.

She gave me a languid look. 'I'd love to.'

A guy behind me coughed signalling his impatience.

'I'll be back later in the week,' I said, knowing too well I had no such intentions.

I left the hospital confused and disappointed but felt better after a couple of minutes, reflecting that I'd made Mioara happy, looking forward to an elusive date.

7

I arrived back home at around half-past-seven, and noted that, as soon as I entered my apartment, I became a little nostalgic. Though very spacious, nicely furnished and welcoming after a long day, that evening the flat seemed impersonal and unfriendly.

I thought about it and I realised that subconsciously, I'd hoped someone would be waiting for me – preferably Kate, or Katarina, or even Rhonda. Or at least a piece of roast pork in the oven. That thought made me conscious that I was hungry.

I helped myself to a glass of wine and did some hard thinking, trying to get Kate out of my mind. What was I going to do about Rhonda? I wondered. And how would Helen react when told of my blunders with Rhonda? After ten minutes of intense reflection and two more glasses of wine, I shrugged and tried Kate's mobile number once more. There was no answer.

I was tempted to call Katarina, but I abstained. I had to get up very early in the morning to pick up Helen from the airport and couldn't afford another strenuous night.

There was another thing I knew I had to do and I wasn't looking forward to it. The least I could do was call Rhonda and apologise for standing her up again. I ate a few slices of cold pork roast and had another half bottle of wine to fortify myself for the very wearing task looming ahead of me. That was calling Rhonda.

At twenty to nine I dialled Rhonda's mobile number.

'So, you're back, Mister Hard-to-Catch,' she answered.

'I'm so sorry that something unexpected happened again — '

'Are you in your flat?' she interrupted.

'Sure … where else would I be?'

There was silence. It took me a while to realise she'd hung up on me. Well, I didn't blame her. But what should I do? I asked myself again. I'd just gulped another glass of wine when my doorbell rang. I opened the door and … there was Katarina smiling at me. Dressed in a short leather skirt and matching jacket, she looked as pretty as ever.

'You drank too much, yes?' she said once she took a closer look at me.

'You know my boss is coming back tomorrow morning and I have to get up early to pick her up from the airport,' I reminded Katarina.

'Is that why you got drunk again?'

Well, she had a point. 'I'm not drunk, I'm just … tired.'

'I'll wake you up, tomorrow morning,' she promised.

I half opened my mouth to say something, when my landline phone rang.

'That must be your boss. Maybe she's back early,' Katarina giggled.

I picked up the receiver. 'This is Cornel Toma.'

'Just checking if you're home indeed,' Rhonda said.

'Where else would I be? I've been home all day,' I replied without thinking.

'No you were not,' Katarina protested.

I covered the receiver with one hand and signalled to her to shut up.

'Is there anyone else with you?' Rhonda asked.

I laughed loudly. 'Of course not. I've been alone all day.' As soon as I said it, I covered the receiver again, but not quite quick enough.

'No, you were not,' Katarina repeated herself.

'Go lock yourself in the bathroom,' I whispered to her.

She grabbed a bottle of wine and a glass and vanished from my view, but not before turning her nose, flinching and making funny gestures at me.

'I thought I heard a female voice,' Rhonda observed.

'Ah, no. It's … the television. I'll turn it down.'

'Listen Mister Television-Addict, could you do me a favour?' Rhonda went on.

'I sure can. Anything you want,' I replied with enthusiasm.

'Go up to Helen's apartment and find a book for me. It's titled "You've Got it Coming" by James Hadley Chase. Ring me straightaway and tell me if you've found it.'

'Sure, I'll go up now,' I promised.

'Do it right away. You may get *distracted* otherwise,' Rhonda said somewhat acidly.

'I won't let you down …' I started to say, but she hung up.

Well, at least Katarina was out of sight, so I didn't have to waste any time telling her what I was going to do next. I fetched the keys to the penthouse and climbed the internal stairs into the hallway that led to Helen's residence. I unlocked the door and went in.

That part of the penthouse adjoining my flat contained the bedrooms – the master bedroom on one side and two smaller bedrooms on the other, with a corridor in the middle. The main bedroom, including the ensuite, the walk-in wardrobe and the dressing-room was larger than the average two-bedroom flat. There was also another full bathroom and a small bar-room on that side of the penthouse.

Once in the corridor, I noted some of the lights were on and the door to the master bedroom was open. As I moved closer to the main bedroom, I heard nice soft music coming from inside. I stepped closer and listened. I heard a woman's voice singing in French, then another woman calling in English, 'Have you found the book?'

My heart skipped a beat. It was Rhonda's voice.

'Come in, Mister Timid,' Rhonda added.

I stepped into the bedroom. She lay on her belly on the king-size bed, reading a magazine. I noticed a bottle of wine and a glass, half full on the night table. But much more noticeable was Rhonda herself, wearing a short, pink slip and … And that was about all she wore.

That silky garment only covered half of her back. Her bottom was naked; her legs long and nicely shaped. She looked very tempting. As she looked up at me, I saw her face was flushed and her eyes glittered.

'Have a seat and listen to this on global warming. It's funny,' she said casually, as if reading witty things to me while naked and exuding sensuality was our usual evening routine.

I sat on the edge of the bed and wondered what all this was about.

Rhonda went on. '"I was staggered in recent days and weeks to hear of the incredible cold temperatures registered in

North America. For example, in the middle of January, in Toronto the maximum temperature was minus 16 on the Celsius scale; in Quebec the maximum was minus 19 and minus 20 in North Dakota. In North Dakota, for 35 days in a row, the temperature never rose above zero. These are unprecedented statistics and similar patterns have recently occurred all over Europe. It makes me wonder: why is this inept idiot, alias Professor Gigolo *(Note 1)*, and the Federal Government for that matter, lying to us about global warming? I don't know where the so-called Professor is coming from – I only know he's going nowhere – but I would suggest that, during the Northern Hemisphere winter, he should be packed in a box and sent to North America, because he needs more than a cold shower to cool him down. And if his brains are going to freeze, no one will notice any difference."'

'That sums it up pretty well,' I said, edgily. I knew Professor Gigolo was an *expert* on the issue of global warming, and was engaged by the Labor Government to provide advice and make publicity in favour of *immediate, decisive action* to combat that phenomenon.

'I think she was too kind to him,' Rhonda replied.

'Who's she?' I asked.

'It's Helen. She wrote this in January. I'll read you a more recent one, from May,' Rhonda said. I gaped at her and I must admit, I'd completely forgotten about Katarina and Kate and everything else on my mind. I was actually about to start drooling with lust.

Rhonda picked up another magazine and continued. "'I hear rumours that there is currently a major rift in the leadership of the Federal Labor Party. The Prime Minister is allegedly accusing Wayne Swine *(Note 2)* of being the source of the swine flu. The allegation is based on the fact that in recent weeks, the Treasurer has been showing acute symptoms of the deadly disease, behaving in a very lethargic, apathetic and pathetic manner. According to Julia Lizard *(Note 3)*, Swine is unable to keep awake, speak, write, think clearly and ... think. There is a great deal of concern that, just in the week before the Federal Budget is due, Wayne Swine keeps asking Treasury officials stupid and even hilarious questions that indicate an utter ignorance of basic economic and finance concepts. Other sources within the Party argue that these deficiencies have always been present and are caused only by the Swine and not by the flu.'"

'That's funny and unfortunately, true,' I said without exaggerating. I wasn't a supporter of the Federal Treasurer either. Instead, as the minutes passed, I observed myself turning into an enthusiastic admirer of the sensual blonde lying practically nude within a metre from me.

'Have a glass of wine, please,' Rhonda said, casually again, apparently oblivious to her nakedness and the effect it had on me.

I shuffled to the bar-room and, aware of Katarina's presence downstairs, on the way, I locked the door leading to my flat. I returned with a glass and a bottle of wine. Rhonda was in the same position, flicking through a magazine and not paying much attention to me. I refilled her glass and poured one for myself wondering what her play was about.

'If you liked the one about the swine flu, listen to this one titled The Mad Cow,' she said and started reading. '"Having heard of the poor lady killed by a cow in England, I thought maybe this tragedy was not accidental. We know that this incident with the cow was not the first one in recent times. So, it looks to me that cows are now jealous because all the media attention is focused on swine and on the lethal things swine can do to humans. According to my sources, the Council of Cows have held an urgent summit and decided to teach the swine a lesson and get back in the news, in style, on the front page. This may also have unexpected and unpleasant consequences in the near future, even at the highest levels of government. I had, until recently, only imagined a cow Prime Minister possibly leading another country, but not any longer. It might be much closer to home, for everyone's comfort. So, attention everyone! Beware of the mad cow!'"

'Is this Helen's too?' I asked.

She looked at me for a long moment and in a way that made me feel it was only then when she started to get naughty ideas. 'What do you think?'

I sipped from the wine and licked my lips. Like the Federal Treasurer, I too had difficulty in thinking and speaking, though my shortcomings weren't caused by the flu. Would Wayne Swine be turned on by this explosively sexy blonde? I asked myself. Why wonder about that stupid geek? I answered my own question. Clearly, I wasn't thinking clearly.

'Found the book?' Rhonda asked.

I'd forgotten about the book. 'What book?'

She giggled. 'Forgotten the book already? Well, if your memory is short, I will remind you. You've got it coming … Mister Tome.'

'Ah … I remember now. That's the title of the book.'

She tittered again. 'It's more than that. I mean, *you*'ve got it coming.'

Note 1: the Government's adviser on global warming and climate change was Prof Ross Garnaut.

Note 2: the Federal Treasurer at the time was Wayne Swan.

Note 3: the Australian Prime Minister was Julia Gillard

'Me?' I asked stupidly, not being able to think of something more intelligent.

'You and me. Come here and make me feel … romantic,' she ordered.

Recalling the very demanding sexual experience I had with Kate last Thursday, the arduous night with Katarina just on Saturday and feeling the lust overcoming me, I wondered if I was perhaps the shallow type. Or worse – maybe I was oversexed.

Well, *foxy lady*, I'm not *that type* of guy, I was inclined to say. Notions like cougars and toy boys and sex slaves came to my mind. I thought of the potentially degrading effect that such *episodes* can have on one's morale and self-esteem. I had to dismiss the temptation, I decided, and resisted it for … well, maybe … about five seconds.

I reached for her and touched her naked bottom. It felt soft, warm and silky. I continued down her legs and I pushed her shoulder gently in an attempt to roll her over on her back, but she wouldn't. I pushed a little harder, but Rhonda was a strong woman. She just wouldn't play the game.

Patience, I thought and began to stroke her body again. Lying on her belly, she was moaning softly. I lay on the bed and aligned my body with hers. I slipped my hands under her silky negligee and caressed her breasts. They felt dense and heavy. I kissed her on the neck. She didn't respond. It frustrated me. Come on, it's a bit late to play the hard-to-get game now, I was inclined to say.

I continued with my foreplay and it seemed to work. With her eyes half-closed and her lips parted, she was moaning with apparent desire and seemed in a trance.

'Nice, very nice …' she murmured.

'Let's make it even nicer,' I suggested.

'What do you mean?' she whispered.

Ah gosh, she was killing me. 'You know what I mean …'

'I don't. Show me,' Rhonda sighed.

I chuckled. 'That's what I was about to do, if you … let me in.'

Her next move got me totally perplexed. She suddenly jumped into a vertical position, looking angrily at me. 'Were you perhaps planning to … fuck me?'

That was the million dollar question. I looked dumbly at her. 'Weren't you?'

She gaped at me with horror. 'Of course not.'

'Why not?' I asked bewildered.

She gave me another angry look. 'Because we aren't married yet.'

That was the last thing I expected from Rhonda Everton. 'But … we don't have to be married for that.'

She shook her head disapprovingly. 'See Mister, that's where you're wrong. I might look an easy catch, but I have my principles and values. In short, forget your naughty thoughts, or save them until the wedding night.'

I was pretty well worked up and just couldn't believe what this bombshell blonde was saying. 'But, why did you call me here?' I asked.

She giggled. 'I said you've got it coming, didn't I? Had you been a good boy before … I mean, last Saturday … we could have got something going, but not under the current circumstances. You're taking me for a sucker and I despise the thought.'

'No, I would never do that,' I protested. 'My great respect and admiration for your moral principles and values will reach new peaks if you … you know … if you … cooperate …'

'If by *cooperation* you mean sex, it's definitely out of the question. I can recommend a cold shower instead. And some more wine will make you sleepy. I want you to sleep here, with me.'

I didn't understand anything anymore. 'But, you've just said that sex was out of the question. And next thing, you're saying you want me to sleep with you. I don't understand.'

She chuckled again. 'When I said I wanted you to *sleep* with me, I meant just that. If you check up the dictionary, to sleep means to be dormant, quiescent, or inactive. It doesn't, in any way encompass activities such as sex.'

'But I like much better the other definition of sleep. I mean, it's much more fun and much more … proactive,' I argued.

'Not negotiable, for the time being. So, have some more wine to make sure you'll be able to sleep and then come back to bed. I am very tired already.' To prove it Rhonda yawned, though she did it in a way that I found very sensual. She probably did it that way on purpose.

'But, what's the point? Why sleep in the same bed with you, if nothing between us is to get going? I may as well go and sleep in my bed.'

'You're not,' Rhonda ordered. 'I want Helen to find us together.'

Tuesday, 31 May

I woke up with a startle, not remembering where I was. I remained still and focused for half a minute. It slowly came to me. I opened my eyes and read the electronic clock on the night table. It said eighteen minutes past eight. The bedroom's door was open, while Rhonda, asleep next to me, was breathing lightly. I tried to put my thoughts together, but it was difficult.

That fact that I'd slept in and didn't pick up Helen from the airport bothered me. But the feeling didn't last long. I immediately panicked, having heard a noise within the apartment.

I jumped from the bed and listened. Clearly, someone was moving around in the penthouse. Was there a burglar? I asked myself. I thought about it and decided it was probably Helen. She must have come home by taxi and she must be quite pissed off with me. What was I going to do? I had to disappear back into my flat before Helen turned up.

I collected my clothes and made it to the bedroom's door. Right then, I heard the door to the corridor being opened from the main entry's hallway. I lost my nerve and tiptoed back and into the ensuite. I locked the door from inside and took a long, hot shower. I actually should have taken a cold one. Once I finished the shower and turned the taps off, I heard voices in the bedroom: female voices and not very soothing or friendly. I stepped out of the shower, walked to the bathroom's door and listened, while putting my clothes on.

'Don't blame me for this,' Rhonda was saying. 'It was your idea.'

'Only you've overdone it, a little. I never thought you'd leave it to the last minute and have it off with him in *my* bedroom, right when he was supposed to pick me up from the airport.'

'And I'd thought you'd have a better sense of humour. I'd actually imagined your face, arriving home and catching your lover in bed with your best friend. I found it *very* funny.'

'Well, he's not my lover,' Helen pointed out.

Of the two of them, Helen sounded more irritated, while Rhonda seemed quite relaxed.

'He's your casual lover,' Rhonda replied.

'Not anymore. Now, he's all yours,' Helen retorted.

'I don't mind sharing. There is plenty of it to share,' Rhonda remarked.

How did she know that? I asked myself. But, even if it sounded complimentary to me, listening to their cat fight, I felt used and abused. Reflecting on it, I realised it was actually the frustration of *not* being used and abused during the night, which annoyed me.

There was a pause, then Helen said, 'Who's knocking on the door at this time of the morning?'

There was silence for the next twenty seconds or so. Helen must have walked out to answer the front door, I thought. I opened the bathroom door and looked into the bedroom. With her back at me, Rhonda was getting dressed. I sneaked from the ensuite close to her.

'You two had a pussy fight?' I said.

She jerked and turned towards me. 'Pussies don't fight,' she said.

'They do much better than that. But cats do fight and pussy or cat is the same thing,' I explained, repeating what Katarina had told me the other day.

'I didn't know about that, but we learn something every day,' Rhonda observed.

'It's a shame I didn't learn anything during the night,' I added.

'What's going on? It sounds like there are several people at the door,' Rhonda said.

Indeed, I could hear several voices, but I couldn't catch what they were saying. 'I'd better go back to my flat before Helen returns,' I said to Rhonda.

'We could have a *quickie* before she's back,' Rhonda suggested, giggling. 'If she wasn't mad enough before, she'll certainly be when she'll catch us in the act.'

She was only half dressed and her bare bottom looked very tempting – tempting enough to entice me, but I knew she was only teasing.

'There is a chance she'll want to join in,' I noted, recalling what Rhonda had just said to Helen about *sharing*.

'Well, you'd find yourself on familiar grounds, so to speak,' she replied tartly.

Was she being jealous? I wondered. 'I think at this moment I'd be much more comfortable on the familiar grounds of my own flat.'

She picked her undies up and put them on. 'See you later, buster.'

'See you, busty.'

I crept out into the corridor and reached the door leading to my flat. I turned the doorknob, but it was locked. I'd locked it last night, I recalled. I searched my pockets for the key, but couldn't find it. I swore softly. What had I done with the key? I couldn't remember. Now, with that door locked, the only way of getting back to my flat was through Helen's front door and I wasn't keen to bump into her yet and whoever else might be at the door.

I leaned against the door and pushed my shoulder very hard trying to force it open. Though I was a pretty strong lad, the hard-timber, *stupid* door remained unmoved. Then I tapped on it, in the elusive hope that Katarina would hear the noise. I stopped, realising it was a better chance that Rhonda would hear the knocking and wonder who might be on the other side of the door.

I slinked back into the master bedroom.

Rhonda, now fully dressed, was making the bed.

She smiled seeing me. 'Having second thoughts already? Please make yourself at home.'

'But that's exactly my problem. I can't get back home through that door,' I said.

She put her index finger to her forehead and paused. 'Let me think. I guess your problem is you have … something sticking out and can't fit through the door because the access is too narrow. Would you like me to take care of your ... problem?'

She was frustrating me. 'Look, I'm not kidding. I don't know what I've done with the key.'

'Have you looked in your trousers?' Rhonda asked.

'You mean in my pockets?'

'No, I mean in your underpants. That's where the key usually is,' she explained.

She was annoying me. 'Look, I don't want Helen to find me here.'

Rhonda paused again, apparently trying to think of a solution. 'Well, you could hide under my skirt, I suppose. But then, there is a chance your *problem* might still be sticking out.'

'Listen, if you find this funny, I don't,' I snapped.

She shrugged. 'Why are you so scared that Helen might find you here? She knows you were here anyway. And we're nearly husband and wife, aren't we? I mean, even if she's jealous, that's her problem. After all, she's the one who pushed us to bed together.'

Well, she had a point. But I was worried about Katarina as well and I didn't want Rhonda to suspect that another woman was waiting for me in my flat. More, I feared Katarina could make her presence known. 'You're seriously considering marrying me?' I diverted.

She chuckled. 'I still don't know if you correspond. It's obvious that you don't meet all the essential criteria and I still don't know about the desirable ones either.'

'What do you mean by essentials and desirables?'

'Some believe that being faithful is essential, but you seem to be the type who enjoys playing around. The desirable criteria are the ones to do with *desire*, if you know what I mean.'

I knew what she meant, but my nerves were still on the edge. Those voices coming from the front entry bothered me. And for some reason, Kate was very vividly back in my mind. That's in addition to Katarina. 'I'm not the type who enjoys playing around,' I protested.

'Sure you're not. That's why you set yourself a double date last Saturday and while two foolish dames were waiting for you, you were probably servicing the third.'

'I was with Luigi,' I said without thinking.

Rhonda raised her eyebrows. 'Ah ... I wouldn't have guessed you had such ... inclinations. Well, I might have to reconsider.'

I then heard footsteps in the corridor.

'You want to take my offer?' Rhonda asked, lifting the hem of her skirt.

'You're making fun of me?' I asked.

She nodded.

Then Helen stepped into the bedroom. She glanced at me and grimaced.

'What was all that about?' Rhonda asked.

'The police, looking for a Cornel Toma,' Helen said.

'The police were looking for me?' I asked incredulously.

'Someone has apparently reported you missing,' Helen replied, glaring.

'But I'm not missing – I'm here,' I pointed out.

'Your sense of observation, like your logic, is remarkable,' Helen noted.

'So, I gather you've told the police he's not missing,' Rhonda said.

Helen nodded. 'That's right. I've told the police he accidentally got into the wrong bed, with the wrong woman.'

I was expecting Rhonda to take that on the chin; instead she proved she could match Helen's sarcasm. 'Certainly the wrong bed but, luckily, the wrong woman wasn't here.'

Where these two having a pussy fight again? I wondered. Well, if they did, I didn't want any part in it. 'I'd better make myself scarce,' I said timidly.

'That's the only intelligent thing you've said so far,' Helen agreed frostily.

'So, who reported you missing?' Rhonda asked, ignoring Helen's comment.

I shrugged. 'I don't know. It was perhaps Luigi.'

Taking advantage that both women had remained silent, I sneaked into the corridor and rushed out of the penthouse.

Back in my flat, Katarina was standing by the kitchen's doorway talking on the phone. Her face relaxed and she beamed at me when I showed up.

I halted and stood opposite her, wondering who she was talking to.

'It's alright,' she said to whoever she was on the phone, while smiling mischievously at me. 'He's here now.'

Seeing the joy in her eyes, I became a little melancholic. There was no question that she loved me and I responded to her feelings by behaving like a jerk.

Gaping at her, it occurred to me that now, when Helen was back and my fake marriage with Rhonda was definitely on the cards, it was the time to tell Katarina that we should stop seeing each other. Yet I couldn't find the necessary strength to break that news to her.

Still on the phone, Katarina listened for about half a minute and nodded. I thought that was unnecessary, as the person at the other end couldn't see her. 'Yes, I'll make sure and sorry for wasting your time.' She then replaced the receiver and looked at me with pretended fury. 'Where have you been?' Though she tried hard to look angry, she couldn't conceal the joy in her eyes.

'Who's that you were apologising to?' I asked.

'Sergeant Dickhead or something like that, from Liverpool police. Maybe Dickson,' she added. 'He lectured me for wasting police time and resources.'

'So, you reported me to the police as a missing person?'

'What else was I supposed to do? I went into the small bed-room and turned the computer on and had a glass of wine. And when I returned to the living room, there was no sign of you. Yes? Where have you been?'

I hesitated. 'It's a long story. But this business with missing persons bothers me.'

'But why? You're here now. You're not missing. Yes?'

'I'm not missing, but a friend of mine is and it worries me,' I said.

'What friend?' Katarina asked.

'You don't know her,' I said cautiously.

'I don't know *her*? So, it's a woman.'

I nodded. 'She's just a friend. There is nothing going on between us.'

'So, why is she missing?'

I shrugged. 'I don't know and it worries me.'

'But, if she's a friend that you care about, you must do some-thing. You can't just sit on your bum and pray that she'll be safe.'

'What would you suggest?' I asked.

'But, it's obvious. You must report her to the police. Yes?'

'Like you just did and caused more hassles than good,' I argued.

'Well, it was different. But, how long is this … friend of yours been missing?'

'It's been five days today.'

Katarina looked at me with horror. 'Five days and you just kept it to yourself? You must be crazy. Yes?'

'Well, maybe I am, but I've done a bit of research in the meantime. I spoke to her best friend and with her father. I'm seeing him again tomorrow.'

Katarina was red in the face. 'Tell me please, what your association with this woman is? But be honest, please. Yes?'

'Nothing romantic, just friends,' I lied.

'But how come you haven't told me anything about it?' Katarina insisted.

I shrugged. 'Well, I had other things on my mind.'

'What's her name?'

I hesitated. 'Ecaterina. She's Spanish.'

'Is that Katarina with an e? Like electronic Katarina?'

'Something like that,' I mumbled.

She paused for a little while and said, 'That's why you were calling me Kate the other day?'

'Yeah … maybe. She was missing already when I called you Kate.'

Katarina gave me an ugly look and reached for the phone. 'Well, I will call the police straight away.'

'Just wait a minute,' I urged her. 'I know you're in the habit of calling the police every five minutes, but this story is a little more complicated.'

'What do you mean by *more complicated*?'

'Well, this Ecaterina is a married woman. If her husband hasn't so far reported her as a missing person, it would be a little awkward for me to do it.'

'I see … So, you're having an affair with a married woman.'

Katarina's assumption made me feel pretty awful, but that

was my nature, I suppose. I couldn't resist attractive dames and sleeping with them gave me a momentary thrill. Invariably, I felt guilty later for whoever I was in a steady relationship with at the time. In Sydney, my only firm girlfriend had been Katarina, but sure, I had quite a few flings with other ladies, whenever an opportunity arose.

I thought of Helen and Kate and said, 'No, I'm not having an affair with a married woman,' which was half true, considering that Helen was single.

Katarina remained quiet, staring at me for a long time. 'Okay, I believe you,' she finally said. 'But still, you must do something about it. Yes?'

'Look, give me another twenty-four hours until I see Doctor Morales again. That's Ecaterina's father. And we'll talk again afterwards.'

She thought some more and read her wristwatch. It was twenty to ten. 'Okay, I hope you know what you are doing. Now, I have to be at uni by eleven. Will you give me a lift to the Strathfield station?'

'I will, but my boss has returned this morning. I don't want her to see us together. You know she doesn't approve of my having sexy female visitors. So, I'll give you a duplicate key and you go downstairs and wait for me in the car. I'll be there in a few minutes.'

Most likely Katarina suspected that my relationship with Helen was more intimate than I wanted her to believe, but she'd never questioned me about it. She probably accepted it as *part of the job.*

'Okay,' Katarina said. 'I'll do that.'

As simple as that. She was that type of girl – so sweet and uncomplicated!

8

Having taken Katarina to Macquarie University, I drove back to Liverpool, fearing a dressing-down from Helen was very much on the cards. Though confident that Rhonda hadn't made her aware of my repeated indiscretions during her absence, I sensed that Helen was cranky.

But on the bright side, as far as Helen knew, I'd been a good boy and followed her instructions, getting apparently intimately *acquainted*, so to speak, with my wife-to-be. The little detail that I was in bed with Rhonda when Helen returned home proved it. So, why was she so pissed off with me? To me, there was only one explanation. Helen was jealous.

Back to my flat, I had a very late breakfast and decided to behave myself and remain on stand-by in case Helen needed me. I turned the television on and waited for Helen to call.

I thought about Kate again and realised during the process that I was getting more detached from her and less interested in her whereabouts. If she'd run away with some lad she was in love with … well … good luck to her. The news that she was in love with another bloke had bruised my pride but there was little I could do about it.

As painful and frustrating as that realisation was, I could now see the positive side of it. With one less woman in my life, my existence was becoming a little less complicated. But, three remaining females in my life were still too many. I thought about reducing the field even further, to only two. The obvious one to get the boot was Helen. Not only was she twelve years older than me; she was definitely not in my class, or rather *I* wasn't in her class.

I certainly fulfilled all her physical needs, but there was a large disparity between us, spiritually. To be fair, I'd never attempted to deal with Helen at that level and I was pretty sure she didn't expect me to fill the gap. Having said all that, I was fully aware that, if Helen was to exit from my life, it was only if *she* chose to do so. I couldn't otherwise do anything about it, unless I was foolish enough to kiss goodbye my very convenient and excessively well-paid job and move out of the deluxe and free accommodation which Helen provided as well.

As for Rhonda … we'd slept in the same bed during the night, though we hadn't slept together. I knew there was a lot more she was able to offer, though for the time being, she still remained a mystery. But, to her credit, she'd certainly taught me a lesson on self-confidence last night: a lesson which I was going to remember for a long time to come. Anyway, thinking of the positives, the big plus about Rhonda was that marrying her would resolve my visa troubles, which had become a huge headache.

Nevertheless, the prospect of marrying Rhonda gave me a knot in the stomach. It was not because she didn't correspond – I was positive she did, in many ways, but … how about sweet and loving

Katarina? How could I do this to her? Now that I was on the right track of getting over Kate, I felt closer than ever to Katarina.

I watched the television without registering much of what was being said, when a piece of news grabbed my full attention. It said, 'Ecaterina Morales, daughter of famous Doctor Juan Morales, has been reported missing from her home. Ecaterina was last seen on Thursday last week, when she was sacked from her part-time job with the men's fashion chain superstore Dowes. Police are intrigued and frustrated that it took someone five days to report the woman missing. Ecaterina, or Kate, as she's known to family and friends, is aged twenty-seven and is described as brunette, five foot ten, or 178 centimetres tall and weighing approximately sixty to sixty-five kilos. She has a light complexion, very short, black hair, and dark blue eyes. At the time of her disappearance she was wearing a white blouse, blue skirt and a jacket of the same colour. Anyone who might have seen Ecaterina, or holding any information which might assist the police, is urged to contact Crime Stoppers on ...'

It took me a while to digest that news. So, someone had reported Kate missing. Who would that someone be? I asked myself. Somehow, I didn't think it was Doctor Morales. He'd barely showed a mild interest when I told him of Kate's vanishing and seemed to be bothered by other things that took a higher priority in his mind.

I didn't think it was Luigi either. Why would he wait four days and then have a sudden change of heart and report her missing on the fifth? I thought Solveig had been spot-on when she'd said Luigi was that type of proud Italian who would never publicly admit his wife had run away from him, most likely with another bloke.

As for Solveig herself, she'd seemed unwilling to get involved in this mess. I wasn't sure what caused her reluctance

– she seemed scared of Luigi and concerned that making the story public would cause Kate more harm than good. She'd even stressed to me not to contact the police about it, as I'd only stir up more trouble. Having revealed that Kate was in the habit of such *escapades*, she wasn't too worried about it and had no plans to report Kate missing.

That certainly ruled Solveig out, which only left two other people who knew of Kate's disappearance. That's Katarina and myself and … it wasn't me.

My endearing thoughts about Katarina suddenly turned into anger. Why had the silly little cow ignored my request and spoke with the police when I'd specifically asked her not to? So far she'd been so sweet, kind and discreet! And now look what she did! She infuriated me.

I prayed that Kate would be located quickly, before the police investigating her disappearance found any link to me. It didn't take me long to decide I wasn't going to assist the police with any information. I had, by any means, to stay out of trouble and out of the public eye. My life and future in this country depended on that.

I then pondered that someone might know of my connection with Kate and dob me in to the police. I thought Doctor Morales was an unlikely candidate. I hadn't specifically told him of my relationship with Kate; I'd only made him aware that Kate was missing. And when I left his office, he seemed, after two shots of liquor, as blank as the Berlin Wall. He probably wouldn't even remember that I was there, if not for his lovely receptionist. She had made a note in her appointment register and was expecting me to turn up tomorrow morning. I wasn't sure if it was a good idea any longer.

As for Luigi, I wasn't worried about him. He certainly wouldn't tell the police that I'd broken into his home and bragged about having had it off with his wife.

Back to Katarina, though I was pretty certain she'd spilled the beans to the police, I liked to believe she hadn't done it with any premeditated malice or intention to make trouble. It had been just an impulsive act resulting from her genuine concern about the wellbeing of a missing woman. So, to sum it up, I thought I was pretty safe with the police, for the time being.

I shifted my thoughts back to Helen wondering if she was having a well-deserved rest. Taking into account waiting time, a flight from Europe to the Australian eastern coast took no less than twenty-four hours, if not up to thirty.

I watched part of a matinee movie, while itching to ring Helen to find out what her plans for the rest of the day were. While hesitating over whether to ring her, a better idea came to me. Helen, just back from Europe must be drowsy and suffering from jet lag. What if I surprised her with a nice home-cooked dinner? It sounded like a pretty smart idea to me.

I knew that sooner or later she'd summon me to her penthouse to express her disappointment in my conduct. So instead of waiting for her reprimand, what if I took a proactive approach and presented myself with a hot, spicy beef casserole, with pasta on the side and a cold, spumante alcoholic raspberry to go with it? Knowing that Helen loved spumante raspberry, I was confident such a treat would soften her mood and smooth her spirits. Yeah, that was definitely the way to go.

What added to my confidence was that my cooking skills were elevated for a single bloke. I'd learned to cook back at home when, as a gourmand teenager I used to watch grandma preparing schnitzels and rissoles and stuffed cabbage, salads and pastas and whatever else.

At a few minutes to two o'clock, I walked to the shops to buy some meat, onions and potatoes – the main ingredients for a casserole. I already had plenty of canned tomatoes and pasta in my pantry. On the way to the Liverpool Plaza, I passed through Westfield and couldn't resist the temptation to stop at Dowes. Solveig was there, not doing anything in particular. Again, she looked very sexy. She frowned on seeing me.

'Hello, Dolly,' I said in a cheerful tone.

'Why didn't you listen to me? Why did you go to the police?' she burst out.

'I didn't. Whoever did it, I swear it wasn't me,' I replied.

She gave me a doubtful look. 'You seemed very much worked up yesterday. I was pretty sure it was you.'

'Well, it wasn't me. I thought about what you told me and I came to the conclusion that if Kate has a lover, it's just … unfortunate. I just can't afford the distraction anymore. I have enough problems on my own, so I decided to call this episode a closed chapter in my life.'

The blonde looked at me with surprise. She seemed pleased by my decision. 'Well … that's good for you. It's certainly the wise thing to do under the circumstances.'

I nodded. 'Yeah … I don't want anything to do with it any longer. But it was nice to meet you during the process. I hope to see you again some time.'

She gave me a sexy smile. 'I'm sure you will. Bye for now.' She turned and walked towards the fitting rooms.

What a pity Helen is back and I've committed myself to cook that stupid casserole for her, I said to myself, watching Solveig's lovely legs and the sensual swaying of her hips.

I returned home at close to three and braised the meat and did plenty of weeping while slicing the onions. I sautéed the onions, wedged the potatoes and mixed them well with the meat and tomatoes. I added salt, pepper, garlic and some other spices and placed the pot in the oven at low temperature to cook slowly for the next two and a half hours.

The aroma coming from the oven assured me that the meal was going to be a definite success. I felt confident that even my very fussy boss would be impressed by the attention.

At half past-five my mobile phone beeped. It was a text message from Helen, saying, 'See you at quarter to six.'

I replied immediately with, 'I have a hot meal in the oven – ready by six. Would you care to have dinner downstairs?'

I waited in vain. No reply came from Helen.

At twenty to six it was time to prepare the pasta. I boiled two litres of water with salt, added three hundred grams of macaroni and turned the heat off.

At ten to six, I was undecided whether I should go up to Helen's or wait a few more minutes, when the doorbell rang. It was Helen herself, dressed in a green, taut sweater and tight matching slacks. Her outfit went very well with her light-brown eyes. She looked relaxed and sexy.

'Welcome back home,' I said, showing plenty of my teeth and my good manners.

She walked past me into the living room and I followed her. I pulled out a chair for her and she sat at the table.

'What were you saying before?' she asked.

'I said welcome back home. I'm glad to see you back.'

'That's right, you didn't have a chance to say it this morning,' she replied coldly.

'I'll give you a drink,' I offered.

'Whatever you have in there smells pretty good,' she remarked.

'Spumante raspberry?' I asked.

She nodded.

I fetched a bottle from the fridge, popped the cork and poured two large glasses. 'Cheers.'

'Is there anything to celebrate?' Helen asked.

I nodded. 'Your return home, I suppose.'

'And your … engagement, perhaps?'

'Ah … I don't know about that,' I said cautiously.

'Did you find Rhonda … satisfactory?' Helen inquired.

'She cooked me a delicious pork roast,' I replied.

'And you're now trying to replicate her success with that … thing in the oven?'

'No, that's not pork roast. It's beef casserole.'

Helen rolled her eyes. 'Very romantic. Anyway, let's see if it is as tasty as it is romantic.'

'Sure, I'll just finish the pasta.'

I drained the macaroni and mixed it with the meat and sauce. The final product, which I served in two very large plates, looked and smelled like it was cooked at a five-star restaurant.

Having tasted the dish, Helen seemed impressed. 'Had I known earlier how good a cook you were, I might have thought twice about pushing you into bed with Rhonda.'

What did she mean by that? I wondered. Was that a hint that she'd rather keep me for herself? 'I didn't cook for Rhonda,' I clarified.

'That's right – she cooked for you,' Helen replied.

'I'm sorry about this morning,' I mumbled.

She made no comment on that. We ate in silence for the next few minutes, then Helen said, 'How about you turn the television on?'

'Would you prefer some music?' I offered.

She shook her head. 'I've been out of the country for several days. I need to get myself up to date with the local news.'

I turned the television on, reluctantly. I was afraid there would be a mention about Kate again. Though Helen had no idea of my connection with her, I just didn't feel comfortable about the whole story. So, with the television on, I kept talking loudly in an attempt to distract Helen's attention from the news.

'Will you have some more casserole?' I asked, seeing that she'd emptied her plate. I had finished my very generous portion a couple of minutes before.

She shook her head. 'I've eaten too much already.'

'Have a little bit more,' I insisted.

'Thanks, but definitely not.'

'Sure. And … how was Paris?' I went on.

'Even better than last time,' Helen said.

'And how's … the tiny fellow?'

'If you mean the French President, he might be small physically, but he's a great man in all other respects. You should know by now that a man's greatness is not always in his body, or in his pants,' she added.

Was she hinting at something? I wondered, but didn't ask the question. 'Yeah, I knew that. Napoleon was tiny as well,' I said. 'But, did he make a pass at you?'

She sighed – an apparent sigh of regret and rolled her eyes. 'So far, I've never been courted by an emperor.'

I was curious to find out if anything had happened between Helen and the well-known womaniser chief of state. Being petite and very sexy, I had no doubt Helen was the type who'd stimulate naughty desires in *the tiny fellow*. I was perhaps a little jealous too of such illustrious potential competition. 'But have you ever been courted by a president?' I inquired.

Helen hesitated. 'Come to think of it, the president of the RSL Club always paid special attention to me. But at seventy-something, he's not really in my age bracket.'

'But how about the French President?' I persisted.

'Even if he'd made a pass at me, I'd be very careful about spreading rumours concerning the French President.'

'But if he did, his actions would be facts, not rumours,' I pointed out.

Helen gestured to me to shut up. 'Wait a minute. I happen to know Doctor Morales.'

I didn't catch what the TV presenter had said about Doctor Morales, but I listened to the rest of the announcement. 'The NSW Police have issued a statement saying that the doctor's daughter, Ecaterina Morales, who was reported missing earlier today, was last seen on Thursday afternoon at the Steak House in Liverpool, where she'd been drinking with a man described as being in his mid-to-late twenties, with dark hair, blue eyes and a very athletic built. The man is believed to be about a hundred and ninety centimetres tall, or six foot three and weighing approximately a hundred and ten to a hundred and twenty kilos. He was wearing dark trousers, a light-blue shirt and a brown jacket. A couple of female observers have commented that Ecaterina's companion was unusually handsome. Fearing she might have met with foul play, the police have serious concerns about her well being. They are very keen to speak to this man and are urging him to contact them as soon as possible. Anyone knowing the whereabouts of Ecaterina, or holding any pertinent information is urged to contact the Liverpool Police Station or ring the Crime Stoppers on ...'

I instantly lost my appetite and probably changed colour in

the face. What happened next to me was probably one of those bouts of delusion the doctors have said I was prone to, at times.

Though the television was on, to me the room appeared to have suddenly sunk into a heavy silence. It felt like watching a silent movie. I kept watching the television screen, pretending to be captivated by what was going on. I actually had no idea what the talk was about. I was afraid to look at Helen. She didn't seem in a hurry to say or do anything, which I found very frustrating. The stillness seemed to last for ages.

'More wine?' I finally managed to ask in a voice which I did not recognise.

Indeed, Helen was not in a hurry to do or say anything. She just ignored my question.

The silence persisted. Peculiarly, the tick-tock of the wall clock seemed to slowly take over, louder and louder.

Another minute passed. I gave Helen a furtive look. She wasn't looking at me, which was a relief. Watching the bubbles made by the sparkling wine in her glass, she seemed absorbed by that phenomenon.

Having nothing better to do, I too began to watch the bubbles in my glass. Then I watched the bubbles in Helen's glass. Though similar, they were different. We were so near and yet, so far apart.

The talk on television began to get louder but not for very long. It gradually faded in a distant background again. Soon, I didn't hear it any longer. I took turns watching the bubbles in both Helen's and my glass. They moved up and down and, in split seconds, burst into nothingness forming a multitude of new, smaller bubbles, like stars in the sky when reaching the end of their astral lives. Like stellar explosions, or supernovas. I found the spectacle fascinating.

I imagined the glasses at an infinitely magnified scale – the size of the cosmos itself. The bubbles in the glasses were like planets and stars which formed galaxies and super clusters. Like in the universe, the larger ones exploded sooner. I thought of a giant star dying and found that miracle like a swan song. Or like the phoenix – the mythical bird reborn from its own ashes.

I gradually distanced myself from everything material around me and thought of time and space and the universe. The time to philosophise just happened to be right.

I saw Helen moving her lips. Was she perhaps talking to me? What was she saying? I made an effort and began to slowly perceive the reality. I didn't like what I saw. The glass was just a glass. The bubbles were no stars – just ordinary fizz.

I liked even less what Helen was saying. 'That man they're looking for fits very well your description.'

I felt threatened and attacked and went instinctively into an aggressive form of defence. *They* were accusing me of something I hadn't done. It was discriminating and unfair. Instead of admitting, *yes, I've been with that woman, but haven't harmed her in any way*, I felt I had to deny everything *they* were suggesting.

'No, I don't think that man fits my description,' I said to Helen.

'Coincidentally, it happened just here, around the corner,' Helen added.

'But there are some two hundred thousand people living in Liverpool City,' I argued.

Helen gave me a long stare. 'I see. Well, if that's the position you're taking, I won't keep you any longer.'

I wanted to be alone, but at the same time, I felt I had to convince Helen she was on the wrong track. 'But stay a little longer. Have some more wine, please.'

'I don't think it's such a good idea. They said the missing woman had drinks with … that man. I wonder what happened afterwards,' Helen went on.

'Nothing happened afterwards,' I jumped in foolishly. 'I mean, I don't know what happened, but I'm sure that nothing bad happened.'

'You're very quick in defending a man you don't know,' Helen said.

'I'm not defending him. I just believe it's unfair that people are already making assumptions which may very well be unfounded.'

'Assumptions which *may* be unfounded,' Helen stressed. 'We aren't quite sure if such assumptions are founded or not – are we?'

'We don't know - that's true,' I agreed. 'What I know is that *until* and *if* found guilty, this man must be presumed innocent.'

'Actually, I don't recall any accusations against this man being made so far. It was just stated that the missing woman was last seen having drinks with this *very athletic and unusually handsome man*,' Helen refreshed my memory.

I just nodded.

'And the police are urging this man to contact them. If I were this man and had nothing to hide, that's exactly what I'd be doing,' she continued.

I was tempted to tell Helen that if I contacted the police, they would certainly check my details and establish that my visa had expired. I'd then be arrested and most likely sent back to Romania. I nearly said it, but I realised that by doing that I would be admitting to Helen that I'd played around with another woman. 'Sure, you'd be doing just that. But you're not that man and neither am I,' I stated.

'I'm glad we've established that. Now, I'll leave you to it. You seem to have quite a lot on your mind.'

Feeling she didn't believe me, I wasn't happy to let her go like that. 'But please stay a little longer. We haven't had the desert yet.'

She stood up. 'Thanks for the meal. It was excellent, but I've left no room for desert.'

I grabbed her arm and pulled her back to her chair. 'Please wait a little. I don't want you to leave like that.'

'I don't know what you mean,' she said.

Still holding her arm, I hesitated. If I tried to convince her that I had nothing to do with Kate's disappearance, I had no choice but to come clean and tell her the full story. I would have to admit that, as soon as she'd departed from Sydney, I picked up a woman and had fun with her. I contemplated that scenario for several seconds and didn't like it.

'Let go of my arm,' Helen whispered. 'You're hurting me.'

I peered at her, not realising that my fingers were squeezing her arm.

'You're hurting me. Please let me go,' she pleaded, looking scared.

I slowly released my grip and let go of her arm.

She sat there, gaping at me with an alarmed look on her face.

I looked sideways, unable to meet her stare. We said nothing for a little while. I picked up my glass and emptied it. The liquid warmed me up, inside. 'Have some?' I asked.

She shook her head.

I took her glass and gulped the spumante. 'I'll get another one. I want to get drunk tonight.'

I stood up and walked to the kitchen. I fetched a bottle from the fridge and opened it. Part of the wine overspilled. It made me laugh very loudly.

I listened to my own laughter and realised it sounded like the laughter of an unstable individual. I took a long pull at the bottle. The feeling was so good.

'Have some straight from the bottle,' I yelled stepping back into the living room. 'It's so much better.'

I halted with my mouth half-open. The room was empty.

I sat on the couch and emptied the bottle very quickly. My mobile beeped. It was a text message from Helen. 'I won't need you in the studio this week. Take some time off and sort yourself out.'

Was that like a prelude to dismissal? I wondered. I couldn't think of a reply. I thought of Kate and of my current position with the police. They had my description, but the key witness was missing. That was Kate Morales herself. According to Kate's best friend, she was more than likely alright, having fun with a bloke, as she was in the habit of doing. Surprisingly, that contemplation didn't make me jealous any longer.

Kate will certainly turn up, sooner or later, as she's always done in the past. That's what Solveig had said and I had no reason not to believe her. Indeed, judging by her actions within the very short time I'd known her, Kate seemed that type of woman. That's why her best friend was not worried about her disappearance. And neither was her husband, nor her father. Why should I be?

As far as I could see, the whole fuss was about nothing. There were millions of bored, unsatisfied wives in this world who indulged themselves from time to time, having a bit of fun on the side to charge their batteries, as they say. Kate was just one of them. It has always happened and it will always happen. There was nothing to worry about.

Tomorrow, or the day after, or … whenever, Kate would turn up, most likely, happy and content. There would be some explaining to do and some embarrassment and maybe apologies would be offered. People will have a good laugh and the whole story would die away in no time. Keep your nerve Cornel Toma and you'll be alright, I encouraged myself.

I drank more, which helped my spirits quite a lot. By quarter-past-eight, I was in a state of euphoria, when my landline phone rang. I listened to the buzz of the phone wondering what it signified. It took me several seconds to work it out – someone wanted to talk to me. But who would that someone be? This second question I found even harder than the first.

Let's take this slowly, I decided, while the phone continued to ring. So, someone wants to speak to me, but do I fancy talking to that someone? I didn't know that, because I wasn't aware who that someone was. I found my logic irreproachable and drank to it. The phone stopped ringing, which solved my dilemma, but only for a few seconds. My mobile began to sing.

My flawless judgment told me it was the same someone trying different tactics. I pressed the green button, without bothering to read the name of the caller on the screen.

'So, you're not at home,' Katarina said.

'How would you know?' I inquired.

'I just tried your fixed line and you didn't answer.'

'So, where am I?' I asked.

There was a pause. 'You've been drinking again?'

'Yeah – I need to drown my sorrows.'

'What sorrows?' Katarina said.

I thought for a little while and the anger got the better of me. It was time to spill the beans, I decided. 'You know, I'm twenty-eight and still single. I need a wife to get permanent residence. I think the French maid will do. Kate would have done as well, but she's disappeared. And someone reported her missing to the police. So, people are now blaming me. They might handcuff me and send me back home before I have the chance to get married. It's all because of a silly girl whom I specifically asked not to talk to the police but she wouldn't listen to me.'

'What are you talking about?' Katarina asked in an anxious voice.

'You know very well what I'm talking about. I'm afraid, because of your precipitated action, our association will have to end. Goodbye, Katarina.'

'But Cornel, please …'

I hung up before she had a chance to continue.

My mobile began to sing again after a few seconds. I let it sing. It stopped and sang again and did the same routine several times. Then, it beeped. I read the text message. It said, 'We need to talk. Please answer your phone. I'll take a taxi and come to your place, if you don't answer your phone. Your boss won't be happy about it but I have no choice.'

I replied. 'No one will be happy. Leave me alone.'

I then turned my mobile phone off and continued drinking.

9

At nine o'clock, my doorbell rang. So, Katarina wasn't kidding, I thought. Well, my reception may not be to her liking, I decided while composing myself an angry facade. I actually didn't have to put a lot of effort in doing that – I was quite cranky already.

I opened the door and my mood changed from anger to perplexity. It wasn't Katarina facing me, as I had expected. There were two blokes in front of me. One was tall, dark and slim, with small, piercing, black eyes and a pock-marked face you wouldn't want to see before going to bed. He looked awfully mean, sadistic and very ugly. He actually reminded me of Cerberus, but a more vicious version of him.

The other, a giant of a man, I'd already met, though I had no idea how he found me. Both were wearing black trousers, white shirts and black jackets.

'Remember me?' the massive one asked with a grin.

'Who wouldn't?' I said, not with a lot of enthusiasm.

'We'll come in, if you don't mind. Or, we'll come in anyway, I should say,' Luigi Maslini went on and pushed me out of the way. The other guy followed Luigi into the hallway and living room. They halted in the middle of the room and looked around.

I left the door open and followed the pair. I thought, if they were about to cause trouble, one of the neighbours might hear the noise, with my front door being open, though that probability wasn't very high. There were only two couples living on the same level with me and I knew one of them was on holidays in the States. The others were pretty old and kept very much to themselves. I very rarely caught a glimpse of them. In addition, the building was of a very high quality and had a top-class acoustic insulation system.

'How did you find me?' I asked Luigi.

'Anyone in trouble with the police shouldn't give their personal details out — not to the doctor or to anyone else, for that matter. But you're obviously too stupid to think of that.'

I recalled the form which Amy had asked me to fill in at the surgery and swore softly, not impressed with myself.

'Nice place, huh?' Luigi said to no one in particular.

'You came all the way from Concord to tell me *nice place, huh*? Or maybe you'd like to rent a room?' I asked.

He fished a cigarette from a packet, lit it and gave one to his mate. They both remained standing, looking around. I noted the slim, ugly guy kept his right hand in his jacket pocket.

'Making yourselves at home?' I asked Luigi.

'Be quiet, or Giuseppe will fix you,' Luigi warned.

'Did you say Giuseppe? I'd have thought he was a male version of Venus of Milos,' I remarked.

Neither of them seemed to appreciate my quip.

'Sit down,' Luigi ordered.

'Talking to me, or to Casanova?' I asked.

Again, my gag failed to make the duo laugh, or even smile.

'Sit down,' Luigi said in a more threatening voice.

'Or what?' I riposted.

An automatic pistol jumped into Giuseppe's right hand. 'Do the fuck what he says,' he snarled. With the pistol pointing at me, he walked to the front door, closed it and returned.

'Aren't you being a little oversensitive?' I asked cautiously and sat on the sofa.

'Listen fucker,' Luigi went on. 'I could very well go to the police and let the cat out of the bag. You know they're looking for you …'

'But you're not going to the police,' I cut him short.

He nodded. 'Know why?'

'Because you're such a sensitive, considerate fella who wouldn't do anything to harm another caring chap. That's unless you're yourself in trouble with the police,' I replied.

'That's crap,' he laughed. 'I'm not giving your game away because we can do business together. I mean, you're going to pay me for this little favour.'

'Blackmail is a criminal offence,' I remarked.

He nodded. 'But not as bad as murder.'

'You know very well I didn't kill your wife.'

There was a pause and when he spoke next, I clearly detected the rage in his voice. 'You did worse than that. You fucked her.'

In one leap, he was onto me and punched me very hard in the face. That thump felt awful. Another savage blow followed to my guts. I cringed on the couch in a state of stupefaction. I felt like vomiting, but somehow I refrained. I realised I should have expected Luigi's move, but the drinks hadn't helped my alertness.

'That's better,' Luigi said. 'How did you like it, fucker?'

Well, I actually didn't. The concept of being bashed in my own home didn't appeal to me.

'Remember what you did the other day to me in *my* house?' Luigi demanded. 'I'm just returning the favour.'

As I didn't say anything, he prompted me with another couple of punches to the head. He could certainly punch, I noted with sorrow. This time, blood spurt from my mouth.

The sight of my own blood infuriated me. It also did another thing – it partly awoke me from my prolonged drunkenness. I leaned forward, pretending to collapse and rolled my body on the wooden floor. I caught Luigi by his legs and pulled as hard as I could, in the state I was in. He fell on his back with a thud that shook the whole building.

With the pistol in his hand, Giuseppe threw himself at me and aimed a sort of Jackie Chan kick at my head, but I shifted a little and he missed it. As he lost his balance, I rose to my feet and hit him a karate chop right on the side of his throat. I'd learned that strike back at home, during the police training course. The gun flew from his hand, his eyes enlarged and his face turned purple. He collapsed unconscious to the floor.

'That makes it two nil, home and away,' I said towards Luigi, but I didn't think he heard me.

I bent carefully and studied his face to make sure he wasn't pretending to be out, to catch me by surprise. With his body in an apparent state of complete numbness, his eyes closed and his face very pale; there was no doubt, he was in Wonderland. The way he looked worried me. I checked his pulse and sighed with relief. Though very weak, it was beating. I then did the same with Giuseppe.

I satisfied myself that though unconscious, both thugs were alive. I collected Giuseppe's pistol using a pair of thin gloves, emptied the cartridge holder and put the gun in Luigi's jacket pocket and the bullets in one of Giuseppe's pockets. Why I placed Giuseppe's pistol in Luigi's pocket jacket, I don't know. I think I did it unconsciously, to confuse the circumstances, just in case.

I opened the front door and dragged Luigi by his legs to the stair head. He was very heavy. I carried him to the other end of the stairway and propped his inert bulk against the wall, as far away from my flat as possible. I touched and felt during the process a very large lump on the back of his head. He must have hit his skull to the parquet, when he fell.

I then carried Giuseppe out of the flat and placed him next to Luigi. The task was much easier – he was some forty kilos lighter than his mate. I'd just finished that chore and was thinking what to do next, when I heard police sirens on the street downstairs. It sounded like a few cars had stopped in front of the building and people were alighting from them. I began to walk down the stairs to see what was going on.

Two men had just entered the building when I reached the ground floor. As both wore police uniforms and service revolvers, genius that I was, I gathered they must be police officers. Several voices outside told me there were plenty more police around the building.

'What's the story?' I asked.

The two officers halted. 'Sergeant Dickson from Liverpool Police Station,' one of them announced. He was about forty, fair, tall and well-built. With a whopping nose and protruding ears, his facial features were somewhat rough, but he looked tough and determined.

'I'm Mister Gib,' I introduced myself in a stupid manner, noting that the effect of the alcohol was still very much present in my system. Having made the blunder, I didn't bother to correct myself saying that my name was actually Cornel Toma.

'This is Constable Morcombe,' the sergeant said, pointing at his colleague.

Morcombe looked very much like Dickson, except he was darker, slimmer, a couple of inches shorter, some ten years younger and three ranks junior to the sergeant. With a turned-up nose and delicate features, he had the effeminate face of a pretty teenage girl.

'You live in this building?' Dickson asked.

I heard a door opening in one of the flats on the ground floor and another one above.

'That's right. What's the fuss about?' I inquired.

'There has been a disturbance reported. Did you see or hear anything?'

I shook my head. 'Nothing at all. I just came out to take some fresh air.'

'Where do you live?' the sergeant asked.

'On the second floor.'

Dickson looked at my face with a lot of attention. 'Have you just been in a fight?'

I noted that Morcombe too was staring at me in a very persistent manner. It gave me the impression that the constable's interest in my face came from a more personal point of view.

I laughed. 'Ah no, not me. I'm the pacifist type. Never been in a fight in all my life. I just had too many drinks and fell on the floor. That's how I decorated my mug.'

By the look on his face, I doubted that the sergeant believed me. 'We'll come upstairs and have a look,' he decided. He signalled to Morcombe and began to move up the stairs.

'Why bother?' I said timidly.

The sergeant kept moving up, not paying any attention to what I'd said, while Morcombe prompted me. 'After you.'

I followed the sergeant and Morcombe followed me, though I didn't feel quite comfortable having the constable so close behind me.

'Who are they?' Dickson asked once he reached the second floor.

Still seated, both Giuseppe and Luigi had opened their eyes and were stirring slowly, trying to revive their limbs.

I joined Dickson on the top of the stairs and composed myself an astonished face. 'Who are they?' I repeated the sergeant's question.

'So, you don't know them?' Dickson probed.

I shook my head. 'Never seen either of these lads in my life.'

'Didn't see them when you walked out to take … some fresh air?' Dickson insisted.

I shook my head again.

'They must have landed here from the skies,' the sergeant observed. He then leaned on the balustrade and shouted very loudly. 'Cooper, Diaz, Tan and Ward present yourselves to the second floor quick smart.'

Four young constables joined us in about twenty seconds. I heard a couple more doors opening on the ground floor and first floor.

'Search these two,' Dickson ordered.

The constables began working on Giuseppe and Luigi.

'This one is armed,' said one of the officers, showing the sergeant the pistol he'd found on Luigi.

'And this one has unused bullets in his pocket,' another added.

I shook my head in apparent disbelief. 'That's incredible – like in thriller movies.'

'Handcuff them both and take them to the station. We'll have a talk with Mister Gib in the meantime,' Dickson went on.

'You're armed as well,' I pointed out to the sergeant. 'You too should be handcuffed and taken to the station.'

'I don't find this funny,' Dickson riposted. 'We'd better have a chat.'

'Well, there is nothing to chat about, because I haven't done anything, I haven't seen anything, I haven't heard anything and I don't know anything,' I said apologetically.

'Is that your flat?' the sergeant asked, pointing at my door which I'd left open.

'How did you guess that?' I asked.

'We'll come in and ask a few questions,' Dickson continued. He didn't bother to ask if his plan suited me.

'But, please, Sergeant Dickhead …' I started.

'Dick-son,' he corrected.

'Sorry, Mister Son-of-a-Gun,' I apologised, laughing. Though aware that the police were likely to ask my ID and subsequently discover that my visa had expired, the drinks I'd had that evening made me behave in an indolent and careless manner.

The sergeant just gave me a stern look. I didn't think he possessed a good sense of humour.

Once inside the flat, he had a look around and scratched his head. Following the fight with the Italians, the living room was in a bit of a mess. At the same time, with the casserole pot still warmish in the oven, a vague welcoming aroma of home-cooked food pervaded the room.

The constable began to whistle, but not very loudly.

'You're sure you don't know those two resting outside?' Dickson asked.

I shook my head. 'As I've said before, I've never seen them in my life.'

'This room looks like a battlefield,' he noted.

'I can explain,' I offered. 'I had a … friend for dinner. I mean, a female friend. I cooked a beef casserole but she didn't fancy it. So, she left and … she didn't reimburse me for the meal, if you know what I mean. I was so upset that I got drunk and head butted myself.'

The sergeant looked suspiciously at me. 'I'd be curious to see how you did that.'

'Well … I don't remember the exact details …'

'I'd just like to see how you could head butt your own face,' Dickson insisted.

I thought about it and found his question tricky. 'Well … how can I put it …'

'If you can't say it in words, just show us how that's physically possible,' Dickson added.

I paused a little and asked. 'So, should I head butt you, or the constable?'

Dickson paused too, probably pondering it, I thought. 'You couldn't do that. You're a pacifist,' he reminded me.

He definitely lacked any sense of humour. Still, I had to come up with an intelligent answer. 'I did it in the mirror,' I explained.

'You said before you fell on the floor,' he reminded me.

'Ah … that as well,' I agreed.

Dickson studied my face again – longer this time – and frowned. 'Are you on the police watch-list for any reason?'

'But that's offensive,' I protested. 'Of course I'm not.'

'Have a good look at his face,' the sergeant said to Morcombe.

The constable gaped at me for several seconds. 'Very handsome,' he decided.

Dickson gave him a stern look. 'Sit down,' he said to me, taking over the host duties.

I sat on an armchair, not happy that he was telling me what

to do in *my* house. That's what Luigi had done a little earlier that evening and … he ended up being sorry afterwards.

The two officers remained standing, looking around.

'Tell us what happened this evening,' Dickson said.

'How about a drink?' I suggested.

'Skip it,' he retorted. He looked at the table and frowned. I hadn't bothered to put away the empty plates, the cutlery and glasses. He picked up a glass and studied it from close range and then did the same with the other.

'So, you had guests for dinner …' the sergeant said.

He was starting to piss me off. 'Is that a criminal offence?' I asked, adopting an unnecessary smart-arse line.

'How many?' the sergeant continued.

He was probably suspecting that Giuseppe and Luigi had been my guests for dinner but was puzzled that there were only two plates, two forks, two knives and two glasses on the table.

'To me, one lady at a time is sufficient,' I continued in the same manner.

He picked up one of the glasses and studied it some more. 'Do you happen to wear lipstick?'

So, he'd detected traces of lipstick on the glass which Helen had used. It helped my case, as it proved that my guest had been a woman. Or, possibly a man who wore lipstick, as the sergeant had just hinted.

'Only on Sundays at the church,' I replied.

My revelation didn't seem to surprise the sergeant. Only the constable flinched a little.

'You know what?' Dickson said.

'What?' I answered.

'Your face is familiar. Are you wanted by the police on any matter?'

'You've asked that before. Of course I'm not,' I said, ostensibly indignant.

'Can I see your ID please?' the sergeant continued.

I fished my driver's licence from my shirt pocket and handed it to him, fearing that my stay in the Southern Land was drawing to a close.

It took Dickson a very long time to read it. Perhaps the English language was not one of his strong subjects. He then showed it to Morcombe. The constable raised his eyebrows, visibly surprised and shifted his stare to me.

'Your ID says Cornel Toma,' Dickson noted.

I laughed. 'Is that offensive as well?'

'You said before your name is Gib,' Dickson added.

'Ah, I'm sorry. That was just a joke,' I explained.

The sergeant paused, studying my face again. It was like he was trying to place me but couldn't remember where. 'What do you do?' he asked.

I shrugged. 'Me? Nothing in particular. I'm just sitting here wondering what *you* are doing.'

'What do you do for a living?' he clarified.

'Ah … I'm Helen Longshanks' personal assistant and body-guard. Helen Longshanks is …'

'I know who Helen Longshanks is,' he interrupted.

'But, did you know I was her assistant?' I inquired.

He didn't answer that. 'I think you need to come to the station with us,' he said instead.

'But why? What have I done?' I protested.

'That's what we need to work out.'

'And can't you work it out without me going to the station?' I argued.

He frowned, perhaps considering that angle. 'Now I remember,' he said after half a minute or so. 'Your girlfriend reported you missing last night. You probably look familiar because I've tried to visualise your description given by her.'

I sighed and thanked God for that. I'd been afraid that my face might seem familiar because of the description given of me earlier on television. 'So, problem solved,' I said with a lot of respite. 'May I mind my own business now?'

My gap of relaxation only lasted a few seconds. The sergeant's answer deflated me. 'You still need to accompany us to the station, I'm afraid.'

I just couldn't believe it. 'But why do I need to go to the train station? What have I done? I don't understand,' I wailed.

'You don't need to go to the *train* station,' Dickson said. 'Just to the police station.' He made it sound as if the train station was a much more dreadful place than the police station.

'Look sergeant. You'd thought before I looked familiar but then you worked out why. I'm not a criminal and haven't done anything against the law. Why should I go to the station with you?'

'Well, maybe you haven't done anything against the law, but maybe you have,' Dickson said. 'That's what we need to work out. We'll just ask a few questions and we'll hopefully clarify this rather bizarre story.'

'But can't you ask me a few questions here? Why go to the station?'

'You may have to provide a formal statement,' Dickson replied unperturbed.

I kept protesting my innocence and made reference to my civil rights as an honourable citizen who paid his rates and taxes, but to no avail. The sergeant was determined to take me to the station, though I thought *determined* was a too kind term, when describing Dickson.

Having said all that, I knew that in the end I had no choice but to submit to Dickson's authority, which I was desperate to avoid. I felt that once at the station, on display among who knows how many officers, it wouldn't take too long until someone worked out I was the man wanted by the police in relation to Kate Morales' disappearance.

While trying frantically to think of a way out, a last-minute idea came to me. 'May I attend the toilet first, please?' I said to the sergeant.

I didn't think he liked my request, but he nodded. 'Okay, but don't be too long.'

So, he was now telling *me* how long I was allowed to spend in *my* toilet, in *my* house. Was that cheeky, or what?

On my way to the bathroom, I passed through the laundry and pushed the emergency button that Helen had installed when I'd moved in the flat. That button, when pressed, activated a sort of alarm bell in Helen's kitchen. She had an identical one in her apartment which triggered a distress signal in my laundry.

I laughed at Helen's idea at the time, arguing that an emergency button in her apartment was all we needed, in case she ever happened to be in danger. I said it was very unlikely that I'd ever be in a situation to be rescued by her. Well, I'd been proved wrong, again.

I remained in the bathroom and listened at the door. I soon heard a woman's voice – it was most probably Helen's. Judging by the inflexion of her voice, I had no doubt that Helen was quite agitated, but I couldn't hear what she was saying. Then I heard a man's voice – most likely Dickson's. I waited a couple of minutes and went out of the bathroom.

Hearing what Helen was saying, I stopped in shock when stepping into the living room.

'You can't just assume he's the man wanted for whatever reason, for the simple fact that his description *might* fit the bloke you're looking for,' Helen was saying.

I think Dickson was as surprised as me. He paused for a little while, probably trying to make sense of what Helen had just said.

'Handsome,' Constable Morcombe came unexpectedly to his boss's rescue. 'That's the key word. Remember what was said about the bloke who'd been seen drinking with that woman?'

The sergeant shook his head.

'I'm certain a witness said that man was unusually handsome,' Morcombe reminded him.

'That's nonsense,' I jumped in. 'Just have a good look at my mug. Do you seriously think this is the visage of a beautiful man?'

'You shouldn't have head butted yourself,' Dickson observed.

Helen had probably just realised she'd made a monumental blunder.

'Did they abuse you, physically?' she asked, peering at my face.

'Ah … just a few kicks and punches in the face and guts. I was surprised though that even Missus Morcombe here is such a vigorous brawler,' I added pointing to the constable.

'I'll ring Captain Walters straightaway,' my boss announced.

'But, wait a minute, madam,' Dickson attempted to stop her.

'Why wait? I'm sick of corrupt police officers abusing their powers, taking bribes and bashing innocent citizens,' Helen declared.

The sergeant grew red in the face. 'He's lying. Neither Constable Morcombe, nor I have ever touched him.'

'The constable has certainly touched my bum,' I said timidly.

Dickson gave me another ugly look. 'You know you may be charged for lying, obstructing police and hindering a police investigation?'

'Leave that aside, sergeant. Better tell me how you can explain these cuts and bruises on his face?' Helen demanded.

The sergeant shrugged. 'We can't and neither can he. He's told us a very interesting story that he had a female guest for dinner who didn't like his home-cooked casserole, which got him so depressed that he head butted his own face into the mirror.'

Dickson's explanation seemed to infuriate Helen. 'How can you talk such garbage, sergeant? For your information, *I* was the one who had dinner with Mister Toma this evening. His casserole was delicious and when I left, he was in good shealth and his face as neat as a new pin.'

The sergeant made a grimace, while Morcombe just nodded. Dickson gave his subordinate an admonishing sort of look. I didn't think he appreciated Morcombe's nodding. Still, for some reason, the sergeant seemed to regain his confidence.

'I've never allowed myself to be pushed around by famous people, be they actors or musicians, politicians or media personalities,' he announced. 'I have a job to do and I'm going to do it, with or without you interfering. Better without.'

'So what's your job tonight, sergeant?' Helen inquired. 'Or, should I perhaps ask, what do you *think* your job is?'

'I have reasonable grounds to suspect that Mister Gib here has, one way or another, broken the law. I mean I believe he's been involved in criminal activities.'

Helen gave him a contemptuous look. 'Is that right? Are you sure you've got your facts right when making these allegations?'

'As I've just said, there is, in my mind, a reasonable suspicion that Mister Gib has committed some sort of crime.'

Though Dickson was now using more official terminology, Helen wasn't impressed. 'Have you been drinking this evening, sergeant?'

'I certainly have not, though it appears that the suspect here has done quite a bit of drinking this evening.'

'So, if you haven't been drinking, why do you keep naming this gentleman Mister Gib?'

Dickson looked puzzled. 'That's the name he's given us.'

'Come on, sergeant. I've just shown you and Constable Morcombe my ID card,' I reminded him. 'Isn't that right, Constable?'

Morcombe nodded. 'That is correct.'

'Could you tell us Constable what your recollection of this man's name is?' Helen asked.

'It's Cornel.'

'Is it Cornel Gib, or Cornel Toma?' Helen continued.

'It's Cornel Toma.'

Helen turned towards Dickson. 'So, do you still believe you've got your facts right, sergeant?'

'Excuse me, madam, may I ask if you're representing Mister Toma as his lawyer? You're behaving like one,' the sergeant remarked.

'As a matter of fact, *I am* a lawyer,' Helen confirmed. 'And as a lawyer I am asking you this. Are you arresting Mister Toma and if so, on what charges?'

While Dickson hesitated, Helen went on. 'If you are, I am reminding you that you must make a statement indicating that Mister Toma is under arrest and the reason for the arrest. But if I were you, I'd be very careful before taking such action.'

The sergeant thought a little but didn't answer Helen's question. Instead, he spoke to me. 'And if I were you, I'd be very careful before making false accusations against the police. Do keep in mind that it's your word against ours and there are two of us …'

'*You* don't forget that I will vouch for him,' Helen broke in.

'And I will make sure I will talk with Captain Walters about you as well.'

Dickson gave me another long look, as if he wanted to register every little detail about my face. 'I have no doubt that we'll see you again.' He then signalled to Morcombe. 'Come on, constable. Let's get out of here, for the time being.'

Morcombe gave us an official salutation and followed his boss towards the front door.

Watching the two police officers leave, I remained in a state of prostration. I kept staring at the closed door, not having the courage to look at Helen, while knowing she was watching me and sensing her eyes piercing through my neck.

I couldn't think of anything to say. I was tired and empty of feelings and emotions. I recalled Kate and our hours of passion – only five days before. So much had happened since then. I desperately wanted to turn the time back while knowing I couldn't do it.

I felt I'd entered a dangerous game and couldn't think of a way out. I felt like I'd been captured by a giant wave and had no idea where it was taking me and where I'd eventually land. Perhaps, back in my country, I feared. Or even worse: in jail for a long time.

For the second time that evening, Helen brought me back to earth. 'What happened?'

I shrugged. 'I don't know what happened.'

'I'm sure you can do better than that.'

'I don't think so,' I said without turning to her.

There was a pause. 'Please find the courage to face me and talk to me, Cornel.'

I turned slowly towards her, but I kept my head down.

There was another, longer pause. 'There is guilt written all over your face,' Helen said.

I kept looking down, not saying anything.

'I don't know why I'm doing this. I must be crazy,' Helen concluded. She strode to the laundry and disappeared upstairs, in her own world.

I walked into the bathroom and watched my face into the mirror, above the sink. I didn't like what I saw. I had bruises and swellings on my lips and cheeks and my eyes looked tired and cloudy. I took my shirt off and poured lots of cold water over my head and face. I kept doing it for a couple of minutes; then I turned off the tap and looked at myself again. I still didn't like me.

The landline phone rang in the living room. I walked to it and picked it up.

'Don't worry, I won't see you tonight,' Katarina said, while crying quietly.

So, as expected, she *is* sorry and crying, I reflected. 'I wasn't worried,' I said.

'The police just took me home,' she continued, whimpering.

I became alert again. 'The police took you home?'

'I was waiting to catch a taxi to come to see you when a hood snatched my handbag and ran off. A guy who was around took me to Parramatta Police Station. They asked for a statement and gave me a lift back home. They were very nice – even called a locksmith who unlocked the door. But now, I have no ID, no money and no phone. What do I do?'

I couldn't think of any intelligent solution. 'Yes, these police officers are always very nice. The ones from Liverpool Station are the nicest.'

She paused for a little while. 'Yes, but this doesn't solve my problem.'

'Police don't solve problems. They *make* problems,' I stressed. 'I know it's unfair for you, because you did help the police with information earlier today.'

She paused again. 'Are you still cross with me?'

'No, I'm not cross with anyone. It's *you* that seems to be very unhappy.'

'Yes,' she admitted. 'But I still love you very much ...'

'Don't worry about that,' I interrupted. 'You have other more important things to worry about. I'd thought at first you were crying because you'd upset me. But I was wrong. To you, your handbag is more important than me. That's why you're crying, not because of me.'

She began sobbing louder. 'I'm crying because you're upset and I can't see you tonight.'

'That's right – not tonight, not tomorrow, not the day after and not ever.'

I replaced the receiver without bothering to say good night. I kept drinking and feeling sorry for myself until the early hours of the morning.

10

Wednesday, 1 June

Though I'd gone to bed physically and morally battered, I woke up just after eight with less than five hours sleep. I was impatient to listen to the news to learn if they said anything more about Kate. They did, in the eight-thirty news.

'In a bizarre twist, Luigi Maslini, husband of the missing woman Ecaterina Morales, was arrested last night while apparently unconscious in a block of flats in the south-western suburb of Liverpool. Coincidentally, Liverpool is the same suburb where his wife was allegedly last seen before she went missing last Thursday. Ecaterina, or Kate Morales, a qualified doctor, also had a part-time job as a sales person with the men's fashion chain Dowes, in the Westfield Shopping Centre at Liverpool. According to the police media unit, Luigi Maslini was charged with the illegal possession of a firearm. A second man arrested at the same time is, according to our sources, well known to the police. The men, both of Italian origin, have so far refused to cooperate with the police.'

That's not too bad, I thought, as there was no mention about the suspect that the police wanted to talk to in relation to Kate's disappearance. My optimism, though, changed immediately to confusion when the radio presenter added: 'Police are urging the man who rang yesterday with information about the missing woman Ecaterina Morales to contact them again.'

What the hell is going on? I asked myself. My assumptions that Katarina was the person who'd informed the police had been wrong.

Perhaps, I thought, I should ring her and apologise, but her mobile phone was gone and she didn't have a landline connection. Well, I would make it up to her ... sometime.

So, who was the man who'd called the police? It couldn't be Luigi, as he was in police custody already and they said that he'd refused to cooperate. As far as I could think, that only left one other option – Doctor Juan Morales. But why hadn't he contacted the police straightaway, after I'd seen him on Monday afternoon and made him aware of Kate's disappearance?

I thought about it and came up with three possible explanations. One was that he kept drinking and blacked out after I left his surgery. Second that he waited until he had official police confirmation that his daughter *was* indeed missing. And third, he might have been too scared of Luigi to contact the police, but acted after hearing the news that his son-in-law had been arrested.

I stepped into the bathroom and kept thinking in the shower, wondering if Doctor Morales had also informed the police about my visit to him on Monday afternoon. As they hadn't mentioned anything about it, I thought it was safe to assume he hadn't. Considering the state he was in when I'd left his surgery, perhaps, he didn't even remember me.

With my mouth and cheeks still aching, I skipped shaving, waiting impatiently instead for the nine o'clock update. Having repeated the same information from before, the news presenter added: 'According to police sources, new information has come to hand about the man who was seen having drinks with Ecaterina Morales, before her disappearance on Thursday last week. Another witness has come forward confirming that a man fitting the same description had picked up Ecaterina at the Dowes store where she worked in the Liverpool Westfield Shopping Centre. The woman, who wished to remain anonymous, said the pair had subsequently walked out of the shopping centre, presumably to the Steak House, where they were seen having drinks together later that afternoon. Police have confirmed that they most likely know the identity of this man and are confident of an early arrest.'

On hearing that piece of news, I went into a sudden panic. A horrible thought struck me. Why are they talking about *an early arrest*? Had the police search for Kate turned into a homicide investigation? Had Kate been murdered? Was Kate Morales dead?

Sweat started to run down my neck and I began to tremble. Though I'd completed the four-year police training course in Bucharest, I found myself incapable to think and reason any more while in an emergency situation. An irrational fear took hold of me, which made me feel paralysed. The fact that the man seen with Kate was also suspected of foul play and probably murder, made me feel like a criminal and act like I *was* guilty.

Instead of thinking about how to defend myself by telling the truth, my only concern was how to escape being arrested.

As my temporary working visa had just expired, I was now an illegal immigrant in the country and had good reasons to fear that, if they arrested me, the federal authorities would send me back home.

As I loathed that scenario, I immediately made up my mind. I wouldn't let the police arrest me. I had to run away, I decided. But run where?

Then I thought of my childhood and teenage years' best mate, Florin Panait, whom I'd promised to visit during Helen's absence. A few years after arriving in Australia, Florin had met and fallen for Remy, a former beauty queen, party girl and socialite, who, tired of her past tumultuous days, was planning a radical change in her life. Her idea was to live a 'solitary' life in the bush.

Her plans suited Florin who was an outdoor lifestyle lover and environmentalist. They married and purchased a very sizeable farm in Sydney's outskirts, somewhere between Penrith and Camden. Florin had told me they lived a quiet life, *far from the madding crowd.*

I had to ask Florin's help, I decided, and do it quick smart. My first impulse was to ring him straightaway, but quickly changed my mind. I had, from now on, to be very careful not to make any wrong moves and give the police an indication of my whereabouts. And I ought to move very fast.

While planning my next move, I instinctively grabbed a cotton piece of cloth and dusted all the hard surfaces in my flat which I thought Kate might have touched. I then vacuumed my bedroom, the bathroom which Kate had used and the furniture in the living areas to make sure any trace of her would be wiped out.

I fetched a couple of travelling bags and stacked them with light clothes, a couple of pairs of sports shoes, toiletries and a few other necessities. Once I zipped the bags, my landline phone began to ring. I watched it ringing, hesitating. Who could it be? Possibly Helen, to remind me I had to do something to come back to my senses. Or, maybe Katarina, trying to make up with me again. Or perhaps … it was the police. My skin crawled at the thought.

The phone kept ringing and I made up my mind not to answer. It stopped after about ten rings. I got hold of my passport and counted the cash I had on me – a little over fourteen hundred dollars. I had to withdraw more money, to hold a cash reserve, just in case, I decided.

I snapped up my passport and the cash, grabbed the two bags and rushed downstairs to my car. I placed the bags in the trunk, got in and took off. As I approached the first intersection, I saw in the rear view mirror two police cars pulling up in front of my building. You've just pulled a fast one, Cornel, I said to myself.

I drove to Westfield and parked on Macquarie Street opposite the shopping centre, in a half-hour limit spot. I assumed the police cars would return to the station via George Street, which ran parallel with Macquarie, and I'd be safe from them for the time being.

Afraid that my bank transactions could soon be monitored by the police, I decided to withdraw a substantial amount of cash. As the daily limit for ATM withdrawals was only one thousand, I had no choice but to walk into the branch of the St George bank, located on the ground floor of the mall.

I strode to the bank with my head down, afraid to look at the hundreds of passers-by. Nonetheless, I had the impression that they were *all* staring at me. I entered the bank and queued on the line with my nerves on edge. I counted thirteen people in front of me, which I found depressing. And the lady at the counter was incredibly slow. She even made small talk with the customers, like "glorious weather this morning", as if that was part of her job description!

Ten minutes passed without the queue making much progress, while I was swearing to myself, fidgeting and checking the time every few seconds.

With my temper boiling, I sensed someone had approached and stopped about a metre behind me on my left. I saw the contour of a man on the corner of my eye and felt his stare fixed on me. I'd usually act assertively, even aggressively in such a situation; but now I lacked the courage to even turn my head to look at him.

The first thought that came to mind was that the police had detected me already. From the little I could see of him, it appeared he wore civilian clothes, but I wasn't sure. He could have been undercover.

He kept looking at me for several seconds, which to me seemed to last ages. I then suddenly froze and my heart nearly stopped. A powerful hand was squeezing my left arm.

'You're under arrest, comrade Toma,' a man said in a hoarse voice.

I felt my pulse accelerating, my mouth very dry and a cold shiver running down my spine. My first impulse was to hit him with a right hook and then flee. But what if there were several of them, behind me? While considering my options, I felt the guy's grip slacken.

'I nearly didn't recognise you,' he said, laughing. 'What happened to your mug?'

I turned towards him – it was Gabriel – a fellow countryman whom I'd befriended a few years back. I forced a smile and replied in Romanian: 'It's been just a little … disagreement.'

He switched to Romanian too. 'Was it about a dame?'

I nodded, and stiffened again. A woman in a police uniform

had lined up in the queue a few metres behind us.

'Whoever it was, he did a pretty good job, but I bet you've returned the favour all the same.'

I nodded again. 'Yeah, Luigi did good and I smashed his face a little too.'

'Don't mess with Italians, mate,' Gabriel offered his advice. 'They're generally small but they don't muck around if they catch you playing with their dames.'

Gabriel was right. All the mess I was in had happened because of a *dame* that I'd played around with. Coincidentally, she was the wife of an Italian.

'Do I look so bad?' I asked.

Gabriel peered at my face again. 'As, I've said, I nearly didn't recognise you. And it looks like you haven't shaved in a few days, which doesn't help either.'

His comment made me feel a little better. The cuts and bruises on my face had swollen over night and as I hadn't shaved that morning my scruffy appearance made me look quite different from the usual *Alain Delon's carbon copy*. I gathered that my description as given out by the police would be somewhat out-of-date already.

'I'll give you a call later in the week. Maybe we'll organise a tennis match for the next weekend,' I changed the subject.

I was actually keen to get rid of him; not that I didn't like him – on the contrary; but I had the impression that chatting with him in a foreign language in that place, where everyone was a stranger to everyone else, attracted a lot of attention. That was one thing that I had to avoid from now on: being conspicuous and attracting attention.

'Actually, I was about to give you a call. I'm having a little party on Friday night, so if you haven't got anything better to do, I'd love you to come,' Gabriel suggested.

Will I still be a free man by Friday night? I asked myself. I noted that, at last, the teller had finished serving an old man who'd been there for the best part of the last ten minutes. 'Yeah, I'd love to come. I'll give you a call tomorrow.'

'Rita is coming too,' Gabriel stressed. 'Remember Rita with big boobies?'

'Sure, I'll give Rita a beep. I mean I'll give you a beep,' I promised.

'Hey, don't you try to jump the queue, young man,' an elderly woman yelled at Gabriel.

'Don't worry ma'am. I wouldn't do any silly things while this pretty police woman is here watching me,' Gabriel laughed.

A few people laughed in the queue.

The police woman didn't say anything.

I didn't have the courage to turn and check how pretty she was. Gabriel's remark made me feel very uncomfortable.

'I should hope so,' the elderly lady replied.

'Okay, mate, I'll talk to you before Friday,' Gabriel concluded.

'See you, Gabe,' I said with relief, as he walked away.

It took another fifteen minutes until I was face to face with the teller. She was probably in her late thirties, brunette, with dark eyes and quite ugly-looking.

I handed her my savings account card. 'I'd like to make a large cash withdrawal, please.'

'How large?' she asked.

'Twenty grand.'

She raised her eyebrows. 'Have you given prior notice?'

'No. Something urgent only came up this morning.'

'I'm sorry. You can't withdraw such a large amount without prior notice.'

'But please – I need that money,' I pleaded.

She shrugged. 'I'd need that sort of money too, but I can't do much about it.'

'But this is *my* money,' I stressed.

'Even so, you should have given prior notice,' she said.

'But how could I have given prior notice when I didn't know until this morning that I needed the money?'

'You can give prior notice now and have the money tomorrow,' the teller offered.

'Thanks a lot, but I need the money today.'

'I'll check with the supervisor,' she said and went away.

A few folks in the line began to murmur their displeasure.

The teller returned within two minutes. 'Five thousand is all we can do.'

'Make it ten,' I said.

She shook her head. 'Five thousand is my best.'

'Is this some sort of auction?' some smart arse in the queue wisecracked.

I hesitated and decided that making a fuss in a public place wasn't a smart idea, considering the circumstances. 'Okay, I'll take five grand.'

'Sure. Can I see your ID please?' the teller demanded.

I hadn't expected that. 'My ID? Why is that? Isn't my card sufficient?'

'This card might not belong to you,' she riposted. 'It's standard procedure to ask for identification when clients make large withdrawals.'

'But this isn't large enough,' I protested. 'Remember I asked for twenty grand and you wouldn't even give me ten?'

'Sorry, it's not negotiable. And I don't understand what your problem is. You show me your ID and I give you the money. It's simple and fair isn't it?'

I didn't find it as simple as that. What if she became suspicious that my face looked different from that shown on the photo on the drivers licence? Maybe she'd check with her supervisor again and … with that police officer lining in the queue … I felt quite uneasy.

I pretended to check my pockets for the drivers licence. 'Sorry, it looks like I left my driver's licence in the car.'

The teller shrugged. 'Just go and get it.'

'But that's ridiculous,' I protested. 'I parked in a half-hour limit spot and I've been in the line for just about half an hour. Now you want me to walk to my car and back, which is another fifteen minutes and by that time I'll probably get a parking ticket.'

'Sorry, but I'm afraid that's not my problem,' she said, untroubled.

She was killing me. 'What *is* your problem then?'

'I don't have a problem. It looks to me like *you* might have one.'

I made an effort to keep my cool and explained. 'I only want some money which I need urgently. It is *my* money and I gave you my card and I'll sign the receipt, so you can check it against the signature on the card. Why is that a problem?'

The teller remained impassive though. 'Sorry, but it's not me who makes the rules. It's the bank's policy.'

Several customers began to murmur their annoyance in the queue again.

I'd already run out of all patience. 'Fuck you and fuck your bank's policy,' I hissed to the teller. I turned around and strode away. A jeer of disapproval followed me from the queuing folks.

I withdrew a thousand dollars from an ATM outside the bank and rushed out of the shopping centre. As I was waiting in front of Westfield to cross Macquarie Street, I noticed a council officer wearing one of those yellow, easy-to-see jackets checking the chalk mark on one of my car's tyres. By the time I reached my car, he'd started writing a parking ticket.

Already infuriated by the bank teller, I yelled at him. 'What the fuck do you think you're doing?'

He gave me a long, tough look. 'Is this your car?'

I noted he was probably just a few years older than me, a little shorter, but very broad. He looked the type who didn't intimidate easily.

'Do you think I'd waste my time talking to you if this wasn't my car?' I replied.

'This car has been parked here for at least forty minutes,' he stated.

'I don't think it's been forty minutes yet. And I'm here now. I also know that you can always apply some discretion, if you have any common sense,' I said, much softer than before.

But he wouldn't take the bait. 'Maybe I could, but I don't have any common sense. Especially when people play tough and swear at me.'

My temper rose again. 'That wasn't tough playing. I'll show you what tough is, if you don't stop writing on that piece of garbage straightaway.'

A few people had already gathered around, watching us.

He halted from writing for a few seconds and gave me another rough look. 'Show me what your idea of tough is,' he said and began writing again.

My fury got the better of me. I made a step forward and was now within inches in front of him. 'You fucking idiot. You've asked for it …'

I hadn't quite finished the sentence, when a marked police car pulled up in the no-stopping zone, just in front of my car. Two constables – one a bloke, the other female – got out and joined us.

I noted by the code displayed in blue paint on it that the car belonged to the Liverpool Police Station's fleet. As I'd just had trouble with two police officers attached to Liverpool Station, that detail made me feel even more uneasy.

'What's the problem?' the male constable, dark and tall, asked.

'This bloke here has overstayed in this parking spot and is now making trouble because I've booked him,' the parking officer stated.

The female constable – a young, pretty blonde – was gaping at my face, frowning. She made me feel very nervous. And more, it suddenly occurred to me that I had more reasons to be nervous. If the police already knew I was the man they were looking for in relation to Kate's disappearance, they were certainly aware of all my personal details, including what car I was driving.

'I wasn't making any trouble,' I said, very softly.

'You were only threatening to belt me,' the council ranger replied.

'You know it's a criminal offence to threaten a government officer and obstruct them from carrying out their duties?' the policeman asked.

'I know that. That's why I didn't punch him,' I said.

'So, your intention *was* to punch him,' the policeman continued.

'Sorry officer, but I don't think I've committed an offence just because of what I might have thought,' I pointed out.

A few approving sounds came from the crowd which had gathered around.

'As far as I can see, you were attempting to frighten this person and you threatened him with using physical force, when he was only doing his job,' the constable went on.

I glanced at the mob around and could see by their body language that they were on my side, which gave me a bit of courage.

'I think you saw wrong. You may ask these folks around,' I said, making a gesture towards the crowd.

Plenty expressions of support came from the mob massed on the sidewalk. That raised my spirits and made me feel much better; not for too long though.

'Can I have your driver's licence?' the policeman demanded.

I felt suddenly sunk. That's it, I said to myself. They'll certainly take me to the station and arrest me, once my identity is revealed. I remained silent, just standing there trying to think of a way out. Several seconds passed. The mob was quiet too and the blonde constable kept staring at me, still frowning, as if trying to remember something.

'Your driver's licence, please,' the tall constable prompted me.

I stayed quiet, just looking dumbly at him, as if I had no idea what he was talking about.

'He's probably disqualified from driving or the car is stolen,' the parking officer broke in.

'He wouldn't care about the parking ticket, if the car wasn't his,' the blonde cop noted.

'Well, maybe he's stupid as well,' the parking officer added.

'We'll find out in a minute,' the policeman said and continued to me: 'Have you had any drinks this morning?'

That was another angle which I didn't particularly like. As I'd had plenty of drinks until three in the morning, it was likely that traces of alcohol were still present in my blood.

'I'll get the drivers licence,' I said, ignoring his question. I opened the passenger door and pretended to search inside the glove compartment, taking my time.

'Any luck, mate?' the policeman yelled at me, once a minute or so passed.

I shut the passenger door and turned towards him. 'It looks

like I've misplaced my driver's licence. It's not there,' I said apologetically.

'That's a lot of crap,' the parking officer exclaimed.

By the disapproving look on his face, the policeman probably agreed with him. 'You're going from bad to worse, mate. But we'll get to the bottom of this in a minute. Can you check this rego on the computer, please?' he asked the blonde.

She made a note of my car's registration on a jotter and stepped to the police car. She sat in the driver's seat and began working on the mobile data terminal.

Several moments of silence followed. The atmosphere was very tense. I felt I was certainly dashed. It would be just a matter of seconds until they found who the owner of the car was. Recalling the two police cars pulling up in front of my flat earlier that morning, I assumed it was likely that a flag against my name had been posted on the police central computer, where the mobile data terminal received the information from. What was I going to do?

'I can tell you my licence number and expiry date. I've memorised these dates when I first got the licence,' I lied to the policeman.

He gave me a dubious look. 'You're positive?'

'Absolutely. No need for the young lady to check the computer.'

'Is that because she might find something you're trying to conceal?' asked the constable.

I felt I was running out of luck. 'I have nothing to hide,' I said.

'Bullshit,' the parking officer butted in.

More and more folks were gathering around, curious to witness the outcome of the incident. There was excitement and anticipation in the air. I was the centre of all the attention.

'I work for Helen Longshanks,' I tried a different line. 'She can vouch for me.'

'Bullshit,' the council officer repeated.

'No need for that,' the constable said. 'We'll get your details in a second.'

Right then, the police woman alighted from the vehicle and stepped up to her colleague frowning.

That's it, the turning point has arrived, I said to myself, noting that several people who'd gathered around were gaping expectantly at the blonde.

'What have you got?' the policeman asked his colleague.

She made a grimace. 'The stupid thing isn't working. It looks like there is a temporary disconnection from the central database.'

The policeman half opened his mouth and remained like that for a few seconds. The blonde gaped at him and shrugged. 'I think we'll have to take him to the station,' she said.

A murmur of disapproval came from the crowd.

The tall constable turned to me and said, 'You'll have to come to the station with us.'

That was one thing I was desperate not to do. Recalling how Helen had intimidated Sergeant Dickson the night before, I thought I'd give it a try as well. 'Are you arresting me officer? And if so, on what charges?' I asked assertively.

Both constables looked at each other, hesitating. 'We're not arresting you,' the blonde said. 'We're just asking you to accompany us to the station to establish your identity.'

'I can tell you my identity and any other pertinent details. Why not take my word for it?'

'Bullshit,' the parking officer said for the third time.

The blonde gave him an ugly look. 'It will only take a few minutes,' she said to me.

'I'm sorry, but I haven't got those few minutes. I'm in a bit of a rush this morning.'

'That's why you've left your car parked illegally for more than forty minutes,' the parking officer remarked.

'Why don't you shut your trap?' I retorted.

The young constables looked again at each other, unsure of what to do next, then the blonde gazed at my face once more and parted her lips to say something.

Right then, her police phone rang. As she answered it, I heard quite clearly what the voice at the other end was saying. 'Sergeant Dickson speaking. There is an armed hold-up at the Valore's bottle shop in Smithfield. They're short in that area, so you need to get there on the double.'

She paused, hesitating. 'We have a guy making trouble here, on Elizabeth Street, opposite Westfield. He's been obstructing a council worker. Should we finish with him first?'

'Has he got a record?' Dickson asked.

She gazed at my face again. 'He might very well have one. He looks like he's just been in a fight, but we can't check his record as he hasn't been able to produce an ID yet.'

There was a pause at the other end. I felt my heart rate going up again, fearing that the sergeant would put two and two together and think of me.

'Has anyone been physically harmed?' Dickson asked.

Once more, the blonde gazed at me. I didn't like her gazing at my face, at that specific point in time. I sure wouldn't mind her staring at me in different circumstances.

'It looks like this gentleman *has* been harmed, but not in this particular incident,' she said.

There was another pause, which made sweat run all over me.

'Just caution him this time and hurry up to Smithfield,' Dickson concluded.

'You've been lucky this time but the fine stays. Let's go,' the blonde said to her colleague. They got in the car and drove off, making a lot of noise with the siren on.

The parking officer seemed quite displeased that the police had let me off so lightly. He was red in the face and looked angry. 'If you keep carrying on like before, I'm sure someone *will* get hurt in *this particular incident*,' he threatened.

'That's one thing we are in agreement, but it so happens that I'm in a bit of a rush right now,' I said and made a step towards the driver's door.

He dropped his booklet on the car's bonnet and pushed me in the chest, blocking my move. 'You're not going anywhere until I finish writing the ticket.'

The people around got excited. 'Just thump the fatso in the head,' someone from the mob encouraged me. Plenty of approving roars followed.

My temper began to boil again. 'Don't worry about writing that shit. I'll throw it in the garbage bin anyway.'

He twisted his face in an ugly grimace. It was obvious that he was itching to hit me. 'Just stay where you are until I finish with you,' he snarled.

I gave him a shove in the shoulder and stepped towards the driver's door once more. He took offence at that. His left hand caught my shirt and pulled me towards him. Next he threw a wild punch aimed at my chin. But his arms were too short and he wasn't very good at throwing punches. I shifted a little backwards and he only punched the air. I then slammed a right hook on the side of his jaw. He went down like he was shot in the head.

There was instant silence in the crowd, then a lot of cheers and applause.

I grabbed the booklet from the car's bonnet, jumped in the car and sped off.

11

I turned left from Elizabeth Street onto the Hume Highway and drove several kilometres towards the southern suburb of Campbelltown, trying to think how to slip through the net without being traced by the police. They certainly knew by now what car I was driving, so I had to get rid of my Mazda CX-9, I decided, which was a shame, as the car was almost brand-new.

Thinking of my plan, I realised that to sell the car I needed the registration papers. Where were the registration papers? I wondered. I pulled up on the side of the road and looked for the papers in the dashboard storage space. This time, I really searched through it, not only pretended. Luckily, the papers were there. I congratulated myself for having been astute enough to store the legal proof for owning the vehicle in the glove compartment, though I knew that keeping that document in the car was otherwise a silly thing to do.

I made a U-turn at an intersection close to the Cross Roads, drove back towards Liverpool and stopped at the Mazda dealer where I'd purchased my car, just a couple of months earlier. I said to the same salesman whom I'd dealt with before that, being in urgent need of dough, I was willing to swap over my four-wheel drive for an older, cheaper model plus about ten grand in cash.

He said that trading conditions were very tough and though my vehicle was nearly new, *any* car lost at least a quarter of its value once driven away from the dealership. He added that he was in the business of *taking* dough from buyers, not *giving* it *away* and he went on and on with that sort of whinging, until I almost began to cry on his shoulder.

I agreed in the end to exchange my 2011, 5000-km-driven Mazda CX-9 for a 2004 model, 180,000 km Mazda 3, plus five grand in cash. Though I knew very well it was an outrageous rip-off, the car salesman assured me he was only doing the deal as a *special favour* to me, though that *very charitable gesture* of his would most likely send him broke, unable to feed his wife, kids, mother-in-law and her dogs. Again, he nearly brought tears to my eyes.

Before driving off, I thought it was time to check my mobile phone and I searched my pockets for it, but in vain. The damn thing wasn't there. I looked for it in my new car, but to no avail. I went back to the dealer's office and told him that I might have left my mobile in the other car. We both had a thorough look, but didn't find it.

The salesman gave me a pitiful look and made a gesture with his hands, expressing his deep sympathy. 'With this awesome deal I've done for you, you had a pretty good day so far, but you can't win all of them. You win one and lose one,' he reflected philosophically.

His observation made me feel a lot better!

By the time I drove away in my newly acquired Mazda 3, it was past midday. My stomach rumbled. I halted at a pub on the Hume Highway and had a beefsteak and a few beers, while thinking of my old buddy Florin.

Hadn't he been lucky? I reflected. Taking into account my accidental meeting with Helen four years earlier and my subsequent settling in Sydney, I considered myself a lucky man, but nothing compared with what had happened to my best mate. Florin belonged to that very fortunate infinitesimal minority who won the lottery, not once, but twice in their lifetime. He won one and a half million in 2004, and the year after that he was the sole winner of a thirteen-million jackpot. That's how he was able to purchase a farm in Sydney's outskirts.

Though I wasn't aware of all the details and circumstances in which he'd married Remy, the little I knew about it bothered me sometimes. Back in those days when he'd fallen for Remy, Florin and I used to keep each other up to date with what we were doing, via the internet and e-mail.

At the time I was still in Romania, a couple of years prior to meeting Helen. Florin was very excited about a new *sensational woman* in his life, one like he'd never seen before, as he was saying. I actually knew that Florin hadn't seen quite a lot of women in his life. To put it better, I wasn't aware of *any* woman in his life. Anyway, he was then quite miserable that *the woman of his dreams* didn't really respond in the same way to his feelings. All that changed after he won the one and a half million at the lotto and then when he hit the jackpot for the second time Remy immediately accepted his marriage proposal.

I suppose it was normal to be sceptical, though I probably had no genuine reasons to suspect unfair play on Remy's part. Especially, because, as far as I knew, Florin and Remy loved each other and lived a very happy life together. Well, if Florin was a very lucky fellow, he certainly deserved his luck, I concluded.

In spite of the troubles I was going through right then, I was excited to spend some time with my old mate. Though we were inseparable as kids and teenagers, I'd only seen Florin three times since arriving in Sydney. Two of those times he'd visited me at my place, and the other time, we'd gone out for drinks in Kings Cross – the city's infamous red district.

I hadn't met his wife yet and I must admit, as I knew Remy was a former beauty queen, I was very curious to come face to face with her. Well, it looked like that time has come, I reflected, unable to think of another hiding place.

I stopped at a bottle shop in Casula and bought a couple of bottles of slivovitz and four cartons of beer. I knew Florin liked a drink and … so did I. I couldn't think of a present for his wife, so I bought her just a box of Swiss bon-bon.

I drove back to Elizabeth Drive and the car hummed down the road which, Florin had told me, led right to his farm. Some twenty-five kilometres further west and the road met the Northern Road, forming the eastern border to his property. A few hundred metres north I located the main entrance to Florin's estate.

The double gate, some six metres wide, reminded me of those Texan ranches from American western movies. The massive vertical posts were joined by a timber beam with a metal sign reading FLORE Farmhouse. I thought about it and assumed that FLORE was a shortened conflation of Florin and Remy. The word was very similar to the noun 'flowers' in Romanian, which was spelt 'flori' but then, the name Florin was also short for 'flori'. Knowing that he was a hopeless romantic, I assumed he'd purposely chosen that name as a symbolic expression of his love for Remy. He'd told me time and time again how sweet and delicate she was. Just like a flower.

I drove in and stopped in front of a house, about a hundred metres further in. The single-storey home, made of hard wood painted in dark brown, reminded me of a cabana in the mountains where my grandma used to take me on holidays when I was little.

I strolled around the dwelling admiring its rustic design and the builder's apparent spotless execution. There wasn't any noise or other apparent sign of activity in the house. I returned to my car and drove a few hundred metres further inside the farm on a long, narrow dirt road.

At that time of the year the ground was covered in thick grass, making a sort of green-brownish pastoral blend. There were goats and sheep feeding happily on both sides of the road. They didn't seem to have a worry in the world.

The ambience was nice, quiet and peaceful and the whole set-up was serene and appealing. In addition to the singing birds, the only noises came from the bleating sheep and goats, cackling chooks and grunting pigs. That was intrinsic part of the country life, I reflected.

I slowed the car and halted next to a huge greenhouse, quite a bit larger than a football field, enclosed by thick plastic, see-through walls. I got out of the car and walked towards the conservatory.

Florin had probably seen me from inside. He rushed out from the hothouse and welcomed me with plenty of enthusiasm. It had been more than eight months since I'd last seen him. We hugged and studied each other.

Short, dark and of medium build, Florin looked the average type of bloke, though I noted that at twenty-eight he appeared quite a few years older than his age. He actually seemed tired and aged; definitely not a multimillionaire happily married with a former beauty queen.

'What happened to your face?' he asked, astonished.

I shrugged. 'It's a long story. I'll tell you later.'

He nodded. 'I'm so happy you've finally made it.'

'Just a few days late,' I replied.

'Better late than never. I hope you'll stick around for a while.'

It could be much longer than you'd expect, I thought, but I didn't say it to him. 'It depends what a while means.'

He thought a little. 'Everything dealing with the notion of time is relative. But let's go in. I'll show you the greenhouse.'

I followed him inside the conservatory, which was quite hot: at least ten degrees warmer than the outside temperature. The roof was also made of a transparent plastic material, which allowed the sun's rays to filter through and warm the inside.

'It's like a sauna in here,' I observed.

He nodded. 'The high temperature helps the plants grow, regardless of the season.'

'What have you got growing?' I asked.

He made a gesture towards a multitude of beds and strata of fertile earth. 'There are some fifty varieties of tomatoes, lettuce and lots of other vegetables and berries – strawberries, blackberries, raspberries, boysenberries …'

Since Kate had explained to me that my surname had its origin in tomatoes, the subject was of interest to me. 'Which tomatoes are the best?'

'If you ask me, it's definitely the Oxheart variety,' Florin said.

I didn't particularly fancy myself being associated with an

ox, but maybe some similarities did exist, I thought. 'So you're self-sufficient here.'

He hesitated. 'I'm *almost* self-sufficient. I still go to the butchers to buy meat, but I only do it in bulk about twice a year.'

I was surprised. 'But I've seen heaps of goats and sheep feeding around and I've heard pigs grunting and chooks cackling as well. Why would you buy your meat from the butcher?'

He nodded. 'There are plenty of ducks too, but I just can't contemplate the idea of killing any of my animals to feed myself. I killed a couple of chooks in the beginning, but I got depressed afterwards and couldn't eat the meat anyway. That's the hardest part of being in this business.'

That was the same compassionate and sensitive Florin I knew, I reflected. 'And I bet your wife is even more opposed to the idea of killing animals than you are.'

Florin frowned and I noted his face darkened. 'Sure, she hasn't killed any of my *pets*, to use her language, but she's … well … I suppose she's the more practical type.'

'What do you mean by more practical?' I asked.

'She blames me for being so … sensitive, though she doesn't use this particular word.'

'So, it looks like this husbandry you do is a hobby rather than business.'

'Well, it's sort of both. I make some money from selling veggies and eggs and there is also plenty of fish in the ponds.'

'Yes, I've seen a big lake on the left when I was driving in. How many lakes are there?'

'There are seven ponds on the farm, ranging from one hectare to several hectares in size. The biggest one is about six hundred metres long.'

'So, how big is the farm?'

'It's about three hundred and twenty hectares, or more than three square kilometres. I'll take you on a tour to have a look.'

'Yes, sure – I'd love to have a look. But you must have paid a fortune for such a huge area.'

'Not really. The land, which is made up of three lots, is zoned as rural and can't be subdivided any further. But it would be worth a fortune if parcelled into residential lots.'

'So are you going to do anything about it?' I asked.

Florin hesitated. 'Well, actually I am not doing anything, but Remy is very passionate about it. She rightly says there is a potential yield of about three thousand development blocks, which is huge, indeed.'

I made a quick calculation in my mind and was astonished by the result. 'So, say that these lots are sold for a hundred thousand each, which is very conservative, that would bring in about three hundred million.'

He nodded. 'A hundred thousand each would pretty much be the margin, if you deduct the development costs. And that's what Remy keeps saying, though the idea doesn't excite me. But she's very persistent and she's now dealing with one of the councillors. Between you and me, I think she's been luring him with some … inducements or sweeteners, as they say. So, you never know … But, let's get out of here. It's so hot that you'll shiver outside.'

We exited the greenhouse and strolled on a narrow alley towards the west. A wooden cabin, close to the greenhouse, was similarly built and designed as the front house, but quite a bit smaller.

'I'll show you the inside when we return,' Florin promised.

We walked on the alley right through the middle of the property, with Florin describing to me the places and things we were passing. A couple of goats unloosed from the herd were feeding leisurely on the grass and came near us stretching their necks out, waiting to be caressed. They were very cute. We stopped and patted their heads, which they seemed to appreciate – when we started to move on again, they followed us.

'See what I mean? How could you possibly kill and eat such an adorable being? I couldn't do it, even if I was starving,' Florin said.

He showed me a very large stable where the sheep and goats stayed overnight and a smaller barn which served as the pigs' accommodation. Two dozen pigs were resting by the barn, close to a swamp. They too got excited seeing us. Most of the pigs got up and rushed to welcome us. Or, maybe they expected food from us. One pig, pink with black spots, began biting at my shoes and pulling at the laces.

We passed a twenty- by thirty-metre fenced pen, for the chooks and ducks, though Florin said that the ducks spent most of their time wandering on one particular pond during the day, which they preferred to the others. Attached to the pen was a very large metal shed where the birds went to shelter after sunset.

Further west, there were some twenty hectares of grapevines, Florin said, explaining that he produced his own homemade wine in a press house near the southern border of the property. There was also a wine cellar underneath the press house, where most of the wine was preserved at the appropriate temperature.

We also had a look at a couple of the ponds located towards the south-western part of the farm. There were stacks of European carp, freshwater catfish and bass in those lakes. A creek, which flowed into the bigger of the lakes, assured the freshwater supply throughout the year, Florin explained.

There was another wooden cabin standing about halfway between the largest of the lakes, the creek, which formed the western boundary of the estate, and another, smaller lake towards the north. It looked exactly like the one located next to the conservatory.

'This is Marin's headquarters,' Florin said.

I was surprised. Florin had never mentioned another bloke living on the ranch. 'I thought it was just you and Remy on the farm.'

'It's too much work for one person. Marin looks after the animals. He's a countryman who's done this sort of thing at home and is very good at it. These days I only work in the greenhouse and even that is a full-time job,' Florin explained.

'So, where is Marin?' I asked.

'He's in town right now, but he shouldn't be too long.'

By the time we returned to the wooden cabin it was getting dark and cooler.

Florin looked at his watch. 'I think it's time for a drink.'

I nodded with enthusiasm. 'I have some stuff in the car.'

'There is plenty of beer and wine in the fridge and in the cold-room,' he replied. 'Let's better go inside.'

'I believe you, but I'm curious to try this new brand of slivovitz which I've just bought from the bottle shop in Casula,' I said.

'I'll have to remind you that I make my own wine,' said Florin.

'You do? And where do you keep it?'

'I have a cold-room in the cabin. It's like the cellars we used to have at home, only it's colder. It's electrically operated and the temperature can be adjusted to go down to as low as minus twenty-five degrees.'

'Minus twenty-five? But why would you need such a low temperature?'

He shrugged. 'I don't, but the facility is there if I ever need to use it.'

I moved my car in front of the wooden cabin, fetched a bottle of slivovitz and a carton of beer from its boot and joined Florin inside. The interior was very cosy, with brown timber beams and floorboards throughout the cottage and rustic pine furniture matching the colour of the beams and the inlay.

'This is my main place of residence,' Florin announced. 'It's got three bedrooms, two bathrooms, one of which is linked to the laundry, an eat-in kitchen, a reception room, a living room and the cold-room, which I just mentioned. It's like a very large pantry, and it's cold, but not very cold. I usually keep the temperature at about zero. The cabin is more than sufficient for me. The main house is just too big, though Remy likes it in there. But ... let's have a drink.'

We sat on armchairs opposite each other in the front living area which, Florin said, he used as a reception room. We tasted the slivovitz and then got stuck into Florin's homemade wine. It was very nice; so nice that we both overindulged. The set-up of the cabin was nice too – airy, simply furnished and very functional.

We spoke of this and that, and well into the evening Florin reminded me that I didn't say how long I was planning to stay.

'You want to get rid of me already?' I asked.

He laughed. 'On the contrary – I want to keep you here for as long as possible. Remember you've promised you'd spend your first holiday on the farm?'

I nodded. 'I did make that promise but my boss hasn't let me go on holidays yet. She just came back from Europe and gave me the rest of the week off.'

'So, you'll be here till Sunday?'

'At least till Sunday. She might give me more time off, but we'll see how we go.'

'We're not going very well with our glasses empty,' Florin observed, while refilling the glasses.

We drank again and the grog made us both hungry.

'I'll get some snacks from the fridge,' Florin offered, when the wall clock ticked nine.

'That would be nice, but I hope you haven't turned into a vegetarian,' I said jokingly, knowing that Florin was very much a meat lover.

'The thought *has* crossed my mind,' he admitted. 'And I swear *I would* become a vegetarian, if I knew that such a radical change could save the millions of animals from being killed for food every day. But I know that's not possible. If, say from tomorrow, I refuse to touch meat ever again, it wouldn't make any difference in this world. So, I eat meat, but I don't kill to eat.'

'I'm glad to hear that. Let's see what you've got.'

Florin stood up and signalled to me. 'We'd better go to the kitchen.'

I followed him and noted he was a little unsteady on his feet.

'Sorry my friend, but I won't be doing any cooking at this hour,' he apologised. 'Had you rung before to tell me you were coming, I'd have organised a proper reception. But for now, we'll just eat what's in the fridge.'

We ate hot-smoked chicken and cold-smoked pork belly, cabanossi and cheese with tomatoes and shallots.

'Very nice,' I said, nearly full, when a thought came to me. 'But what about your wife? Shouldn't you have dinner together?'

He made a gesture with his hand whose meaning I didn't catch. 'She went shopping to the city. If she hasn't come back by now, she might be sleeping in town at one of her girlfriends'.'

'I remember you told me she was sick of the city life and that's why you moved onto the farm,' I said.

He paused, trying to find his words. 'Remy is not easy to please. And she's a little bored here. Anyway, let's go back to the living room and have another drink.'

I could see he wasn't comfortable to talk about his wife and, once in the living room, I changed the subject. We spoke about our childhood and recalled some of the pranks we'd played during those wonder years. And we kept on drinking steadily.

Just before eleven, Florin excused himself and went to the bathroom. He switched on the radio, listening to the eleven o'clock news.

I remained alone, asking myself questions. Why did he say that the wooden cabin was his main place of residence? And he'd also complained that there was too much work on the farm for one person. Did he mean that Remy didn't take any interest in the day-to-day running of the farm? And why was he reluctant to talk about his wife? The little he'd said about her wasn't too flash either. And where was Remy? I was a little intrigued.

At the same time, I was in two minds over whether to tell Florin of my troubles right then and of the real reason I'd decided to visit him. I knew I could rely a hundred percent on him, but … would he panic if he knew I was hiding from the police? And how about Remy? How would she react if she found out that their visitor, a bloke whom she'd never seen before was possibly a murderer wanted by the police?

As it turned out, I didn't have to worry about telling or not telling Florin of my current, very shaky situation. He came from the bathroom looking very different. Paler and more tired, he actually looked terrible. He sat opposite me and stared at the floor for a while, without saying anything. He made me feel uneasy.

'What happened in the bathroom?' I asked. 'You look very worried.'

He looked me straight in the eyes. 'That's because *I am* worried.'

'I can imagine that. I'd be stressed too if I had such a huge place to take care of, but you've only changed within the last ten minutes or so,' I pointed out.

'I listened to the news. They said that the man believed responsible for the disappearance of the missing woman Kate Morales, has been identified as being a Romanian national named Cornel Toma, currently on a working visa in Australia.'

Florin's statement was like a cold shower to me. The effect of the grog seemed to suddenly evaporate. As I'd done the evening before with Helen, I looked down, not able to meet Florin's eyes. 'It could be another Cornel Toma,' I said stupidly.

'They gave a description of this Cornel Toma, which fits you, spot on. And they described the car he's driving, though I noted that you came here in a different car. Still, I recall you told me you were very proud when you purchased your Mazda CX-9, a few weeks back. That's the car they said Cornel Toma was driving – a black, Mazda CX-9, 2011 model.'

'What else did they say?' I whispered.

'They urged anyone who knows of Cornel Toma's whereabouts to contact police on the hotline and warned people not to approach him, as he's believed to be vicious and very dangerous. They said he bashed to the ground a parking officer this morning. Is that where you got these bruises on your face?'

I shook my head. 'That creep got what he deserved. He tried to punch me, but I do have my pride. I wouldn't let a jerk like him touch me. That's why I belted him – I was provoked, or rather, I was in self-defence.'

'Is this the version of events you're going to tell the police?' Florin asked.

Florin's question upset me. His words, rephrased in my mind, were a pretty good indication that he intended to blow the whistle.

'So, are you going to turn me in to the police?'

He laughed – a nervous laugh. 'Are you being serious? How could I do such a thing to my best friend? Have you forgotten all those years when we were like brothers and all the stuff and pranks we did together? You can't be serious. Would you hand me over to the police, if I were in your situation and came to you to ask for help?'

'No, of course I wouldn't,' I mumbled. 'It's just that I can see you're very stressed about it.'

Indeed, Florin looked very tense. 'Of course I am very stressed, but that's because I love you and I'm worried about you. But otherwise, regardless of what you might have done, the thought of turning you in to the police would never ever cross my mind.'

Florin's declaration made me feel a little better. Still, I thought it was safer to probe his loyalty once more, asking. 'Even if I might have murdered someone?'

His straight, plain answer gave me more reassurance that I could rely on him. 'I don't believe you've murdered someone. But, even if you have, I'm sure you only did it in a moment of rage, or when you've temporarily lost your mind and not as a premeditated act.'

'Thank you, my friend. This means a lot to me,' I said and I meant it.

He shrugged. 'You don't have to thank me. I am not doing you any special favour and I'm not making any sacrifice. It's just the way I feel about it and it can't be any other way.'

'Well … I will remember that,' I mumbled again.

'Have another drink?' he asked.

I shook my head. 'Thanks, but it's time to tell you what really happened between this Kate Morales and me. I'll try to keep my head clear to get the facts straight.'

'You don't have to feel under any sort of pressure to confess, but if it makes you feel any better, please go on and tell me.'

I told Florin of my accidental encounter with Kate the week before, of the time we spent together, of my sudden infatuation with her, of her disappearance, of me breaking into her house, of Solveig, of Doctor Juan Morales, of Kate being forced into a prearranged marriage which she hated, of Helen's plan about me marrying Rhonda, of Luigi and Giuseppe, of Sergeant Dickson's visit at my place and so on, but not quite everything. A few things, which I thought didn't portray me in a very positive light, I kept to myself.

Florin remained quiet, looking thoughtful for a long while. 'So, you haven't killed anyone,' he finally said.

'Of course I haven't.'

'Not even at home, in Bucharest?' he asked.

'Do you think I'd be now here, talking to you, if I had?' I replied.

He shrugged. 'Everything is possible in Romania, if you work for the Securitate.'

'No, that's not true any longer,' I protested. 'Things have changed a lot since you left. But, you sound like you don't believe me.'

'Of course I believe you. What I don't understand is, if you're innocent, why you don't come clean. Why not go to the police and tell them exactly what happened, as you've just told me?'

'I didn't do it in the first place because I didn't want my boss to find out that I was playing around with another woman. I've told you that her plan for me was to marry Rhonda and she'd asked me to stop seeing other dames and get cosy with Rhonda.'

Florin made a dismissive gesture with his hands. 'I've gathered that. But now, things have become very complicated. You're now being accused of kidnapping and suspected of murder. These are extremely serious offences. Is hiding certain indiscretions from your boss more important to you than defending yourself from kidnapping and murder allegations?'

I hesitated. I hadn't told him that my working visa had expired, fearing that he'd be reluctant to shelter an illegal immigrant. But now, as I had no answers to the argument he'd just put to me, I had to tell him the full story. 'You're right,' I said. 'But things are even more complicated. Though I'm innocent, they'd still arrest me, if I go to the police.'

He frowned, looking confused. 'Why would they?'

'Because I'm now an illegal immigrant in Australia. My visa has expired.'

Florin's face and eyes turned even bleaker. 'Even so, it's still better to quash any potential kidnapping and murder charges ...'

Right then I heard a car door being slammed outside.

Florin jumped from his seat with a look of panic on his face. 'That must be Remy. If she's heard the news, she might put two and two together and work out who you are. We won't tell her who you are, nor that you're Romanian. So, you're not Romanian, but she'll work out that English is not your first language. You're ... Serbian and your name is ... Novak Ivanovici.'

I heard the front door being opened and footsteps on the floorboards. They sounded like the footsteps of a woman wearing high heels. A few seconds later a woman, who looked like a top-class model, made her entry in the living room. She stopped and hesitated at the sight of me. She seemed taken aback by my presence, which made me wonder.

Knowing that she must have seen my car parked close to the cabin's entry, I doubted that her surprise was genuine. Or, maybe she'd expected to find someone with Florin, but hadn't imagined that someone to look like me.

That aside, my heart skipped a beat at the sight of her. I gaped at the woman and, assuming she was Remy, I understood why Florin said that his wife was nothing short of sensational.

She wasn't a classical beauty, but what struck me about her was her extraordinary sex appeal. Though she didn't carry any excess kilos, she had fully rounded hips and breasts and she stood at about five-foot-ten tall. The best adjective that came to mind for describing her body was voluptuous. Or perhaps lascivious.

Her face was oval, with large, almond-shaped brown eyes and long, straight black hair reaching to her breasts. She had an oversized mouth with full, provoking lips, high cheekbones and a small nose with pulsating nostrils which added to her striking sensuality.

Her complexion was light and her perfect teeth resembled those shown by Colgate in TV advertising. In fact, I found everything about her perfect. In a few words, she was the most sexually attractive woman I'd ever seen in my life.

The expression of her face and her body language radiated confidence and self-assurance. She knew she was irresistible and that fact of life appeared to suit her very well, I thought.

'That's Remy, my wife,' Florin said to me and continued to Remy. 'This is my friend, Novak.'

I stood up, waiting for Remy to offer her hand, which she didn't.

'You've never mentioned before of a friend named Novak,' she observed, having studied my face for several seconds.

She sounded sure of herself, but still her voice was pleasant. It went well with the rest of her. I knew she was half Filipina and I guessed it was that exotic half of her mother's side which gave her an irresistible sex appeal.

'That's right,' Florin said. 'I haven't seen Novak for quite a few years and didn't know anything about him. And now he happens to be here on a temporary visa.'

'Is he Romanian?' Remy asked.

I noted she was being rude asking a third party questions about me while I was there. She just ignored my presence, which hurt my self-esteem. I wasn't used to that sort of reception, as I normally attracted a lot of attention from the other gender.

'No, Novak is from Serbia,' Florin said. 'We met in Bucharest when he was visiting, many years ago and we remained good friends since then.'

Remy stepped to the leather sofa, sat on it and crossed her legs. Her moves were sensual and luscious, or maybe that was just my perception.

Florin and I also took our seats. And she continued to question Florin about me, as if I was only a lifeless object or wasn't in the room at all. 'Does he speak Romanian?'

I half opened my mouth to reply but Florin was quicker. 'Novak comes from that part of the country known as the Serbian Banat or Vojvodina, which has close ties with Romania. Banat is a Romanian territory, on the Serbian border.'

'Thank you for the information, but I still don't know if he speaks Romanian,' she said.

Though extraordinarily attractive, her manners irritated me. 'Why would that be of interest to you?' I broke in.

She gave me a quick glance and I could see the fury in her eyes. She then shifted her eyes to Florin and raised her eyebrows, as if saying, *you haven't answered my question*. He looked at me and then at her. From the way he looked at her, there was no doubt that Florin adored his wife.

'I don't speak Romanian,' I answered for Florin.

Again, she glanced very swiftly at me and it was quite clear from her body language that she'd taken a strong aversion towards me. I must admit, I was intrigued.

'How about a drink?' Florin suggested.

'Thank you, but there is something about your Serbian friend that makes me feel uneasy,' Remy replied, looking at me with her lips pouted. It was a cold, disapproving look.

She was baffling me with such offensive comments and I had to make a powerful effort of will to keep my cool.

'There is nothing to feel uneasy about,' Florin said, unconvincingly.

The atmosphere was weird and tense – nothing you would expect in a situation when a bloke introduces his best friend to his wife.

Remy just read her wristwatch and said. 'I should have stayed in the city overnight.'

'You know … Novak will be around for a few days,' Florin said cautiously.

She pursed her lips, obviously displeased at the news. Her dislike of me was very blatant and she did nothing to conceal it. She stood up. 'Well … I'll let you keep him company.'

'Don't worry about me. I'll be alright by myself. You better go to bed with your wife,' I said to Florin.

'He's staying here, with you,' Remy retorted in a surprisingly strong manner – this time addressing her words directly to me, and referring to her husband as a *he*.

'Sure I'm staying here,' Florin muttered, while Remy turned around and walked briskly away, without saying good night.

He rushed after her and they both went out in the dark.

That went extremely well, I said to myself, scratching my head.

I poured myself another drink and thought of Remy. What a bitch! The fact that she looks out of this world doesn't give her the right to behave like a bully, I thought. And poor Florin ... He was certainly wrapped around her little finger and she had him eating out of her hand. That's the impression I got, having spent less than ten minutes in Remy's company.

Well, at least Florin is fortunate enough to go to bed with her. Going to bed with such a doll must be quite a thrill, I reflected. Your thoughts are crossing the line, I immediately admonished myself. As fabulous as she looks, she's the wife of your best friend and to you she is and she must remain just the forbidden fruit, I concluded.

A few minutes later Florin returned. 'Sorry about that,' he apologised. 'Remy can be like that at times.'

'It's alright. You don't need to apologise,' I said. 'But I don't want to cause you any trouble with your wife. I think it's better for everyone if I don't stick around any longer.'

'But ... where would you go?' he asked.

I shrugged. 'To a motel or a caravan park.'

He hesitated. 'No, I won't let you go. You've had far too many drinks to be able to drive and I wouldn't drive either. You'd better go to bed and we'll talk in the morning. I'll show you to your bedroom. It's not five-star accommodation but it's comfortable enough.'

In the state I was in right then, comfort was the last thing on my mind. I had many other things to worry about; not least the police. Interesting enough, I wasn't too concerned about Kate any longer. I was instead disturbed by Remy.

12

Thursday, 2 June

I woke up with a headache on Thursday morning and heard
Florin moving around in one of the bathrooms. I heard the radio
on in his bathroom, which prompted me to step into the other
bathroom, keen to listen to the news. I had no luck – there was
no radio in there.

I had a shower and skipped shaving again and walked into the
kitchen. Florin was already there, waiting for me at the kitchen
table.

I joined him, taking a seat.

'You slept well?' he asked.

I'd actually tossed and turned in bed all night. In addition to
all my other troubles, there was something very serious which
worried me, but I wasn't going to tell it to Florin. 'Yeah, I slept

pretty well,' I said. 'And you? Did you join your wife in the main house?'

He shook his head. 'No, I didn't join Remy and please, don't feel guilty about it. Believe me, it's nothing to do with you.'

I was surprised to hear that, but I didn't feel guilty. There were other things on my mind that I felt guilty about. 'Anything interesting in the news, this morning?' I asked.

'Would you rather have breakfast first?' Florin suggested.

'No, I'm not that hungry. What did they say in the news?'

'Well, I can tell you the news is quite exciting this morning. You were in the news again. I listened to the same piece of news twice and I memorised as much as I could,' Florin assured me. 'I even made some notes.'

He produced a piece of paper from his shirt pocket, unfolded it and read to me. '"They said that there was another bizarre twist concerning the circumstances surrounding the missing woman Kate Morales. A woman, who identified herself as the popular fashion designer Rhonda Everton, has come forward and told the police that she'd met Kate Morales last Saturday, which was two days *after* her reported disappearance. Miss Everton stated to the police that she and Kate had met in the apartment occupied by Kate's alleged kidnapper, believed to be Romanian national Cornel Toma, personal assistant to radio broadcaster Helen Longshanks, who also lives in the same block of flats in Liverpool. According to Miss Everton, Kate who had introduced herself as Mister Toma's girlfriend, was in good spirits, joyous and relaxed, apparently unconcerned about all the fuss she'd caused." What do you make of that?' Florin asked.

'That's … something,' I mumbled.

Florin seemed puzzled by my lack of enthusiasm. 'Well … aren't you excited? It looks like you are in the clear.'

I just nodded. 'It looks that way, doesn't it?'

I actually knew very well that I didn't have any reason to feel pleased. It was obvious that Rhonda had confused Katarina with Kate last Saturday, when they met in my flat. I hadn't told Florin that detail and now I decided to keep it to myself.

'So, what are you going to do next?' Florin asked.

Good question, I said to myself. Recalling last night's talk with Florin, I had the impression he was maybe expecting me to leave, which I wasn't prepared to do. Something was keeping me there and I knew, it wasn't the fear of being caught by the police. 'Well … I'd say it's better to wait for a little while to have the story confirmed and see how things develop from here. Hopefully Kate will surface sometime soon and then everyone will know that I'd always been innocent.'

Florin appeared disappointed. He probably expected a much more positive reaction from me. 'Yes, sure, there is no rush, but I thought … Never mind.'

'Did they say anything else?' I asked.

Florin frowned, trying to recall. 'As a matter of fact, they did. They said that the man suspected of Kate's abduction is missing as well and, considering that the woman *kidnapped* is married, police believe that the victim and her abductor are having an affair and may be hiding together, most likely in a love nest, but for the time being their whereabouts was anyone's guess.'

'I wonder where Kate is,' I said, just to say something, knowing too well that all those speculations were false.

'Well, she's certainly not with you,' Florin noted.

I nodded. 'I wonder what she's doing right now.'

I was actually wondering what *Remy* was doing right then. Though her behaviour towards me had, so far, been absolutely pathetic, I was itching to see her again. Thinking of Remy, I realised that less than a week after my sudden infatuation with Kate, I was already haunted by the idea of another woman. The woman who happened to be the wife of my host and best friend.

In mid morning I was in front of the cabin taking some fresh air, when Remy turned up in a golf buggy. She wore tight slacks, which emphasised her curvy hips and her long legs. I noted that in the daylight she looked even more stunning and provocative than the night before.

She only gave me a casual glance and pouted her lips, apparently displeased with what she saw and she walked into the cottage.

Staring at her from behind, I noted her waist was very narrow and her torso too small compared with her exceedingly long legs, but in a very alluring fashion. Her waist-to-hip ratio looked more than perfect to me and though in strict modelling terms her hips were probably a shade too pronounced, being a tall woman, it suited her very well. From my point of view, I thought that feature only added to her striking sex appeal.

I remained outside to give Florin and Remy some space, but I only did it with a lot of reluctance. I strolled to the greenhouse and back, willing to bump into Remy again when she returned to her buggy.

I had a look at the buggy noting it was battery operated, which meant less noise and a smoother drive compared to the ones running on petrol. Studying the cart, I hesitated and climbed into the driver's seat. I did it from a sudden, childish impulse and maybe, the fact that Remy had just sat there minutes before, had added to my compulsion.

I'd only been there for a minute or so, when Remy came out of the cabin, alone.

I immediately got out from the buggy and she gave me an angry look. 'Sniffing around?' she asked, unimpressed with me meddling in her stuff.

'Sorry, I've never driven a battery-operated one,' I mumbled.

She smiled mischievously while mounting the driver's seat. 'I am surprised. I'd have thought you'd seen and done just about anything one can think of in this world.'

'I'd thought so too, but only until last night,' I replied.

She raised her eyebrows. 'What happened last night?'

I hesitated and decided to give her a hint. 'Last night I realised that even the best of friends can't be trusted in certain circumstances.'

She gave me a long stare. 'I thought you and Florin were just friends, not *best* friends.'

'This thing which I realised last night applies to both friends and best friends.'

'Have you told Florin that?' Remy asked.

'Should I?'

She shrugged. 'It's your call. He's *your* best friend, not mine.'

She switched the engine on and drove away.

I remained still, looking at the buggy moving away at low speed until it vanished from my view. As I walked towards the cabin, I noted a curtain being drawn back in the reception room.

Florin and I spent most of the day in the greenhouse tending to his plants and vegetables. While Florin was very passionate and meticulous about it, I found that type of work boring and uninspiring. We had a frugal lunch in the cabin and listened to the two o'clock news. They didn't say anything about Kate or me, which I thought was good news.

After lunch, we continued working in the conservatory for

another couple of hours. Later in the afternoon, Florin excused himself saying he had to handle some things in the kitchen.

I lay on a paved alley among the strata of vegies, enjoying the warmth from the sun, intensified by the transparent plastic roof and walls. I closed my eyes and tried to think of nothing. I'd already dozed off when a deep male voice startled me.

'Good afternoon, Mister. Enjoying yourself?'

I propped myself in a sitting position and looked up. Standing in front of me was a giant of a man, aged probably in his early forties. I blinked my eyes to have a better look. Dark and hugely built, with a very large head and a full beard, this guy looked very much like the Italian actor Bud Spencer from those 1970's spaghetti westerns with Terrence Hill. The right and left hand of the devil, as they were known; only this guy was a little bigger than Bud.

He was more than four inches taller than me, which made him about six foot seven or a little over two metres and a quick estimation told me he weighed some one hundred and forty kilos. He wore blue work overalls, with rolled-up sleeves revealing a pair of hairy, enormous forearms.

As I just sat there with my mouth half open, looking dumbly at him and without answering his question, he repeated it: 'Are you enjoying yourself?'

As the question was put in Romanian, I answered automatically in Romanian. 'Yes, it's nice and warm in here.'

'I am Marin, the shepherd,' he continued in Romanian, stretching out his hand.

I stood up and shook his hand. His hand felt heavy like lead and his grip strong like a screw vice. 'Glad to meet you. Florin told me about you.'

'May I ask what your name is?' he demanded.

The short nap seemed to have caused me a memory lapse. I just couldn't remember what name Florin had given me the evening before. 'I am … I am … shit, I have another memory slip.'

'Does this usually happen to you?' Marin asked.

'No … well, I mean … yes … it's since I had a … a minor accident,' I raved.

'Was that when you messed up your face?' he inquired.

'No … that happened before. I mean … it happened afterwards,' I continued my ramble.

The giant peered at me doubtfully. 'Should I ask Florin to call a doctor?'

I forced a laugh. 'Ah no … I'm good, only I don't remember my name.'

'Perhaps … Goran Ivanisevic?' Marin suggested.

Why did he mention that name? I wondered. Was it accidental? Still, on hearing the name of the Croatian former tennis superstar I recalled that Florin had given me a similar Slavic name. I snapped my fingers. 'That's right, that's me.'

The giant arched his eyebrows. 'You mean you're Goran Ivanisevic?'

'No, I am Novak Ivanovici.'

'I thought you didn't speak Romanian,' he noted.

I bit my lower lip and swore in my mind, unable to say something which made any sense. Luckily, at that moment, I saw Florin entering the greenhouse.

'Look, Florin is back,' I said in English. 'You wanted to see him?'

Marin turned his head in the direction of the gate, hesitated and walked slowly towards Florin, who had stopped near the entry checking something on the ground. Once Marin got near to him, they chatted for a couple of minutes, but I couldn't hear what they were saying.

I shrugged, picked a ripe tomato from a tendril close by and bit from it. It was sweet and juicy. Normally, I'd have been impressed by its organic flavour, but not that afternoon. I must admit, the encounter with the giant shepherd had unnerved me a little.

Florin and I only spent about forty more minutes working in the greenhouse; though saying that I *worked* was a bit of an overstatement. Just before five, to my relief, he suggested that we should call it a day.

As we entered the cabin, I smelled a nice aroma of baking meat, garlic and other spices coming from the oven. 'So, that's what you said before you had to handle in the kitchen,' I said. 'What's in there?'

'Yeah, I put the meat in the oven about an hour ago. I'm cooking a meat pie and roasted lamb shoulder. Remy will hopefully dine with us this evening.'

'It smells yummy,' I complimented him.

He laughed. 'It's the garlic. No matter how bad a cook you are, any dish will smell yummy if you add garlic to it. But since we've established before that you don't speak Romanian, it's better if we only talk in English. You know, just to get used to it.'

I hadn't thought of that. 'You think I made a mistake when I told your wife that I didn't speak Romanian?'

Though Florin didn't answer the question directly, I understood from what he said that he didn't approve of my denying that I spoke Romanian. 'I told Remy that imaginary background about you coming from the Serbian Banat to justify why you *did* speak Romanian, but you spoiled the whole story when you said you *didn't* speak the language.'

'Sorry mate, but if I said a lie, your story was fabricated too,' I pointed out.

'Have a seat and let's have a beer,' he suggested.

We sat at the kitchen table.

'How about something stronger than beer to start with?' I proposed.

He shook his head. 'If Remy is coming to dinner, I want to be sober tonight, but you can please yourself.'

I thought a little and decided he was right. 'No, beer is okay, thank you.'

At the same time, I sensed that Florin was quite excited and even nervous about Remy possibly dining with us that evening, which made me wonder. Weren't a husband and wife supposed to eat together as a matter of fact?

He grabbed two half-litre Amsterdam cans from the fridge and handed one to me. We clinked the cans and drank.

Florin nodded his approval. 'Nice beer. Where were we before?'

'I said a lie and you fabricated one last night,' I reminded him.

'About you coming from Vojvodina?'

I nodded. 'That's right.'

'I just explained why. The intention was to follow the trumped-up story with a truth, which I didn't have the chance to say.'

'So, you said half a lie,' I pointed out.

'Or, in better words, I said half a truth. Remember, half a truth is always better than a straight lie. Anyway, it's too late now.'

'It is too late, indeed,' I admitted. 'I've been caught out already.'

Florin nodded. 'I know. Marin mentioned it to me.'

'He seems quite a ... an interesting character,' I remarked. 'Where's he coming from?'

Florin laughed. 'Believe it or not, he's from Banat. That's the Romanian Banat, not the Serbian one.'

'But how did he settle in Australia?'

'He defected more than twenty years ago, when Ceausescu was still ruling the country. He came with the weightlifters team and refused to go back. They granted him political asylum.'

'But you said before he was a shepherd in Romania.'

He nodded. 'He was, until the age of fourteen or so, when a weightlifting trainer spotted him by chance and took him to Bucharest. Marin was very big since he was a kid.'

'I can see that. He must have been a super heavyweight,' I said. Florin nodded.

'And … did he achieve much here?'

'He didn't, because he was in jail for a few years. He got involved in an argument with a group of youths in a pub. They set him up when he left. A brawl broke out and he hit one of them too hard and killed him. He was found guilty of manslaughter and spent three years in jail.'

'Those blokes must have been pretty stupid to have got in a fight with him. I mean, I'm not a wimp, but I'd be thinking twice before having a go at him. He looks quite … lethal.'

Florin laughed. 'As a matter of fact he's still a big kid. At his age, he's still addicted to spaghetti movies. You know, those movies we couldn't have enough of when we were kids, with Clint Eastwood and of course, the ones with Bud Spencer and Terence Hill. That's what he does all day, when he's not looking after the animals. He's watching movies.'

'Was he an Aussie? I mean was he an Australian citizen when this happened?' I asked.

Florin laughed. 'That's a very good question. Actually, he'd just been made an Aussie that very day. He was celebrating the event with a friend at the pub when this thing happened.'

'He was very lucky, if you can call that luck. Had he not been a citizen, they'd have packed his bags and sent him back home.'

'That's right,' Florin agreed.

'So, how did you employ him?'

'Well, it was only by chance. One of Remy's girlfriends had met Marin and she was aware of his background. She also knew that Remy had just married a Romanian who purchased a farm. That was me. So, she introduced Marin to Remy. He worked as a bouncer at the time and like Remy, he was sick of the city life. It so happened that right then I needed someone to look after my beasts, so it all worked out pretty well. Now, I have no worries at all about my sheep and goats and pigs.'

Florin grabbed the tray with the roasting lamb from the oven, turned the meat on the other side and put it back in the oven. He then fetched another baking tray from the fridge and placed it in the oven. 'That's the meat pie. It takes less time to cook than the lamb,' he explained.

'How about some more beer?' I suggested.

He took a couple of cans from the fridge and handed one to me.

'So, this lamb you're cooking is not from your herd?' I asked.

Florin shook his head. 'It's from the cold-room, but I bought it from the butcher.'

I was a little intrigued. 'I can see you're well supplied, but still, with all the livestock you have on the farm, buying meat from the butcher seems a waste of money. And sure, by the look of him and considering his background, Marin wouldn't have any qualms to slaughter a lamb or a kid.'

'You're right, but I won't let him do it. He and Remy always make fun of me about that.'

'You mean your wife blames you for not killing your beasts?'

He nodded. 'She calls them my pets. And she calls me a dupe.'

Considering Remy's very soft feminine appearance, I had

some difficulty apprehending that. I just couldn't imagine such a silky looking creature contemplating in cold blood the killing of lambs, kids or piglets to fulfil her basic needs. 'What time is she coming?'

Florin checked the time. 'She shouldn't be too long. I'd better lay the table.' He fetched some plates, cutlery and glasses and laid the table in the living room.

'Why don't we eat in the kitchen?' I asked. 'There is plenty of room in here.'

His answer stunned me. 'This evening is a special occasion. It's not that often that my wife and I have dinner together.'

I had to admit, I too was very impatient to see glamorous Remy again.

A couple of hours later we were still waiting for Remy. We'd watched the six o'clock news on Channel 7 and later on ABC. There had been no mention of me or Kate. I guessed that Rhonda's statement to the police that Kate was alive and well had got the media confused and put a big question mark on the whole storyline.

I noted that Florin had already forgotten about being sober and had started drinking quite heavily in the past hour or so. He had some slivovitz on top of the beer and was tipsy already. So far, I'd stuck with beer and I was in a better condition than he was. It was nearly eight o'clock.

'Time to switch the oven off,' Florin decided.

'You don't want your dishes to be cold when Remy arrives,' I remarked.

He smiled bitterly, looking past me. It was a sad, depressed look. 'She's not coming.'

'But you said before she *was* coming,' I reminded him.

He smirked. 'If she hasn't turned up by now, she's certainly not coming. She should have arrived at six. It's nearly eight already.'

That news depressed me a little. 'I'm sorry. I was looking forward …'

'Even after that frosty reception last night?' Florin asked.

'Well … it's okay. I forgave her. She's your wife, after all …'

Florin downed another shot of slivovitz. 'That's right. She's my *frosty* wife.'

His remark startled me. 'Maybe I shouldn't say it, but she looks nothing like frosty.'

'That's what everybody thinks, but believe me, it's not the case.'

He made me curious. 'You mean … she's sort of … like … frigid?'

'Even worse than that.'

'What's worse than that?' I asked.

He paused and poured himself another shot. 'Men are repulsive to her. She's a lesbian.'

That was a huge blow. 'She's a lesbian? So … you two … you don't do … stuff together?'

He didn't answer that.

'But … lesbians can still do … things with men,' I insisted.

He nodded. 'We sort of did, after the wedding. It was a disaster.'

He got me more and more perplexed. 'You mean you waited until the wedding?'

'I know it's hard to believe these days, but that's exactly what happened. Remy insisted that, as a strict catholic, she wouldn't have it any other way.'

Again, curiosity got the better of me. 'And … sorry to ask. You don't have to answer …'

'I know what you're going to ask,' Florin interrupted. 'No, she wasn't a virgin.'

'So … you mean … nothing happened after the wedding?'

He sighed, took a can of beer from the fridge and sipped from it. 'She has allowed me in bed with her a few times, but … she was so cold that … I just couldn't do it.'

'I see. They call it inhibition, I think.'

'She calls it impotence,' Florin retorted.

I visualised Remy in my mind and couldn't comprehend how *any* bloke could not perform in bed with her. 'Sorry to hear that. And … how about kids? I know you always wanted kids.'

'She's not ready to have kids, though she's thirty already.'

'Is she? I didn't know she's older than you. But it doesn't really matter these days. And I know, women prefer to have kids in their mid and late thirties these days.'

'That's right. She wants to have kids sometime later. For now, she's just obsessed with rezoning the land.'

'But to have kids … you still have to … you know?' I pointed out.

'Not necessarily,' Florin answered. 'She can get pregnant by using IVF.'

I'd never heard of that. 'What's IVF?'

He frowned, trying to focus. 'I think it's *I Value Fucking*, if I remember well.'

I looked dumbly at him.

'No, I don't remember well. It's in-vitro fertilisation – or something like that,' Florin added.

'I see … something to do with artificial insemination.'

He nodded. 'Exactly.'

I was perplexed to hear that such a doll was planning to conceive by means other than the traditional course. But then, if she was a lesbian, it shouldn't be a surprise. *Men are repulsive to her,* I recalled what Florin said. It was normal that she disliked men, I thought, trying to accept her adversity towards me as a fact of life.

Florin had a couple more shots of slivovitz while we ate and only a can of Amsterdam after the meal. Hardly keeping his eyes open, he just couldn't cope anymore. Before ten o'clock he shuffled his way to his bedroom. Moving unsteadily with his head slumped between his shoulders; he looked like a defeated man. Staring at him, I had a distinct feeling that what I'd learned from him that night was only a part of his real life drama.

I listened to the ten o'clock news and then I did the dishes and some cleaning around the kitchen. I had another couple of drinks and, as they hadn't mentioned anything about me in the news, I had no looming things to worry about, at least for the time being. So I focused my thoughts on Florin and his wife.

What a story! I just couldn't believe that such a gorgeous-looking sexy doll like Remy despised men and found them repulsive. Why was Florin staying with her? Sure, with his millions, he could easily find another wife; perhaps not as sensational-looking like Remy, but still a very desirable one.

And how about Remy herself? Why was she being complacent in that sort of weird and artificial relationship? Was it perhaps because she wanted a slice of her husband's money? Though I didn't fancy that scenario, I admitted in my mind that it could well have been the case.

After the eleven o'clock news, which had again been indifferent to me, I covered with tinfoil what was left of the lamb roast and the meat pie and put them in the fridge, deciding to call it a day as well. Just as I walked through the living room towards my bedroom, I heard a key turning in the front door. Unusually for me, I panicked hearing that sound. For some peculiar reason, I thought the night-time visitor was Marin – the giant shepherd.

I stepped towards the entry, prepared for possible trouble. As the door opened, my mouth fell open at the sight in front of me. The visitor wasn't Marin.

She still wore tight slacks which underlined her sexy form, but it was a different outfit from the one she wore in the morning. Though it was the third time I saw Remy in the past twenty-four hours, I couldn't help marvel at how stunning she looked.

She gave me a cursory glance and walked past me to the living room. Her hips touched mine on her way, which sent my heart rate up and my blood going. She had a look around and stepped into the kitchen. 'Had dinner already?' she asked.

'It's passed eleven,' I said apologetically. 'Florin said you were supposed to come at about six. But there is plenty left in the fridge, if you want some.'

She twitched her nose. 'I'm not here to have dinner.'

'Why are you here?' I asked.

She laughed. 'Is he smashed already?'

'You mean your husband?'

She didn't answer that. She propped her bottom against the kitchen sink and gave me a long, languid look. 'I came to check on how the two of you were getting along.'

Staring at her I wondered if she consciously played the femme fatale role. It certainly suited her very well. 'We're getting along very fine,' I said.

She smiled contemptuously. 'I thought so. Do you sleep in the same bed?'

I stared at her, saying nothing. We were facing each other, a couple of metres apart.

'Do you sleep in the same bed?' Remy repeated her question.

I paused, thinking of an appropriate reply. 'You know, like the majority of males, I happen to be attracted to women. But it's a shame that a few of the most extraordinarily good-looking females don't fancy the other gender.'

As soon as I'd said it, I regretted it. I certainly wouldn't have said it if not for the drinks.

But Remy didn't seem offended. 'That's good news, if I can believe it.'

My mouth was again quicker than my brains. 'You're very welcome to test me.'

She crossed her arms and smiled provocatively. 'Are you going to the markets tomorrow morning?'

'Markets? What markets?'

She arched her eyebrows. 'So, Florin hasn't told you …. He goes to the Flemington Markets every Friday and Saturday.'

Florin hadn't mentioned that to me. 'What's he doing at the markets?'

'He sells vegetables and eggs. Not that he needs the money, but it gives him a sense of purpose, I suppose. Nevertheless, he's very stingy, or at least he's very stingy with his wife.'

'I doubt that Florin will go to the markets tomorrow. He was quite upset before and had plenty of drinks,' I said.

'Did he confide in you?' Remy asked.

I shrugged. 'No, not really. Only bits and pieces.'

She pouted. 'My advice is, don't believe in everything you hear.'

'I don't. I only believe in what I see.'

She gave me another sexy smile. 'What do you see?'

'I see a very different woman from the one I met last night.'

'Your sense of perception is not too bad,' she said, still smiling.

'Would you perhaps like a drink?' I suggested.

She paused and pursed her lips. 'I would, but I won't.'

'Why not?'

'Because one drink usually leads to another.'

'Are you afraid by what another drink might lead to?'

The smile vanished from her face and her eyes darkened. She was suddenly distant and cold like an iceberg: *frosty*, as Florin had said. Without looking at me, she moved towards the exit. As she passed by, inches from me, I felt an urge to get hold of her and take her in my arms. But sanity prevailed on time. I followed her into the reception room and she kept walking.

Before reaching the exit, she stopped and turned towards me. I noted her eyes were on fire. 'I am not afraid of anything,' she said and walked out.

I went to bed well aware that I'd just stepped on very dangerous ground. Having flirted with my best mate's wife gave me a distinct feeling of guilt. That feeling persisted well into the early hours of the morning. Thinking about it, I couldn't fall asleep and it annoyed me.

Well, you shouldn't feel guilty, because nothing happened, I kept saying to myself, trying to snap out of my state of remorse. And, more importantly, nothing was going to happen.

I reflected some more and decided that, even if I wanted to, nothing could possibly happen.

My best friend had just told me that Remy was a lesbian.

Still, even so, I fell asleep nurturing erotic thoughts about her.

13

Friday, 3 June

On Friday morning, as I walked to the bathroom, I noticed the door to Florin's bedroom was wide open. He wasn't there. Having had a look in the other rooms, I determined he wasn't in the house at all. I recalled Remy saying that he went to Flemington on Fridays and Saturdays and assumed he was at the markets. I was surprised. I wouldn't have thought that, in the state he was in last night, he'd be capable of getting up so early and attend to business duties.

I spent some time in Florin's bathroom, which was equipped with a radio. The other bathroom wasn't. I listened to the eight o'clock news. They said nothing about Kate or me.

I brushed my teeth, had a shower and, inspecting my face in the mirror, I decided to skip shaving again. My few millimetres of beard gave me a different look and made me harder to recognise. Having a different look wasn't a bad thing, I thought, at least until all the mess with Kate Morales came to some sort of conclusion.

Wearing only a pair of boxer shorts, I stepped into my bedroom to get dressed. As it turned out, I didn't need to put any clothes on …

Laying under a pink bed sheet, Remy was waiting for me.

Considering that the woman offering herself so overtly to me was none other than my best friend's wife, it did cross my mind that the sensible thing to do was to ask her to get out. No matter how stunning she looked, Remy *was* the forbidden fruit, after all.

But again, acting sensibly was not high on my priority list. Once she parted her lips and gave me a look full of naughty promises, I knew there was no going back from that point.

With very brief breaks, we made love until three in the afternoon, when Remy reluctantly announced. 'It's time for me to go.'

She looked content and radiant. For the past several hours, she'd been so loving and tender that I wondered how it was possible that the very same woman had given me such a cold and rude reception only a couple of days before.

And I told her so. 'I can't believe you're the same woman who said to me she was feeling uneasy with me around, just a couple of days back.'

'I wasn't making it up,' Remy replied. 'I mean I did feel … perturbed by you, though *perturbed* is probably not the most suitable word. You know, it's not only you, blokes who have erotic fantasies when meeting someone attractive. It happens to women as well.'

I knew that, but I just wouldn't have thought that when we met, on Wednesday night, Remy was having erotic fantasies about me. 'How many did you have?' I asked.

She looked puzzled. 'How many what? You mean how many lovers?'

I didn't like her question. 'I won't ask you that. I don't need any more reasons to get jealous. What I meant was how many times you climaxed today.'

She laughed. 'I don't know. I was too busy with other things to count, but I'd say I've come many more times than you, and that's for sure.'

'So, you're not ...' I left it in suspense.

'I'm not what?'

'I thought you might be ... frigid.' In fact, the word I had in mind was lesbian.

She chuckled. 'Do I look like I'm frigid? And did I behave like a frigid?'

I shrugged. 'I don't know. Never been in bed with a frigid.'

'I bet even if you had been she'd have turned into a whore and very quickly,' Remy complimented me.

Her comment pleased me. 'You think so?' I said just for the sake of hearing it again.

She moaned. 'I have no doubts ... By the way, if I were one, what would you pay me for the services I ... rendered today?'

'If you were *what*?' I asked.

She hesitated. 'A ... top-class prostitute. What do you think I'd be worth for one day's work?'

'Well ... I think you'd be worth a huge pile of dough. To be honest, I haven't known anyone with such amazing ... talents. I've been with plenty of dames before, but I've never experienced such unbelievable ... acrobatic abilities.'

'I did gymnastics,' Remy explained. 'I missed making the Olympic team by a whisker only.'

'Ah … I see. But … a gymnast with such incredibly long legs … it's very unusual.'

She paused. 'This may be a desirable feature in bed, but it wasn't on the beam, for example. I had to work much harder than the smaller girls with shorter legs.'

'I wouldn't have imagined you as a gymnast, though I must admit, when watching women's gymnastics, I sometimes wondered of the tricks they could do in bed.'

'Well, I hope I did satisfy your curiosity,' Remy said. 'But I'm curious too. Tell me how you would value my expertise. How much would you be willing to pay for today's work?'

'I'm afraid I don't have enough money on me to remunerate such a wonderful performance.'

'What have you got?'

'About … seven grand.'

'You'd need much more than that,' Remy remarked.

'The most I could afford would be about ten times as much. That's all I got in the bank.'

She grimaced. 'Even that amount wouldn't be enough.'

She paused and added. 'If you're curious to see what a frigid does in bed, I'll show you.'

'I can't imagine you being a frigid,' I said.

'I can behave like one,' Remy assured me. 'I'll show you next time.'

'When is next time?'

'Tomorrow is Saturday. Florin will certainly follow his routine and go to the markets again. Poor thing,' Remy said smiling contemptuously.

It was past five o'clock when Florin returned from the markets. He looked exhausted, but pleased. 'Beer,' he ordered, as he entered the reception room and slumped into an armchair. 'Plenty of cold beer for the working class.'

I handed him a can of Amsterdam, which he emptied in about twenty seconds. 'Oh gosh, how good a beer can be after such an exhausting day,' he exclaimed. 'How was *your* day?'

I took a seat into another armchair, next to Florin. Trying to think how my day had been, I felt a knot growing in my stomach: thrill, delightful memories and guilt, all at the same time.

I just shrugged. 'Nothing out of the ordinary. How did you go at the markets?'

He paused for a little while. 'How did you know where I was? I didn't tell you last night that I was going to the markets.'

Good point, I thought, panicking a little, but I recovered pretty quickly. 'That's right – you didn't. Why didn't you tell me?'

He shrugged. 'I just forgot. And when I got up in the morning, I opened the door to your bedroom to check if you were up. You were sleeping like a baby and I didn't want to wake you.'

His words made me feel terrible. He was so altruistic, gentle and considerate. And me … I was the biggest jerk on earth. He'd welcomed me in his house, he'd fed me and sheltered me; he'd let me sleep in and in return, when I woke up, I screwed his wife for the rest of the day!

'I'd have gone with you,' I said unconvincingly, 'but I didn't feel very well. I had too many drinks last night.'

He peered at my face. 'You do look very pale,' he noted.

Indeed, I didn't feel well. Feelings of guilt and words of shame were jumping around in my head. *I am pale because I stayed inside, all day long, in bed with your wife*, I answered his observation in my mind. *What a mongrel I am.*

'Just have a few drinks and I bet you'll feel like brand-new again. And you can come with me tomorrow. I'm going to

Flemington every Friday and Saturday. I've never missed one day in more than four years. Come with me – it's good fun,' Florin encouraged me.

And I bet I had, in one day, more fun with your wife than you had in four years, I continued in my mind, but I didn't say anything.

'Seriously, come with me tomorrow. It's good fun,' Florin repeated his offer.

Nothing is good fun, compared to what Remy does in bed, I reflected. *Still, I should come with you, if I had any sense,* my brain told me, but my heart said *no way.*

Remy had hinted earlier of another intimate encounter on Saturday and the temptation was too much for me to resist. Recalling how she had performed in bed, the remorse I felt just a minute earlier was suddenly gone, replaced by a feeling of excitement. So, I had to invent a reason not to go to the markets.

'I'd like to come with you, but I can't,' I told Florin.

'What's stopping you?' he asked.

'I was in the news again today,' I lied. 'They said the police had re-emphasised to the public that I was very dangerous and not to be approached if spotted and they were still searching for me. I wouldn't risk going to such a crowded place like the markets, where there is a fair chance that someone could recognise me.'

Florin seemed disappointed. 'I only listened to the news in the morning, while driving to Flemington and on my way back. They didn't mention anything about you.'

'They did in the morning, at nine, ten, eleven …' I reinforced my lie.

He shrugged. 'Well … you still didn't tell me what you did all day.'

I walked to the kitchen and got two cans of beer. I needed a little time to think about my answer. Had I told him that my day was most likely even more exhausting than his, he wouldn't have believed it. I had to make up another lie. 'Not a lot. I woke up late and had a good look around the farm. I walked to the main road and back to the lakes and so on. I probably covered nearly half a marathon in a few hours. But I didn't see your wife at all.'

Florin nodded. 'Remy's not that fond of the farm. She spends a lot of time away with her girlfriends in the city and lobbying the council with the rezoning application.'

'Is there any chance with that?' I asked.

He shrugged. 'I'm not up to date with it. And to be perfectly honest, it doesn't interest me that much.'

Knowing that Florin was very good at finance and business, his apparent indifference to a project potentially worth three hundred million amazed me.

I sipped from the beer and remained quiet. I noted, a few minutes later, that in his armchair, Florin had dropped his head to his chest. He'd just dozed off when I heard a knock on the front door. I went to the door and opened it.

It was Marin. He came in walking slowly, the floorboards creaking under his weight. He stopped as he entered the room and gazed at Florin. Florin opened his eyes very slowly. He seemed not to know where he was.

I took my seat next to Florin and yawned.

'You've finished out there?' Florin asked, seeing Marin.

The giant pulled a chair from under the table and sat on it, facing both Florin and me. 'All finished for the day,' he said.

'Any news?' Florin queried.

'We have another baby. Being a boy, I named him Abbot, as you'd suggested,' Marin said, snorting. Florin joined him and they both had a good laugh.

'Who had a baby?' I asked.

'Lizard, one of the lady sheep,' Florin said.

That was our Prime Minister's surname. 'You mean Lizard, as in Julia Lizard?'

'You've guessed right. That's why we called her son Abbott,' Florin replied with a grin.

Florin and Marin had a good laugh again.

'Have a drink? Florin suggested.

'Wine,' Marin said.

'Please help yourself, my friend. I'm just too tired. And so is Novak. He says he's walked kilometres today,' Florin explained.

As Marin raised his eyebrows, I sensed danger coming from him. 'He did?' Marin asked. 'When and where?'

'All day … around the farm,' Florin said looking at me for confirmation.

'How come I didn't catch a glimpse of him all day?' Marin continued.

A tense silence followed for several seconds. I stood up and stepped into the kitchen. I grabbed a can of beer from the fridge and snapped its metal ring, pretending not to have heard Marin's comment. As I returned to the living room, humming a tuneless song, the phone rang.

Florin picked it up. 'Florin Panait speaking.'

'You said you're Sergeant Dickson from Liverpool police?' he asked after a few seconds. 'Good evening, Sergeant. How can I help you?'

He listened for a little while and went on. 'Sure I know Cornel Toma, but I haven't seen him in a long while. The last time I saw Cornel was … let me think … yes, I think it was October last year, if I remember well.'

Florin paused, listening, and asked. 'Is he in some sort of trouble?' He walked with the cordless receiver into the living room.

I remained alone with Marin, which for some reason made me feel uncomfortable. A couple of minutes passed in silence.

Marin went to the cold-room and returned with a bottle of wine. He seemed very familiar with the cabin's set-up and the facilities. He unscrewed the bottle and took a long pull straight from it. I heard Florin talking on the phone, but I couldn't catch his words.

'Who is Cornel Toma?' Marin asked in Romanian.

This time I was prepared. 'Sorry, I don't speak Romanian.'

'You did, the other day,' he pointed out.

I decided it was time to tell him a little story, which I'd made up in my mind. 'To tell you the truth, I understand Romanian and can speak the language a little, though I'm not fluent and I prefer not to,' I said in English.

Marin gave me a doubtful look, but replied also in English. 'Why not?'

'Because I'd rather practise my English and hopefully, improve it. Plus, my Romanian is a little … broken and some folks make fun of me, which I don't particularly like. I'd thought Florin would have told you.'

He frowned. 'He hasn't. So, are you Romanian?'

I shook my head. 'I'm from Vojvodina, just over the border. We do speak Romanian over there, but it's actually a different dialect. I mean, it's very similar, but not identical.'

I'd actually just made that up; as I had no idea what sort of dialect they spoke in the Serbian Banat. I only realised after making the affirmation that I'd been very careless again. I recalled Florin telling me that Marin actually came from Banat. Though that was the Romanian Banat, it was a good chance that he'd know what dialect they spoke over the border, I feared, but it worked.

Marin nodded and took another long pull at the bottle. 'So, what's your game, Novak?'

I made a surprised-looking face. 'I don't know what you mean.'

He paused, staring at me, apparently reflecting. 'I know there is something phoney about you. I can feel it. And I'm going to find out.'

He gulped what was left in the bottle and stood up.

'On the same subject, I'd say there is something phoney about you,' I said.

He looked down at me, grinning. 'Is there?'

'If Florin hasn't told you my background, how did you know that I wasn't supposed to speak Romanian? Is perhaps your source … Remy?'

Marin just released a dismissive sort of snort and walked out.

A few minutes later Florin returned and replaced the receiver to its cradle. His eyes were bleak and he had a worried look on his face. He fetched a beer from the fridge and slouched in his armchair.

'Was that the police?' I asked.

He nodded. 'Sergeant Dickson from Liverpool Station.'

'They know I'm here?'

'They're only fishing, I guess. I think I fooled him, this time.'

'What did he say?' I asked.

'He asked all sorts of questions and then he asked the same questions again, but rephrased them, trying to pick up inconsistencies in my answers. I know they do this sort of cross-checking.'

'You think they suspect that I'm hiding here?'

Florin shrugged. 'Hard to tell. I'd say they don't, but it's their job to check all possible avenues.'

'They might turn up and have a look on the farm,' I said.

'They might, but they have to get a search warrant, which they're usually reluctant to do, unless they are quite certain that they'll find what they're looking for.'

'So you reckon I'm safe here?'

Florin nodded. 'Yep, for the time being, I'd say you're safe here.'

'How about Marin? I'm pretty sure he doesn't like me,' I pointed out. 'I don't think he'd have any misgivings to turn me in.'

Florin paused, collecting his thoughts. He drank from his can and said, 'Don't worry about him. He's very loyal to me. He wouldn't do anything which I don't want him to do.'

'He might suspect that I'm not who I pretend to be,' I added.

Florin nodded. 'Even so, he wouldn't do anything, knowing that I'm sheltering you.'

'He's been quite blunt in showing his dislike of me,' I continued.

Again Florin paused, reflecting. 'Marin is very big physically, but unfortunately, not a lot is happening upstairs. His problem is that he thinks, with you here, I'm paying less attention to him. It's a sort of … childish jealousy. But, as I've said before, you don't need to worry about him.'

Before falling asleep that night, I thought again of how good a mate Florin was to me. I thought of all the troubles I caused him and all the sacrifices he made for me. And how I responded to that? By screwing his wife! And having no qualms to doing it again! What a jerk I was!

As it turned out, the next day, screwing was the last thing on Remy's mind.

Saturday, 4 June

On Saturday morning, Remy arrived half an hour earlier than the previous day, which made me think she was so horny that she couldn't wait any longer. I was very impatient too, having slept very little during the night, filled with excitement and desire.

I'd woken very early that morning and waited in my bedroom until I heard Florin leaving the cottage. It was before five o'clock and still dark outside. I'd listened to the news, gone through the morning routine, had breakfast and then paced the kitchen back and forth, wondering what tricks Remy was going to teach me in bed later that day and planning a couple of new tricks myself.

I quickly posted myself by the front door when I heard the door handle being turned. Once Remy entered the hallway and closed the door, I caught her from behind and held her tightly, caressing her breasts and expecting her to drop her pants to the floor. Surprised to feel her body stiffen at my touch, I released my grip and let her free.

She turned to me and said, 'No fun today. I'm not playing, I'm afraid.' She walked past me into the reception room, threw her handbag into an armchair and took a seat, crossing her legs and looking cool and composed. That's in addition to looking extremely desirable.

I followed her noticing she wore a sort of business outfit: blue slacks with a matching jacket and a white blouse under-neath. Her shoes and handbag also matched her slacks and jacket. Somehow, I didn't think she'd dressed like that just planning to have sex.

I took a seat opposite her, wondering what was going on. She'd simply stunned me. 'No fun today? What do you mean?' I queried.

'You need a dictionary to check what fun means?' she said coldly.

'I know what fun means, but I thought …'

'You thought wrong,' she interrupted.

'But ... why are you here?' I asked perplexed.

She frowned, looking upset and unhappy. 'I shouldn't have done what I did yesterday. I thought about it and though the sex was wonderful ... '

'It was more than wonderful,' I added.

Remy put her hands to her temples and shook her head looking depressed and miserable. 'But it's not right. I can't live like that. I can't be with you while I am officially his wife.'

'I know ... I don't like it either and I feel bad cheating behind Florin's back. But ... what else can we do?'

'We need to do something. I feel I am falling for you,' Remy whispered. 'I'd never thought it could happen to me. And now, when I know it has happened, I just don't know what to do. I only know that something needs to be done.'

'I don't know what you mean,' I said shyly.

She raised her head and looked at me. 'Do something, Novak. Just think about it. If you want to be with me, you must do something. We must do something.'

I nodded. 'Yes, we'll do something.'

She stood up. 'I have to go now. And I need some cash, please.'

Her request came as a bit of a shock. 'You need some cash? What for?'

'It's for a business venture,' she replied candidly.

I noted it had taken her no time at all to come out of her state of misery. 'Sorry ... you've lost me. What's this business venture to do with me?' I asked.

'A share of the profits, perhaps,' Remy said.

'What are you talking about?'

'Has my husband mentioned to you about our rezoning application?' Remy asked.

'He did ... but, that's a huge project ...'

'It is,' Remy interrupted. 'And he doesn't give a shit about it. I have to do all the hard work while he kisses his dear piglets' snouts and arses. I am meeting a councillor today and he asked for … an inducement.'

'But that's way out of my league. I mean, compared to me, you have plenty of dough …'

'*He*'s got plenty, not me,' Remy corrected. 'I mean my husband. I've told you he is very stingy. And I was crazy in the head to hook up with him.'

'Why are you staying with him if you're not happy?'

She fished a cigarette from her handbag and lit it. It surprised me, as I hadn't seen her smoking before. It was probably her business image, I thought.

'Because we're sitting on a gold mine,' she said. 'If I can get this application approved, I've hit the jackpot. It means a lot to me. But I can't do it on my own. I need a partner to share some of the costs and enjoy the profits together. But, I will find someone else, if you're not interested …'

I paused, reflecting. 'And how much do you need?'

'Today, I need ten grand.'

'I haven't got ten grand in cash.'

'What have you got?'

I recalled telling her that I had about seven grand on me. 'About seven grand.'

'That will have to do for now,' Remy said. 'I'll tell him that's all I could find.'

I went to my bedroom and counted the money. It took me a few minutes to count seven grand in fifty-dollar notes. When I returned to the living room, Remy was standing up, looking impatient. I handed her the money; but not with a lot of enthusiasm.

234

'Do I need to count it?' Remy asked, snapping the notes.

I shrugged. 'I counted it, but you may double-check.'

She put the money in her handbag and gave me a grin. 'I must trust you, I suppose. We're partners, aren't we?'

She turned around and left in a rush.

I watched her leave feeling deflated. It wasn't only Remy's rejection; it was the recognition that I only had a couple of hundred dollars left on me, as well.

Not knowing what to do next, I stepped out of the cabin and strolled towards the main road. It was sunny but a little cool. No wonder: winter had just arrived.

It took me several minutes to reach the Panait official residence, about a hundred metres inside from the Northern Road. I stopped by the house and listened at one of its side doors. Perhaps Remy was still at home, I thought. I turned the door handle very slowly. It was locked.

I paced around the house and checked the main entrance. That door was also locked. I then walked to the six-car garage which was detached from the house. A golf cart was parked in front of one of the three double doors. I lifted the rolling door up.

Stationed inside was a vintage Dodge as big as a bus and a small tractor. A faint smell of gasoline told me that an engine had just been switched on in there, not too long before. I assumed Remy had just driven off to spend my money! That thought didn't please me a lot.

I strolled back to Florin's cabin and sat on a bench, under a pergola, at the back of the house. A small, black-and-white bird landed on a wooden beam at one side of the pergola, just a couple of metres from me. I looked at him assuming it was a male. He reminded me of a robin.

The little thing studied me with apparent interest, cocking his little head from one side to the other. He then began to chirp with passion. I wondered where his girlfriend was. Perhaps she was on a spending spree, I thought. He didn't seem concerned by that; he went on with his singing, stopping from time to time to stare at me, probably expecting my approval. He made me smile.

Watching the little fellow, I tried to empty my mind of Remy and of my other worries. There were some other things which mattered in life, besides the irresistible charm of a sexy woman.

This tiny creature offered me companionship while asking nothing in return. Someone once told me, this sort of affection was akin to unconditional love: a concept more powerful than true love, which may, very quickly, turn into hatred, they say.

I spent several minutes gazing at the bird and listening to his passionate tunes. Eventually he took off as suddenly as he'd turned up. I watched him fly away and prayed for his wellbeing in my mind. Feeling he might, at that point in time, be my only friend, I thought I ought to give him a name. I named him Robin.

The rest of the weekend passed slowly, eventless and even boring. Florin and I got drunk again on Saturday night and once more on Sunday. Marin the shepherd didn't bother us and Remy didn't show up either. On Sunday night, when, after several glasses of homemade wine, I asked Florin where she was, he just shrugged and said Remy usually spent her weekends in town.

His apparent lack of concern puzzled me. How could a bloke remain indifferent to the whereabouts of his wife, when that woman happened to be one of the most extraordinarily tempting dames; I just couldn't comprehend. I was intrigued and, more than that, I was restless, longing for Remy.

I wondered where she was right then. It seemed that ages have passed since she'd physically vanished on Saturday, though she'd remained on my mind and in my thoughts. As hard as I tried, I found it difficult to recover from the impact she'd made on me. It was something which had never happened to me in my adult life. Not even with Kate.

What was so special about Remy? I asked myself. We'd made love and it had been wonderful. Then, I'd felt terribly guilty and now I wanted her again so badly! I wanted Remy not only in bed; I wanted her as a permanent fixture in my life. I needed her to fill a vacuum in my existence – an emptiness that I hadn't been aware of until the very day we met. I wanted her to be my wife. The thought scared me, because it all had happened so quickly.

But how could she be my wife when she was married already? And more, she was married to my best friend. What did she mean when she'd said that *we must do something*? She'd hinted that we had to do something to be together, but I had no idea what she'd meant by that. Did she mean that she had to get a divorce? But, if that was the case, how did I fit into that? Was Remy perhaps thinking that we should come clean and admit to Florin we were having an affair? I knew I would never have the guts to ever face Florin with that confession.

14

Monday, 6 June

On Monday morning I woke up with a bad headache, symptom of a severe hangover. 'I feel pretty rotten this morning,' I told Florin when he welcomed me in the living room.

'You should stick with beer,' he replied laughing. 'It looks that my homemade wine is too strong for you.'

He was right, I thought, though the truth was that I'd knowingly overindulged the night before, to drown my sorrows. I'd been frustrated and cranky and ... I clearly missed Remy.

At the same time, the fact that I only had very little cash left on me made me very uncomfortable. Being a guest in Florin's home, I felt I should share some of the costs. As his cold-room was stacked with food and wine, I'd planned to maintain the beer supply, but now, with just a couple of hundred dollars left in my pocket, I wasn't inclined to spend any more.

With those thoughts circling in my head, I was in a depressed state of mind. Florin, on the other hand, looked positive and optimistic. Though much smaller than me physically, he didn't seem affected by the grog. He was in good health and spirits. With his work overalls on, he couldn't wait to get out and get his hands dirty.

'Are you coming with me, or staying inside this morning?' Florin asked.

'By the way I feel right now, I think I'll stay in the whole day, not only this morning,' I said.

'Well … I'm heading off. Take care.'

He walked out.

I went to the bathroom and listened to the eight o'clock news on 2HS, which was Helen's radio station. They said after the news that Julia Lizard – the Australian Prime Minister – had accepted an invitation to attend the 2HS studio and would be chatting with Helen following the nine o'clock news on the subject of global warming and carbon tax.

That announcement made me realise that I hadn't heard Helen's voice in nearly a week and I missed her a little. Having nothing better to do, I decided to listen to her talk with the PM.

Having listened to the interview, I felt my blood boiling. I knew I wasn't a very smart bloke by any standards, but this redhead holding the highest office in the country made me feel a sort of Einstein. Such arrogance and utter incompetence I hadn't seen in all my life.

Later that morning I was in two minds over whether to contact Helen or not. On the one hand, having heard my boss on the radio, I was a little nostalgic about her and, also, I was curious to find out if she had any news from the police at her end of the town. On the other hand, I was afraid that her reception might not be to my liking. And I was aware that contacting Helen entailed a risk as well, because the police could have been monitoring her phone. Considering that angle, I decided that I was most likely oversuspicious.

I made up my mind after watching the half-past-eleven news on Channel 7. They mentioned on the news that CCTV security cameras images just released by the police showed Kate Morales leaving the Westfield Shopping Centre in the company of a man, believed to be the Romanian national Cornel Toma. Those few seconds of images shown on television, taken on the 26th of May, which was the day when Kate disappeared, were very obscure and inconclusive. Police were asking anyone who recognised the man accompanying Kate in those shots to come forward immediately.

I thought about it and concluded that, although those CCTV images were very blurry, they were good enough for someone who knew me to suspect that I was the man hunted by the police. With that in mind, I thought it was time for me to admit to Helen that I had met Kate, but not to tell her the full story.

I waited until lunchtime, when Helen finished her show and then dialled her mobile number from Florin's fixed-line phone. Besides my own phone numbers, I remembered Helen's mobile and landline number too. I'd also memorised Katarina's mobile number, though that didn't help me, as her mobile had been stolen and she didn't have a landline connection. With my contact list stored on my mobile phone and my phone missing, I couldn't remember any other phone numbers.

My boss answered immediately. 'Helen Longshanks speaking.'

'Hello Miss Longshanks,' I said timidly.

She paused. 'You're being very formal this afternoon. Where are you?'

I wasn't going to tell her that. 'I'm still in … the Southern Land.'

'I see … Why did you call?'

'I called … I thought it's time to tell you the truth.'

'I'm listening,' Helen said.

'Well, I don't know why I told you before that I didn't know this Kate Morales. I mean, it's sort of true that I didn't know her. I only met her that Thursday – after you'd flown to Europe. We had a chat and a few drinks at the Steak House and … that's all.'

'Hmmm … you're sure that's all?' Helen asked.

I hesitated. 'Well, she sort of fancied me and wanted to meet again, but knowing that you'd lined up Rhonda for me, I wasn't keen. And then … she vanished.'

'I see … So, if that's the case, why are you hiding?'

'Well, it's because a lot of people have already made up their mind that I'm guilty for … who knows … Abduction, seduction …. and even murder. And whatever I say, they won't believe me. So I better not say anything and wait until Kate turns up. Then everyone will know that I am innocent and that I've always been innocent.'

'It's a nice story,' Helen said.

'And true,' I added.

'So you maintain that your relationship with Kate was … platonic only.'

'Yeah … that's right.'

'She never came to your place and never undressed for you?'

'Ah no, no way,' I was quick to deny.

There was a long pause. 'You know, Cornel, I am very disappointed in you.'

'But why? Why don't you believe me that I'm telling the truth?'

'Because the police have searched your flat, a couple of times.'

'They have?'

As I'd dusted and cleaned the place very thoroughly before I fled last Wednesday, I was confident that I'd wiped out any of Kate's fingerprints. 'Well, I don't think they could possibly have found any evidence that Kate was there.'

'Why are you so confident that they didn't find anything?' Helen inquired.

'Well ... because she wasn't in my flat.'

'It's true the police didn't find any of Kate's fingerprints. But they found something more ... let's just say, more *pertinent*.'

'Which is?' I prompted her.

'A pair of black, very tiny, sexy undies.'

Stupid me; I'd forgotten about that! She'd left her panties on the floor, when she bolted from my flat that evening. Now I recalled putting her pants in a drawer to keep it as a souvenir. Still, I wasn't ready to confess. 'But how would they know that those undies belonged to Kate?'

I heard Helen laughing on the line. 'I am surprised you're so ... let's say naïve, particularly, considering that you did a police training course. Or don't they use DNA evidence in your country?'

She got me with that one.

'In this particular case, the DNA tests proved beyond any reasonable doubt that those undies had been worn by Kate Morales,' Helen went on.

Well, she left me speechless.

'There is one more thing,' Helen added.

I didn't say anything; I just didn't know what I could possibly say.

'Rhonda wants to talk to you,' Helen continued.

'I don't have her number,' I mumbled.

Helen told me Rhonda's phone numbers, which I noted on a piece of paper.

I thanked her and found the courage to add. 'You know, that story about Rhonda telling the police that she met Kate a couple of days after Kate went missing is not true.'

'I know,' Helen replied and hung up.

Tuesday, 7 June

I woke up still sullen on Tuesday morning, cranky that once more Helen had caught me out with a lie – a lie which I didn't have to tell. What added to my bad mood – or perhaps, was the main cause for it – was that I hadn't seen Remy in the last couple of days and I missed her a lot.

As usual, Florin was already up when I turned up in the kitchen and unlike me, he was in a very good mood. He looked well fed and clean dishes sat on the dish rack.

'Sorry not to have waited to have breakfast with you but I'm in a rush this morning,' he apologised.

'What's up?' I asked

'I forgot to tell you last night that I'm seeing my old man in the city today. He wants to have lunch and catch up. We do get together from time to time.'

'And … your mother?'

'I'm seeing Mum separately. I've told you they divorced, a few years back.'

Yes, he'd told me that, I recalled. He'd also told me that his mum, who'd kept her husband's family name, was a senator with the Federal Greens Party and a Greens activist.

'And how is Mister Panait senior?' I asked.

'He's actually doing very well and still makes plenty of dough as a mining consultant.'

Florin's father was a mining engineer which, obviously, caused an ideological conflict with his former wife's views, as a Greens activist.

'Well, please say hello to Mister Panait from me,' I said.

'I certainly will. He always asks about you and so does Mum. They say I'm very lucky to have such a good friend. Though, I'm not so sure about that,' Florin added, laughing.

I hesitated and asked. 'And is Remy coming with you?'

'Ah, no. She doesn't get along well with either Mum or Dad.' Half an hour later Florin was gone.

Alone and with nothing to do, I flicked through a magazine, while trying not to think of Remy, at which I did not succeed. There was no doubt in my mind that I was infatuated with her and I didn't like it – neither the feeling, nor the idea.

Involuntarily, lyrics from an old French song, which I'd often listened to when I was a kid and lived with my grandparents, kept replaying in my ears: *Tu es la femme de mon ami*, which translated meant both You are my friend's woman and You are my friend's wife.

I listened to the nine o'clock news and was relieved not to hear anything about me. I then hesitated whether to keep the radio on for Helen's program, which followed the news. I thought about it and turned it off. I just wasn't in the mood. Actually, I wasn't in the mood to do just about anything. Except perhaps ... being with Remy.

Though it was early in the morning, I gulped a glass of slivovitz and sat on the sofa in the reception room, determined this morning to sort out what went wrong in my head and make a resolution.

I knew I was infatuated with Remy and I knew that my obsession meant trouble, with a capital T. It was a sort of animal attraction which didn't do me any good. She had, at the snap of her fingers, made me part with seven thousand dollars already, after just one intimate encounter.

What else was she capable of making me do? I feared Remy spelled trouble for both myself and Florin. Being aware of all that, logic and common sense told me I had to end my obsession with her. It was simple, wasn't it? But … easier said than done.

I knew that however hard it was, I had to put a stop to playing around with Remy. I ought to end it, no matter how cruel to me it was. It took a lot of deliberations in my mind, but I finally resolved that ending my affair with Remy was the only option.

Sitting on the sofa, going through those reflections again and again, I dozed off. Before falling asleep, I swore in my mind I wouldn't fall for Remy's charm again.

Faint sounds coming from the hallway woke me up. I then heard footsteps on the floorboards approaching. I stirred but refused to open my eyes. I felt soft lips touching mine and small palms caressing my neck. Then, shoes being kicked off and a rustling sound of a dress being thrown away. I opened my eyes very slowly to see a bra and pair of undies landing on top of a dress on the floor. And then … the promises I'd just made in my mind and my resolution to never fall for Remy's charm again went out the window in an instant.

A couple of hours later, while we both lay naked in my bed, I felt that saying no to Remy represented the most accurate definition of the word *impossible*.

'Did you walk here?' I asked Remy.

'Of course I didn't. It takes several minutes walking here from the front house and there are much better things to do in several minutes.'

'So, you came on your buggy?'

She nodded.

'Isn't that … risky?' I asked.

She raised her eyebrows. 'Why?'

I thought it was obvious. 'Marin could see you.'

'Don't worry about him. I know his routine, anyway. He usually watches video movies for kids and wanks at the same time. Otherwise, he's with the animals in the north-western corner of the farm, between two of the lakes. He says the grass tastes better over there …'

'He eats grass?' I asked.

Remy ignored my question. 'And the water is sweeter. He can't see the cabin from there. And I parked at the back.'

'I still think there is a risk involved,' I said.

'There is a risk involved in anything we do. Even getting out of the bed is risky.'

'Why?' I asked stupidly.

'You may slip and fall on the floor.'

'I was being serious,' I pointed out.

'Me, too,' Remy replied. 'But if you're not happy with me visiting you and find it too risky, I won't bother you again.'

I remained quiet, aware that was an opportunity I should take advantage of. I could tell Remy right then that she should stay away from me. I should, if I could find the power of will.

A few minutes passed in silence. I thought Remy was dozing off when she suddenly jumped from the bed and began to collect her clothes. She reminded me of Kate, that Thursday night … Only, unlike Kate, Remy did put on her undies, while I was watching her dumbly.

Once she fastened her bras, she sent me into a panic. I leaped from the bed and caught her in my arms. 'What are you doing?' I exclaimed.

'I'm leaving,' she stated the obvious.

'Please don't,' I begged her, while strengthening my grip on her body.

I felt her harden in my arms. 'Let me get dressed,' she said with sparks of fury in her eyes. 'I am a risky proposition to you, so I'll leave you alone.'

'There is no way I'll let you go,' I riposted.

'I'll scream,' she threatened.

'No one will hear you. Marin is two kilometres away.'

'I wish he was here. I know you are scared of him.'

'Well, he *is* sort of scary,' I admitted while holding Remy in my arms.

'So he is. But … let's say he did something to me … like he raped me one day and you just saw him doing it. What would you do? I guess you'd be too scared to do anything,' Remy answered her own question.

Imagining that scenario, made me see red before my eyes. 'I'd kill him,' I assured Remy and, at that moment, I meant it.

I felt Remy's body relax. 'Would you kill for me?'

'I would,' I promised.

Her arms began moving slowly up my body, caressing my torso and she stretched up on her toes to reach my lips.

Late that evening, Florin returned home very plastered. Though Remy had left a few hours earlier, his question, as he entered the reception room, stunned me. 'Has Remy been here?'

I froze for a few seconds. 'Remy? You mean your wife?'

He slumped onto the sofa and yawned. 'Do you know any other Remy?'

I frowned pretending to focus if I knew of another Remy. 'I actually do and you do to, if you think about it.'

Florin arched his eyebrows. 'Do I?'

I took a seat in an armchair. 'It's remy – the game, which we play at home. I don't know how they say it in English.'

'Ah … that's rummy in English. But it's not a smell of rum I feel in here. I thought I smelled Remy's perfume.'

I swore in my mind, realising, too late, that I should have aired the room.

'I can't smell anything,' I said. 'But now, that you've mentioned it, I think *there is* a smell of rum, but it's coming from you.'

Florin laughed. 'No, I didn't drink rum.'

'But you drank quite a bit,' I observed.

'Yeah … I know I drank too much and I shouldn't have.'

'Did you say hello to Mister Panait from me?' I asked.

He frowned. 'I didn't.'

I made a gesture with my hands, to indicate to Florin that I didn't mind. 'That's alright. We all forget things.'

Florin paused for several seconds. 'I didn't forget.'

I gaped at him, surprised. 'You just didn't think it was necessary?'

He shook his head. 'No, it wasn't that either. I just didn't think it was a good idea to tell Dad that I'd seen you recently.'

The penny dropped. 'I see. He's heard of me in the news.'

Florin nodded. 'He has.'

I expected him to elaborate on that and say that his father didn't believe I'd done anything criminal. Florin didn't offer any further explanations.

'So, your father thinks I've done something bad?'

Florin hesitated. 'Dad says he remembers you as a good kid, but with a bad temper. He still recalls you belting a couple of boys who had bullied me, when we were little. He believes, whether you're a menace to the community or not, you're certainly not a risk to me. I think, by saying that, he implied he knew you're hiding on my farm.'

I thought of our childhood days and I became nostalgic. I was, in those years, very fond of Florin and I admired him for being smart at school, which I wasn't. And he valued my physical qualities. Then we formed a successful sort of partnership. He often did the school assignments for me and I protected him from bigger boys.

And now *he* was the one protecting me from the police, while I was being a jerk, screwing his wife in return, I reflected. 'How about a drink?' I suggested.

Florin shook his head. 'I had plenty already and I mixed beer with heaps of wine. I'd better not have a third different drink. I'm actually pretty tired and I'll hit the sack in a minute.' He stood up, stretched himself and went to his bedroom.

Though it wasn't ten o'clock yet, I felt tired too. I had another couple of beers and went to bed. Before falling asleep, a crazy thought struck me. That evening, Florin had driven a long way from the city while being well over the legal alcohol limit. If the police had stopped and tested him, he'd have spent the night in a police cell. And I could have spent mine with Remy.

I fell asleep ashamed of myself.

I awoke just after midnight and noticed on my way to the bathroom the lights in Florin's bathroom were on, though I didn't hear any noise. Ten minutes later, on my way back to my room, the lights in his bathroom were still on. Fearing Florin wasn't feeling well, I knocked on the door. Nothing happened. I turned the handle and stepped in. No one was in the bathroom. He probably forgot to switch the lights off, I assumed.

Still, I listened at his bedroom door and was surprised not to hear him snoring. He always snored pretty badly, particularly after too many drinks. This time though, his bedroom was very quiet. I turned the door handle slowly and opened the door. I waited a few seconds to adjust my eyes to the dark. No one seemed to be in there. I turned the lights on. The room was empty.

I checked all the other rooms in the house. Florin was not in the cabin. I then stepped outside. Florin's 4WD was parked in front of the house. Where was Florin? I wondered. I walked to the back of the house to check if his buggy was there. It wasn't.

I came back inside and sat on a chair, collecting my thoughts, wondering where he'd gone in that drunken state and at that time of the night. The only possible explanation I could think of was that he'd gone to see Remy. The thought filled me with bitter jealousy.

I tried all night to accept the idea that it was normal for a married bloke to have intimate moments with his wife, at least from time to time. Though it was a fact of life, I refused to accept it. I felt that both Florin and Remy were cheating on me!

I wanted to believe that the physical contact with Florin was repulsive to Remy and she only did it, unwillingly, to discharge her duties as a wife, but I wasn't convinced. A thought began to take shape in my mind. Florin was the villain; I was the victim and Remy … she was the damsel in distress awaiting to be rescued.

Wednesday, 8 June.

On Wednesday morning I reluctantly rang Rhonda on her land-line. I didn't expect her to be at home at nine in the morning, but she was.

'I'll be very quick,' Rhonda said when she heard my voice. 'I won't ask you where you are or what happened to your mobile phone. I just want you to know that you are not alone during this difficult period in your life.'

I liked hearing that plenty. 'Thanks a lot, Rhonda. I'd have thought you didn't want anything to do with me, anymore.'

'Don't be childish, Cornel. I know you haven't done anything bad. I mean, there is nothing criminal in having sex with an attractive woman. And I'm sure that's all it was. It was unfortunate for you that other circumstances which you weren't aware of have caused this otherwise trivial story to make the headlines in the news, but I'm sure it will all be sorted out very soon.'

'I wish I was as confident as you are.'

'Yes, I'm confident we'll get to the bottom of it. I'm working on it.'

I wondered what she meant by that but I didn't ask. 'There is something I wanted to tell you,' I said instead. 'It's about the girl who you met in my flat that Saturday. She's not Kate Morales.'

'I knew that,' Rhonda replied.

'You knew?'

'I knew.'

She amazed me. 'So, you intentionally lied to the police?'

'No one would be able to prove that,' Rhonda said. 'From the description of Kate Morales, I gathered she looks quite similar with the other girlfriend of yours, also named Kate. So, if the police work out that the woman I was referring to was a different Kate, I'll just say it was a mix-up.'

Thinking about it, Rhonda made sense. Kate and Katarina could easily be confused for sisters. 'I see what you mean. But I still don't understand why you lied to the police.'

'To confuse the things and give you some breathing space,' Rhonda replied. 'In the meantime, my man is doing some good work in the background.'

'You said your man? Who's your man?'

She laughed. 'I didn't mean my husband or my boyfriend. I'm still available, but that's another story. I hired a private eye. *He* is my man. He's already done a lot of digging and sooner or later, he'll come up with something. He's very good and I have a lot of confidence in him. I should have a report from him pretty soon. As you are out of reach, so to speak, you'll need to call me again. I hope the news will be good when we talk next.'

I hadn't expected Rhonda to go through all that trouble because of me. 'But … this private eye will cost you quite a bit of dough,' I pointed out. 'Why are you doing this?'

I heard Rhonda sigh on the line: a very loud sigh. 'You men are pretty thick at times. It's because you and I are to get married. Remember that?'

I tried to say something, but she'd hung up.

Though a guest in Florin's house and in spite of my efforts to do otherwise, I knew I was gradually distancing myself from him. Following his escapade on Tuesday night, I avoided in the next few days bumping into him as much as I could. I began to come out of my bedroom only after I heard him leaving the cabin in the morning and I stopped helping him in the greenhouse.

We only ate together in the evening, not saying much to each other. I then retired early to my bedroom, reflecting and drinking alone. Florin certainly knew there was something not right with me, but he didn't pester me about it. He was that kind of guy. At the same time, I blamed my bad mood and lack of participation on not feeling well.

It was actually true. I missed Remy and felt addicted to her.

15

Friday, 10 June.

By Friday morning when Florin went to the markets, my bad mood deteriorated further. And if I thought the last couple of days had been terrible, Friday morning went even worse.

Waiting for Remy, while pacing the reception room back and forth, I was like a time bomb ready to explode. My nerves were stretched to the limit. And what made it much worse, Remy was late.

She finally arrived at twenty to one in the afternoon. Seeing her looking incredibly delicious, my bad mood suddenly evaporated.

'I'd thought you'd forgotten about me,' I panted.

Wearing a short floral dress under a sports jacket, she was, I thought, the embodiment of everything desirable in a woman.

'Waiting only makes it more exciting,' she said, parting her lips and giving me that voluptuous look.

Watching her, I instantly forgot about everything else, impatient to take her in my arms. Right then she was the only thing that mattered. Just enjoy the moment, mate, I said to myself.

A couple of hours later, when my sexual drive had somewhat subsided, I decided to tell Remy what was biting me. Lying in bed on one side to face her, I asked casually, 'You had a good week?'

She shrugged. 'Nothing special. I still didn't get anywhere with the council.'

'Well … at least Tuesday night must have been good,' I added.

She frowned. 'Tuesday night? Why Tuesday night? If I remember well, Tuesday was quite a … prolific day, but that was during the day, not the night.'

Well, at least she was flattering me, admitting that Tuesday was prolific, I noted, but still, that wasn't sufficient to keep my grimy thoughts in check. 'So, the night wasn't as good as the day?'

'Should the night have been as good?' Remy asked.

'I don't know, but I'm curious to find out. Has he performed to your satisfaction?'

She gave me a confused look. 'What are you talking about?'

It was time to be forthright with her, I decided. 'I know Florin visited you on Tuesday night.'

She frowned. 'Did he? How come that you know and I don't?'

'Maybe you just don't want to admit,' I retorted.

She pouted, looking irritated. 'Let's get this straight. What makes you think that my husband came to see me on Tuesday night?'

'Florin was in the city all day, with his dad. He came back late, pretty well plastered and retired to his bedroom unusually early. I accidentally discovered at midnight that he'd gone out.'

'He could have gone anywhere,' Remy pointed out.

'I don't think so. I went outside and had a look. His car was parked in front of the house, but his golf cart was missing.'

'So, what's your point?' Remy asked.

'My point is, he couldn't have gone too far in his buggy.'

She laughed. 'That's very good detective work, Mister Sherlock Holmes. Except it doesn't prove anything. And then, let's say for the sake of the argument that Florin wanted to see me. Why would he sneak out of the house to hide his escapade from you?'

Good point, I admitted. She was his wife, after all. 'Well, maybe he felt that I'd be a little … jealous,' I said, unconvincingly.

She laughed again. 'That's a lot of garbage. And one more thing, to put your mind at ease. Maybe I shouldn't say this, but since you are such a fool, I'll add that you're crazy to suspect that Florin has been with me.'

'Why am I crazy to think that? Though I do feel terribly jealous about it, I can't change the fact that he's your husband. And you happen to be too damn attractive. Why wouldn't your husband want to be with you? Or, why wouldn't *any* man, for that matter? Isn't that normal?'

She gave me a contemptuous look. 'No, it's not normal for him.'

'Why not?' I asked.

'Because he's got a lover.'

Though she said it so naturally, I found it difficult to comprehend that scenario. Florin has got a lover! How could he?! Married to the most sexually attractive doll you'll ever see on earth and having a lover! It was something I just couldn't figure out.

On Saturday, Remy turned up at the cabin very early – less than an hour after Florin had gone to the markets. I was still in the bathroom when she arrived and had a very enjoyable surprise when I walked in the living room.

Lying on the sofa, she was flicking through a magazine wearing only a bra, black stockings and suspenders. She was obviously enjoying the warmth in the living room. I actually found the air conditioning in the cabin was set a few degrees too high.

Generously done up, with her full lips coloured in intense red, Remy definitely knew how to turn a bloke on.

'So you decided to make up for the time we lost yesterday,' I said.

She looked up and gave me one of those languid composed looks. 'I'm eager to compensate for the time lost today, after lunch.'

I didn't know what she was talking about. 'What do you mean?'

'I have to leave before lunchtime.'

'Why so early? Florin won't be back until six or so.'

'Forget Florin,' Remy said. 'I have to see that councillor in the afternoon.'

'On a Saturday?'

She nodded. 'Come here, Novak. I'm very horny this morning.'

A couple of hours later Remy was still very horny. And I was giving signs of exhaustion, which she certainly noticed. 'Why would you like me to stay any longer when you seem to have run out of ammunition already?' she asked tartly.

Still, she was able to prove she had the talent to arouse me again.

Shortly before eleven she suddenly snapped out of her erotic trance and became business-oriented. 'I need some money,' she said very candidly, while she began to put her clothes on.

Her request came like a cold shower to me. 'You need money again? What for?'

She paused a little. 'For buying myself a vibrator.'

Was she making fun of me? 'Why do you need a vibrator?' I asked stupidly.

She gave me an amused look. 'In case you didn't know, women do .... You know, they do *things* with a vibrator, when they are frustrated. Anyway I've told you before I had certain obligations towards certain councillors.'

I didn't say anything.

'And I thought I'd mentioned to you that, if this project of mine comes off, we could share the profits just between the two of us,' she added.

She had mentioned that, but I couldn't quite understand her thinking. 'But ... how about Florin? He's your husband, isn't he? And sure, if this project pays off, you'll have to share the profits with him, not with me.'

She was sitting on a chair, fully dressed, looking cool and composed. 'Why should I share anything with him? What's he doing about it?'

As far as I knew, he wasn't doing anything about it, but I didn't tell Remy that.

'You know what he's doing?' Remy went on.

I just shrugged.

The fury was already showing in her eyes. 'I'll tell you what he's doing. Nothing, absolutely nothing. That's what he's doing. Even more, he pulls the strings behind my back lobbying other councillors *not* to approve the rezoning.'

'But why would he do that?' I asked, amazed.

'Because he knows if I get a share of the money, I'll drop him like a hot potato.'

Though Remy had hinted at that before, it was the first time she'd said it explicitly. I must admit, I enjoyed hearing it. Though she didn't say she'd ditch Florin because she was in love with me, I assumed that was the idea.

Even so, I couldn't help thinking that Remy's plans were unfair and I said so. 'But still, this is his land. He was the one who purchased the farm.'

'He did,' Remy acknowledged. 'But it was *me* who saw the potential in the land and the opportunity to make big money. And *I* am the one who does all the dirty work with the council.'

Wondering what sort of dirty work Remy was doing while lobbying certain councillors, as she'd put it, depressed me. Still, I asked the question. 'What sort of dirty work?'

She grimaced. 'You didn't answer my question.'

'What question?'

'I asked if you could lend me some money.'

I hesitated. 'I haven't got any cash right now. Seven grand was all I had and I gave it to you.'

She made an impatient gesture with her hands. 'That money has gone. But sure, you still have some cash in the bank.'

I recalled boasting to her that I had seventy grand in the bank. What a fool I was! 'I can't withdraw it,' I said.

'Why not?' Remy asked with visible signs of annoyance.

I couldn't tell her that I suspected my account was probably monitored by the police, so I had to invent a lie. 'I can't withdraw it because … it's because that money is in a term deposit. And I forfeit the interest if I withdraw it before the term is up.'

She grunted contemptuously. 'Big deal. You'll probably lose a couple of grand, if that. How about your share of three hundred million? Isn't that more appealing to you?'

I still couldn't understand how Remy was planning to share that money with me and that's what I told her. 'I'm sorry, but I can't see how I could get any of that dough. It's money that belongs to you and to Florin and I am not entitled to any bit of it.'

'You keep saying that,' Remy remarked. 'And maybe it seems that way, on face value. But you should view this from another angle … use lateral thinking, so to speak.'

I shrugged. 'I don't know what you mean by that.'

She pursed her lips, surely not impressed with my intellectual abilities. 'I can see that. Anyway, as far as I recall, I have mentioned to you that we must do something about resolving this … love triangle, so to speak. But you don't seem to remember. Needless to say you haven't even bothered to think about it. That's the least you could have done.'

She was putting me under a lot of pressure and I felt very uncomfortable. 'Sorry, but I still don't know what you're getting at.'

'Aren't you going to shave any time soon?' You look sort of … scruffy, which doesn't do you justice, as you're such a handsome man otherwise.'

I knew she was right. I'd trimmed my beard a little, but hadn't had a full shave in more than a week. 'Yeah … I've just been lazy lately,' I said absently.

She nodded. 'I've noticed you're getting lazy in bed as well.'

She had a point there. The truth, which I realised last week, was that I couldn't keep pace with her. It was also true that she was very demanding.

Amazingly, her body language changed within seconds, once more. She was suddenly gentle, loving and caring. She got up from the chair and sat on the bed next to me. She put one hand in mine and with the other began caressing my chest. 'A marriage doesn't have to last forever,' she said.

She's certainly falling for me, I thought. She's planning to divorce Florin because she wants to be with me. Curiously, that thought didn't make me feel guilty towards Florin any longer.

'But, if you plan to divorce Florin, you'll maybe end up with half of his fortune, so the three hundred million gain you're talking about, would only amount to a hundred and fifty,' I pointed out.

Remy stopped caressing my chest, withdrew her hand from mine and made a grimace. 'If Florin and I separate, I won't get anything at all.'

That was a bombshell. 'What do you mean you won't get anything at all? You're his wife and, as far as I know, if you separate, you should get half of his assets.'

She grimaced again. 'Not if there is a prenuptial agreement in place, which there is, in this case. Florin was very adamant about it, when we got married.'

So Florin wasn't as mesmerised by his wife as I'd thought, if he'd insisted on that arrangement. He certainly knew how to take care of his financial affairs, I reflected. But if that was the case, why was Remy dreaming about getting three hundred million dollars? 'So, you'll get nothing if you separate, which means a divorce is not an option. But what happens if you stay with him?'

'This prenuptial agreement only applies in respect of the money and property he brought into the marriage. What we make afterwards is still subject to a fifty-fifty division.'

'So, I was right before saying that you'd only get a hundred and fifty million, not three hundred,' I emphasised.

She glanced at her wristwatch and parted her lips, giving me that sensual look again; I knew very well what that meant. 'I want the whole lot … only for you and me,' she whispered, while pulling me close to her.

I became conscious, after Remy had left, that somehow she'd hooked me with her proposition. Though I still had no idea of how she planned to get her hands on that fortune, the more I thought about it, the more appealing her idea became. Three hundred million was a lot of dough. Not even Helen had that sort of money – or at least I didn't think she had.

The fact that Remy's scheme implied we'd deceive her husband and my best friend did bother me, but Remy had said that Florin had a lover. So he deserved what Remy was planning for him, I thought, though I wasn't quite convinced. I knew that whatever happened between Florin and his wife was none of my business. Still, being infatuated with Remy and having an affair with her, I *made* it my business.

I went outside to the back of the house and sat on a bench under the pergola, nursing a glass of slivovitz while collecting my thoughts. I realised I'd become complacent with the idea that Remy and I were lovers. And I was determined that we were to remain lovers and maybe more ... I didn't feel guilty any longer. It was because I'd been made aware that Florin had a lover.

I had become contented to reside in my best mate's house while cheating with his wife. I reflected on it for a long while. There was nothing wrong with that, I concluded. Remy's revelation about Florin cheating on her had come at the right moment for me. It made me feel that Florin deserved what he got.

My affair with Remy was in retaliation to his infidelity. I had nothing to feel ashamed about; I had a good excuse. I was blameless. Only I had to behave in a more convincing manner towards Florin. He wasn't a fool and my aloofness in the past few days could arouse his suspicion.

Deep in thought, I hadn't seen little Robin sitting on the same beam at the side of the pergola where I first saw him the previous week. I only noticed him when he began to chirrup. I smiled at him and he stopped chirping. He looked at me, probably wanting my attention.

I had to be friendly with Florin again, I continued thinking. Behave friendly with him, while dreaming to steal both his wife and his money! What a disgusting, two-faced jerk you are, Cornel Toma, I said to myself. But that thought only lasted one moment.

That evening I cooked Florin a nice dinner. He accepted my gesture with grace and gallantry, without showing surprise or asking any questions.

In the week that followed, Florin and I were back to normal, so to speak. Or at least, on face value we were. I made a considerable effort and started to help him in the greenhouse again. We spent most of the time together, chatted about this and that and had drinks in the evening.

At the same time, as the days passed so slowly, I couldn't wait for Friday to come quicker. While counting the days and the hours, I started to think of Abel and Caine.

Thursday, 16 June

On Thursday evening, while Florin was having a bath, I thought it was time to give Rhonda a call. It had been more than a week since we'd last spoken.

'I thought you'd be at Helen's,' I said, surprised that, at half past seven in the evening, Rhonda answered her landline, which meant she was at home.

She paused a little. 'Helen and I haven't been the best of friends, lately.'

'Ah … I'm sorry to hear that.'

'Don't worry about it. Anyway, I'm glad you called. I have some news for you.'

'Has your private eye made any progress?'

'He has. The news is about Kate's husband – a dubious character named Luigi Maslini, whom I know you've met.'

'Yeah ... we've met briefly,' I confirmed.

'This Luigi, who's now in police custody, is apparently part of a racket involved in human trafficking. More precisely, they recruit young women, mostly from Asia, which they place in illegal, five-star brothels in Sydney and Perth.'

Recalling the automatic pistol which I'd discovered in Luigi's house and the fragments of conversations with his Italian mates, I wasn't surprised by Rhonda's news. 'I see. So, how does this racket work?'

'Luigi and his mates target young attractive migrants who don't have a visa or have arrived in Australia illegally ...'

'So, he could solve my problem, too, as I am in the same situation,' I interrupted.

'But you're not a woman,' Rhonda said flatly, ignoring my irony.

'That's discrimination,' I said.

'They offer these ladies a job and a guarantee they'll stay in Australia. It's a two-way traffic between Sydney and Perth, or a relocation of the women who have lived in one of the two cities and are wanted by the immigration authorities, to the other end of the country. As you know, Sydney and Perth are some four thousand kilometres apart.'

'And ... your private eye has discovered all that?'

'I told you he's very good.'

'You did, but ... I don't know how this is going to help me.'

'I'm confident one thing will lead to another. My man has been in contact with the police, he says, and they're working on it too. There will be something in the news, very soon.'

'And ... is there anything else?' I asked.

She paused. 'Helen has hired a replacement for you.'

That news disappointed me. 'Ah … she has?'

As Rhonda didn't answer, I added, 'This thing which you mentioned before, that you and Helen haven't been very friendly lately … why is this?'

'I'm not sure. It may have something to do with you.'

Though Rhonda's answer was vague, I had a hunch that it definitely had something to do with me.

Friday, 17 June

On Friday morning, while lying in bed next to Remy, she shocked me once again. 'I need fifty grand urgently,' she announced, just seconds after having another raucous orgasm.

'You need *fifty* grand?' I asked perplexed.

'Why are you surprised? I've told you already, haven't I?' Remy asked.

'You did, but … I thought you were kidding …'

She propped herself in a sitting position and gave me a stern look. 'We are partners, aren't we? I mean we're business partners as well.'

I noted her breasts looked firm and heavy; her nipples still erect.

I remained quiet.

'You can't just enjoy having a good time and do nothing in return,' Remy went on. 'You need to do your bit to earn your share as well.'

'But … fifty grand is huge …'

'I'd have thought it's a fantastic investment. Who wouldn't dream of putting fifty grand in and getting one hundred and fifty million in return?'

Though I did like the idea, the fortune Remy was talking about seemed somewhat vague and abstract to me. It was time to find out exactly how she planned to get that money, I decided. 'Before I do anything, I need to know all the details.'

'What details?' Remy asked.

'I need to know *everything*. You've always been very ambiguous about it. Before I put any more money in, I have to know the nitty-gritty. What's the plot? How exactly do you plan to get this money and share it with me? And how can you keep Florin out of it?'

She pursed her lips and reflected for a minute or so. 'I need to know if you're in this with me before I can tell you.'

I remained silent, hesitating. We were in a vicious circle. I wanted to know Remy's plan before committing to her and she demanded my commitment as a condition of telling me what her plan was.

Of the two of us, Remy proved she had the upper hand. Sensing my hesitation she capitalised on her advantage in a decisive manner. 'But if you decide to stay out of it, we must put a stop to any other form of association between us.'

That was one thing I didn't want to hear. 'You know I couldn't do that. I am with you.'

'Definitely?'

I nodded. 'Yes. Just tell me what the plan is.'

Remy reached for her handbag on a chair, fished out a cigarette and lit it. She drew at it and exhaled smoke into the air. 'There is only one way to get all the money for the two of us and keep Florin out of it,' she said.

'But you said that divorcing Florin is not an option,' I pointed out.

She blew out more smoke and watched it dispersing in the air.

She didn't seem in a hurry to elaborate. 'Florin must meet with an accident, or something like that,' she finally said.

I was speechless, not believing what she'd just said. I was completely horrified. It took me a good couple of minutes before I was able to speak again. 'Are you being serious?'

'Are you being … shocked?' she replied.

I nodded. 'Yes.'

'Well, you must get used to the idea. Or, did you think that getting three hundred million dollars was as easy as snapping your fingers?'

I considered that. 'No, of course it's not that easy. But … murder is too much for me.'

'It's not murder as such,' Remy said. 'You just need to arrange an unfortunate accident. That's all. The rest will take care of itself.'

The coolness and indifference with which she was asking me to arrange a fatal accident for my best friend, who also happened to be her husband, sickened me. 'You mean … you mean *me*? You want *me* to murder your husband?'

Remy gave me a serene, detached look. 'Yes, that's the idea.'

I felt I needed oxygen. Her nonchalance was unbelievable under the circumstances. 'But … how could I do such a dreadful thing? I mean … could you do it?'

She grimaced with contempt. 'For three hundred million, I'd slit my mother's throat.'

I stared at her for a long while and pinched myself, hoping I'd wake up from a bad dream. It didn't happen. It wasn't a dream.

Remy got out of the bed and put her clothes on.

I made no attempt to stop her.

I wanted her to leave, but she didn't.

She pulled up a chair and sat on it, a metre away from the bed. She studied my face in silence for maybe half a minute. I guessed

I didn't look too flash.

'What do you say?' she asked.

'I'm not doing it. I'm out,' I said convincingly.

She grimaced. 'I don't quite understand. It wouldn't be the first time you killed someone, would it?'

'What do you mean?' I asked angrily.

She stood up and stepped to the door. She opened the door and turned to me. 'You know very well what I mean, Mister Cornel Toma. You have a week to reconsider. Bye for now.'

She walked out, leaving me utterly stunned.

So Remy knew who I was. How did she find out? I wondered. The obvious answer was Florin, but somehow I didn't think he'd revealed my identity to Remy. She could have heard of me on the radio or television, or perhaps she'd read something in the papers. I had no doubt the story of Kate's disappearance had been covered in the newspapers.

Or perhaps ... There was another possibility that worried me. It was obvious that Marin suspected something wasn't right with me. He'd made it clear – twice, as a matter of fact.

One other thing bothered me about Marin. Was there a secret connection between Remy and him? Though I had no obvious reasons to suspect that Remy and Marin were having an affair, the thought was present in my mind. It was perhaps Marin's primitive look and raw physical strength emanating from him which made me feel that Remy, with her insatiable libido, could seek sexual gratification in the shepherd's arms.

Remy remained a mystery to me: a huge question mark. My thoughts and feelings towards her were confusing and conflicting. A sort of love-and-hate affair. Her physical touch was divine. She was so skilled and passionate in bed. I loved being intimate with her and I craved for her body and her touch. The thrill of being with her had become addictive and obsessive. But I never knew what to expect from her on other fronts.

Having replayed in my mind the talk I had with her that morning, I began to understand that, in spite of her strikingly sensual appearance and wild behaviour in bed, sex was not the most important thing on her mind. I wondered if she'd instigated the whole affair with me just to get me on her side in her plan to deceive Florin. The thought hurt my ego.

I was now quite certain she'd married Florin with the sole purpose of ripping off his fortune. And I began to see the other face of her: determined, tough and ruthless; ready to do anything to achieve her goals. Recalling her words *for three hundred million, I'd slit my mother's throat,* I shuddered with revulsion.

At the same time, the manner in which she'd told me she knew who I was made me very uneasy. If I refused to play her game, I concluded, she'd have no hesitation to doublecross me as well.

I thought about it for a couple of hours and made up my mind. Even if I had to turn myself in and go to jail, I wasn't going to side with Remy, I decided. Though mesmerised by her, the asking price was too high. I had to talk with Florin and warn him of his wife's deadly intentions. Having resolved that, I felt much better afterwards.

One thing still worried me: I didn't know how I was to spill the beans to Florin without admitting that I'd been intimate with his wife.

The news that Remy knew who I was wasn't the only surprising piece of information I became aware of on Friday. I listened to the five o'clock news rather absent-mindedly, my thoughts still occupied with Remy and my next course of action. My apathetic state of mind changed very quickly once I heard one of the items on the news.

'There have been recent astonishing developments in the case of the Sydney missing woman, Ecaterina Morales,' the news presenter began. 'According to information from the New South Wales Police, Luigi Maslini, the husband of Ecaterina, has been charged in relation to a human trafficking racket operating between Sydney and Perth. Mister Maslini, who had just been released on bail for firearm possession, was allegedly involved in organising the recruitment, transportation and placement in exclusive brothels of girls and young women who were illegal immigrants in the country. In a joint police operation, simultaneous raids in Perth and Sydney have resulted in several other arrests. Following these arrests, a Chinese national has come forward with sensational information about Luigi Maslini's wife – none other than the missing woman Ecaterina Morales. According to this man, who also operates an exclusive escort agency in Sydney's south-west, Ecaterina was employed by his agency as a luxury call-girl on a casual basis. She'd been allegedly scheduled to work at his agency on the night of her reported disappearance, but she never turned up. It is still unclear whether Luigi Maslini was aware of, or was involved in, his wife's illegal employment and in her subsequent disappearance. Police investigations are currently continuing in both Sydney and Perth.'

Wow! Kate Morales – the delicate, pretty, charming woman I'd nearly fallen in love with was a high-class prostitute! I never ever could have imagined that. It only showed how little I knew about women. Recalling how she'd bolted from my flat that Thursday evening, saying she was due to begin her night shift and my ensuing search for her at the Liverpool Hospital, I could only smile. I'd just found out that Kate had told the truth that she was due to begin her night shift that Thursday, but in a very different workplace. I had been so naïve and she'd taken me for a sucker!

But what did that news mean for me? I shrugged. The fact remained that, prostitute or not, Kate Morales was still missing. And the main suspect was still me. But, at that point in time, I was more concerned about Remy.

Ironically, having heard the news about Kate I felt a lot better. Recalling my sudden infatuation with her, I knew I'd only got over her because I'd subsequently met Remy. So Remy was my saviour. She'd saved me the embarrassment of falling in love with a prostitute.

I thought of *The Lady of the Camellias*, that novel by Alexander Dumas about the doomed prostitute with the heart of gold and her well-meaning and equally doomed naïve lover which I read when I was a teenager and thanked Remy in my mind that she'd rescued me from a potentially similar misfortune.

At seven in the evening, Florin and I had finished dinner and were having drinks in the living room, as we did most evenings. That particular night though, Florin was unusually quiet and withdrawn, which didn't suit my plan to have a heart-to-heart chat with him. I asked him a few questions about how he'd gone at the markets, but my attempts to arouse his interest weren't working. He just sat in an armchair and sipped from his glass looking absent and faraway.

It took more than an hour and several glasses of wine until he gave me an opening, though the way he did it absolutely stunned me.

'I hear that my wife has been visiting you in the cabin when I go to the markets,' he said casually, without even looking at me.

I was perplexed, but instinctively knew that denying what

Florin had said wasn't an option. He must have got his facts right before saying it. I had to think very quickly and come up with a reasonable and believable explanation.

'Your wife feels lonely and … neglected,' I answered.

He frowned and looked at me. 'Has she confessed to you?'

I nodded, looking down. 'She has. She isn't very happy, as you know.'

'Why isn't Remy happy? Or, what reason did she give you for not being happy?' Florin asked.

I hesitated. 'Well … she said there is another woman.'

He grinned and remained quiet for a while. 'Do you believe her?' he finally asked.

'I had no reasons not to believe her,' I replied.

Florin paused again. 'There is no other woman,' he said after a minute or so.

He said it so convincingly that I didn't know what to believe any longer. But Remy had been very convincing too and until now, I'd been sure her story was true. Or maybe I just wanted to believe Remy's version because it suited me. Clearly, one of them was lying. Was it Florin or Remy? Having no idea what to say, I remained silent.

'So, there is nothing going on between you and Remy?' Florin went on.

Though I'd planned to tell him the whole truth, including my affair with Remy and her determination to steal his money, I just couldn't find the courage to do it. However, I had to warn him to beware of his wife without confessing that Remy and I were lovers, I decided. 'No, of course there is nothing else going on between us.'

Florin gave me a doubtful look. 'So, why did she come to see you?'

'She knows who I am,' was the first thing which came to mind.

Florin nodded, thoughtful. 'It doesn't surprise me.'

'And she … warned me … or rather she threatened me that she wouldn't keep it a secret. In case she might go to the police, I thought I'd better come clean and follow your advice …'

'What advice?' Florin interrupted.

'You know, the first evening when I came to the farm, you said that defending myself from kidnapping and murder allegations was more important than risking being arrested and sent back to Romania. So, I decided to turn myself in to the police and tell them the full story, even if that means I will be sent back home.'

I'd decided earlier in the day to take that course of action, fearing that Remy would blackmail me threatening to reveal my identity if I didn't help her with her murderous plot. My thinking was that, by turning myself in to the police, I'd cancel Remy's upper hand on me.

Florin stood up and walked to the cold-room. He returned with another bottle of chilled wine and filled our glasses. He then took his seat into the armchair and sipped from his glass.

I waited for him to say that he agreed with me, or at least to say something, but he didn't.

'Well, don't you think that I should go to the police?' I prompted him.

'I don't think it's such a good idea,' Florin replied.

'But it was *your* idea,' I stressed.

'My idea was based on the assumption that you were innocent,' Florin said.

He depressed me with that. 'But I *am* innocent,' I pleaded.

He downed his wine and refilled his glass. 'I am sorry to say this, but I don't know what to believe anymore. I did believe that you were innocent then, but now …' He left the rest in suspense.

'What's changed since then?' I asked.

He hesitated. 'I'm sorry, Cornel, but I don't know if I can rely on what you're telling me. You're saying there is nothing going on between Remy and you, but Marin tells me otherwise.'

'But I've just told you there's nothing going on. Do you believe Marin rather than me?'

'Please don't be offended,' he answered.

Though I knew very well I was in the wrong, his words hurt me. It was Marin's word against mine and he believed Marin. How could he? I downed my glass and stood up. 'Well, I thank you a lot for your hospitality. I better go and pack my things …'

'Don't be silly,' Florin said. 'You're welcome to stay here for as long as you like. Please do.'

Now he got me confused. 'But … I don't understand you. If you believe that I'm having an affair with your wife, which I am not, why are you asking me to stay?'

He looked past me and grinned. 'Please sit down.'

I took my seat and waited for him to explain. He refilled our glasses and frowned as if trying to find his words. 'You sure have noted that my marriage is … let's say peculiar. The truth is I knew from the very first day when you arrived here that you'd be seduced by Remy. I mean, with her looks, it's almost impossible for *any* bloke not to be seduced by Remy. So I don't blame you for that. Having said that, I also knew she wouldn't do anything stupid to risk a divorce.'

Florin paused and drank from his glass. 'I'd better rephrase that. I meant to say *I'd thought* she wouldn't risk a divorce. I was very confident of that. I also told you she was a lesbian, trying to keep you away from her. I'd thought I had it covered, but I was wrong.'

I meant to contradict him and say he wasn't wrong; to say that

Remy and I *weren't* having an affair, but I couldn't do it – the words just wouldn't come out.

'Anyway, what baffles me is I can't work out what makes her so reckless,' Florin continued. 'I understand that she feels the need to … to have a lover, but her behaviour is just … it's too blatant and even defiant. It's true that I do have reasons to suspect it's not the first time she's played around, but she's been very discreet in the past. But now … Why isn't she concerned any longer that I'll get a divorce? What's changed? Has she perhaps fallen in love?'

He wasn't asking me directly, he was only expressing his own thoughts and fears, trying to make sense of what was going on; but I answered him anyway: 'Of course she hasn't.'

'I don't think so either,' Florin went on. 'As far as I know Remy, she isn't the type to fall in love. She never fell for me either, though I don't blame her for that.'

Why did you marry her? I was tempted to ask.

As if reading my mind, Florin went on. 'I always knew she only married me because I had money and she was sick and tired of what she was doing. She wanted a quiet, comfortable life and she got it. But she didn't get everything she wanted. I was smart enough to put a prenuptial in place. So if she ever thought to ditch me for a handsome hunk, she'd get no money at all. And now, she's suddenly giving me the divorce motive … I just don't get it …'

I know why, I said to myself, and you'll be horrified to hear her reasons. But listening to Florin's sad monologue, I changed my mind and decided not to tell him. The seed of treachery was already planted in my mind.

I was in a dreadful state of mind for the next few days, both morally and physically. I hardly ate anything, but drank heavily instead. I isolated myself within the cabin and again, discontinued helping Florin in the greenhouse. I just didn't know what to do.

My good intentions to come clean and confess to Florin were now dead and buried. My best friend had hurt me badly by choosing to trust Marin rather than me. I felt rejected and betrayed. At the same time, contemplating Remy's murderous plot gave me such awful nightmares that I was scared to go to bed and I only fell asleep when excessively drunk.

On top of everything else, I didn't know what to believe or whom to trust. How was it possible that Florin, while suspecting that I was screwing his wife, took my liaison with her so lightly? He'd even acknowledged his empathy and assured me I was welcome to stay in his house for as long as I liked! There was definitely something that didn't make sense.

What was I going to do? However hard I thought about it, I couldn't work it out.

Florin didn't help either. He just went on with his daily routine and left me alone with my thoughts without interfering in any way. I didn't know if his apparent indifference was in response to my total withdrawal from any activity on the farm or to his suspicion that Remy and I were having an affair.

In a strange change of heart, once Friday approached, I prayed that Florin wouldn't go to the markets, which would prevent Remy from visiting me. As hooked as I was on Remy's sexual charm and talents, now I knew she wanted a firm commitment from me and I wasn't ready to see her.

On Friday morning though, once Florin went to the markets, I knew I had no choice but to face the music.

16

'What's your decision?' Remy asked as soon as she showed up in the reception room at a few minutes past eight. She looked cool and relaxed, sure of herself.

'Have a seat, please,' I replied with a knot in my stomach, not knowing what else to say.

She sat on the sofa and crossed her legs. I gazed at her registering she was as sexy as ever; only now, for once, sex was not on my mind.

'Where did you park your buggy?' I asked.

'At the back, as usual.'

'Did Marin see you coming?'

She shrugged. 'I'm not concerned about him.'

'I am,' I said.

She gave me a contemptuous look. 'I know.'

I walked to the front door, opened it and left it wide open.

As I returned to the reception room, looking puzzled, Remy said, 'Isn't it a little cool to leave the door wide open?'

'It's better this way,' I replied curtly.

She made a face and lit a cigarette while I took a seat in an armchair, remaining quiet.

'I am waiting,' Remy reminded me, once a couple of minutes had passed in silence.

Though I disliked the idea, I thought one option to keep Remy off my back was to offer her the money to progress her rezoning application. While not convinced of her venture's success, Remy had a point when saying that a fifty-grand outlay returning a one-hundred-and-fifty-million windfall gain was an exceptional investment. Perhaps, too good to be true, but I'd decided to take the risk. 'How about I give you fifty grand?' I said.

Her eyes brightened. 'Have you got the dough on you?'

I chuckled. 'Of course I haven't got fifty grand in cash.'

'You could have got it in a week, had you been fair dinkum with your proposition,' she remarked.

'I don't know about that. My bank account may well be monitored by the police.'

She stubbed her cigarette out. 'So, you may not be able to get the money anyway.'

I shrugged. 'I'll give it a go.'

'Let's go to the bank,' she said at once.

I stared at the ashtray and said, 'No wonder your husband knows you've been seeing me in the cabin.'

I expected Remy to be surprised and ask details about my statement, but she wasn't and didn't. She just grimaced and stood up. 'Who cares?'

I took the ashtray, emptied it in the toilet, flushed the toilet twice and returned to the reception room. Remy was standing up waiting, apparently impatient. Wearing a dark green frock cut two inches above her knees, she looked at her irresistible best.

'I think it's better if you drive me to the bank in your car,' I said to her.

'Which bank?' she asked.

'St. George.'

'Okay, let's go,' she said and moved towards the door, swaying her hips.

Keen to get out of the cabin as quickly as possible, I followed her outside and saw Marin in the distance. Though he wasn't looking in our direction, I had no doubt he was aware of Remy's presence. 'He must have seen you coming to the cabin,' I said to her.

'Who cares?' Remy said again.

We walked around to the back of the cabin, where Remy's four-seater golf cart was stationed. Realising the unnecessary risk we'd taken, I said to her, 'We should have gone out the back door, so Marin wouldn't have seen us.'

'Who cares?' she said for the third time.

Once we reached the front house and alighted from the buggy, Remy gave me one of her well-composed looks. 'You're not in a … playful disposition this morning?'

Though an involuntary rush of blood went through my crotch, I found the moral courage to shake my head. 'It costs too much. I can't afford it.'

'You know very well it's worth every cent.'

'I never paid for sex before,' I riposted.

She grimaced. 'Well … I hope your mood will change later.'

I didn't tell Remy that I was actually inhibited knowing that

Florin suspected we were having an affair. I feared he could very well set a trap to catch Remy and me in the act, which would give him the evidence he needed for a divorce.

We got in to Remy's Audi A6 TDI Quattro and drove off.

'Nice car,' I said, just to say something.

'It's the only little luxury my husband has ever let me have.'

'Where are we going?' I asked as we headed east on Elizabeth Drive.

'The Liverpool Branch of St. George is the one I am familiar with.'

'But I live in Liverpool and the police are looking for me. I don't think going to Liverpool is such a good idea.'

She pressed the accelerator further down making the car shoot off like a bullet. 'Don't worry. They won't look for you in places where you're not expected to show. Plus, with a beard fully grown, you're not easy to recognise.'

It was past nine o'clock when Remy parked her car on the corner of Elizabeth and Northumberland Streets in Liverpool. The few minutes' walk to Westfield seemed to take forever. It made me very nervous. Being the first time I was in public with Remy, I hadn't anticipated the amount of attention she received from males of all ages. Men were staring and gaping at her like she was the Pope walking the streets with his gear off.

As we were approaching Dowes – the place where my nightmare had begun just one month earlier – I felt my heart thumping on my ribs. I wondered if Solveig was there, but didn't have the chance to check. Though the way to the bank was shorter if we'd passed by Dowes, Remy diverted to the left and made a detour, rejoining the main alley some fifty metres further on.

'How do you plan to get fifty grand in cash?' she asked once we reached the St. George branch.

'I will need to talk to the manager, I suppose.'

'And if your account is being monitored?' Remy reminded me.

I shrugged. 'It looks like I have to take the risk. What else can I do?'

'There is always a risk in whatever we do, but there's no need to overdo it,' Remy said.

'What do you mean? How else can I get the money?'

'Let's do a little test first,' Remy suggested. 'Just try to withdraw some cash from the ATM. If your account is under surveillance, you won't be able to access it.'

We stepped to the ATM. I inserted my card in the slot and entered the PIN, with Remy watching me.

'Your year of birth?' she said, and went on when I said nothing: 'You shouldn't use your year of birth as your PIN. It's easy for someone to take a guess, if they know you.'

I was stunned at how quickly and expertly she'd registered my PIN.

I entered the amount and pressed OK.

'You're sure it's the correct PIN?' Remy asked, reading the message on the screen.

I read it too. It said: *Your transaction could not be completed. The PIN you entered is incorrect. Please re-enter your PIN.*

'I'm positive but I'll try again.'

I inserted the card again and re-entered my PIN. My second attempt also failed.

I swore softly. 'It looks like I'm stuffed. I'll try once more.'

'Don't,' Remy stopped me. 'It's obvious that your access has been blocked. The machine will confiscate your card if you try again and then you'll need to talk to someone within the branch to get it back, which is probably not a bright idea.'

She was right, I decided. 'So, what do I do?'

She thought for a moment. 'Are you using internet banking?' I nodded. 'Let's go to an internet café. Maybe they overlooked that aspect.'

We found an internet café on the ground floor, not too far from the bank. I paid the girl in attendance a couple of dollars, realising I only had very little cash left on me. We sat at a computer and Remy brought up the St. George website on screen. She then passed the mouse to me.

'But I can't withdraw cash using internet banking,' I pointed out.

'You hopefully can make an electronic transfer,' she replied.

'Make a transfer to where?'

'Just log on first. I'll give you the account details once you're logged on,' Remy said.

'But, even if my access isn't blocked, they will, sooner or later, work out that some money has gone from my account. They'll trace the receiving account in no time,' I said in a low voice.

'Don't worry about it. Just do as I say,' Remy ordered.

Noting that she was treating me like I was a child, I entered the access number, security number and password.

'Bingo!' Remy said excitedly.

It worked. My savings account and visa credit card details came up on the screen.

'Go to transfers and payments,' Remy ordered.

Once I clicked on Transfers and Payments, Remy took over. She snatched the mouse from my hand, saying, 'You're too slow.' She then added a new payee. I tried, but couldn't memorise the BSB and account number, but the payee's name left me perplexed. It said Solveig Anderson.

Was it a coincidence? I wondered as we walked back to the car. Was this a different Solveig? I didn't know Solveig's surname and

I guessed there were hundreds of Andersons in Sydney, but probably not many of them were named Solveig. I was quite certain this Solveig was the same one I'd met last month. What was the connection between Kate's girlfriend and my best friend's wife? I had no idea and was baffled. The *It's a small world* saying didn't make much sense in a city of four and a half million people.

'Keen to hang around for a while, since we're here already?' Remy interrupted my thoughts.

'Too much exposure might be risky,' I replied.

Remy ignored my comment. 'Want to have a look at Dowes?'

'Dowes? Why Dowes?' I asked, suddenly alert.

'It's the best fashion store for men, as far as I know,' Remy replied.

'Only I don't have any money left,' I noted bitterly. I was suddenly depressed that most of my savings had evaporated at the touch of a button. Though I reluctantly agreed to part with fifty grand to help Remy with her business venture, I would never have done it, had I known the money was going to Solveig Anderson.

Without stopping, Remy opened her hand bag and fished out a few banknotes. She handed the money to me. 'There is five hundred bucks. It's a present from me. I mean, I won't need it back.'

I took the money and said. 'You're very generous, considering that you just took a hundred times as much from my account.'

'That money wasn't for me,' she pointed out.

'I know. It went to Solveig Anderson.'

'You were not supposed to see the payee's name,' she admonished me.

Well, at least Remy had just proved she wasn't greedy; I tried to calm myself down. She'd said she needed fifty grand for business and that's all she'd transferred out of my bank account. A greedy person would have wiped out the lot, but she left a balance of about twenty grand.

We reached Remy's car and boarded it, remaining silent for the next few minutes, while Remy exited the car park and drove around the block until she joined the main road.

She searched through the glove box while driving and produced an LG mobile phone. She handed it to me, saying, 'This is another freebie from me. It is essential that from now on, we can communicate, if needed.'

I took the phone and began playing with it. 'What's the number?' I asked.

She told me the number. I added it into the contact list and then asked hers.

She hesitated. 'It's better if you don't call me. I'll ring you, if necessary.'

I nodded. 'And who's paying the phone bills?'

'It's prepaid. You have nearly three hundred dollars worth of credit. It should suffice for a while. That's if you don't ring your girlfriends overseas.'

Her comment made me feel homesick. I was suddenly longing for the girls I'd been with in the past. I thought of Cristina, Adriana, Sanda, Daniela, Liliana … There had been quite a few of them – young, pretty and vibrant.

'Thinking of your girlfriends overseas?' Remy interrupted my nostalgia.

'Is this Solveig Anderson a young attractive blonde?' I asked, ignoring her question.

Remy pursed her lips. 'I guess any woman with such a name would be a blonde.'

That's a good politician's answer, I thought. 'But is she a councillor?'

Remy paused. 'I don't know if she does counselling these days as well.'

'But, you said you needed the dough to bribe one of the councillors to approve the subdivision,' I reminded her.

'Dealt with that already,' Remy stated.

She was simply killing me. 'So, why did you pay Solveig fifty grand?'

She paused again for several seconds. 'It's part of the scheme.'

'What scheme?'

'What do you mean what scheme? We've just dealt with the small fish. Now, we're going for the big one,' she said, while driving west.

'We're going for the big fish?'

She nodded. 'Forgot the three hundred million already?'

There was something I didn't quite grasp. 'But ... I just paid you fifty grand because I didn't want to be part of your scheme. I mean, the fifty grand was to help you with the rezoning application, but also in return for your silence.'

She shrugged. 'Was it? I didn't get that impression. If that was your intention, you should have articulated it. I thought you parted with the dough to show your commitment to my plan.'

She stunned me again. 'So, you still want to ... to get rid of your husband?'

Remy nodded. 'Of course I do. And you do too. You just don't want to admit it, but subconsciously, you want my husband to ... vanish ... forever. Then, there will be only you and me. And three hundred million dollars.'

She shut me up with that one.

A few minutes later, Remy turned the radio on. 'Let's listen to the news.'

They said something about Julia Lizard and the dysfunctional

Labor Government and then, the bombshell. 'Missing Sydney woman Ecaterina Morales has been located at the other end of the country,' the female newsreader announced. 'Four weeks after Ecaterina, daughter of the famous doctor Juan Morales disappeared in Sydney in mysterious circumstances, she was found safe and well in a waterfront mansion in Perth, which was empty and listed for sale. Ecaterina's resurfacing follows a number of arrests in both Sydney in Perth, including that of her husband, Luigi Maslini, accused of being involved in a human-trafficking racket operating between the two cities. It has been alleged that Mister Maslini was part of a well-organised criminal syndicate which recruited underage girls and young women to work in high-class exclusive brothels. It is not known yet if his own wife is a victim of the same criminal operation herself. Ecaterina has been taken to the Royal Perth Hospital to undergo health tests and will remain under medical supervision overnight. According to our sources in Perth, she is otherwise relaxed and in good spirits.'

Wow! I couldn't believe my ears! After four weeks of hell, I was at last in the clear. I had no more reasons to hide and lie and pretend that I was someone else. I was me again! Well, on second thoughts, that wasn't quite so. I still had to deal with my visa situation. Yet I was glad knowing that nothing sinister had happened with Kate. I felt so much better, for a change.

But Remy received the news so badly that she nearly lost control of the car.

'Easy!' I yelled, grabbing the steering wheel with my right hand. 'We don't want an accident right now.'

'We do, but a different one,' she said. She was suddenly worried and glum-looking.

'What's wrong?' I asked. 'The good news seemed to displease you.'

She nodded. 'Now that you're free again and this … Kate piece of work is alive and well, you don't need me anymore. You probably can't wait to see her again.'

She had a point, I thought. Not that I wanted to ditch her for Kate, but the fact that I wasn't a suspected murderer wanted by the police anymore, meant that Remy was no longer in a position to blackmail me into doing what she wanted me to do. Unless she knew of my other problem – that my visa had expired and I was now an illegal immigrant. But she didn't know that and I wasn't going to tell her. Instead, being suddenly in a very good mood, I felt the need to compliment her by saying, 'Even as a high-class escort, this *Kate piece of work* is not as good as you.'

'No one is as good as me,' she replied. 'And I will prove it to you again and again.'

I was afraid of that. Or, maybe I was waiting for it. Fearing that I was about to give in to her sexual appeal once more, I didn't say anything else for the rest of the trip back to the farm.

We reached the farm at a few minutes past eleven. To my dismay, Remy passed the front gate and kept driving on the Northern Road. Several kilometres further north, she turned left on a sec-ondary road and entered the new estate of Glenmore Park. She stopped on a loop street in front of a brick-veneer cottage.

She unbuckled her seatbelt and put a hand on my left leg. She rubbed it gently and said, 'Please look at me, Cornel. I know you want me now. However hard you try to refrain from your desire, I know you're craving to have me. And I do too. I want you, Cornel, and not only now. I want you forever in my life. Plus, there is another naughty trick I can't wait to show you today.'

'Where are we?' I asked.

'This is a bungalow,' Remy stated the obvious. 'I share it with a couple of my girlfriends, as a … it's a sort of a … holiday retreat. I noticed this morning you were scared to be alone with me on the farm. I assume Florin has said something to you …'

I nodded. 'He has. He knows we're having an affair and so does Marin. He's puzzled that you're not trying to cover it. And so am I.'

She giggled, with a look of satisfaction on her face. 'It's part of my revenge plan. I love seeing him humiliated. He's always put me down and disgraced me. He's been mean and stingy for years, knowing that I had to take all the crap he's been giving me and put up with it. Otherwise, he threatened to divorce me and leave me with no money. Now, that I know what I have to do, it's my turn to give him hell. And I enjoy every minute of it.'

I considered that and could see her angle, though I didn't know what she meant when saying she'd been disgraced and humiliated. Anyway, it wasn't my business and that's what I said to Remy. 'But, this has nothing to do with me …'

She stretched her arms around my neck and kissed me on the lips. 'It has, Cornel, it has … We are in this together.'

Once I felt her touch, all my fears and inhibitions evaporated. She felt warm and receptive. Her sex appeal was just too much. And I hadn't had her in a week.

My interlude of ecstasy after consuming another breathtaking episode in bed with Remy didn't last very long.

'Have you worked it out?' she asked while lying next to me in the queen-size bed.

'You mean if I worked out how you did this … naughty trick?' I asked, still mesmerised by the experience.

She paused for a while. 'There are still plenty of naughty things I'm going to teach you. But as I've said before, I find this situation unbearable. I can't focus my energy on you while my *dear* husband is still around. We must do something to get rid of him.'

I just lay there looking into the ceiling, not saying anything.

'Can you imagine just you and me ... free and uninhibited? We'll be able to make love every day ... whenever we feel like, with no need to hide from ... whoever and without feeling we're cheating,' Remy went on after a couple of minutes.

'That's assuming we're not in jail serving twenty years or even life,' I added.

Remy moved on her side towards me and raised her head, propping it on her hand. 'It's going to be an accident. Have you thought of a scenario?'

'I haven't and I can't think of one.'

'I have,' she said, unperturbed by my lack of participation.

I closed my eyes and replayed in my mind the news about Kate which I'd heard in the car. I found it difficult to comprehend that she was an escort.

'How about you suggest to Florin a fishing expedition on Sunday?' Remy continued.

Preoccupied with my thoughts about Kate, I hadn't quite caught what Remy had said. 'What was that?'

'You should challenge Florin to a fishing contest on Sunday,' Remy rephrased her suggestion.

Glad that she was changing her line to something constructive, I opened my eyes. 'That's not a bad idea. Florin and I used to go fishing with grandpa, when we were kids.'

'There is plenty of fish in these ponds on the farm. The best fish are in the biggest lake, in the south-west. That's because the creek flows into that lake. It keeps the fresh supply of water moving and so do the fish.'

As I was a passionate fisherman, she'd caught my interest. 'So the fish aren't fat, like they are in the artificial lakes.'

'Exactly,' Remy said. 'The biggest pond is more than six-hundred-metres long and about half as wide.'

'That's pretty big,' I said, already captivated by the idea.

'It's big enough to fish from a boat. There are a few boats on the farm,' Remy continued.

'You're on,' I said excitedly and took her in my arms. I was actually more excited about the fact that I was a free man again, but the fishing expedition appealed to me as well.

'Easy,' she said laughing. 'It's not me you're going fishing with. It's Florin.'

'I know, but it's your idea.'

I was now on top of her and she moaned softly under my weight. I was about to kiss her, when she said, 'The pond is three-to five-metres deep, just a few metres away from the bank. Once you're in deep water, you could accidentally fall from the boat.'

I stopped and frowned. 'Why would I fall from the boat?'

She smiled enigmatically. 'Not you. Florin. You know he can't swim.'

In the afternoon, I felt confident enough to drive to the bottle shop in Casula. While driving, I thought of Remy's idea. Though still excited by the latest developments about Kate and preoccupied with my visa situation, Remy's plan had taken priority in my mind. Her general idea didn't enrage me any longer, but I couldn't consider the *means* by which she proposed to get rid of her husband. The ease with which she'd asked me to push Florin from the boat, knowing that he couldn't swim was staggering.

Making use of Remy's money, I bought two more bottles of slivovitz and a few cartons of beer. While driving back from the bottle shop, I reflected some more of what Remy's scheme would entail. Well, maybe the act of pushing him into the lake wasn't so hard in itself, I thought, recalling Remy's words. *You just give him a shove pretending it was accidental. Then you panic, not knowing what to do and, until you recover, in a minute or so, he's gone already.*

But, how could I just watch him screaming for help while pretending not to see and not to hear him? How could I make out that I'd lost my nerve and couldn't think of what to do when he knew very well that I was a top-class swimmer? How could I watch my best mate go under the water without attempting to help him? No, I wasn't going to do it, I decided.

Back on the farm, I cooked a pork roast, which was nearly ready when Florin arrived from the markets, close to seven in the evening.

Once he entered the cabin, sniffing the nice aroma coming from the kitchen, Florin grinned, obviously surprised and pleased by my attentive welcome. 'You must be feeling much better this evening,' he said.

'I thought it's time for me to move on. You've been too nice to me and I've abused your hospitality already,' I replied.

He slumped into an armchair, looking tired. 'What do you mean that you've abused my hospitality?'

'I mean I've stayed much too long in your home.'

He made a dismissive gesture with his hand. 'But I wanted you to stay. I've told you several times, haven't I?'

'How about a shot of slivovitz?' I asked.

He looked surprised. 'I'd thought we'd run out of it.'

I nodded. 'I bought some more today.'

He seemed surprised again. 'Are we celebrating anything?'

I fetched a bottle of slivovitz and was about to open it, when Florin stopped me. 'No, not for me, thank you. I'm very thirsty.

I'd rather have a beer.'

I took the bottle back to the kitchen and grabbed two cans of beer. I handed one to Florin and sat on an armchair. We drank the beer and Florin repeated his question: 'Are we celebrating anything?'

'Well … as I've said before, I think it's time for me to move on.'

'You mean you're planning to leave?' Florin asked.

I nodded. 'Yep … that's the idea.'

'But, you haven't resolved your problems with the police yet,' Florin noted.

'I have,' I replied.

'You have? When? And how?' he asked, surprised.

I told him the news about Kate. He already knew of her husband's arrest and of the human trafficking racket in which Luigi Maslini was involved.

'Well, that's … something,' Florin said, having listened to my account of events. 'It shows you that, in many cases, women are not what they seem to be.'

I was tempted to say his observation applied to his wife as well, but I didn't. I just nodded.

Florin stayed quiet for a little while and then pointed out. 'This news is excellent, but you still haven't resolved your other problem, have you?'

I nodded again. 'That's true, but I can't fix my visa from here. I have to go to the city.'

'So, is this a farewell dinner?' Florin asked.

'The farewell dinner will be on Sunday. I thought I'd better leave on Monday.'

The farewell dinner might be for you, I continued in my mind. The truth was that I hadn't made up my mind of what

I was going to do on Sunday, but I'd decided that regardless of what happened, it was time to say goodbye to the place. The circumstances were appropriate and I was very impatient to get going.

'I'm sorry to see you go,' Florin said.

I'd be sorry to see you go too, I thought, but I didn't say it.

We ate and had more beer.

Once we finished the dinner, Florin excused himself, saying. 'Sorry for not keeping you company this evening. I've had a very long day and it won't get any easier tomorrow. I will see you tomorrow evening.'

He went to his bedroom just before ten, which was very unusual.

I did the dishes, tidied up and retired within one hour. I was tired too, both physically and emotionally. So many things had happened in one day. And I still had no idea what was going to happen in the next couple of days.

Saturday, 25 June

On Saturday morning, I shaved for the first time in three weeks and walked to the front house, where Remy picked me up, as we'd agreed on Friday.

'You're even more handsome without a beard,' Remy complimented me once she had a good look at my face and nodded her approval. She hummed to herself, seemingly very happy, while driving to her holiday retreat villa, where we'd spent a few hours the day before.

It was nearly half-past-nine when we got there. The single-level house was just a few years old, I guessed, surrounded by similar near-new properties. It contained a reception room, living room, kitchen, laundry, bathroom and three bedrooms.

Two of the bedrooms had an ensuite, which I found unusual for such a small house. The place was clean and tidy, with simple, modern furniture. I had the clear impression that no one lived there on a regular basis.

'So, you own the house?' I asked Remy, once I'd had a good look around, which I hadn't done the day before.

She hesitated. 'Not quite. I only own one-third of it. It's my only asset besides the car and Florin is not aware of it.'

'And who owns the remaining two-thirds?'

'Two of my girlfriends.'

'But you've said Florin didn't give you any money. Where did you get the money?' I insisted.

'Too many questions,' she replied. 'There are better things to do than talking …'

And we did those better things for quite a long while.

A couple of hours later, I told Remy I couldn't and wouldn't push Florin into the lake. It took me a while to explain why I couldn't do it. She listened to my reasons patiently, then nodded and said, 'We've passed the first hurdle.'

She'd stunned me once again. I'd have thought she'd be cranky and contemptuous towards me, labelling me a coward or wimp, or something like that. Instead, she was sympathetic and understanding. 'You're a good man, Cornel,' she whispered, with a dreamy look on her face. 'And by the way, I never thought you killed Kate Morales,' she added.

'Thanks, but … what do you mean when saying that we've passed the first hurdle?' I asked.

She smiled. 'Just that. That we've passed the first hurdle.'

'But we haven't. If I'm not doing what you've asked me to do, it means we haven't resolved anything yet.'

'We have,' Remy replied. 'What we've achieved is that although you are refusing to push him into the lake, you are considering other options in your mind. It's not that you're discarding the idea, you're only rejecting the means to deliver the plan.'

I didn't say anything. I thought about it and I realised she was right. I remained confused thinking that, although it had just been proved I wasn't a murderer, she still considered me a potential assassin. The thought worried me.

But Remy didn't give me much time to feel sorry for myself. She unexpectedly began to show signs of a mental crack-up. 'I keep praying to God to help us and give us his blessing,' she began with tears in her eyes. 'I pray he will listen to us and, with his blessing, I know we will succeed.'

I couldn't find the guts to say anything. She simply amazed me. As far as I was concerned, praying to God to bless the slaying of another human being was the most dreadful sin.

'I want to be free, Cornel,' Remy went on. 'You sure do understand what being free means. The past few years have been a nightmare for me. I keep praying to God to end this nightmare. It has to end, tomorrow night. I can't take it anymore.'

I still didn't say anything.

'I need to choose my own destiny, Cornel,' she went on. 'I've been spurned and humiliated for too long. You probably don't understand, but you will, one day. I want to be with you, my love. I must leave this nightmare in the past and have a family with you. We must marry, Cornel.'

Her plea moved me. I hadn't seen that side of her yet. She was much more than a sexy doll, I decided. Her looks didn't do her justice. When seeing her, men only thought of sex. And women … they probably saw a threat – an unfair opponent with whom they could not compete. I'd thought that too, but now … not any longer. It was the first time I saw Remy emotionally hurt and I was moved. She was a human being after all.

'You're so strong and so handsome, my love. You're everything a woman needs in a man. I want you to father my children,' she continued. 'It's my maternal instinct which urges me to have kids with you. I want my kids to wear your genes, Cornel. You can't blame me for that.'

'Why would you want your kids to have my genes?' I asked with apparent modesty.

'Because I love you and I always will. I fell in love with you the very first time I set my eyes on you. That's why I was so rude to you that night when we first met. I knew I was falling in love and I was angry with myself for giving in to your charm.'

Remy's apparent fervour and her desire to become my wife flattered me. I suddenly saw another, better solution to my visa problems and permanent residence status in the country. With this better proposition from Remy, I had no need to marry Rhonda.

Yes, Remy was a better proposition – one which came with a three-hundred-million dowry as well. I'd be a fool not to take it.

With those thoughts on my mind, I looked at Remy in a different way. And she probably read my mind. Sensing my hesitation, she was back to business very quickly. 'You know, the most humanly and painless way they kill crabs or lobsters is by freezing them,' she said casually.

I became immediately attentive. 'Why are you telling me this?'

'The temperature in the cold room can go down to minus twenty-five Celsius,' she continued, paying no attention to my question.

I recalled Florin had told me that. 'So …?'

'The electrical gadget which adjusts the temperature is located in the laundry. Once the temperature is set, it cannot be changed from inside the cold room. The room can be locked and unlocked from both the inside and the outside.'

'Well, no one would want to look themselves in the room from inside, if the temperature is minus twenty-five,' I said.

'That's exactly the idea,' Remy said.

'What idea?' I asked.

'The idea is that someone could adjust the temperature to minimum twenty-five and then send someone else in the cold room, making sure the key is in the outside lock, where it usually stays. Once that someone else goes in, the first someone locks the door from outside, so the other someone is trapped inside.'

Understanding what she was getting at, I remained speechless.

'The room is only about twelve square metres, so it won't take too long until he's frozen. It's a very peaceful passing and there is no pain whatsoever.'

'Very humane, indeed.'

She nodded, apparently missing my sarcasm. 'Once you've made sure he's gone, you adjust the temperature back to a fraction above zero, which is the usual, and unlock the door.'

I noted she wasn't using the third person any longer. Now she was conveying that it was *me* who had to execute her plan. I was aware, though, that compared to the previous morning, there was a hell of a difference as far as my relationship with Remy was concerned.

Now, as Remy's trump card was gone, she was not in a position to threaten me with blackmail any longer. It was my own choice whether to put her plan into practice or not. I had, though, a strong incentive to stick to Remy's plot.

She said she wanted to be my wife and her proposal flattered me. According to Helen, marriage was the solution to my permanent residence status here. But to marry me, Remy would need a divorce. And a divorce would take at least a year. I couldn't afford to wait a year in my situation. Something had to happen very quickly: something which would annul Remy's marriage and liberate her instantaneously. Like an accident to her husband. That's exactly what Remy wanted. Without telling her, I recognised in my mind that we both had the same objective.

'So the hypothetical person who does the deed is me …' I murmured.

She just nodded again. 'You'll first need to get him drunk on Sunday evening, which I know it's not hard to do. He always loves to get drunk. Only on Sunday, it will be the last time he does it.'

Back on the farm on Saturday afternoon, I was more confused than ever. Reflecting on Remy's suggestion, I realised I was sliding on a dangerous slope. My mind was chaotic. I couldn't distinguish good from bad, right from wrong and fair from biased any longer.

On the one hand, the thought that I was considering murdering my friend frightened me silly. On the other, I found the idea of marrying Remy exciting and captivating. Not only would that solve my visa troubles, but as Remy had said the day before, we'd be the perfect couple – the envy of the world. Bound together as husband and wife, we'd be the pick of the bunch. With Remy's looks and mine, imagine our children! And imagine the life we'd live with three hundred million in the bank!

There was a little detail to deal with, though. Well, it wasn't really a *detail*. Let's say it was an *obstacle*. A *major obstacle*. But, as Remy had said, one can't expect that getting a three-hundred-million fortune was as easy as snapping one's fingers. Who wouldn't be willing to commit a murder for three hundred million? Many would do it for just one million.

And, it wasn't murder as such. As Remy had suggested, I only had to arrange an accident. An accident is just an accident. I mean, it could, by definition, happen anyway. And he wouldn't feel a thing. No pain, no torment and no agony. He would die like a giant crab.

The seed of treachery was growing firmly in my mind.

17

It was Saturday night. As he did the evening before, Florin went to bed early and I followed suit. I lay in bed reflecting, unable to sleep. I was in disarray. The only thing I was positive about was that I had to leave that place. Leaving the farm was also part of Remy's scheme. But my problem was I still didn't know whether I was going to stick to Remy's plan. Though she was very confident that her plan was risk-free and foolproof, as she'd put it to me, I still had my reservations.

'What if Marin turns up when Florin is locked in the cold-room?' I'd asked her in the morning.

'It's very unlikely,' Remy had assured me.

'Why is it unlikely?'

'How many times has Marin come to see Florin since you arrived here?' Remy had asked.

'Well ... he only came once.'

'That's once in more than three weeks,' Remy had stated.

'Once in … twenty-three days is about a four-percent chance. That's why I'm saying it's a low probability.'

'But how about *after*?' I'd insisted.

'After what?'

'After they find him … you know … frozen. Marin will certainly know that I was in the cabin with him. It won't be hard for anyone to work out what happened.'

'You won't be there when they find him,' Remy said.

'Where will I be? In heaven, with him?'

'Listen very carefully,' Remy said. 'This is how it's going to work. You set the temperature at minus twenty-five just after Florin has had his lunchbreak and gone back to the greenhouse. At this time of the year, he usually finishes in the greenhouse at about five. When he comes back to the cabin, the temperature in the cold-room would have settled at its minimum. You eat and have drinks, as usual. And you must get him drunk by eight …'

'I'll probably be drunker than him,' I interrupted her. 'Being in that very stressful situation, I'm sure I'll be drinking like a fish.'

Remy had given me a reproachful look. 'Do that, if you want to kiss goodbye the three hundred million. And me as well,' she'd added and paused, looking angrily at me.

'Okay, okay … go on,' I said.

'So, at about eight, when he's well plastered, you find a reason to send him into the cold-room. You know, just tell him that you'd like a certain brand of wine from the cold-room and you're too lazy to get it yourself, or something like that. He'll sure go in there to get it for you. You must also ensure that the key is in the outside lock. Once he steps in, you just lock the door. That's all you need to do. Then, you pack your things and wait. He should be gone by eleven at the latest. At eleven, you change the temperature back to the usual zero or so, unlock the door and leave the key in the lock. You then drive here. I'll be waiting for you.'

I'd been amazed at how cool and detached she'd been when dictating to me the details of how I was to murder her husband.

'But before I leave the cabin, I must ensure he's ... you know ... he's frozen,' I'd pointed out. 'I must enter the cold-room and have a look. What if he isn't dead?'

'He will be dead,' Remy had assured me.

'How do you know?'

'Though very stingy, you've probably noted that he's not concerned about saving on electricity. He always likes to keep warm and overheats the cabin, day and night. That's a bit of a womanly thing, if you ask me and it's not the only one of his. Anyway, you know he's always very lightly dressed. You've got the idea?'

I nodded. Indeed, inside the cabin Florin usually only wore shorts and a singlet. Dressed like that, he wouldn't last too long at minus twenty-five.

Still, I hadn't been convinced. 'But, there will be a police investigation afterwards. The police will certainly find out that we were lovers, which won't look very good at all.'

'That's alright. We'll have to admit to that, anyway,' she acknowledged. 'But you don't need to fear anything, because you'll have an alibi.'

'What alibi?'

'Me,' she replied promptly. 'I will swear that at the probable time of Florin's passing, you were with me for hours.'

'So who do you think will be suspected for his murder?'

Remy had shrugged. 'I'm positive they'll come to the conclusion it was an accident which wouldn't have occurred if he hadn't been drunk. You know, it happens a lot in winter in the cold countries, where drunks fall asleep and freeze on their way back from the pub.'

'But if Florin was allegedly by himself, is it credible that he got so drunk alone?'

Remy had nodded. 'Definitely. We'll tell the police that earlier that day I'd confessed to my husband I was having an affair with you. He'd made a scene, which caused both you and me to leave the farm. Alone, depressed and feeling sorry for himself, he got very drunk and careless. He went into the cold-room to get more grog and fell asleep. It ties up with the rest.'

With those thoughts on my mind, I heard a movement in the cabin. I read in the dark the digital clock on the night table. It showed four minutes to eleven. Though I'd had quite a few drinks, I became vigilant very quickly. It was probably because of the stress I was under.

I jumped from the bed and listened at the door. Someone was moving around in the living room. It must have been Florin. But what was he doing at that time, when he'd crashed to bed less than one hour before pretending to be very tired? I opened the bedroom door very slowly and stepped into the living room. Right then, I heard the click of the front door being closed. So, Florin had gone out. He must have been much fresher than he'd made out to be. He'd fooled me again, it seemed.

Where had he gone? The same horrid thought I had when Florin vanished at night nearly three weeks before, felt like a knife piercing through my heart. What if he'd gone to see Remy? The thought filled me with raging jealousy. This time, I was determined to find out.

I was instantly alert, ready for action. I walked to the front door and, without turning the lights on, listened attentively expecting to hear a car engine being switched on. I didn't.

I hurried back to my bedroom and turned the radio on to the

eleven o'clock news, just in case. There was nothing of interest in the news, only the unusual cold temperature in the Sydney's west: just two degrees above zero.

I got dressed, stepped outside and had a look. Florin's car was parked next to mine. His golf cart was missing. He couldn't have gone very far, I thought. Perhaps to the front house, to see Remy.

Without giving it a lot of consideration, I set out on the dirt road towards the mansion. The night of late June was crispy cold. Imagine what minus twenty-five was like if plus two felt so cold, I reflected. I kept walking briskly, wondering if Florin was with Remy. Somehow, I was sure that's where he was.

Perhaps he'd decided to get a divorce and was giving her the news right then. Or … maybe they were both laughing behind my back, while having fun together. Recalling the hostile reception she gave me on the night when we first met, I thought maybe Remy had always lied to me. Perhaps she'd set a trap for me, to prove to her husband what sort of character I was. But why would she do that? And, if that was the case, she'd gone *very* far trying to prove her point. Well, one never knows what to expect from women, I concluded.

After a few minutes of rapid walking, the contour of the front house appeared clearly in the bright glow of the moon. As I came close to it, I had a feeling that the mansion was deserted. The quiet was complete and there were no lights visible inside at all.

I tiptoed to the front door and tried the handle. It was locked. I walked to the garage and lifted the door up. I waited a little to allow my eyes to adjust to the dark. I then surveyed the garage. The vintage Dodge, the small tractor and Remy's golf cart were stationed inside. Remy's Audi was missing. And there was no sign of Florin's buggy either.

So, Florin had gone to some other place. And Remy was out

too. Another filthy thought struck me. What if Florin and his wife were having a rendezvous at her villa? As Glenmore Park was too far to walk to, I had no choice but to hit the road back to Florin's cottage; slowly this time, still reflecting. I recalled Florin saying that Remy usually spent her weekends in the city. But what was she doing there, alone? Or … maybe she wasn't alone. The thought enraged me further.

With those grubby thoughts occupying my mind, I reached Florin's cottage but kept walking towards the western border. Some fifteen minutes later, I reached the cabin where Marin resided. On seeing it, I stopped in a state of confusion. I wondered why I was there. I shrugged. As I was there already, I stepped to the cabin and had a look at it from close range.

I suddenly stopped. There were two golf carts parked side by side in front of the cabin. One was Marin's, the other belonged to Florin. I stayed there still, for a couple of minutes, thinking. The penny dropped.

I then circled the cabin, taking great care not to make any noise. Except for one room, the rest of the cabin was plunged into darkness. Though I'd never been inside the cabin, I knew from its design, identical to Florin's, that the only window, dimly lit right then, was that of the master bedroom.

Things began to make sense. Florin had a lover, Remy had said. Florin, on the other hand, had categorically denied there was another woman in his life. I'd always believed that one of them was lying. I knew now they had both told the truth.

Back at the cabin, I had a few more drinks and considered the latest state of affairs with mixed emotions. On one hand, I was relieved and grateful to Remy for being faithful to me. And on the other, I was disgusted by Florin cheating on her. I couldn't comprehend that he preferred that Bud Spencer look-alike brute to his delightful wife. I finally understood her frustration and humiliation.

I'd always had my doubts about her, but these were now in the past. I accepted in my mind that she'd constantly been honest with me. I finally believed that she was in love with me, that she wanted to have kids with me and was keen to share a three-hundred-million fortune with me. All those things she'd said to me must have come from her heart. And it made me feel good.

I felt she'd been considerate and caring. We shared a special bond and I had to do something for her, to recompense her honesty and faithfulness. I recognised, at last, that in our association, she'd given more than she had received from me.

I'd only given her money – fifty grand, or fifty-seven, to be precise, but what was that compared with the millions she was prepared to share with me? And she'd given me much more in return than money: trust, love and honesty. That ought to be rewarded.

It was past five in the morning when, with those thoughts bouncing around in my mind, I fell into an uneasy sleep. Aware that Florin hadn't returned to the cabin, I dreamed that I'd transformed him into a snowman and he was begging me to turn him back to life.

I woke up shaking and in a pool of sweat at just after nine.

Sunday 26 June

On Sunday morning, I was a packet of nerves: more jumpy than ever. Knowing that the moment of truth had nearly arrived, I just couldn't cope with the situation. I stayed in bed for a long time, replaying in my mind the dream which had awakened me.

Though just a dream, it seemed so real. It truly frightened me.

How could I deal with *the real thing* when only a dream had unnerved me so much? I lay in bed still sweating, trying to pull myself together. Ten more minutes passed, then twenty … half an hour … forty minutes … I still lay there, not knowing what to do.

The cabin was quiet; the only noises I perceived were those of the bleating sheep and goats, somewhere in the distance. Then I thought I heard little Robin singing, but even his joyous chirping failed to make me smile this time.

I listened to the ten o'clock news and again one hour later, without comprehending much. Words, as well as time, seemed to have lost their meaning.

More minutes passed. A sudden idea came to me. I could perhaps run away. I could pack my things and bolt, without telling anyone. But, if I did run, I'd part my ways with Remy, and I hated the thought. And where would I go anyway? Back to my flat in Liverpool? How would Helen welcome me? I wondered. There was only one way to find out.

I dragged myself from bed into the living room and dialled Helen's number.

'Helen Longshanks speaking,' she answered.

'Hello, Helen, it's me.'

'You sound like half-dead,' she observed. 'I would have thought you'd be extremely happy.'

'I am,' I replied, with the same level of enthusiasm.

'Well … you're certainly not showing it.' She paused a little. 'By the way … I'm glad it's all over and I owe you an apology.'

'No problem … I spoke to Rhonda the other day. She said …'

'That I found a replacement for you,' Helen cut me off.

'Yeah, she did say that as well. So, I have no job, for the time being.'

'You have a wife instead,' Helen replied. 'Rhonda is quite excited about the news. As far as I can see, she can't wait to tie the
knot with you. You need to hurry up.'

'But I'd thought you two have ...'

'Maybe we have, but it's now in the past. As you probably
appreciate, an affair between two women is much more ... how
should I put it ... let's say, it's much more *inoffensive* physically
than that between a man and a woman, or between two men, for
that matter.'

That wasn't what I'd intended to ask, but I was glad that Hel-
en clarified that aspect for me. I was actually surprised that Helen
and Rhonda were very close again. 'How about my flat? I mean,
do you mind if I come back?' I asked.

She paused again. 'It's not a good time right now. Taking advantage of your absence, I decided to give it a face lift. The flat is
now undergoing major renovations and it will take several weeks,
if not months until it's finished.'

'I see ... Well, thank you for that. I'd better let you go then.'

'You didn't say why you called,' Helen remarked.

'Ah ... I just wanted to hear how you were. I'm glad that
you're well ...'

'I'm glad too. Anyway, as you're not very talkative this morning, which is consistent with your recent behaviour, I won't ask
any other questions. If you ever feel the need to confess ... you
know where to find me. And remember – Rhonda is waiting. I'd
hurry up if I were you.'

'Sure ... I'll give Rhonda a call.'

'Please do. By the way, how's your Mazda 3 going?'

How the hell did she know about my Mazda 3, I wondered.
Trying to work it out in my mind, I remained quiet.

'In case you wonder how I knew about it, the transfer of the registration papers came in the mail. I paid for the transfer and I also took the liberty to insure the car,' Helen explained.

'Thank you, Helen.' Those thoughts had never crossed my mind.

'I knew, with so many things on your plate, you wouldn't bother about those little details,' she added. 'Anyway, I'm glad that you remembered me and called. Better late than never.'

'Yeah … I've been busy and I didn't have a phone …'

'I know it's becoming more and more difficult with these modern gadgets. You know, technology draws us closer to the ones far from us, but puts a barrier between us and the ones close to us.'

I mumbled something, which not even I really understood.

'Goodbye for now, Cornel,' she said.

Though she hung up before me, I replaced the receiver very slowly. That didn't go very well, I thought. Helen had basically confirmed that my job had gone and my flat was unavailable. I could probably find shelter at Rhonda's, but right then it wasn't the best time to fool around with two women at the same time. Things were complicated enough as they were.

I reflected on it and concluded that I had to stay put and obey Remy's instructions. The fact that I had nowhere to go meant that the train of events could not be stopped. Providence was telling me that I had to go ahead with Remy's scheme.

I stepped into the kitchen out of mere habit but I immediately realised I didn't feel like eating. But, how about a drink? That sounded like a pretty good idea. With shaking hands, I poured myself a large glass of wine. I drank it in one gulp and repeated the process. I felt much better afterwards.

I then remembered I'd promised Florin a farewell Sunday dinner. But cooking was the last thing on my mind. How was

I going to justify to him that I hadn't felt like cooking? I wondered. What excuse should I invent? Well, it didn't really matter. Even if he was to remain disappointed, he wouldn't have a lot of time to dwell on it. The thought made me shudder.

I drank another glass of wine. It felt so good. I wondered where Remy was. I felt the need to talk to her, to hear her reassurance. Too bad; I couldn't. She said it was safer if I didn't call her and maybe she was right. But why wasn't she calling me? Well, for the same reason, I assumed. Still, I'd have very much preferred if she did call.

I read the time and suddenly went into a panic. It was lunchtime already and Florin could pop in any minute now. So what? I said to myself. Why was I panicking? Was it perhaps because this could be his last lunchbreak ever? I shuddered again. I wasn't ready for it. I needed to drink more. And I did. But, having downed another glass of wine, Remy's words came back to haunt me. *For three hundred million, I'd slit my mother's throat.* That line scared me silly.

At half past twelve, I put some clothes on and bolted from the cabin. I knew that facing Florin was too much for me. I strolled east on the dirt road, as I'd done the night before. I reached the front house and noted the door to the garage was open. Remy's Audi wasn't there. I tried to remember if I'd rolled the door down last night but I couldn't.

But what difference did it make? I mean, Remy wasn't there anyway. Well, it did make a difference, I answered my own question. If I had closed the door, it meant Remy had come back to the mansion and left again afterwards. Maybe she left in a rush later, forgetting to close the door. But if I hadn't closed the door … well, I didn't know what happened since last night. Perhaps Remy had returned, or maybe she hadn't. But where was she right then? Why wasn't she with me?

I walked to the main road, stopped at the double gate and noted on the timber beam the sign made of metal letters. On reading it, I winced in shock. The sign read FLOMAR Farmhouse. I wondered if I was going crazy. I could swear the sign said FLORE Farmhouse only the day before: FLORE, the contraction of Florin and Remy. It wasn't hard to guess that FLOMAR was another contraction: Florin and *Marin*.

Though the afternoon was chilly, I began to sweat again. Things were happening on the farm. The dynamics were changing. I could only guess that Florin had made his mind up to come out into the open. The FLOMAR sign was defiant – the exact word which Florin had used when talking about Remy cheating on him. He must have decided he'd had enough of her cheating and chosen to side with his lover.

Guessing that a divorce was imminent, I pictured in my mind the three hundred million landing in a Florin and Marin joint bank account. I saw Remy leaving the farm in disgust. I saw her ditching me with contempt. I imagined myself a lonely jobless drunkard, impoverished and miserable and feeling sorry for myself. I saw Remy's and my dreams evaporate in nothingness forever.

I made an effort of will and pulled myself together. I couldn't let that happen. Not for Remy, not for me and not for our beautiful offspring. I had to do what a man has got to do. I had to do it for Remy. And for us. To get Remy and her dowry: the three hundred million dollars. I swore loudly at the FLOMAR sign and strode back to Florin's cabin.

A warmish plate left in the kitchen sink told me Florin had just had his lunch. He must have gone back to the greenhouse only minutes before. I had another glass of wine and thanked God for not making me face Florin. I knew I had to see him later that day, but probably not the day after. And never afterwards.

I went into the cold-room and searched through the meat compartment. Even with a jumper on, I shivered in the cold. I wondered again of how cold minus twenty-five must feel. Florin will find out soon, I thought. But he'll never live to tell the story.

There were stacks of frozen meat stored in an industrial freezer, but I needed a fresh piece for my dish. I knew he kept a few pieces of fresh meat for current consumption.

I looked for a piece of beef to cook my speciality – a stew or casserole. That's what I'd cooked for Helen to welcome her back from overseas. That feast had later proved to be our last dinner together. Now I decided to prepare the same dish for Florin. The last supper.

I found a nice chunk of chuck steak, which suited my purpose. Before preparing the casserole, with a knot in the stomach, I turned the temperature in the cold-room down to minus twenty-five. The time was ten minutes to two. Once the dish was ready to go into the oven, I got stuck into the wine again.

18

It was quarter past five when Florin returned from the green-house. He hadn't shaved that morning and looked tired, but in good spirits. 'So, the farewell dinner is on. Smells absolutely delicious,' he observed, while getting a whiff of garlic.

'Let's hope it tastes as good as it smells,' I said. The wine I drank since late morning had raised my spirits considerably. I was in a state of callousness, no longer jittery at the dreadful task looming ahead of me.

'What's to drink?' Florin asked, taking a seat at the kitchen table.

'I'd strongly recommend a few shots of slivovitz before dinner is ready.'

'How long till then?' he asked.

I pondered it. 'I'd say about an hour.'

'Good. Let's have some slivovitz.'

I grabbed one bottle and filled two fifty-millilitre glasses. I then joined Florin at the table, with the bottle of slivovitz within easy reach.

Florin raised his glass and clinked it to mine. 'Let's drink for your good fortune, Cornel. Let's drink for new beginnings. Whatever you choose to do, whether you want to be with Remy or not, I wish you good luck and pray for you to succeed.'

On hearing his weird, totally unexpected wish about Remy and me ending up together, I swallowed the wrong way and spilled some of the drink.

He downed his glass and I was quick to refill it.

His words had startled me and moved me as well. He was so unbelievably altruistic. And me … I didn't know how to describe myself. Insensitive, ruthless, cruel … My only excuse was that I had a mission. It was for a good cause. Good cause? Was it really good? Doubts and hesitation got hold of me again.

'You're still going to leave tomorrow?' Florin asked.

I nodded. 'Yeah, it's time for me to go. Now there is nothing keeping me here any longer.'

He gave me a long look, but didn't say anything.

'I mean … of course I'd love to keep you company, but there are things I need to do in town. You know … my visa,' I added, realising my gaffe.

Florin emptied his glass again and poured himself another shot. 'A man has got to do what a man has got to do,' he said looking somewhat lost in thought.

He distressed me with that remark. It was the exact line I had in mind a few hours before, when I concluded I had to go ahead with Remy's plan. Those fears from the morning were now returning to me. 'Not necessarily,' I mumbled.

Florin gave me a strange look. 'I don't know what you mean.'

I shrugged. 'Me neither.'

We drank and Florin talked of trivial things. I only nodded and spoke very little – mostly yes and no. I watched him with compassion. He seemed disturbed and sad. He kept talking in a low voice, but soon I didn't hear him any longer. I had my own thoughts to deal with, giving me hell. His fate was in my hands. Right then I was a sort of god. I was to decide whether he lived or died.

I tormented myself but couldn't reach a decision. I wished I could pass the buck. But there was no one to pass it to. I wasn't a religious person, but I believed in fate, or in divine intervention. I thought about it and found a possible solution.

I couldn't just send him to his death, as Remy had planned. I couldn't do it in cold blood. I wasn't God. He had to make that decision himself. He had to choose whether he lived or died. I won't send him in. But if he went in the cold-room of his own accord and for whatever reason ... that would be different. That way he'd seal his own fate. I only had to do the rest: to lock the door. It shouldn't be so hard. That way, I was not the executioner. I was the gravedigger only. In the state of drunkenness I was in, I thought, that role wasn't so terribly dreadful.

By half past six, the half-litre slivovitz bottle was almost empty. Though Florin had drunk most of it, I was very dizzy too. It must have been the wine I drank before. And, by the look of him, Florin wasn't in a better state. Most likely, he was worse.

'This stuff is strong,' he noted in an indistinct voice.

I had to make a considerable effort to come out of my reflections and pay attention to what he was saying.

'You know, I'll start making my own slivovitz next year,' he announced, much louder this time. 'There are plenty of plum trees on the farm.'

I nodded, but remained quiet. I was pretty sure, for some reason,

Florin would go into the cold-room that night.

'I'll do it for sure, next year,' Florin reinforced his plan.

Perhaps, but my bet is that you won't, I said to myself. You won't do anything at all tomorrow, let alone next year.

'You're very quiet this evening,' Florin observed.

'Yeah … I feel funny. It's like an end is approaching and I don't want it to happen.'

'You don't have to leave,' Florin said. 'It's not too late to change your mind.'

Once more, his words brought fears and doubts to my mind. 'It's not too late?' I asked in a very low voice.

He smiled. 'Of course it's not. Please don't.'

His plea reminded me of the dream I had that morning. Florin the snowman, begging me to bring him back to life. I felt emotional and weak again.

At that moment, my mobile phone began to buzz in my pocket. It was just an ordinary buzz, not a song, or one of those modern themes which most young people use these days. Having forgotten about it, I was as surprised by it as Florin was. I just sat there dumbly, not knowing what to do.

'Is that your mobile or mine?' Florin asked.

I shrugged, noting he must be pretty well plastered if he didn't know whose phone was ringing. As I made no attempt to answer it, Florin searched through his pockets and produced his mobile. He stared at the small gadget curiously like it was the first time he was seeing it. He switched it off and put it back in his pocket. 'It's not mine. It must be yours,' he observed.

'Is it?' I asked, feigning surprise.

He nodded. 'Aren't you going to answer it?'

The buzz of the phone stopped as suddenly as it had started.

'No need – it's stopped,' I said.

'I thought you'd lost your mobile,' Florin remarked.

I paused nodding. 'Yeah … but I just bought another one.'

He shrugged. 'You think that casserole is ready?'

I jumped from my chair, stumbled and fell faced down on the kitchen floor. I got up slowly feeling very intoxicated. I took the pot from the oven. 'Let's eat.'

'We'll eat in here,' Florin announced. 'The living room is too far.'

He was definitely smashed if he couldn't walk a few metres to the living room.

I was very wobbly too, but even after consuming a heap of alcohol, I didn't feel like eating. I placed on a large plate a very generous portion for Florin and sat opposite him watching him eating. He was so drunk, he didn't notice that I wasn't eating.

I reached for my glass but, recalling Remy's threat, *do that, if you want to kiss the three hundred million good bye. And me as well* … I changed my mind. I had to stop drinking, I said to myself. I'll stuff everything up otherwise. I loathed the thought of losing Remy. But was I prepared to pay the price? The price was Florin's life. And the weighing scale was heavier on Remy's side.

Watching Florin enjoying his dinner, I thought of The Last Supper again.

The alcohol had made me speak my mind. 'You two are getting a divorce?' I asked, once Florin had just finished his meal.

He looked surprised. 'The news travels fast these days.'

'So, it's true,' I said.

I could see by the expression on his face that Florin was upset. 'Why are you asking? Don't you trust what Remy tells you?'

'It's not from Remy I know,' I replied.

He gave me a doubtful look. 'Only she knows.'

'And Marin?' I asked.

He looked at me surprised. 'And Marin.'

'I saw the new sign at the front gate,' I continued.

He quivered, but recovered quickly. 'Ah … Marin just put it up this morning.'

'It's not hard to work out what FLOMAR means,' I went on.

Florin paused, looking at the window, to the darkness outside. He was probably trying to find his words. 'I'm sorry, Cornel,' he apologised, after a minute or so. 'I'm sorry for lying to you, but it was … it was too hard for me to come clean. I had this … this *thing* for many years. I do love women … I mean, I love beautiful women and that's why I fell for Remy. I'd thought, being such a superb specimen, it would work with her, but it didn't. I still love her, but it's only platonic.'

'I understand,' I said, though I didn't.

He drank from his glass and remained quiet for a long while. 'You know, this may come as a surprise to you, but I'm not jealous of you,' he stated unexpectedly. 'I've never been jealous of you. I remember when we were in high school all the girls swarming around you, craving for a date with you. You were so strong and handsome …'

Thinking back of those times, I recalled Florin being weird and withdrawn with girls. I'd always believed he was just shy and lacked confidence. Now I knew the real reason.

'No wonder Remy fell for you, though it's my fault as well,' Florin went on.

His statement intrigued me. 'What do you mean it's your fault?'

'I'd told Remy of you … you know – how macho you were. That was quite a while back. I didn't know then that one day you two would meet face to face … You know … I was always proud of you, since we were kids. That's why I boasted to Remy about you. I couldn't have known …'

His speech was very slurred. 'Okay, maybe I *was* a *little* jealous,' he continued. 'You know, that night when you and Remy met, I knew exactly what happened. I knew she only pretended to dislike you. She managed to put on quite a convincing act, but she never fooled me. I knew she was craving to go to bed with you. The writing was on the wall.'

I didn't say anything. There wasn't much point in trying to deny his observations. Much too late for that. I could have confirmed it, but that wouldn't have made any difference. The writing was on the wall, as he'd just said.

He emptied his glass, looking sad and miserable. I thought he was about to fall asleep, when he added, totally out of the blue. 'If you think that you and Remy can have a future together, you have my blessing.'

What an irony, I thought. He's giving me his blessing to take his wife away from him, while she is asking God to help us take him out of this world.

He stood up slowly, unsteady on his feet and walked out of the kitchen.

'Where are you going?' I asked.

He stopped for a moment. 'We need to have a proper cele-bration.'

'What do you mean a proper celebration?'

'Pop open the champagne. There is some French champagne, somewhere. I'll grab a bottle,' he said while moving on through the living room.

'Grab a bottle from where?' I called to him.

'The cold-room,' he yelled back.

My heart skipped a beat. That was the sign I was waiting for.

It's now or never, I said to myself and followed in Florin's footsteps.

I crept into the living room and saw the door to the coldroom open. The light inside was off. Some glow from the living room partly illuminated the area. I noted the key in the outside lock. I couldn't see Florin, but I heard him saying something. I thought he was swearing.

I moved close to the cold-room. My heart was racing like mad. I was within reach of the six-inch-thick door, panelled in metal and thermally insulated.

I still couldn't see Florin, but I heard him quite clearly this time. 'Where the hell is the fucking champagne?'

I was surprised he wasn't swearing at the cold. It must be freezing in there, I thought. Perhaps he was so drunk, he didn't feel the cold. Right then, I wouldn't have felt it either, I guessed, while sweat was running down all over me.

I heard him fumble inside. I stretched my arm and noted it was shaking very badly. My legs – my whole body was trembling.

With Remy and the three hundred million dollars on my mind, I made an effort of will and pushed the door closed. I turned the key in the lock and then dropped it in my pocket.

I leaned my back against the metal door. That was all. It hadn't been so hard, after all, I told myself. Yet I was still shaking all over.

I looked at my watch, my hand visibly trembling. It was eight minutes past eight. I stayed at the door, still shaking for a good couple of minutes. I didn't hear any noise inside. 'God forgive you, my friend,' I murmured in a low voice.

I walked to the kitchen and downed a large glass of wine. I knew I shouldn't drink any more, but I needed it. And the job was already done. I had to collect myself. There was nothing more to fear, I encouraged myself. I sat on a chair and felt my heart rate gradually slowing.

I thought of my next move and of my future with Remy. I imagined my life with her, as husband and wife. I saw in my mind the two of us walking hand in hand, whispering words of love. I saw a happy ending to our love story. I drank another glass of wine and felt reckless and dreamy afterwards. The good times were about to come, I reassured myself.

At ten minutes to nine, the landline phone began to ring in the reception room. It gave me a huge startle. I rushed to pick it up, but stopped one metre from it. Who could it be? I knew it wasn't Remy. She said she'd only ring me on my mobile and never on the fixed phone.

I watched the phone ringing and retreated slowly. It buzzed for a long time, then stopped and began to ring again. I swore at it, but it didn't stop. Why didn't he have an answering machine?! Because he doesn't need one, I answered myself. He doesn't need anything, anymore. The buzz eventually stopped.

I walked to my bedroom, fetched my two travelling bags and started to pack my things. I'd just finished packing when I heard loud knocks somewhere in the house. I suddenly froze, fearing it was Florin desperate to escape from the deadly trap. I then realised it was someone knocking on the front door. I panicked and had no idea what to do. I stood there and listened, stone-still in fright. The time was twenty-five past nine.

Suddenly the knocks ceased. A few seconds later, they started again. And louder this time. Whoever knocked on the door was very persistent. I had to do something, and quickly, I decided. I bolted from my bedroom towards the front door but stopped while passing the laundry.

I entered the laundry and, with my hands trembling, I fiddled a little with the knob adjusting the temperature in the cold-room.

It seemed to take ages until I turned the adjustor up to a fraction above zero. The man, or perhaps the woman, at the front door kept pounding on it. I thought it was most likely a man.

Whoever it was, he was very impatient. Fearing he'd soon take the door off its hinges, I rushed to the lobby and distinguished a massive outline through the glass.

Still shaking severely, I unlocked the door.

Marin burst in, pushing me out of his way. He went through the reception room, living room; back to the kitchen and then checked all three bedrooms. I followed him through the house, keeping a couple of metres behind.

'What's this?' he asked in Romanian, seeing my travelling bags zipped up by the door in my bedroom.

'These are my travelling bags,' I said quietly, also in Romanian.

'Don't be a smart arse, or I'll give you a good smack,' he retorted. 'I know what these are, but where are you going?'

'I'm leaving tomorrow, so I've packed my bags.'

'Where is Florin?' Marin asked.

I paused and replied very slowly. 'I was wondering too. We both got drunk earlier and I fell asleep. I thought he did too. But when I woke up, he wasn't around any longer.'

Marin stepped out of my bedroom and surveyed the bathrooms and the laundry. I noted him checking the cold room's temperature adjustor. He was agitated and seemed angry. 'How can you explain that his car and his buggy are here, but he isn't?' he demanded.

'I don't know and I'm not trying to explain. I'm just telling you he's not in the cabin.'

Marin glanced towards the cold-room and stepped close to it.

That's it, I said in my mind. Florin will start screaming for help, and that will be the end of me. I thought of making a dash for the door, but my legs felt like rubber.

Marin turned the handle to open the door, but it held. My heart was pounding at an incredible speed. If Florin was still alive, he'd certainly start screaming.

'Where's the key?' Marin asked. 'It should be in the lock.'

I just shrugged. I couldn't find enough strength to articulate a single word.

'Gimme the key,' Marin demanded in a threatening tone.

I shook my head in terror and murmured. 'I don't have it.'

Marin studied my face. 'What's going on? There is something not right here. I can smell a rat and I'm never wrong. He's not answering his mobile and, when I rang a little earlier, nobody answered the fixed line either. Just tell me what's going on, you jerk.'

'Sorry,' I mumbled. 'I was asleep, as I've just said.'

'You'll be asleep forever if you don't spill the beans.' He stepped close to me and I was pretty sure he was going to belt me.

'No point fighting,' I whispered.

He suddenly produced a mobile phone from his pocket and fiddled with it a little. An eerie instrumental sound I was familiar with filled the room in an instant.

While holding the phone in his left hand, Marin announced. 'This will last three minutes and ten seconds. You have three minutes to make up your mind. Tell me what's going on, or else. If you're still quiet once the piece is over, I'll smash your head in. You may choose to do the same and have a go at me. You're more than welcome, if you do.'

Having recognised the tune, I admitted it was one of best I'd ever heard – the Russian band PPK performing their finest song: 'Resurrection'. I found it distinctive, emotional, even spinechilling and yet so beautiful. I wouldn't have expected Marin to have such a sophisticated musical taste. I realised, while mulling over it, I'd been flippant and condescending about him. I should have given him more credit.

At the same time, it wasn't hard to work out, even in my state of drunkenness, that Marin was actually attempting to re-enact a high-tension scene from the 1960s spaghetti western with Clint Eastwood *For a Few Dollars More*, which I'd seen a couple of times.

In that movie, villain El Indio had a musical pocket watch which he played before engaging in gun duels. *When the chimes finish, we begin*, El Indio was in the habit of saying. And that's what Marin was doing now. Just like El Indio in that movie, he seemed to have gone into a trance, listening to the tune and watching his little gadget as if hypnotized by it.

The seconds passed very slowly… one minute, then two …

I listened to the song, knowing I was unable to challenge Marin once the tune was over. I found the music as touching as that of Ennio Morricone's in the movie, but to me the stand-off between Marin and me lacked the suspense and tension which he intended to generate. I knew, at that moment, I wasn't fit to fight Marin, nor was I willing to.

Another minute passed.

Then the music finished. 'No guns, just fists,' Marin said, dropping the phone to the floor.

I stood in front of him, watching him dumbly, while the now-defunct sounds of 'Resurrection' were still echoing in my ears.

Marin scratched his beard with his left hand while his right slammed with surprising speed into the side of my head. The smash, which I could hear as a colossal bang in my head, sent me reeling back, falling onto the floor. I tried to get up, but stumbled and fell back.

I heard Marin snorting with contempt. 'I'd thought you'd be a little better than that, but what a piece of shit you are.'

My manly pride was telling me I should get up and smash his face, but I just wasn't up to it. I lacked the energy and the willpower. Again, I was battered both physically and emotionally. And, I had to admit, I couldn't fight him anyway, even if I was in top condition.

'Come on, dickhead. Get up and show you're a man,' he tried to incite me.

It didn't work. I had other worries on my mind. I wondered if Florin had died. The fact that he wasn't screaming for help told me he might have passed away already.

I propped myself in a sitting position and pulled a chair from under the table. I sat on it and wiped my mouth with the back of my hand. I was surprised not to see blood.

I felt weak and defeated. And worse, the thought that I'd just killed a man, and my best friend at that, suddenly hit home.

'What a mongrel you are,' Marin said with condescension, while picking up his mobile from the floor. 'You took advantage of your friend's kindness and went ahead with your animal instincts. You had to fuck his wife, no matter what. I'd warned Florin the first time I saw you that you were a jerk, but he wouldn't listen. He knows now, but it's too late ...'

That's right: it's too late. Now everything is too late for him, I said to myself.

'The good thing out of this is that he's now ditching her and she won't get a nickel,' Marin continued. 'That's all she always wanted. Money – that's all. That dame is bad news. You two deserve each other.'

And you are taking on her conjugal duties, I was inclined to say, but I couldn't find the energy.

He stared at me and scratched his chin. I thought he was going to hit me again and I couldn't do anything about it. In the state I was in, I couldn't defend myself.

He then stepped to the cold-room and tried the handle once more.

My heart went up to my throat. But no one screamed from behind the heavy door. He must have died, I thought. That thought brought another wave of cold sweat down my spine.

He walked back into the living room and stopped in front of me. 'Stay here. Don't go anywhere,' he threatened. 'I'll get the key and I'll be right back.' He then walked out.

What did he mean, he'd get the key, I wondered. I stood up and walked to the front door, which he'd left open. I saw in the moonlight Marin striding west. Probably to his cabin, to get a duplicate key to the cold-room, I assumed. As his cabin was identically built to Florin's, I presumed Marin also had a cold-room with a matching key.

I had to leave before he returned, I decided. I grabbed my bags and dropped them in the car. That's all I had to do. I was ready to go. I hesitated and walked back inside. I had to check if Florin was dead. I unlocked the door to the cold-room but couldn't find the necessary strength to look inside. I left the key in the lock and bolted from the cabin.

I drove out of the farm and turned left onto the main road, heading north with mixed feelings. The fact that I'd just killed my best friend made me feel the most disgusting grub on earth.

But on the other hand, I was relieved it was all over. I couldn't wait to see Remy. Now I needed her more than anything I'd ever needed. I needed her reassurance that I'd done the right thing. I'd done it as a supreme act of love.

With those thoughts on my mind, I pressed the accelerator. The time was ten minutes past ten. The night – miserable: cloudy and windy, with a cold drizzle.

The speedometer reached a hundred and ten in an eighty zone. There was about fifteen more minutes until I'd reach Remy's villa. I'll leave Kate and Helen and Rhonda and Florin and all that mess in the past, I told myself. I'll start all over again. With Remy my wife and three hundred million in the bank, I'll move mountains and more! Nothing and no one will ever stop me.

Unless … I heard the siren of a police car approaching. Knowing I was well over the blood alcohol limit, I instantly made up my mind. I wouldn't stop. I wouldn't let them prevent me from meeting Remy. I had to get to her, no matter what. No one was going to stop me.

I pressed the accelerator down. I was now driving at a hundred and thirty. Even so, the police car kept getting closer. I pushed the accelerator further. The speedometer showed one hundred and fifty. A couple of minutes passed. I didn't hear the siren any longer. I sighed with relief.

I suddenly discerned, but too late, a marked police car blocking the road. I hit the brakes, while frantically trying to keep control of the steering wheel.

The car skidded, spun around and went off the road. It rolled a couple of times, ending up on the grass, on the side of the road. Amazingly, the crash caused me only a few minor scratches.

I was arrested for high-range drink-driving, trying to evade police and driving at more than forty-five kilometres over the speed limit. My Mazda didn't display any registration either, the police constable noted. My driving licence was suspended on the spot, my car was confiscated and I was taken to the Penrith Police Station.

They checked my record and found that, in spite of being cleared of recent kidnapping accusations, I was flagged on the computer as violent and potentially dangerous. There were also charges of assault and inflicting grievous bodily harm pending against me, following that incident with the parking officer in Liverpool. They locked me in a cell overnight.

Surprisingly, the officer in attendance didn't search my pockets, allowing me to keep my mobile phone. I didn't know if that privilege was standard procedure, or happened thanks to a police oversight. I checked my mobile phone. I only had a missed call, earlier that evening. Nothing else. It didn't say who the caller was. I read the number again and again. I was certain I'd seen that number before. I knew it wasn't one of my contacts, but I recalled the number because it was unusual, with two pairs of three identical numbers repeated.

I nearly fell asleep, but I suddenly awoke, recalling where I'd seen that phone number before. I was positive the call which I'd missed earlier that evening had been sent from the same number which had rung me the previous month and suggested that I drop in to Dowes to meet Kate.

I finally fell asleep wondering why Remy hadn't called.

I dreamed that I shared the cell with a snowman. 'Relax,' the snowman said to me. 'He's dead. You have nothing to fear. You did a swell job.'

I woke up trembling, knowing my best friend was now as cold and lifeless as a snowman.

19

Monday, 27 June

Having been drunk at the time of my arrest, the police only in-
terviewed me on Monday morning and released me on bail in
the afternoon. Rhonda, whom I'd rung in the morning, paid the
bail money and picked me up from the police station. She drove
me in silence to her flat in the inner-west suburb of Burwood
and offered to put me up for as long as I needed.

Like Helen, Rhonda owned a very large penthouse apartment
in a luxury block of flats. Burwood was a much more desirable
location, compared to Liverpool. The three-bedroom apartment
was furnished with much taste and as stylish as you'd expect from
a highly prominent fashion designer.

Having shown me my bedroom, Rhonda behaved with gallant
consideration for the rest of the evening. She left me with my
thoughts, not asking any questions, which I greatly appreciated. I

had a shower and shaved, but I still felt like hell. Perhaps sensing there was something seriously wrong with me, Rhonda left me alone.

I watched the seven o'clock news on ABC, while Rhonda prepared dinner in the kitchen. They didn't say anything on television about Florin, which made me assume his body hadn't been found yet.

I thought that didn't make much sense. Marin must certainly have found him last night. Maybe he hadn't raised the alarm yet, or maybe the news hadn't reached the media.

The other question that gave me nightmares was what happened to Remy. Why hadn't she made contact yet? Was she, I thought, perhaps in trouble? Has that brute, Marin, worked out it had been Remy who plotted to kill Florin and gone after her? These questions tortured me.

Before eight, the dinner was ready. Though I didn't feel like eating, it smelled so good that I finally gave in to Rhonda's persistent invitation.

'In the state you're in, it's mandatory to eat,' she pushed me again and again and I eventually gave in.

I ate a piece of New York steak, cooked rare, juicy and very tender. I had a few bottles of beer and felt exhausted afterwards. At ten, when Rhonda ordered me to bed, I was afraid she'd come and share it with me. I thanked God that she didn't.

Tuesday, 28 June

On Tuesday morning, I woke up very early and checked my mobile phone. A text message, sent nearly twenty-four hours before, said: *You're a spineless pile of garbage. I don't want to see you again. Good bye, Novak.*

The message, sent from the mystery number which had called but missed me on Sunday night, wasn't signed. So who was the caller? Could it have been Remy? No, I rejected the idea. That text couldn't have come from her. I didn't quite understand the content, but she wouldn't have called me Novak and wouldn't have talked like that.

Besides Remy, only two people knew of my alias. One of them was dead. The other one was Marin.

So, if the caller wasn't Remy, it must have been Marin. But he had already found out what he'd always suspected – that I was Cornel, not Novak. Why would he call me Novak?

And why had I only received the text message twenty-four hours late? I recalled a few other instances, when text messages had been delayed due to technical problems within the telecommunications network, or perhaps blunders of the phone carriers.

What added to the puzzle was that neither Remy nor Marin could possibly have been the one who urged me to go and meet Kate at Dowes. My meeting with Kate had happened more than a month before, at which point in time I didn't know either Remy or Marin. The whole thing didn't make sense.

I shrugged and went out to buy the morning paper. I sat on a bench in the Burwood Park opposite Westfield and flicked through the paper. There was nothing about Florin. What an ironic situation! I thought. With Kate, the news and accusations had kept coming, pointing the finger at me though I'd been innocent. And now, I'd just killed my best friend and no one in the world gave a damn about it – or still the body had not been found.

However, although they didn't say anything about Florin, the name Panait *was* mentioned in the newspaper. A small article said that prominent green activist, Natasha Panait, a senator in the

Greens Party and Florin's mother, had issued a discussion paper outlining her position and proposed measures to remove man-made greenhouse gas emissions from the atmosphere and thereby reduce the effects of climate change and global warming.

The discussion paper was available for public comment on the internet and an open forum was organised on the upcoming weekend to publicise those green initiatives and gain public support. Being interested in the subject, I made a note on a piece of paper of Ms Panait's contact details and the date and place of the public forum. I vaguely remembered her as a very passionate and opinionated chemistry teacher in my childhood. Nevertheless, I recalled her as a young, pretty woman, but … so many years had passed since then.

Thinking of those wonder years, when Florin and I were inseparable, I felt nostalgic and wished for those times to return. Though I felt an instant urge to make contact with Ms Panait, I knew that the Florin subject would undoubtedly come up in the discussion. What could I possibly tell her? That I'd killed my best friend and her son?

I walked to the shops and stopped at the St. George Bank to withdraw some cash. I only had about two hundred dollars on me. This time, I was relieved that the PIN was accepted, but … stupor followed afterwards. I read the screen unable to comprehend what it said. There should have been about twenty grand left in the account.

But the ATM's screen showed a zero balance.

At first, I thought it was the bank itself which had cleaned my account on orders received from the police. I went into a silent rage, feeling like killing someone. I was so enraged that my immediate impulse was to walk into the manager's office and strangle that person, whoever they might be. I just didn't care anymore.

I started towards the office, but halted before reaching it. I suddenly realised that I'd already killed someone. Was this perhaps the price I had to pay? A human life for twenty grand?

I turned around and walked out, reflecting. It slowly occurred to me that it hadn't been the gods who'd punished me by taking the money. A more likely explanation was that it was Remy. She must have memorised my internet security details and emptied the account.

Refusing to believe she'd done it maliciously, I wasn't angry any longer. I was only depressed. She had to be given the benefit of the doubt, I decided. Perhaps she knew what she was doing. It was perhaps, part of *the scheme*. That's how she had justified the fifty grand payment to Solveig. The scheme should bring in three hundred million. That money she was willing to share with me, I reassured myself – though I found my own arguments pretty weak.

I wandered along Burwood Road to the Hume Highway intersection and back to the park with my mind filled by doubts and frustration. Was Remy the one who'd emptied my account? Why wasn't the news of Florin's death coming out? Why wasn't Remy calling me? Perhaps that was her very reason, I decided. Not having the confirmation of her husband's passing, she had to wait to get the green light first. Yeah, that must be the reason. I rushed back to Rhonda's flat. Maybe the news Remy and I were waiting for had just come out.

I found the flat empty. At ten in the morning, Rhonda had already left. There was a note for me, on the kitchen table. It said: *I'm sorry I had to go. Everything you need for breakfast and lunch you'll find in the fridge. I hope to be back in time for dinner. Please have a rest and try to relax. It's not the end of the world.* It was signed: *Rhonda – your loving wife to be.*

Why was Rhonda being so nice with a jerk like me? I shrugged and switched the television on. The first image I saw perplexed me. The round, pretty face of Helen Longshanks filled the huge television screen. I learned a little later there was a televised debate that morning on the subject of carbon tax, with the main protagonist being Wayne Swine, the Federal Treasurer.

I only partly watched the debate, my mind being occupied with other things. Even so, I found within five minutes the rubbish coming from the Federal Treasurer much too annoying. As usual, Wayne Swine was at his best, making a fool of himself. I switched off the television. That ignorant clown could certainly amuse me, but not at that point in time.

I sat on the couch feeling absolutely miserable. I had no money, no shelter, no car and no job. I'd just killed my best friend. The woman whom I desperately loved seemed to have taken my last cent and snubbed me. And everything else was in a mess with me. I had no idea what had happened to Florin's body. And where Remy was.

Right now the only human being who cared for me was Rhonda. While grateful to her, I felt embarrassed taking for granted all she was giving me. She'd even washed my things and ironed them the night before. I knew there was a price to pay. I knew, in the end, Rhonda expected me to marry her. But was I willing to marry Rhonda?

Conflicting thoughts went through my head. Now with Florin dead, Remy was free to be my wife. I had to take Remy over Rhonda; there was no question about that, but where the hell was Remy? Associating Remy with hell scared me. What if Remy *was* in hell?

I recalled the panic I went into when hearing of Kate's disappearance, fearing she'd been murdered. Since then, Kate had turned up alive, but … what if, in a perverse chain of events, now Remy was the one murdered? I thought of Marin and shuddered.

I shuffled to the liquor cabinet and grabbed a bottle of whisky. I usually didn't drink whisky, but now … it didn't matter. I took a long pull at the bottle and then another one.

I sat on the sofa and thought of Helen. She'd been so good to me. She'd brought me to this country and given me a job and a place to stay. She'd even arranged a wife for me and had only asked loyalty and support in exchange. I'd lied to her and behaved like a teenager full of hormones. Now, I was sorry. But was I sorry for her, or for me?

I drank more whisky and thought of Katarina. I thought of the wonderful time we'd had together, of how caring and loving she was. Now it seemed so far in the past. What was she doing now? I'd been so unfair and cruel to her. Now I was sorry.

The time for regrets had come. I took another guzzle of scotch. It only depressed me further, but I had nothing better to do. I kept drinking until I fell into a dreamless sleep.

The smell of grilled meat woke me. I opened my eyes and looked into a blank nothingness. It took me a while to realise it was a ceiling. My head was clear of alcohol, but I had a nasty hangover. I slowly remembered where I was.

I heard someone moving around in the kitchen. It had to be Rhonda, I thought. I read the time. It showed twenty minutes to six. I'd slept for hours. I closed my eyes and lay still, trying to think of nothing.

More minutes passed; then I heard footsteps approaching. They stopped. Next a palm touched my face: a very gentle touch. I opened my eyes and looked straight into Rhonda's blue eyes. She sat on the couch and her body touched mine. Her face looked concerned.

'Did I just wake you?' she asked.

I shook my head very slowly.

She was so considerate and kind. I'd never known that side of her and it was a nice revelation. It just didn't match her usual easygoing attitude and looks. But why was she so kind to me? I didn't deserve her gentleness.

I felt, for the first time in my life, a sudden, perverse urge to punish myself. But how? Beat my head against the walls? Drive nails through my hands? Kill myself?

'Dinner is ready,' Rhonda whispered to me, while her hand caressed my face.

Her touch made me flinch. The left side of my face hurt.

'That's a nasty bruise,' Rhonda noted. 'Been in a fight over a woman?'

'And lost her,' I answered.

Her hand halted on my face. She then withdrew it slowly.

'Are you hungry?' she asked.

'I'm not hungry. But I wish I was dead.'

'Don't talk like that. What's wrong? What's got you in such a mess?' she asked.

I raised my bulk to a sitting position. Rhonda moved back a little, but remained on the sofa, her body still touching mine. I looked at her. She wore a satin dressing-gown revealing several inches of her thighs. I noted she had lost quite a bit of weight and it suited her very well. She parted her lips and her nostrils twitched. She had *that look* in her eyes.

I recalled, about a month before, she'd taught me a lesson. I'd wanted her badly then, but she wouldn't play. Now … I sensed she was willing. But now, *I* was the one not eager to play. I had to punish myself. But resisting Rhonda's sexual charm was too light a punishment. It had to be something much more powerful than that. I made my mind up very quickly.

'I have to tell you something,' I said weakly.

She smiled. 'It's alright. I understand if you don't feel like it.'

'It's not that,' I murmured.

She scowled. 'What is it?'

'I have to confess my sins.'

She paused. 'I don't know if I want to listen. I have a feeling I will regret it if I do.'

I nodded. 'You must listen. You're the only human being who cares about me.'

She paused again, staring at me with an air of concern. 'Tell me,' she finally said.

I began with that Thursday of May when I met Kate Morales. I told her why I'd run away and sought refuge at Florin's farm. I told her of the affair I began with Remy, of Remy's idea to murder her husband and split his fortune between the two of us.

And I told her the rest – but not quite everything. I told her how I killed Florin in cold blood. I told her I'd done it because my stake in the plot was a whooping fortune of a hundred and fifty million dollars. I didn't tell her I'd fallen for Remy and planned to marry her. I only wanted to punish myself, not to hurt Rhonda's feelings.

I noted while talking, the expression on her face gradually changing; from interest and concern, to surprise, shock, then horror and fear. Once I finished my confession, the colour on her face had completely drained. She looked as white as a sheet. She withdrew and cringed towards the other end of the sofa.

Her pupils were enlarged and she looked very scared. She made a visible effort to articulate a few words. 'Tell me it's not true.'

I nodded. 'I wish I could turn the time back … but I can't.'

I saw instant tears forming in her eyes. 'Why did you tell me this?'

I shrugged. 'I had to tell someone.'

'It's the most horrific thing one has ever told me. Why? Why did you tell me?' Rhonda demanded with a tremor in her voice.

'Because … you had to know what I am capable of doing.'

She bit her lip while tears rolled down her cheeks.

I reached for her, but she flinched further back. 'Don't touch me.'

She began gasping, her breasts moving up and down rapidly. 'You stink of grog. Go have a shower. Go wash your sins away.'

With Rhonda watching me terrified, I hobbled to the bathroom.

When I came out, some twenty minutes later, Rhonda was gone. A note on the kitchen table said. *You had the nerve to murder your best friend and blow your own trumpet afterwards. You shouldn't have confessed to me and I shouldn't have listened to you. But now, as you say, it's all too late. Now I don't know what to do, but Helen will know. I'm going to see her. You'll find me there, if you dare to face Helen. If not, just go away and lock the door from outside. Just as you locked the cold-room. And drop the key in the letterbox.*

The fact that the note wasn't signed suggested Rhonda's contempt and disgust towards me. And it was obvious that by asking me to lock the door from outside, she wanted nothing to do with me anymore. The only human being who cared about me was now gone from my life forever. I was now on my own. But that's what I wanted, didn't I? To punish myself.

Now that I was sober, I had to think of my next move. I wasn't going to face Helen. With Rhonda it hadn't been so hard, but Helen was a different kettle of fish: tough, determined, even ruthless when circumstances required. I wondered if Helen or Rhonda, or both, would alert the police. I couldn't do much about that if they did. Unless …

An audacious thought crossed my mind. I could silence them forever. I was a killer already. I'd just killed my best friend. They say the first killing is the hardest. But when you've done it once, it becomes routine. That's what I was taught in Bucharest, at the police academy.

I thought about it. Yes, I could go to Helen's, pretend to ask forgiveness and … There was no problem in overpowering both Helen and Rhonda, but, how exactly would I finish them off? A cold-room would be easy, but Helen didn't have a cold-room. Strangle them? Stab them in the heart? Beat them up to death?

I walked into the kitchen, thinking. The dinner which Rhonda had prepared was on the kitchen table. Grilled, thick slices of sirloin, with salad and pasta on the side. Amazingly considering my state of mind, the sight of the expensive cut of beef made me instantly hungry. I placed the meat in the microwave to reheat it and began to eat the pasta. I then consumed all the meat: more than a kilo of it. I probably did it instinctively: the instinct of self-preservation. With very little money left, I sensed I might never enjoy such a nice meal again.

The oversized portion of meat made me thirsty. And sleepy. I had a couple of beers and craved for more. I knew though I must not overindulge. And I must not stay too long in Rhonda's flat.

I thought of Rhonda and Helen again. They both had been so good to me. How could I possibly contemplate harming Helen or Rhonda? I couldn't find an excuse. Well, it had been just a passing thought. Or, perhaps the hunger had caused me a temporary lapse of reason.

But how about Florin? What excuse did I have then? He'd

been more than a brother to me. And still, I killed him in cold blood. I wished it too had been just a thought, but I knew it wasn't. How was I capable of doing such a horrible thing? I did it for a woman, I answered myself. It hadn't been my flaw; it was the woman's. These are the things women do, I reflected.

I had to move on, I decided. I turned the television on, just in case there was some news concerning me. I switched between channels trying to catch a news update. I did, after about ten minutes. There was nothing on the news highlights about Florin, Remy or me.

I walked into my bedroom and packed my things, as I'd done less than forty-eight hours before. This time, I crammed as many things as I could in one travelling bag only. I had to be mindful that I didn't have a car and two bags were too much to carry.

It was past eight o'clock when I heard a police siren outside. I had to hurry up. Before exiting the flat, I had another look around, to make sure I didn't miss anything. A bunch of keys on a decorative saucer in the living room caught my attention. I picked them up and studied them. A key to Rhonda's BMW was in the bunch. I knew she had two cars – a Honda Sport and a BMW sedan 5 series. Without too much thinking, I removed the key from the ring and put it in my pocket.

I walked out, locked the door and rushed downstairs to the basement using the emergency exit. Worried by the police siren, I didn't take the risk to drop the key to the flat in the letterbox downstairs, as Rhonda had demanded.

I found the BMW parked in the garage. I got in and drove out into the night noting the petrol tank was nearly full.

I exited into a side street and, curious to see if the police were after me, I turned back onto the road where the entry to the block of flats was located. I drove along the road, passing the building at very low speed, but I didn't see any police car around, nor did I hear the siren any longer. Maybe that police car wasn't after me. Or maybe the car was unmarked and the siren had been switched off.

I drove south and turned left onto Liverpool Road towards Ashfield, not having any idea where to go. Just before reaching the Frederick Street intersection, an idea came to me. I turned left on Frederick Street and left again on Parramatta Road, towards Harris Park.

There was one more human being whose help I wasn't ashamed or embarrassed to ask. That was sweet and loving Katarina. Enjoying the smoothness and comfort of the BMW, I drove west feeling confident that Katarina would shelter me and look after me.

I thought, in the next twenty minutes, of how unstable my personality was and how treacherously I could go off the rails. How could I have ever contemplated murdering Helen and Rhonda?! The question baffled me. Though I'd come back to my senses in no time, discarding the idea, the thought still worried me.

How revolting and repulsive Remy's idea to murder her husband had been to me at first, but I was the one who ended up killing him! I had all the reasons to be worried about my state of mind. I always knew there was a dark side to my personality and that I did foolish things at times, but murder was taking it too far. I shuddered, making an effort to empty my mind of those dark reflections and to think of something nice. I thought of Katarina.

I hadn't seen her in more than a month and I missed her. I had no doubt she longed for me too and she'd be thrilled to see me turn up from nowhere. I loved those touching reunions, like you see in the movies. As I approached Katarina's address, I became emotional.

While being aware that Katarina had no answers to the troubles I was going through at the time, I still looked forward to the support I expected from her.

Was I going to confess to Katarina as well? No way, I decided, already regretting my hasty resolution to come clean to Rhonda. The truth was that, although I'd felt a sudden urge to punish myself, I hadn't anticipated Rhonda's extreme reaction. Now it was too late.

But Katarina … she was something else. She was the one who *really* cared about me. I knew she loved me deeply and I'd been a jerk with her. I'd thought Rhonda cared about me too, but it looked like I was wrong.

As for Kate, it had been just a very brief affair and it should never have happened.

And with Remy … I just didn't know.

With those thoughts on my mind, I reached Katarina's flat at nine-thirty-five. I stood in front of the door and, hearing the television was on inside, I sighed with relief. It meant Katarina must be at home.

I pushed the doorbell button, smiling in excitement. She'd get such a surprise seeing me.

Indeed, when Katarina opened the door, she stood there with her mouth hanging open, like I was a phantom.

I too stared at her, liking what I saw. With her hair wet and ruffled and wearing a tight dressing-gown cut well above her knees, she'd put on a couple of kilos, which made her look more voluptuous. She'd probably only just stepped out of the shower.

We remained like that, staring at each other and not saying anything for several seconds.

'Hello, remember me?' I finally asked.

She nodded slightly but remained silent. The joy and excitement of seeing me which I'd expected from Katarina didn't eventuate. Perhaps she was too emotional and needed a little time to recover, I thought.

'May I come in?' I continued.

Katarina appeared startled by my request but didn't shift from the door to let me in. Well, she probably wanted our bodies to make contact and that's why she hadn't moved.

'I'm so tired and thirsty,' I added, making a miserable-looking face.

It didn't work. She only arched her eyebrows, without saying anything.

'Is everything alright?' I asked intrigued.

She nodded.

I didn't know if she meant that everything was alright, or something wasn't right.

Finding her behaviour peculiar, I thought it was time to ask a reassuring question. 'You still love me as much as I love you?'

At last, she said something: 'It's too late.'

'What do you mean it's too late?'

She stared at me with sadness in her eyes.

An alarm bell went off in my head. There was something seriously wrong.

More seconds passed in silence again.

A voice then broke the silence. 'Who's there?'

It was a male voice, coming from inside the flat. I felt like someone tipped a bucket of ice down my back.

'It's a mistake,' Katarina called back.

She closed the door very slowly.

The last thing I saw before the door was fully shut were tears forming in her eyes.

I climbed down the stairs, my heart heavy and my mind empty of thoughts beyond the realisation of how reckless and stupid I'd been! I had to lose her to recognise how dear she was to me.

I got in the car but couldn't bear the thought of leaving that place. I drove only fifty metres further and stopped in a spot where I had a good view of the windows to Katarina's flat.

The light in the living room was on. I watched the window as if mesmerised for more than one and a half hours, until the light was switched off and the side of the flat I could see fell into darkness.

Another half an hour passed. Then the light in Katarina's bedroom came alive – but switched off a few minutes later. Then it was replaced by a dim one – most likely a bedroom lamp.

I fell asleep in the driver's seat, sometime after two in the morning. I woke up in a state of acute anxiety a couple of hours later. The dim light in the bedroom was still on and suddenly, thinking about what she was doing in there, my mood changed from depression and anxiety to rage. I felt an urge to kill someone.

I rolled the car window's down and let a wave of crisp night air in. The cold air calmed me down and actually made me sleepy. I moved to the back seats and rolled the windows up, but not completely. I lay on the soft leather seats and fell asleep.

I woke – it was morning; close to nine o'clock.

The blinds to Katarina's bedroom were closed. She must still be sleeping, I thought, after a very late night. The anger got hold of me again. I was so furious that I considered, for a little while, going back up to her apartment and confronting her new man. I'd give him a belting to remember for the rest of his life, I planned in my mind.

That impulse didn't last too long. My thinking took another turn. That unknown bloke, the object of my fury whom I'd never seen and couldn't visualise, began to materialise in my mind as Marin. He was the *real* villain, I decided.

Enough of being pushed around and being treated like crap, I said to myself. It's time I did something proactive. It was Marin who bashed me the other day, and insulted me, and sent that cheeky text message: *You're a spineless pile of garbage.*

It must have been Marin who sent it. Who else could it have been? And that was just the final drop that filled the glass. He'd corrupted Florin into homosexual promiscuity and humiliated Remy. He'd persuaded Florin that I was a useless bum. It had been Marin who'd caused Florin to distance himself from me and take his side. Were it not for Marin, I wouldn't have killed my best friend, I concluded.

I suddenly felt an urge to face Marin in a decisive fight. I'd never been bashed by a single guy in my adult life and, even recognising that this Romanian version of Bud Spencer was bigger and probably stronger than me, I was keen to risk it. The time to do something about Marin had come. Revenge was all of a sudden my highest concern.

To take revenge on evil Marin, I had to return to Florin's farmhouse. That was the only possible place where my planned life and death clash with Marin could occur.

But … was this maybe an excuse for me to go back to the farm? Maybe my real reason was that, not knowing what happened to Remy and why the news of Florin's death hadn't come out, I couldn't stand the pressure any longer; I had to find out, even if that was the last thing I did on earth.

I didn't care if, this time, Marin bashed me to death or if I killed him. I'd already killed my best mate. Another murder didn't bother me.

I drove to the nearest McDonald's, had breakfast and used

the bathroom. Then I walked to an internet café, paid two bucks and downloaded that PPK's Resurrection song which Marin had played last Sunday on my mobile phone. I would confront the giant in style, I decided, and give him a taste of his own medicine. I didn't care if that implied killing him. I was a killer already.

20

I drove south on Elizabeth Drive, as I did, that very day, four weeks ago. Four weeks seemed like a lifetime. So much had happened since then.

I reached the front double gate of the farm at just after midday. I parked inside the gate, got out of the car and read the sign FLOMAR on the timber beam, with mixed emotions.

I was, on one hand, glad that the FLORE sign had been replaced. That's because FLORE signified the union between Florin and Remy and I didn't want Remy to be united with any other bloke. Not even with a corpse. I wanted her for me only and I'd already killed for that.

On the other hand, FLOMAR reminded me of Florin and Marin, which was also a union. A union of which I didn't approve. But did it really matter? Florin was dead, so it didn't matter anymore. But Marin was most likely alive. My mission now was to unite them in death.

I walked on the dirt road, stopped at the front house and had a look around. The house seemed lonely and deserted, as it had always been. The vintage Dodge, the small tractor and Remy's golf cart were still parked in the garage. Her Audi wasn't there.

The afternoon was cloudy and warm. I kept walking west on the narrow, country road. Like then, one month ago, the ground was covered in thick, brown-greenish grass. Like then, sheep and goats were bleating in the distance. The farm was as peaceful as ever.

I could have driven through, but I needed more time. Time to put my thoughts together. And add more drama to the upcoming confrontation; like in the movies. The same classic flick which Marin had played on Sunday I now had in mind. With the 'Res-urrection' tune saved on my mobile phone, I imagined myself as a Clint Eastwood hero.

I kept walking imagining an overconfident Marin waiting for me. I'd been no match for him, just a few days before. Why would today be any different? Because, today *was* different, I encouraged myself. Today I felt my role in Florin's death had been instrumental only.

I wasn't the moral killer. I knew it was actually Remy, but chose to blame Marin instead.

I imagined a scenario where the police charged Marin with murdering his boss and the courts found him guilty. I pictured in my mind the distressed wife of the victim weeping in front of the television cameras. With her breathtaking looks, she'd capture the hearts of millions of viewers.

But she only had eyes for one man. That man was me. Well, that was something. It made me feel so good. We'd then go through the process. A love story would unfold. The devastated widow finding new love with her husband's best friend. Unusual, but ... yes, like in the movies. Thrilling, exciting and ... moving.

The fairytale would continue. The rezoning application would come through. The land would be sold. The deal would make headlines in the media. *Widow of slain Romanian entrepreneur overnight becomes one of the richest women in the country.*

There would be a lot of talk of me as well. *Romanian Cornel Toma, former assistant to radio personality Helen Longshanks, teams up with countrywoman Remy Panait in a three-hundred-million-dollar deal.* Or something like that.

Well, the details were not that important. What mattered now was that I had to fix Marin. For good. Then another thought struck me. If I killed Marin, he couldn't be charged and found guilty. *I* could be charged instead. My thoughts and logic annoyed me. Stop dreaming and get on with the job! I said to myself.

I kept walking, noting the country road seemed even narrower, the grass more brown than green, the sky dull and grey. Even the birds and the beasts were quieter than ever before. It was perhaps just my impression. Maybe because Florin was no longer around. And Remy? She wasn't on the farm, for sure, but where was she? I had to find her. But first, I had to deal with Marin.

I reached Florin's cabin at a few minutes to one. At that time, he usually had his lunchbreak. I noted his golf cart parked by the cabin, just as it had been when I bolted from the farm last Sunday. His car was there too. Where else would it be? Its owner was no longer around.

I walked to the front door and stood there, reflecting, recalling my time spent in there with Florin. Those thoughts didn't do me much good. I turned the handle. The door was unlocked. I took a deep breath and stepped inside. I glanced around noting the cabin was tidy and clean, just as Florin used to keep it. Only now there was no Florin anymore.

I passed through the reception room and the living room. I then had a look through the bedrooms, the bathrooms and the laundry. The small electronic screen displaying the temperature in the cold-room showed one tenth of a degree above zero.

I stepped close to the cold-room and stood by the heavy door, hesitating.

Last Sunday I hadn't had the courage to open that door. Now I had to do what I hadn't done then. I had to enter the cold-room. A few days had passed. He must have been found and probably buried. Unless … maybe the forensic police hadn't finished with him. Or, even worse. What if Florin was still in the cold-room? Perhaps something had happened to Marin on Sunday night. Something that prevented him to return to Florin's cabin.

That would explain why the news about Florin's passing hadn't come out. It would also explain why Remy hadn't made contact yet. Not hearing the news she was waiting for, she probably suspected that I hadn't carried out the task, or something had gone wrong. She'd probably decided to keep a low profile until she heard something in the news.

I stood there, staring at the door, not daring to touch it. The key was in the lock, just as I'd left it on Sunday night. I had to open the door, I tried to encourage myself, but I didn't have the guts to go ahead with it. I needed a drink, I decided.

I could have grabbed a drink from the cold-room. There was plenty of wine in there, but for that, I needed to go inside. A much simpler option would be to get a drink from the kitchen, but I rejected that easy option. It implied cowardice, so I wasn't going to do it. Still, I remained undecided for another minute or so.

It took me a while, but I eventually took a deep breath and turned the door handle. As usual, it was unlocked. I opened the door very slowly, expecting it to creak. I didn't know why I expected the door to creak, as it never had. I stepped inside, prepared for the worst. The light inside switched automatically on, as it always did.

A thought came to me in a flash. *On Sunday, when Florin had walked in there, the light in the cold-room was off.*

Something wasn't right, but I didn't know what.

A familiar image welcomed me: countless casks and barrels of wine, pork hams, specks, and sausages hanged on metal pegs, chesses and jars of pickled cabbage, capsicum and tomatoes and so on. But otherwise, the room was empty.

Florin's frozen body wasn't there; not even a snowman was there.

His body must have been found and removed. But why hadn't the story hit the press? I felt Marin must have held the clue.

A crazy idea hit me. What if Marin had had his own reasons to get rid of his master? What if Marin had finished the job which Remy had masterminded and I failed to complete?

And worse, what if Remy, unsure of my commitment, had also persuaded Marin to join her plot? A reinsurance policy, just in case, as they say. Clearly, I had to face Marin.

Forgetting about the drink, I walked out of the cabin to the greenhouse. That's where Florin used to spend most of his time. He was so passionate about it. While knowing he couldn't possibly be there, the urge to enter the huge artificial garden was too much.

As I'd expected, Florin wasn't there, or at least, I couldn't see him. No wonder: the greenhouse was nearly one hectare in size. If he were still alive, he could be anywhere; perhaps laying between strata of vegetables enjoying an afternoon nap, or concealed from view under a tall plant. I knew, though, that this was just wishful thinking. He couldn't be there for the same reason he couldn't be anywhere. The only place he could be was in a morgue or six feet under.

I exited the greenhouse with a bitter taste in my mouth. I strode west, noting two flocks of sheep and goats mingled together feeding on both sides of the dirt road.

I didn't spot Marin. I kept walking to his cabin.

I reached his bungalow at close to half past one. I halted a few metres from the entry and considered my next move.

I stepped to the door and knocked on it. I waited about ten seconds. Nothing happened. I knocked on the door again and waited. Again, there was no answer.

I tried the door handle. It offered no resistance. I pushed the door open and stepped in.

The cabin was quiet and seemed empty. I hadn't been in there before, but it felt familiar. The lobby led into the reception room, there was the kitchen on the right and the living room in front. It was identical to Florin's and nearly as clean and as tidy.

Having expected it to look like a pigsty, I was surprised. Once more I'd thought of Marin with contempt. I was in the habit of doing that and he kept proving me wrong, I observed.

I halted in the living room and looked around trying to spot some item of interest. I didn't know what; just something which would give me a clue of what was going on or of Marin's whereabouts.

An item on the coffee table caught my attention. Or, rather *two* items. Two mobile phones lying side by side.

There was something not right with those mobile phones. I focused, trying to work it out. I couldn't. The feeling that one of the mobile phones held an important clue persisted.

My reflection was suddenly interrupted. I heard a door being shut in the bedrooms section. Next, footsteps were coming my way. It had to have been Marin.

Another moment of truth had just arrived.

I fished my mobile phone out, which I'd set on 'music' and pressed the enter button. The eerie sound of the 'Resurrection' song instantly filled the room.

The footsteps stopped in the corridor, somewhere between the bedrooms.

I was in a spot where I could see the door to one of the bathrooms and a couple of metres inside the vestibule separating the bedrooms, but no further.

Not being able to see beyond that point frustrated me, but I was reluctant to move. I stood there, listening. The only sound I heard was the awesome music.

I waited for Marin to make his appearance.

He didn't seem in a hurry. He must have known it was me. Who else would play that tune, just days after he'd done that very same to me?

The seconds passed. Twenty seconds, half a minute ... a minute.

And still, Marin wasn't showing. Should I move to him? I wondered. Though on a high, determined to fight him to death, I was still cautious. I knew I had to be at my very best to have a chance against Marin. I felt brave and bold and prepared to even die, but I was not suicidal yet.

More seconds passed ... another minute. So he was very cautious too. He must be scared as well. Now he was showing due respect, I thought and felt more confident.

The tune was approaching its conclusion.

With seconds left from 'Resurrection', Marin stepped in from the corridor.

Wearing only a pair of homespun peasant trousers, and with his huge chest bare, he stopped about three metres in front of me.

The song ended with some lyrics spoken in Russian, of which I didn't understand a single word. We gaped at each other, saying nothing.

I pressed the back and enter buttons on my mobile phone.

PPK's song filled the room once more.

More seconds passed in silence.

I was amazingly calm in that situation and so seemed Marin.

Facing me, he appeared perturbed by the song, but only vaguely aware of my presence.

He gave me the impression he was in a trance; like he'd been on Sunday night, when listening to the same very song.

We were facing each other, like Lee Van Cleef and Gian Maria Volonte in that movie. This time though I had the impression that Marin was the one reluctant to make a move.

'Nice number,' he said, eventually. He'd said it very softly, with no menace in his voice.

'What number?' I asked aggressively.

'The Clint Eastwood number. You're doing it nicely,' Marin replied.

I wondered if he was making fun of me. 'Yeah ... sure, but not very original,' I said.

He shrugged. 'It needn't be. Mine wasn't either.'

'You mean ... on Sunday night?' I asked.

The giant nodded.

What happened next, I never understood. For some mysterious reason, I mellowed in an instant. My murderous intentions suddenly disappeared. It was perhaps another bout of delusion. Or, maybe Marin's remorseful expression and his gentle tone had abruptly softened me.

But his soft approach didn't make any sense. The fact that I'd murdered his master and lover still stood. Why was Marin behaving like *he* was the guilty one?

I pressed the stop button on my mobile. With the song being cut off short, Marin's face showed a shade of disappointment.

I stared at him and he looked down.

'What exactly happened on Sunday night? I can't quite remember,' I said, softly this time.

He fidgeted from one leg to the other, seemingly embarrassed. 'Would you care to have a seat?' Again, he spoke very tenderly.

Was he perhaps trying to catch me by surprise?

I turned around, wondering if he'd king hit me from behind. He didn't.

I took a seat on an armchair and Marin eased his bulk onto the floor. I had the impression he'd done that because he wanted me to look down at him. And I did.

'What were you saying?' Marin asked, apparently absent-minded.

'What happened on Sunday night?' I repeated myself.

'I'm sorry for Sunday night,' he whispered.

I'm sorry too, but it's too late, I was tempted to say. 'I don't understand anything,' I said instead.

Marin looked at me thoughtfully. 'I owe you an apology.'

'You owe me an apology?' I repeated astonished.

He nodded. 'I shouldn't have thumped you and I'm sorry. I'd had a hunch something wasn't right, but ...' He left the rest in suspense.

Of course something wasn't right, I said to myself. To Marin I didn't say anything.

'I thought you were lying to me,' Marin continued, looking embarrassed.

I didn't understand what he was getting at. Was this some sort of play, part of a punishment plan? Of course I was lying, I said in my mind.

'You were right about Florin,' Marin went on.

I didn't know what he meant by that. 'What do you mean?' I asked.

Marin paused and scratched his chin. 'Florin did fall asleep on Sunday evening. Indeed, he was so drunk he couldn't remember much. But he did remember he'd gone into the cold-room to look for something and for some strange reason he locked himself in. He then fell asleep. That's why the key wasn't in the lock. It was in Florin's pocket.'

I was completely stunned. Why was Marin telling me these fairy tales? I knew very well it wasn't true and Florin could certainly testify if he were alive. Which he wasn't.

And how could Marin believe that any human being, no matter how drunk they were, would lock themselves in a room at minus twenty-five degrees? It just didn't make any sense. More, how could Marin possibly know what Florin had done on Sunday night?

'How would you know what Florin did that night?' I asked.

'Because he told me so,' Marin replied candidly.

He must have gone nuts, I assumed. 'Florin told you so? How could he?'

It was Marin's turn to look baffled. 'I don't know what you mean. He just said so.'

What did he mean, *he just said so*? I felt an electric shock going through me and the hairs on my arms stood erect. Let's take this slowly, I said to myself. It's either that Marin has completely gone off the rails, or maybe this conversation was only taking place in my imagination.

That probably made sense, I thought. I'd just imagined myself being a character in that movie, though I wasn't sure which one. Was I impersonating the colonel bounty hunter, or the villain El Indio? I liked to believe I was the colonel, but judging by my actions, I was rather El Indio.

I opened my mouth to say something, but stopped. There was a noise coming from the bedrooms area.

Marin stood up from the floor and pulled a chair from under the table. He sat on it and I could see the timber frame bending under his weight. He looked embarrassed.

Next, a pair of footsteps were approaching. I knew a third character was due on the stage. Just like in the movie.

I instantly understood why there were *two* mobile phones on the coffee table; one of which looked familiar. Because there were *two* people in the cabin.

One was Marin. The other one, due to appear, was perhaps the Man with No Name, played by Eastwood himself.

Then, I abruptly remembered. He did have a name. His name was Manco. I suddenly got dizzy and very confused. That was his name in the movie. *That one* was Manco. But *not this one.*

The last thing I recalled was the face of someone whose name I knew wasn't Manco. The face gradually disappeared behind a veil of mist. For the second time in my life, I fainted.

I heard voices which seemed somewhere in the distance. I listened but couldn't distinguish what they were saying. I didn't know where I was. I only knew I was very tired. I made an effort, but couldn't open my eyes. I fell into a semiconscious state again.

I dreamed that Marin and I were locked in a deadly confrontation. He was playing his pocket watch. *When the chimes finish, we begin*, he was saying. I tried to draw my gun, but my arms wouldn't move. I didn't even have a gun, but Marin did. Next he was going to slay me. I couldn't even run away from him. My legs felt heavy like lead. I was just a sitting duck at the giant's mercy.

Then, as it happens in dreams, it wasn't Marin facing me any longer. It was the villain El Indio himself. He looked more deadly than Marin. I just watched him, resigned, my eyes saying *just do what you have to do and get over with it*. I couldn't fight him and, even if I could, what was the point?

I didn't know what the point was. I was tired of everything and everyone in this world. El Indio, grinning, watched me, enjoying my agony. As the chimes of his pocket watch were approaching the end, I jerked violently and screamed. 'No!'

With sweat running down my face, I came out of the dream. I felt a soft pillow under my head and heard voices again. Were those the same voices? I didn't know. I forced myself to stay awake. I didn't want to fall asleep. I feared if I did, El Indio would finish the job.

Where was the Man with No Name? I asked myself. Why wasn't he coming to rescue me? Then, the miracle happened. I felt a hand touching my forehead.

'His fever has nearly gone,' a voice said.

'Give him a slap. Maybe he'll wake up,' another voice said.

A palm slapped my open hand very gently. I opened my eyes with difficulty. I didn't know where I was. I only remembered that I'd fainted.

It had happened once before, when I was about to complete that police academy training in Bucharest. I collapsed during the final exams. I'd finally passed the exams, but only just. I never recalled afterwards anything that had happened before passing out. Several hours from my life had been wiped out forever. The medical tests didn't give any clue.

And now, it happened again.

'Where am I?' I whispered.

'Bingo,' a voice said next to me. It was the first voice again.

I made an effort and raised my head a little. I felt terribly dizzy and my whole body was shaking. Someone was sitting on the sofa next to me.

'Is it you?' I whispered.

'I'm not sure you know who *you* are, at this moment, let alone me,' the same voice answered.

'I know who you are. You rescued me from my dream,' I said.

'His mind is still wandering. He's hallucinating,' the second voice said.

At that point, I realised the man who'd just spoken was Marin. He was the second voice. As for the first one, I still had difficulty comprehending the situation.

'You're right – he's hallucinating,' the reply came from the sofa. 'Keep an eye on him. I'll be back shortly,' the voice added.

I saw a silhouette standing up and moving away. I dropped my head on the pillow and remained quiet, trying to make sense of what was happening. I fell asleep again.

I woke up not remembering where I was. It took me a few minutes to recall I was in Marin's cabin, but not much else. I noticed it was dark outside and read my wristwatch. It showed twenty-past-six. So, I'd been there, in and out of consciousness, for nearly five hours.

I heard someone moving around in the cabin. It must be Marin, I thought. So, I was alone with Marin. Strangely, I didn't fear him any longer, nor did I long to kill him.

Then I thought of Remy. That thought gave me enough strength to snap out of my prostration.

I stood up and walked to the kitchen, where I'd heard noises before.

Marin stared at me, raising his eyebrows. 'Feeling better?'

'What happened to Remy?' I asked, ignoring his question.

He paused frowning, as if trying to make up his mind. 'There will be a divorce.'

'But now, there is no need for a divorce,' I pointed out.

He shrugged. 'I don't know what you mean, but Florin has made up his mind. It's definite.'

'Why do you keep talking like that?' I asked.

Marin looked at me inquiringly. 'You're sure you are alright?'

I actually wasn't alright. I felt dizzy and weak and my hands were still trembling. 'I wouldn't mind a drink.'

He paused and shook his head. 'Not such a good idea. A drink in your current condition could do you more harm than good.'

I pondered that. Well, maybe he was right. 'Why were you saying a divorce is definite?'

He scratched his neck with abnormally thick fingers. 'Maybe definite is not the right word. As far as I know, nothing in this world is definite. Everything is relative.'

I smiled bitterly, noting he was philosophising, which you wouldn't expect from an uneducated shepherd. He was rather talking like Florin, probably replicating fragments from his master's observations.

'Death is not. Death is absolute,' I said.

Marin nodded. 'I feel bad being in the middle … part of the divorce motive.'

I knew what he meant by that. It was a very weird love triangle. But I was still unsure why he kept talking about a divorce.

'On death, a marriage is dissolved as a matter of course,' I added.

'If such an event occurs, which is not the case here,' Marin added.

I heard the front door opening, then footsteps approaching.

I looked that way and I remembered the same scene had already happened earlier that day. Only then, the footsteps had come from the other direction; from inside the cottage.

It was déjà vu, but still, it didn't make any more sense than it had made before. The gods must be crazy, I thought, at the sight of the weirdest apparition I'd ever encountered.

Yet, the veil of mist was starting to disperse.

I suddenly understood. Marin's talk of a divorce now made sense. His apology made sense too. And his fairytale.

The guy in the kitchen door, watching me with an inquisitive air, wasn't a ghost, or a product of my imagination. It wasn't an optical illusion, or just a photo on a funeral stone. It wasn't a carbon copy of Florin either.

It was the shock of my life and yet, such a relief. Somehow my best friend hadn't died. The real Florin Panait was there, right in front of me.

Still, I couldn't understand how it could possibly be him. 'So, it's true,' I murmured.

He frowned at me. 'What's true?'

Good question, I thought, realising I didn't know what was true or what was real anymore.

I felt a weakness in my legs. I sat on a chair at the kitchen table.

Florin stepped into the kitchen and leaned against the stove, watching me.

Marin was taking turns looking at Florin and me.

An awkward silence followed, for maybe a couple of minutes.

Florin then broke the silence. 'It's true.'

It was my turn to frown at him. 'What's true?'

He leered. 'Everything Marin told you. I did fall asleep that night. I was so drunk …'

I knew what Florin said couldn't be true. 'But, how could you fall asleep at minus …'

I stopped in time, realising I'd nearly given myself away. I was about to say *minus twenty-five*, when the temperature in the cold-room should have been only about zero.

I noted a smile of contempt on Florin's face. 'Go ahead,' he encouraged me.

I gazed at Marin. He scowled nervously.

'I was very drunk too,' I continued.

'Lucky me,' Florin said. 'I'd certainly have dropped dead and you wouldn't have been able to save me if the temperature had been … If the temperature had been what you were about to say.'

He paused and looked me in the eyes.

I stiffened. But how could he know what I meant to say? He couldn't possibly know the plot. On the other hand, I doubted he'd have survived if he'd fallen asleep as drunk as he was, even at zero, let alone minus twenty-five.

Florin then shifted his eyes from me to Marin. He made me very edgy. Was this his tacit signal to the giant to finish me off? I wondered.

'It was only by accident I found on Sunday evening that my cold-room wasn't working,' Marin stated. 'The power supply had been disrupted. I tried to ring Florin on his mobile to ask if his cold-room was working. He didn't answer, so I tried the landline, but no one answered it either. I went into a panic and … you know what happened next …'

I knew what had happened next. But, what a coincidence! The loss of power occurring right on the night when there should have been no slip-up at all. I just couldn't believe it.

To my amazement, Florin immediately confirmed that the

power disruption last Sunday had not been a coincidence. 'Marin's assumption was that, if my cold-room was working, he obviously had a problem with his, as both cold-rooms are on the same electrical circuit,' he explained. 'It's a separate circuit which only supplies power to the cold-rooms. As it turned out, there had been a sudden surge of consumption on Sunday afternoon, which the network was unable to sustain. So the safety catch went off and the power was disconnected.'

Then I understood. Sweat started to run down my ribs.

How ironic! It was me who'd planned to murder Florin and, at the same time, it was also me who had unknowingly saved his life. The power supply would not have been cut if I hadn't tampered with the temperature adjustor.

If that was not divine intervention, nothing was. My mouth was suddenly very dry and the weakness in my legs seemed to get worse.

'What would cause such a sudden surge of consumption?' I asked, feeling I had to say something.

Florin's answer made me regret asking the question. He gave me an intent look. 'Good question,' he said grinning and then took his time before continuing: 'Let's say that for some reason, someone set the temperature adjustor to the minimum. That's minus twenty-five Celsius. We never ever needed such a severe cold in there and I suppose the electrical generator would struggle to deliver that chill.'

The colour must have drained from my face, for Florin asked: 'Are you feeling okay?'

I wasn't. 'No, not really.'

Marin was frowning, as if he'd just uncovered something he hadn't thought of. 'But who'd do that?' he asked.

Florin shrugged. 'It's just hypothetical. I'm not an expert but that's what the electrician explained to me on Monday.'

'What would have happened if the power had been on when you fell asleep in there?' Marin asked.

Florin grinned. 'Well, I'd have been made into a snowman, I suppose. But, as the power was off, it was quite pleasant and a little warmish in there. So, I slept like a newborn baby. The power supply must have been disconnected quite a few hours before.'

He was right. I recalled myself fiddling with the temperature adjustor before two in the afternoon. And it was past eight in the evening when I locked the door and trapped him in the cold-room. More than six hours had passed.

Thinking about it, I recalled a little detail to which I didn't pay attention on Sunday evening. Had I been more careful and less drunk, I should have registered it. When Florin had gone into the cold-room and left the door open, I should have felt a strong current of cold air coming from inside, which I didn't. Had I noticed that detail, it would have told me something wasn't right.

And now, the fact that the light in the cold-room was at that time off made sense, too.

I thought at the time it had been divine intervention which sent Florin into the cold-room. Now I began to comprehend that the divine intervention had actually been the sudden surge of consumption. But that was the essential part of the scheme. I mean, achieving minus twenty-five in there could only occur through a huge amount of electricity consumption, which in turn caused the loss of power. In other words, Remy's plan was doomed from the beginning.

But where was Remy? Was she aware that I'd failed? Had she been in contact with Florin since Sunday? I was dying to ask the question, but felt awkward about it.

Then another thought came to me. 'Why did you send me that text message on Monday?' I asked Marin.

The giant gave me a confused look. 'What text message?'

I fished my mobile phone out, opened the message and handed the phone to Marin.

He read it and smirked. He then read it loudly. 'You're a spineless pile of garbage. I don't want to see you again. Good bye, Novak.' He passed the phone to Florin.

Florin read it and leered. 'It was sent from Remy's mobile,' he said.

He placed my mobile phone on the kitchen table and leaned against the stove with his arms crossed to his chest.

His words hit me right where it hurt.

'But why would Remy say those nasty things to you?' Marin asked.

Because she learned that I failed, I answered in my mind. She must found out that Florin was alive and she became disgusted with me. She probably believed that I'd lost my nerve and hadn't even tried to send Florin to his death.

Was I sorry? No, I wasn't. I mean, I was relieved that Florin was alive and that I wasn't a killer. But I was sorry that I'd disappointed Remy. Which feeling was stronger? I wasn't sure.

Would I try again? I asked myself. No, I would not. I would think of some other option to protect Florin's life and keep Remy for me.

'I'm sorry my friend,' Florin said in an indifferent tone.

I looked up at him and understood why he had his arms crossed to his chest. Having read a book about body language, I knew his posture implied resentment.

'I told you once, Remy spent most of her weekends in town,'

Florin continued in a monotonous voice, while looking out the window, right like he'd done on Sunday night. Like then, it was dark outside.

He appeared bored telling that tale. 'On Sunday night, she turned up here, unexpectedly. It was well after midnight. Marin and I were up, in my cabin. I was still a little plastered, but not too badly. I told her I'd instructed my lawyer to file for a divorce. I told her I'd gathered all the evidence I needed to prove she was playing around and it was certain that the court's decision would favour me. With that prenuptial in place, she wouldn't get a cent from me.'

He paused and said to Marin. 'Could you give me a drink?'

Marin grabbed a can of beer from the fridge and took one for himself. I noted neither Florin nor Marin asked me if I wanted a drink.

Florin sipped from his can and went on. 'Remy took the news pretty badly. She got very angry and bolted. I guess she sent that text to you, just to get the frustration off her chest. Otherwise, what reasons would she have to be so rude to you?'

I had a distinct feeling Florin knew very well why his wife had been so angry and rude to me. He spoke in a very clever way to make me understand he knew, but keep Marin out of it. He probably feared that Marin would take me apart, if he became aware of my betrayal.

Now I had a pretty good idea of what had happened on Sunday night. Frustrated that I hadn't turned up at her villa, Remy couldn't stand the tension any longer and drove to the farm to find out what was going on. Finding Florin alive, she assumed I'd chickened out and given up without trying to kill him. No wonder she was disgusted with me. Her text message was unequivocal.

If her intention was to hurt me, she'd definitely succeeded. At the same time, I was glad that I'd failed. I'd nearly done one of the most horrific things one can think of: kill my best friend to steal his woman.

Another thought struck me in a flash. If that insulting text message had been sent by Remy, it meant that *it was Remy who'd arranged my encounter with Kate.* The text I'd received back in May to go to Dowes and meet Kate had been sent from the same number.

It meant, were it not for Remy, I wouldn't have met Kate and wouldn't be in this mess right now. But there was something which didn't add up. At the time when I'd come across Kate, Remy and I hadn't met.

Trying to work it out, I remained silent, looking down for several minutes. Florin and Marin were also silent. Except for the whirr of the fridge, the whole cabin was quiet. I thought again of the place where nothing ever happened. And yet so much had happened.

I wasn't what you'd call a sensitive person, but I was receptive to atmosphere. Glancing towards Florin, I felt he was hostile. He wanted me to leave.

As for Marin, his remorseful mood had changed. He didn't look apologetic anymore. I thought he looked a bit confused and perhaps suspicious.

I was tired and didn't feel too well. The fact that I'd fainted a few hours before worried me. The fact that Florin most certainly knew I'd tried to get rid of him, made me feel terribly low.

And Remy's snub had come on top of everything else. Like Helen, Rhonda and Katarina, the woman who'd caused all this mess had deserted me.

I was alone, out in the cold.

I was craving for a beer but didn't have the guts to ask for one.

Feeling my request would be denied, I chose to spare myself the humiliation. It was time for me to go.

I stood on my feet, a little unsteadily. I glanced at Florin.

He looked me straight in the eyes. His eyes were sad.

I couldn't stand his stare.

'I'd better leave you two,' I said, weakly.

Neither Florin nor Marin said anything.

'I'll see you sometime,' I murmured and shuffled my way out.

I knew in my mind I'd never have the guts to face Florin again.

As neither Florin nor Marin had offered me a lift, I walked back to the front gate, alone.. The nippy air did me good physically, but not otherwise. I had no idea what to do and where to go. Still, I thought I was lucky I had a car, albeit a stolen car. I was aware the police could arrest me at any time if they stopped me for whatever reason. I was driving without a licence and had stolen a motor vehicle. As well as being an illegal immigrant.

I didn't really care. At least, if they arrested me, I'd have some place to sleep. A bed in a cell was better than in the car. The men in blue left me alone. I ended up sleeping in the car again; that if you could call it sleep.

21

Thursday, 30 June

In the morning, I followed the same routine as the day before. I had some breakfast at McDonald's and made use of their facilities. I then bought a newspaper and read it in the park. There was no mention of Rhonda's stolen car but I did find some interesting news.

A small article talked about Kate's husband, Luigi Maslini being under investigation by the Crime Commission. The columnist said that the object of the Commission's investigation was Luigi's fortune, including a two-million-dollar mansion in Concord West and a luxury boat, which were allegedly acquired with proceeds from organised crime. Those allegations didn't surprise me. I always found it odd that a couple with no children lived in such a huge house.

Sitting on the bench, feeling as down and as low as never before in my life, I asked myself which of the current misfortunes I had experienced lately upset me the most. Was it the fact that I didn't have a job nor a place to stay any longer? That I'd lost all my savings: seventy-seven grand of it and I didn't have any foreseeable prospect to make any money? Was it the fact that I'd been ditched by both Rhonda and Katarina? Was my gloomy mood due to the guilt I felt because I'd attempted to murder my best friend? Was my depression caused by his knowledge that I'd betrayed his trust? Or … perhaps, I just regretted that I had failed. Had I succeeded, I'd be with Remy now.

I didn't know the answer and it annoyed me. I certainly knew I was missing Remy. Where could I find her? A sudden thought hit me. Why not look for her at her villa?

Filled with excitement, I strode to my car and drove towards Glenmore Park. Though all indications were that Remy had ditched me for good, I wanted to believe it wasn't true.

She must love me more than she treasured all that heap of money, I tried to convince myself. She'd told me I was special to her and she'd certainly shown her feelings for me, time and time again. I mean, in intimacy. How could she possibly be so passionate if not because she loved me? Sure, with the failed attempt on Florin's life and a divorce now imminent, we could certainly kiss the three hundred million good bye, but we still had each other.

That was the most important thing when two people loved each other, I reassured myself. That fortune would certainly have helped, but we had to go on with our lives and look for other opportunities together.

Mixed feelings were going through my heart when I reached Remy's villa, shortly after eleven in the morning. Excitement at the prospect of seeing her, frustration of not knowing what was going on, fear she wouldn't be there, or she'd give me the cold shoulder, if she was there.

I pulled up near the kerb, noting another car was parked on the driveway. It was a small, newish Toyota Corolla. Though I hadn't seen that car before, I felt another surge of excitement. Perhaps, like I did when I needed money, Remy had exchanged her luxury Audi for a cheaper model and pocketed the difference, I thought.

As I got out of the car and moved on the pathway, my morale got an unexpected boost. A bloke next door, whom I hadn't seen, yelled to me from the front of his garage. 'With that gorgeous dame waiting for you, I wish we could exchange places, mate.'

His words could only mean one thing: Remy was in the villa, probably waiting for me. I turned to the bloke, my heart pounding in my ribs.

He was probably in his early fifties, red in the face, bulky with a sagging belly.

'Thanks for the complement, but I don't know about exchanging places with you,' I said.

He chuckled and winked at me. 'I don't blame you mate. I wouldn't either.'

I nodded and walked onto the patio to the front door. My heart rate went up to well above a hundred per minute. I knocked on the door and I listened intently. I heard after several seconds footsteps which sounded like those of a woman wearing high heels.

Clearly, Remy was there. Her love for me must be genuine, I thought. In spite of my failure to execute her plan, she was still waiting for me. Sure she loved me. I saw, for a few seconds, a happy ending to our love story. Remy must have come to her senses and probably regretted her idea of killing her husband. She must have realised that true love was above money and material things. Love was all that mattered and with passion on our side, we would make it.

The footsteps stopped at the door. I perceived through the glass a woman's silhouette. I felt the emotion overcoming me. A positive emotion, not like the one I'd experienced when I locked Florin in the cold-room. I wanted the moment to last for ages: Remy and me, one metre apart, on either side of only a petty material object.

The moment only lasted a few seconds. The door opened. The first thing that hit me was the scent of a woman's perfume. Then, the silhouette materialised.

The woman gaping at me from the doorsill was as stunningly attractive as I'd expected, but she was blonde. Solveig Anderson.

Solveig kept gaping at me, obviously surprised; probably as staggered as I was at seeing her. Wearing a tight, short green dress, nicely moulded on her hips, she looked as sexy as Claudia Schiffer on the catwalk. I noticed though, she seemed far from happy. Her mouth was tight and the dark rings under her eyes were very visible.

'What are you doing here?' she asked.

I remained dumb for a few seconds, then I retorted, 'What are *you* doing here?'

'I happen to own this house,' she replied. 'Or, rather a share of it.'

After more dumb seconds, things began to make some sense. 'Ah …'

'You seem disappointed to see me,' she said.

Indeed, I was disappointed and my face must have shown it. 'I was expecting to see … someone else,' I muttered.

She paused, frowning and then nodded. 'I think I understand.'

'But since you're here, I want my fifty grand back,' I said, taking a gamble.

I wasn't sure if the money which Remy had transferred from my account had gone to *this* Solveig, but my gamble paid off.

Solveig paused again and waved at me. 'Come in.'

I stepped inside and followed her into the living room.

She lit a cigarette and sat on a sofa. I pulled up a chair and sat in front of her on the other side of a coffee table. I noted a sheet of paper on the table. I picked it up and perused it. It was a list of clothing garments, some household appliances and other miscellaneous things; like an inventory. Some items had a tick against them, others didn't.

'What's this?' I asked.

'I'm packing my things. I have to vacate the place.'

I shrugged, read my watch and announced. 'I haven't got a lot of time. But I won't leave until you give me my money back.'

'So, that fifty grand came from you,' Solveig said, more to herself.

'And I want it back,' I reinforced my demand.

She shook her head. 'You're such a sucker. Like any other bloke who fell for Remy's charms. I sometimes wonder what sort of gear she's got to make such an impact on men.'

Though impatient to get my money and leave, Solveig's comments about Remy made me curious. 'So, you two know each other,' I stated the obvious.

She grunted and walked to a liquor cabinet. 'You want a drink?'

I shook my head.

She returned and sat on the couch with a large glass half-full with some sort of liquor. She took a large swig from the glass and rolled her eyes in a dramatic manner. 'I'll tell you a little story.'

'I'd rather have my fifty grand back,' I reminded her.

Solveig shrugged. 'I didn't know that money came from you.'

'You know now. So, give it back to me,' I said.

She smiled bitterly. 'I wish I still had the fifty grand, but I don't.'

'What do you mean you don't? The money was only transferred to you last Friday. You couldn't have possibly spent fifty grand in a few days.'

She nodded. 'I didn't spend it as such. I gave it to … someone.'

I was already angry. 'Don't tell me crap. I don't believe a word you're saying.'

She stood up and arranged her dress. 'Come with me,' she said and walked towards the bedroom area.

Maybe she wanted to mellow me with a sexual proposition. 'I won't take the bait,' I raised my voice. 'I want my money back, and I won't settle for anything less than that.'

She kept walking and I followed her. We entered a small bedroom made into an office where a computer was on. Without sitting, she brought an internet banking screen up, did some typing and beckoned to me. 'Come here, have a look.'

I read the screen. It showed a banking transaction effected on Sunday. A fifty-thousand transfer from Solveig Anderson into another bank account, with the description 'From Solveig with Love'. The name of the payee made me see red before my eyes. It said Diego Morales.

'You believe me now?' Solveig asked.

I had to make a strong effort of will not to strangle her. I turned around and walked through the living room towards the exit without saying anything. I was about to explode.

'Hey, wait a minute,' Solveig shouted, while trailing me.

I stopped and turned, facing her, trying hard to control my temper.

She halted too. 'She's such a work of art, isn't she?' Solveig went on, with fire in her eyes.

I twisted my mouth, not finding my words. 'Why are you saying *she's* such a work of art? *You* paid the money to that jerk, not her.'

Solveig pursed her lips and remained silent. I looked at her and I could see she was about to have a nervous breakdown. She was suddenly very pale and tears were forming in her eyes. 'You're right. I gave the money to Diego, but Remy tricked me into doing it,' she whispered.

'She must have pulled quite a fast one to make you part with fifty grand at the snap of her fingers,' I said sarcastically.

Solveig nodded. 'She did. She's very good at that.'

I sighed loudly, just able to control my fury. 'So, what's your proposition now? You'd like us to hold hands and weep together?'

She wiped her tears with the back of her hand. 'Let's go for a drive. I'll take you to a place of interest. And I'll tell you a little story on the way.'

My first impulse was to tell her to go to hell, but I changed my mind. She wouldn't have gone to hell anyway and I was curious to hear what she had to say.

'You know, there is a very fine line between love and hatred,' Solveig began while driving Rhonda's BMW towards the M4 motorway.

She offered to drive and I'd protested at first, pointing out she'd been drinking. She'd then said she was okay and I let her drive. I thought if the police stopped us for whatever reason, *she* might be the one to get into trouble, not me. Soon though, I was sorry I'd let her drive, for I noticed she was trembling slightly.

'So, you're in love with Diego,' I said.

She paused, and tears began to roll down her cheeks. I handed her a tissue and she wiped her tears away. I felt pretty rotten myself. If there is one thing that melts my temper down, that's seeing a woman crying.

'I've told you the story of Kate's life,' Solveig continued. 'Everything I said to you is true, but I only told you half of the story ...'

'But what's this to do with Remy and my fifty grand?' I interrupted.

'It has. Just listen,' Solveig assured me. 'I told you that Kate and I were like sisters, since we were very little. I spent a lot of time at her place and, like most of the other girls at that age, I had a crush on her brother as early as I can remember. He was five years older and looked so ... adorable.'

'He won't look so adorable when I smash his face,' I said.

Solveig let that go. 'Not long before I turned thirteen, something terrible happened.'

She paused and tears formed in her eyes again. We had already entered the motorway, and with Solveig driving in such a messy state of mind, I was worried about our safety.

'Please take it easy,' I said gently.

She nodded. 'One day, Kate, who was a few months younger than me, told me Diego had raped her.'

The hairs on my back prickled. 'For God's sake, but he's her brother!'

Solveig nodded again. 'That's what I said to her at first. But, though feeling ashamed and guilty, Kate went on with it. I was sickened at first, but then, I got used to the idea.'

'You mean ... he continued to rape her?'

Solveig shook her head. 'It wasn't rape any longer. It was consensual sex.'

'That's … unbelievable,' I murmured.

'And it gets worse,' Solveig continued. 'As Kate kept confiding in me, I began to feel jealous. I wanted that to happen to me as well. And I told Kate of my fantasy. As Kate and I were sharing everything, she told her brother of my desire. So, Diego did it to me as well. It happened on the day when I turned thirteen. It was his birthday present for me, he said.'

'When you turned thirteen?' I asked, not believing my ears.

'That's right. And of course, he kept doing it to me. And in return, I gave him more than Kate could ever have done. I fell in love with him. By the time I was fourteen, I wanted him for me only and I told him so. I was exuberant when he stopped sleeping with Kate, though I learned later that he'd done it rather from boredom, not because I'd asked him to do so. I also learned later that sometimes, when he came home late and drunk, he still visited Kate in her bedroom. That went on until Kate had a crush on another boy, when she was fifteen. Then, I believed that Diego was mine and mine only, at last.'

'Which wasn't the case,' I broke in.

'Of course it wasn't the case. With his looks, girls and women of all ages kept throwing themselves at him in droves, willing to fulfil his most perverse sexual needs. He sure made the most of it …'

'Slow down,' I said, spotting a marked police car in the side window. 'There is a police car less than a hundred metres behind.'

She braked, but too suddenly. The car behind nearly bumped into us. Luckily and probably aware of the police car, they didn't make a lot of fuss.

'Sorry,' Solveig said and went on. 'As the years went by, our encounters became more and more casual. I began to see other guys, but never ceased to adore the man who'd made me a woman.

And it so happened that our affair began to flourish again nearly ten years after it had begun. By then, Diego was already deep into trouble over his gambling debts.'

We were now passing the Minchinbury housing estate on one side and Rooty Hill on the other.

'So, he needed money, that's why he was willing to give it another go,' I took a guess.

'Exactly,' Solveig confirmed and continued. 'But his renewed attention to me made me so happy. When Diego gave me the second chance, both Kate and I were about to complete a degree in medicine. Kate was already working at her father's surgery, but Diego had different ideas. One night, he came home drunk and raped Kate once more. He excused himself afterwards saying he'd only done it because he had to assess if she was good enough for a top class escort. He'd just met a guy who ran an exclusive escorting agency for millionaires. Diego said he'd showed the guy a photo of Kate and he was interested. So Diego asked his sister to take an escort job to help him pay off his debts.'

'Which I know she did,' I jumped in. 'It was in the news.'

The police car was now tailing us, which made me quite nervous. If Rhonda had reported her BMW missing, the police would certainly pull us over.

'Kate would have none of it, in the beginning,' Solveig went on. 'She took a part-time job at Dowes instead, but Diego wasn't happy with that sort of money. He threatened Kate he'd tell their father of the incest, if she didn't give in to his demands. Kate still refused and Diego told their father, Doctor Morales, the story.'

'Now, I understand why the doctor was so depressed and apathetic when I saw him,' I said, half-listening, while watching the marked police car in the side window.

'He began drinking very heavily and lost interest in everything after he learned of the incest. He became just a shadow of what he used to be,' Solveig continued, with her hands tight on the steering wheel.

'But once this Diego mongrel kept his promise and told Doctor Morales the grim story, he'd used his trump card already,' I remarked. 'What persuaded Kate to still take that escort job?'

Solveig smiled bitterly. 'You don't know Diego. He's very cunning. He threatened his father that if Kate didn't do what he'd asked her to do, he'd take the story to the media.'

'But he'd have certainly gone to jail for paedophilia, if he did.'

As we passed Toongabbie, the police car changed lanes and overtook us. Lucky; or perhaps Rhonda had not reported her car missing yet.

'That's right,' Solveig continued, 'but Diego said he didn't care if he went to jail. And Doctor Morales knew his son was capable of anything. So, with his heart broken, he begged his daughter to keep that very sordid story private. That's why she took that job, which paid a lot of money.'

'What sort of money?' I asked.

'Five grand an hour,' Solveig said.

I whistled admiringly. 'That must certainly be a *very* exclusive agency.'

'It is for millionaires only and even for billionaires. Anyway, a couple of weeks after Kate took the job, Diego asked me to join her. To cut a long story short, I did.'

She left me with my mouth open. 'You and Kate worked together?'

Solveig nodded. 'Sometimes we did a trio act with an old fart, or a foursome and made a little fortune in one night.

The very candid manner in which Solveig talked about her job as a call girl amazed me. At the same time, a soothing thought crossed my mind. With her looks, Remy would be the cream of the crop as an escort, but she had enough decency not to get involved in that sort of racket.

'And how much of the money was yours? I mean, how much did the agency take?' I asked.

'It was generally fifty-fifty, unless we negotiated some other percentage in advance.'

'And all that money went to Diego?'

'Most of it,' Solveig said. 'But it was never enough for him. That's why, being in debt to a poker syndicate, the Morales agreed to marry Kate with Luigi. It happened two years ago. I've told you that part of the story already.'

'You did. But sure, once Kate was married, she had to give up that job,' I remarked.

'Not completely,' Solveig said. 'As I've told you before, her marriage proved to be a disaster from the very beginning. And Luigi spent a lot of time on the road, driving from Sydney to Perth and back. So Kate had plenty of time on her hands.'

Recalling my encounter with Kate and how sweet and delicate she looked and behaved, I had difficulty comprehending Solveig's story. And how about Solveig herself! It's true she looked a top fashion model, but I wouldn't have guessed she was in the escorting business.

I even recalled fantasising about a trio act with Kate and Solveig at the time, not having any idea they were actually doing it. Well, you never know with women. But now, my utmost concern was Remy. And Solveig's story had made no mention of her.

We were now nearing the exit from the motorway to North Strathfield.

'Where are we going?' I asked.

'To meet Diego,' Solveig replied calmly.

Her words sparked another bout of anger in me. 'Meet Diego? Where?'

'In Ashfield. I'll give them a call a little later.'

'Give them a call? What do you mean give *them* a call?'

'Just be patient. It will all be revealed. Very soon.'

'How about Remy?' I asked. 'You've told me quite an extraordinary story, but where does she come into this?'

Solveig sneered. 'I bet you won't like this part of the story.'

'Maybe I won't, but tell me anyway,' I said.

We exited the motorway and turned into Parramatta Road.

'Kate and I met Remy when we started at that … establishment and we befriended her.'

Solveig's statement horrified me. 'You mean … you mean Remy was an escort as well?'

Solveig grinned. 'Did you think she was the Virgin Mary? With her exotic looks, she was actually the most expensive one.'

She left me bewildered. 'You're positive?'

'As positive as I am that my name is Solveig Anderson.'

I did some calculations in my mind. 'But … that would have been 2007. Remy was already married in 2007.'

Solveig nodded. 'So she was, but she whinged that her husband was weird and very stingy.'

Those details were correct, so it must be true, I thought. I felt gutted.

'Kate and I became so close to Remy that we bought a house together,' Solveig carried on. 'Though a big chunk of Kate's and my money went to Diego, we managed to put a little aside, but not enough to buy a house on our own. So we purchased it together with Remy, as tenants in common. That house brought me a lot of bad luck. Things were going so well between Diego and me, until one day, I took him to see the house. It so happened that Remy was there. Once Diego set his eyes on her … you can imagine the rest from your own experience.'

Indeed, it wasn't hard to imagine, I reflected bitterly.

'Making use of her talents, she had Diego tamed in no time. Cunning as she was, she played the hard-to-catch game until she drove him absolutely insane. Being used to all women chasing him, he found himself in an unprecedented situation, where *he* was obsessed with Remy, begging her to go to bed with him. I just couldn't believe my eyes seeing Diego getting mad when Remy flirted with another guy at a party. Since hooking up with Remy, he became a totally different man from what he'd always been. She played it very smartly and got him wrapped around her little finger. Now, Diego does whatever Remy wants him to do. It's just incredible.'

'I don't think I want to listen anymore,' I said utterly deflated.

Paying no attention to me, Solveig continued. 'Once she became aware of Diego's financial troubles, Remy came up with a very bold idea. Knowing that the Morales had sold Kate to Luigi, she suggested that Kate could be sold again. To a billionaire.'

'Sell Kate to a billionaire?' I repeated dumbly.

'Like in the movies,' Solveig added. 'No one knows the full details, but there is a strong suggestion that a mining tycoon in Perth, known only as Don, was involved. His people had contacts with the poker syndicate to which Luigi was a member. There is anecdotal evidence that one day, this Don happened to see Kate and was mesmerised by her. Somehow, Remy became aware of his obsession with Kate and took the chance, when the opportunity arose. She is that sort of woman.'

I was beginning to see that.

'She told Diego of her idea and he jumped at it. One night,

Diego, with whom I was still desperately in love, agreed to see me. Being drunk and careless, he told me of his plan. So I became part of it. You understand now?' Solveig asked.

I shook my head. I didn't understand and I was worried by Solveig's driving. In Strathfield, on Parramatta Road the traffic was chaotic.

Solveig sighed, stuck in traffic. 'It was Remy, Diego and I who organised Kate's kidnapping and her delivery to Western Australia.'

I found that unbelievable. 'Like in the movies. How did you do it?'

Solveig grinned. 'It was sort of funny. Diego, who despised his brother-in-law, had befriended an associate of Luigi named Alberto, who *also* had a grudge against Luigi. So Diego told Alberto of his plan to trade his sister knowing that Alberto had close connections with a group of billionaires, one of which was Don. Alberto, who hadn't seen Kate, went to Dowes that very day when you and Kate met. He wanted to see Kate face to face, to make sure she was worth all the risk involved with the potential kidnapping. That's where you came inadvertently into play and nearly spoiled the whole thing.'

Solveig's revelations continued to bewilder me.

'I had received a text message saying to go to Dowes and meet Kate,' I explained. I purposely didn't tell Solveig I knew who'd sent that text.

'That's right. It was part of the plan. We needed a scapegoat. And Remy concocted a scheme to line up an obvious suspect for Kate's disappearance. She said she knew of a handsome, macho-man friend of her husband, whom she was positive Kate would fancy. This guy also happened to be a womaniser, so all we needed to do was arrange an *accidental* encounter between Kate and him. Unfortunately, it so happened that both you and Alberto turned up to Dowes at the same time. Though it was essential to the plan that you and Kate were to meet, the timing you turned up at Dowes couldn't have been any worse. Anyway, it worked out in the end. Remy had taken a gamble and it worked. You know the rest very well.'

'I do, but how do you know what happened at Dowes that day?'

'I was there,' she clarified.

'I didn't see you,' I said.

'You didn't because you were too preoccupied with Kate,' Solveig explained.

I was perplexed. So, the fatso whom I'd nearly punched for making trouble to Kate was this Alberto that Solveig was talking about.

I also recalled hearing a man's voice answering his mobile and announcing he was Alberto Gazzara when I was hiding in Luigi's mansion. I knew then that I'd heard that voice before but couldn't remember where. Now, it made sense.

I remained silent for several minutes, reflecting. Solveig was quiet too, apparently absorbed in her own thoughts. I felt sorry for her.

We were moving along towards Ashfield at a snail's pace.

The winter sun was shining softly.

'So, this Alberto double crossed his business associate and kidnapped his wife,' I repeated in a loud voice what was going on in my mind.

Solveig nodded. 'Not only that. The billionaire client whom Diego thinks is Don, worried of the publicity Kate's disappearance was making in the media, postponed paying the agreed price. He said he'd pay up once the dust had settled, which didn't eventuate.'

'How much was he supposed to pay?' I inquired.

'Ten million, which was to be split between Alberto and Diego.'

'Wow! And how about you and Remy?'

'Remy, as the architect of the scheme, was pledged one million from Diego's share. As for me, as I only had an auxiliary role, Diego reluctantly promised to pay me one hundred thousand.'

'And I was the sucker in the middle,' I said, more to myself.

'I'm sorry,' Solveig apologised. 'If I knew then what I know now, things would have been different. But I was hooked at the time and I was capable of doing anything to please Diego.'

Thinking about that day when I ran away fearing the police would arrest me, I recalled they said on the news that a man had contacted the police about Kate, which had puzzled me at the time, as I assumed the police informer had been Katarina. Subsequently, an anonymous woman had given my description to the police.

Now, wondering if Solveig knew anything about it, I asked her. 'At the time when Kate vanished, they said on the news that a man and then a woman, who wished to remain anonymous, had contacted the police with information about the alleged kidnapper, assumed to be me. You know anything about that?'

'Sure I do,' Solveig replied candidly. 'The man was Diego and the woman was me. We had to do something to give the police a hint and put them on the wrong track. You were the obvious suspect anyway. We only emphasised the facts.'

I shook my head once more. The story was incredible.

'So, the money from that billionaire never arrived?' I asked.

'We still held high hopes, but not after Kate was found. It was apparently a private eye who did a lot of work in the background and gave the police the clue. I have no idea who put him on the job and why he came into the play,' Solveig stated.

I had a pretty good idea who paid him and why, but I kept it to myself. I only thanked Rhonda in my mind for doing that for me. I certainly didn't deserve that favour. At the same time, I had difficulty absorbing such extraordinary information. There were still things I didn't know, or couldn't follow, so I kept asking Solveig more questions.

'How exactly was Kate kidnapped and from where?'

She paused and frowned. 'I'm sorry I did that to you and I'm more sorry for Kate. You two were tailed that afternoon when you hooked up. Alberto and another guy waited for many hours by your flat, while you and Kate were having fun inside. When she left to begin her shift at that joint in Liverpool, they grabbed her from behind and stuck a handkerchief drenched with anaesthetic to her nose. They pushed her into a car and … the rest was easy.'

I should have followed Kate downstairs, I thought. It would have saved a heap of trouble, but too late now. 'And I became the main suspect,' I said.

Solveig shrugged. 'You'd been the last person who saw Kate before she vanished. It was normal that you were the likely perpetrator.'

If not for Rhonda, I'd probably be awaiting trial for kidnapping and possibly murder right now, I reflected. It was ironic that Rhonda had fought so hard those homicide allegations and I subsequently confessed to her of another murder. Though that confession had proved unfounded afterwards, I still wondered if I was guilty or not. Even if not guilty at law, I knew very well that no one in this world could ever acquit me as far as my own conscience was concerned.

I felt a sudden impulse to tell Solveig that I *was* actually guilty, but I refrained in time. *She* was the one confessing, not me. And there was one more piece of information that I had to find out from Solveig. Not that it mattered anymore, but just to set the record straight.

'You've told me then Kate had a lover,' I reminded her. 'Was it true?'

'Sorry,' Solveig apologised. 'Kate didn't have a lover. But you were quite worked up at the time, so I had to discourage you from trying to find Kate, just in case you uncovered something.'

It wasn't you who put Kate out of my mind, I reflected. It was Remy.

We were approaching Croydon, the suburb before Ashfield, where Solveig had said we were to meet Diego. A knot was slowly forming in my stomach.

'You said we'd meet Diego this afternoon,' I reminded Solveig.

She nodded. 'Actually, I'd better not tell him in advance. He might not appreciate my call. It's going to be a surprise.'

The day has been full of surprises already. But I was not any closer to getting my money back. 'You still haven't told me why you gave my money to Diego,' I prompted Solveig.

Solveig sighed. 'He needed the money for a business proposition.'

We were now queuing to turn right from Parramatta Road onto Frederick Street, in the heart of Ashfield. 'And why did Remy pay fifty grand to you?' I insisted.

'She pulled a fast one. I was desperate to raise a hundred grand to help Diego purchase a business, so I told Remy I was considering selling my share of the villa. Knowing I'd do anything to please Diego, she offered to purchase my share but said the maximum she could afford to pay was fifty thousand. That was much less than what my share was worth, but we eventually agreed on fifty-five. She paid five grand in early June …'

'That was my money too,' I interrupted, recalling how Remy had persuaded me to spare seven grand, which she said she had to give to a councillor. So she lied to me, paid five grand to Solveig to exchange the sale contracts and pocketed the difference.

Solveig shrugged. 'I'm sorry again. I bet she said to you she needed that money for something else. Anyway, the contracts were ready to settle, which happened last Friday, when Remy paid the fifty grand. She knew very well that money would end up back in her pockets, via Diego.'

To me, something didn't add up and I told Solveig so. 'I can't understand why you gave Diego the money, when he'd ditched you for Remy.'

Solveig blinked her eyes and her mouth tightened. She was no longer helpless and namby-pamby. She seemed suddenly strong and determined. 'He'd told me he wanted me back. He said his affair with Remy had been just a fling and he regretted it. He'd realised I was his true love. But, of course, he needed money. He promised he'd paid his debts off and was planning to buy a business. I didn't believe him at first, but he showed me the papers. To his credit, and I must say, to Remy's credit, he seemed to have grown up, at last.'

Solveig turned left on a leafy side road off Frederick Street and pulled up in front of a small federation cottage. She switched off the engine and lit a cigarette. I noticed her hands were steady. It was close to one o'clock.

'What are we doing here?' I asked.

Solveig exhaled smoke out the driver's window. 'Just having a little break.'

We sat in silence for a couple of minutes; then I asked, 'What's next?'

She flicked her cigarette stub out the window and searched in her handbag. It was a very large handbag. She produced a small bottle of whisky and swallowed about half of its contents in one gulp – about one hundred millilitres of liquor.

'You won't be driving back,' I stated.

'No, I don't think I'll be driving back,' she agreed.

She put the bottle back in her handbag and fished out a cheque book. She started writing a cheque. 'Is it Toma with one M or two?' she asked.

'One M, like in Remy,' I replied.

Solveig grimaced and handed me the cheque.

I took the cheque and read it. It was drawn to Cornel Toma, for five thousand dollars.

I looked at her inquiringly.

'That's the least I can do for you. It's about all I have and I won't need it anymore.'

I folded the cheque and put it in my pocket, without thanking her. I'd only recovered a small percentage of the dough Solveig had got from me, via Remy. That's if the cheque wouldn't bounce.

As if reading my mind, Solveig assured me. 'I can guarantee you that the cheque will be honoured. Five grand is the minimum balance I must keep in my account.'

I still didn't thank her. 'So what sort of business is Diego buying?'

She scowled. 'His share in a partnership. He needed a hundred grand from me, but I could only raise fifty. So, he took the money first and told me off afterwards. He said fifty grand was useless to him and he didn't want to see me again.'

'That's nice of him,' I said. 'And what's this partnership about?'

'It's a brothel in Newtown.'

I wasn't surprised. It had to be something either illegal or sleazy. A brothel was both. 'And who's the other partner?'

'Remy Panait.'

22

Solveig lit another cigarette and sucked the smoke in. We both remained quiet for a few minutes. An old man exited from the small federation cottage. Seeing him, Solveig pulled the driver's window up. He walked passed us, peering curiously at Rhonda's luxury BMW. With the car's windows being tinted, he couldn't see us. He kept walking towards the main road.

There was no one else on the street. Solveig opened the window again, flicked out the cigarette butt and turned on the engine. She drove very slowly along the road. I was about to remind her she wasn't supposed to drive, when she stopped the car about two hundred metres east at the other end of the street.

She left the engine running, which annoyed me. I looked at her admonishingly. She didn't appear to notice. She seemed to be absorbed in her thoughts. I shrugged and remained quiet.

Except the smooth purr of the engine, there were no noises of any kind. A strange silence seemed to have suddenly enveloped the neighbourhood.

She read the time and turned off the engine. 'Let's go.'

'Go where?' I asked.

'To see Diego.'

I felt the knot in my stomach growing. And so was my anger.

We got out of the car and Solveig handed me the car key.

The day was glorious: sunny and warm for that time of the year. I'd noted the car's thermometer showing twenty-three degrees.

We walked back some sixty metres west and crossed the road.

'Here,' Solveig signalled, stopping in front of a large, two-storey federation house. 'Here I spent a good part of my childhood and my teenage years,' she said.

'Is that where you lived?' I asked.

She smiled bitterly. 'It's Doctor Morales's house. Here Kate and I played when we were little girls and shared our thoughts and our dreams …'

So how did you have the audacity to arrange your best friend's kidnapping? I was tempted to ask, but I refrained. Coming from me, it would have been like Satan reproving sin. I'd done worse than that. She'd done it for a man; I'd done it for a woman. We were both in the same boat.

'Here I first fell in love and I became a woman …' she whispered dreamily and moved on.

The metal gate at the front was wide open. We strolled on the paved pathway to the main entry and read a similar metal plaque with the one I'd seen at the doctor's surgery in the city. It said Doctor Juan Morales lived there and it listed his qualifications. The only difference was that Kate's name wasn't on the plaque.

I had a close look at the house. Its shabby appearance suggested that a facelift was long overdue. I noted the whole joint needed quite a bit of maintenance work. There were large cracks on the walls, the gutters had leaked, the paint on the wooden windows and doors had peeled off and the lawn hadn't been cut in weeks.

Solveig walked around the house into the backyard and I followed her. I turned after a few metres and looked back at the house. I was pretty sure I saw a curtain moving in a room upstairs. I shrugged and followed Solveig.

She halted some thirty metres further in front of a smaller one-storey dwelling, the size of an average two-bedroom villa. I assumed it was the granny flat that Doctor Morales had mentioned to me. It looked newer than the house in front, but also in need of maintenance work.

So I was about to meet Diego Morales. I'd been waiting for this moment.

I wasn't sure what I was going to do. I only knew I despised him. The rest would come as a matter of course, I reflected.

Solveig stepped to the front door and beckoned to me. 'Stay behind and leave the talking to me. Don't do anything until I give you the signal. And don't do anything stupid.'

I nodded. 'Would this Diego baby be home?'

'He usually sleeps until two in the afternoon,' Solveig replied. She rapped on the door.

I waited about a metre behind, on her left.

Some twenty seconds passed. I heard footsteps inside, approaching the door.

'Who's there?' a male voice asked aggressively.

Solveig nodded to me. She probably meant to confirm that the guy who'd just spoken was Diego. 'It's me. Please open,' she said.

I heard a key being turned in the lock. The door opened slightly.

'What the fuck you want?' Diego demanded.

'Please let me in,' Solveig begged him.

'I've told you to leave me alone, haven't I? I'm busy,' he said.

'I got the other fifty grand for you,' Solveig announced.

There was a pause; then the door opened wide.

A tall, dark guy appeared in the doorway. 'Come in,' he said, softly this time.

I stepped to the right and had a good look at him.

He was about six-foot-one tall, dark with a round, tough-looking face: piercing, brown eyes, a high forehead and straight nose. I had expected him to be more handsome, but maybe he looked better than I perceived. Perhaps I was biased.

He looked quite a bit like Elvis in his youth and maybe that's what made women drop their pants at the sight of him. Unlike Elvis, there was something wild and brutish about him.

His eyes narrowed and flickered with anger when he saw me. 'Who's he?' he barked.

I was tempted to offer him my hand and give him a smack on the mouth when he stretched his, but I'd promised Solveig I'd be good and wait for her signal before taking any action.

I noted he was very well stacked and looked the sort of bloke who'd enjoy picking a fight, rather than back off from it.

Dressed in a white T-shirt and shorts, he showed broad shoulders, big arms and a well-developed chest. His legs, like his neck, were very thick. I guessed he spent quite a bit of time in the weights room, though I wondered when if he slept until two in the afternoon. Still, that day, at just after one o'clock, he was up and seemed alert.

'Let us in and I'll explain,' Solveig said.

'Who's he?' Diego repeated his question.

'You want the money, or not?' Solveig retorted.

He moved a little aside and let us in.

We entered a small reception room smelling of tobacco and furnished with a sofa, three armchairs, a liquor cabinet and a coffee table. There were four glasses on the table and a bottle of Metaxa, nearly empty. There was also a packet of cigarettes and an ashtray full of stubs. I peered at the ashtray and noted traces of lipstick on some of the stubs.

Diego pulled the curtain aside to one of the two windows in the room. He then glanced angrily at me and asked Solveig. 'Got the dough?'

She took her time lighting a cigarette and exhaling the smoke towards him. 'I thought you wanted to know who he is,' she reminded Diego.

He shifted his eyes to me, studied me for a few seconds and asked. 'What's your story, dummy?'

I didn't say anything. In a surprising way, I was now very calm. I didn't fear him, nor did I feel like smashing him. He was indifferent to me. Maybe because I'd expected Diego to be a semi-god – which he clearly wasn't. I felt I had the upper hand on him and I was somewhat disappointed.

'Is he a deaf-mute or something?' Diego asked.

'You'd be amazed to learn what he is, or rather *who* he is,' Solveig said.

Diego looked like he was losing patience. I saw his cheeks getting reddish and a vein pulsating on his temple. 'Spill it,' he barked.

The three of us were all standing around the coffee table and the atmosphere was getting tense. I heard a curtain rustling and felt a gush of fresh air flowing in the room.

'Want to take a guess?' Solveig asked.

Diego frowned and blinked his eyes. He then sneered with apparent contempt. 'Got yourself a lover already?'

Solveig returned his contemptuous smirk. 'Not me. He's Remy's lover.'

My eyebrows flew up. I was perplexed by that. And I wasn't the only one.

The change in Diego's facial expression was dramatic. The leer on his face froze, replaced gradually by doubt, astonishment and shock. 'Are you crazy?' he demanded, in a hoarse voice.

'You're the crazy one, if you believed Remy wasn't sleeping around,' Solveig riposted.

I saw the colour draining from Diego's face. He sat on the sofa very slowly and whispered, 'It's not true. You're making it up.'

'You're trying to delude yourself,' Solveig retorted. 'What do you think Cornel is doing here? He can't wait to take Remy back to his place.'

By then, I understood Solveig's game and decided to go along with it. I found the idea of giving Diego a hard time appealing.

Diego gazed at me. 'What are you doing here?'

'Where is Remy?' I asked. 'It's not the first time she's been naughty , but this time I'm going to smack her bottom very hard.'

He looked at me incredulously; then shouted towards the bedrooms. 'Remy!'

A surge of excitement went through me. So, Remy was there. That's why Solveig had said *I'll give them a call* on our way here. She'd always known Remy was at Diego's bungalow.

Looking bewildered, Diego lit a cigarette and sucked on it. He stared at the floor for several seconds; then shouted again, much louder, this time. 'Remy!'

More seconds passed; then I heard a door being opened and footsteps coming from the hallway. With only a short, red chemise on, Remy appeared in the room. Like always, the sensuality coming from her was overpowering.

Half asleep, she could hardly keep her eyes open. 'What's going on?' she murmured.

With rage showing clearly on his face, Diego asked. 'Who's he?'

She blinked her eyes and peered at me. It took her a few seconds to realise who I was. 'What are you doing here?' she demanded, suddenly alert and clearly displeased.

'So, it's true,' Diego exploded. 'He's your lover, isn't he?'

She paused, apparently trying to comprehend what was going on. 'It's a set-up,' she finally said. 'This whore is setting me up, so that she can take you back from me.'

'You can keep him,' Solveig replied. 'I've had enough of him. I only thought it's fair enough that he knew what you've been up to.'

'You're jealous,' Remy bellowed. 'You're jealous because I'm better than you. That's why you've staged this nonsense. You hope Diego will ditch me, but he won't.'

She gazed at him inquiringly, but he avoided her stare. The seed of distrust was definitely planted in his mind.

'Where do you know him from?' Diego demanded.

Remy hesitated. 'He's a friend of my husband. I mean my ex.'

'The one you lined up as the scapegoat, when we snatched Kate?'

I thought I saw from the corner of my eye a shadow moving about the opened window. It only lasted a split second, but gave me a creepy feeling.

'That's right,' Remy was quick to confirm. 'He never had a clue. He's always been a sucker.'

'So, what's he doing here?' Diego demanded.

Remy shrugged. 'Ask the blonde whore.'

'As opposed to the brunette one,' I butted in.

I saw Diego's face redden. 'So, you're not a deaf-mute after all ...'

He studied me again. He then stood up and stepped towards

me, very slowly. 'You're pretty good with your mouth. Let's see how good you are otherwise.'

My recent indifference towards him turned quickly into anger. I waited for him to make a move, prepared to give him a hiding to remember for the rest of his life.

When he was about a metre from me, the front door creaked. We all looked at the door. It opened very slowly.

Wearing a white blouse and a pair of brown slacks, Kate Morales walked in.

She looked tired and a little older. Besides that, she was as lovely as when we'd met at Dowes that afternoon of May. Her hair had grown a little longer and her dark-blue eyes were inquisitive. I noted a very large, beige handbag on her shoulder. It was identical to Solveig's.

She gazed at me and managed a shy smile. 'Long time no see.'

I nodded but, with the emotion overcoming me, I had difficulty in speaking. She was as loveable and fetching as I remembered her.

Kate glanced at Solveig and nodded slightly. She then shifted her eyes to Diego.

'When did you come back home?' he asked.

'This morning. I thought it was time to see you,' Kate said.

'I'm so glad to see you back,' Remy declared, with a wide smile on her face. She then frowned and said to Solveig. 'I think you two should leave now.'

'No, I'd rather have them stay,' Kate said. 'It's time Diego and I have a chat and I want them to hear what I've got to say.'

'But … this should be in the family,' Remy protested.

'Are you family?' Kate asked.

'Well … Diego and I are getting engaged.'

Kate smiled enigmatically. 'I don't think so.'

Diego, his fury apparently gone, was fidgeting uneasily. 'I don't know what you mean.'

'You'll know very soon,' Kate replied. 'I'll be very quick and to the point.

She paused, as if to collect her thoughts, and went on. 'I've had, in the past few weeks, enough time on my hands to look back at my life. It may come as a surprise to some of you to hear that the only daughter of Doctor Juan Morales had been sexually abused from a very early age ...'

'Come on, don't be so dramatic,' Diego interrupted.

'Abused by none other than her older brother,' Kate continued.

'Come on, who can believe this crap?' he interrupted again.

'Solveig can testify,' Kate went on. 'She knows it too well. She's also been raped by Diego from the very day she turned thirteen.'

We all looked at Solveig. She nodded.

'I went along with it for years and for the sake of my father. But there are limits to everything. When my own brother conspired with his new slut to have me abducted and traded like a piece of meat, it became too much. I'd been sold already and couldn't take it any longer.'

'That's nonsense,' Remy broke in. 'These are very serious allegations. How can you blame us for your own misfortunes?'

Kate looked at her with condescension. 'These are facts, not allegations.'

Remy's face had grown red. 'Can you prove anything of what you're saying?'

'Not in a court ... not yet,' Kate answered. 'But there will be no need for a court.'

I noted Remy and Diego warily exchanging glances.

'Thanks to my brother and his slut, I was sedated for a few

days after being abducted. The guys guarding me day and night played poker and talked. That's all they did. They thought I couldn't hear anything, but I did. I didn't understand a lot, but Remy's and Diego's names were mentioned time and time again. The context was unequivocal. My brother and his whore had arranged my abduction. There is no question about that.'

I stared at Solveig. She looked very calm, with a relaxed smile on her face. I'd had some doubts about her story before, but now I was certain she had told the truth.

I took turns watching Remy and Diego. Remy seemed defiant; Diego bewildered.

The five of us were standing around the table, tense and quiet, like we were waiting for a jury's decision.

The verdict was not to be made by a jury. It would be by one of us.

'Let's say, for the sake of the argument, that what you're alleging is true, which it is not,' Diego broke the silence. 'What is your point?'

Very calmly, Kate dropped her handbag on the coffee table and fished out a silver-coloured pistol. She aimed the gun at Diego and said, 'This is my point.'

Then, bang, bang, bang! Three shots hit Diego right in the middle of his chest.

He looked at his sister in horror.

A red spot suddenly appeared on his white T-shirt. It grew and spread out, like a giant spider stretching its legs.

He tried to say something, but it was too late. Instead of words, a stream of blood came from his mouth.

23

Friday, 1 July.

On Friday morning, I bought the newspapers and drove to a natural reserve on Henry Lawson Drive. I usually went there when I wanted to be alone. I sat on a bench and read the papers.

Under sensationalised headlines, Diego's murder had made the front pages in the city's papers. There were three articles in the main papers, titled *Deranged kidnapping victim kills brother*, *Tragedy hits the Morales again*, and *Kidnapping Victim Turns Killer*.

I read the papers and thought of Juan Morales. I wondered if his son's murder was a tragedy to him. Or perhaps just a relief. I thought of Kate, too. The papers said she handed herself over to the police, shortly after the murder.

I recalled her dropping the gun back in her handbag and walking very calmly out of her brother's bungalow. She'd even smiled and waved at me. Maybe she *was* deranged.

Solveig had remained very calm, while Remy was screaming hysterically. I'd bolted from the house and Solveig followed me. I'd driven west along Liverpool Road, not knowing where to go.

Neither Solveig nor I had said anything for nearly half an hour. We were both in shock; Solveig probably more than I was.

I had realised in the past half an hour that Remy was gone from my life forever and I had mixed emotions about it. My heart was hurting badly. Nonetheless, I felt a sort of peaceful relief engulfing my spirit. I knew there was no going back from that point.

With Solveig, things were even more definite. *Death is absolute*, I recalled myself telling Marin, at the time when I'd thought Florin was dead.

'Where are you going?' Solveig had finally asked, while we were waiting at the Hume Highway – Woodville Road intersection. Her eyes were misty, but otherwise she looked composed.

I shrugged. 'I don't know. I have nowhere to go.'

We kept silent for more minutes.

'Come to my place. I live alone,' Solveig said, when we were in Warwick Farm – the suburb before Liverpool.

I didn't know what to do. Though somewhat embarrassed to take her offer, I knew it would be for a limited period only. It was just a matter of time before the immigration authorities located me and sent me back to Bucharest.

'Where do you live?' I asked.

'Right here, in Warwick Farm. Turn left on Bigge Street and then left again.'

Later that evening Solveig had made another shocking confession. 'It had to be either Kate or me. Kate was quicker again,' she said.

I told her I didn't understand.

Solveig picked up her handbag, brandished it before my eyes and asked, 'Did you notice Kate's handbag was identical to mine?'

I said I had.

She reached into the handbag and produced a silver pistol. 'The pistols are identical, too. We purchased the pair many years ago, just in case. Neither Kate nor I have ever used the pistols. Then, one day, we both decided it was time. But she was quicker.'

I said I still didn't understand.

She smiled bitterly. 'I'd made my decision in the morning, before you arrived in Glenmore Park. I was determined to shoot Diego dead today.'

We'd talked about trivial things for the rest of the evening and retired in separate rooms. I thought of Solveig and me. We were similar in many ways. We'd both betrayed our best friends for whatever reasons. It was only by accident that we'd both failed. Or perhaps, it'd been divine intervention. By chance, we'd both remained in the clear. But being blameless didn't make either of us any better.

I read the articles telling of Diego's murder and remained on the bench, looking absently around. Then I saw little Robin. Watching the cute, little bird and listening to his tweeting made me smile. *Life is made of little things*, I recalled reading somewhere.

I thought of the other Robin, that I'd met on the farm. Or maybe it was the same Robin. Whether he was the same or not, I knew I was not the same Cornel Toma anymore.

I flicked through the rest of the pages and noticed another piece of interest. It talked about the public forum organised by the Greens Senator Natasha Panait, on the subject of climate change. The meeting, which I'd forgotten about, was taking place that weekend. Though sceptical about the topic, I felt an impulse to see Florin's mother, whom I only vaguely remembered. I hadn't seen Natasha Panait since I was a kid.

In the evening, having had a few drinks, I thought it was fair to tell Solveig what I'd done when I was a guest in Florin's house. I felt an urge to confess to her, just as I had confessed to Rhonda. I knew I was taking a risk, but I couldn't keep it to myself any longer. She had to know who I was, even if she was going to kick me out, as Rhonda had done.

This time, I didn't keep anything out. I told her everything and I told her I did it for the charms of the woman I loved. I only referred to the woman as *she*. There was no doubt Solveig knew very well who *she* was.

She listened calmly, without asking any questions and without interrupting in any way.

After I finished, Solveig remained quiet for a long while. She didn't say she loathed me and she didn't say she understood. She didn't say she was sorry, either.

Later that evening, before I went to bed, she said. 'These are the things men do.'

I nodded and added. 'The things men wouldn't do, if not for the things women do.'

That line though, didn't make me feel any better. I knew very well that blaming my irrational actions on the things women do was just a pathetic excuse.

Solveig looked past me and whispered. 'I'm sorry that Kate killed him. I'm not sorry for him or for Remy. I'm not sorry for me either. I'm sorry for Kate.'

That night, Solveig and I could have become lovers. I felt she'd do it if I made the first move. I also felt she was quite indifferent about it. Perhaps she just needed a distraction.

I wasn't ready for it. Something didn't click. Something wasn't right. We'd both been through a lot recently. Though she put on a brave face, I knew she was hurting inside. And so was I. We both needed time. Time to forget and to heal.

Saturday, 2 July

The public forum took place in the open at Parramatta Stadium, which was nearly full to capacity, more than twenty thousand people. There were several speakers sharing a lot of nonsense, as far as I was concerned.

Ms Panait though, was the only one who succeeded in captivating her audience. She certainly knew what she was talking about and had quite a charismatic approach. I still didn't believe that crap about global warming, but I was impressed by the way she conveyed her ideas.

It was only by sheer determination that I got hold of her after the debate concluded. I made my way to the stand where she was taking questions and giving autographs and I waited patiently for nearly two hours until the last of the fans were dispersing.

I stood there watching the Greens senator, some ten metres away, wanting to introduce myself but not daring to approach her. I feared she might be aware of my attempt on Florin's life.

Dressed casually in a pair of blue jeans and a sports jacket over a white blouse, I thought she'd preserved herself amazingly well.

She was slim, with short, brown hair and an oval pretty face, with brown eyes and a turned-up nose. It was a shame that Florin didn't take after her, I thought.

I moved towards her and stopped just three metres short, unable to find the courage to talk to her. She looked up and spotted me. Well, she certainly wouldn't recognise me, I thought, but I remained speechless when she called my name.

'That's Cornel, isn't it?' she said in Romanian.

I stepped towards her filled with emotion – mixed emotion: fear of being reprimanded and excitement of seeing her after so many years.

'Good afternoon, Ms Panait,' I said, also in Romanian.

She smiled and offered her hand. 'Don't be so formal. Please call me Natasha.'

I shook her hand and kissed it. It was an old Romanian custom, to kiss the hand of a woman; particularly an older woman. It showed attention and respect.

This time she laughed, which made me relax. Considering her warm reception, it was safe to assume she didn't know anything about my recent indiscretions.

'Don't do that,' she protested, though I felt she enjoyed the attention. 'No one does such things these days.'

'How did you know it was me?' I asked.

'I've seen you a couple of times on television, with your boss,' she explained. 'But the real thing looks even better. Gee, what a handsome young man you are.'

I must have blushed, for she added, 'I usually don't compliment males, but with you it's a different story. You're like my own son.'

The son, whom I nearly killed, I said in my mind.

A few folks, part of her entourage, were waiting around, tapping their feet and glancing at us.

'You must be very busy. I won't keep you,' I excused myself, signalling towards those folks.

'No, not at all,' she assured me. 'If you can wait a few minutes, I'll just sort out a few things and then I'd love to have a chat. That's only if you don't have anything better to do.'

I shook my head. 'No, sure … I'd love to.'

The truth was, I was excited to see Florin's mother again, but even more thrilled to meet Senator Natasha Panait.

Twenty minutes later we were strolling out of the stadium together. It was past four o'clock. We walked down O'Connell Street through the Parramatta CBD and ended up at an Irish pub on the Great Western Highway. We chatted, ate fried sausages and drank tap beer.

It was the first time in weeks when I felt relaxed and had a great time. By seven o'clock, full of beer and in a state of euphoria, Ms Panait and I had overcome the etiquette, the history and age barrier between us and become the best of friends.

I still don't know if what happened at the end of the evening had been caused by her kindness, compassion, too much alcohol, or ... something else.

Learning that I didn't have a job, nor a valid visa any longer, Ms Panait, who'd already persuaded me to call her by her first name, offered me, the *obvious solution* to my problem, as she referred to it. Not very original, but still, mind blowing!

'You see ... I am single and, at the moment, unattached. Sometimes, I feel very lonely. You're desperate to find a solution to stay here. Let's form a partnership to help each other. I mean, if we get married, I won't be lonely anymore. And it will solve your visa problem too.'

I was absolutely stunned.

After many deliberations in my mind, I went ahead with it. There were obviously lots of moral obstacles between us, but altogether, I decided that the marriage achieved my ultimate goal. It kept me in the country. I had to put myself first and deal with the consequences later.

On the second-last day of July, a marriage celebrant pronounced

Natasha Panait and Cornel Toma husband and wife, in what was supposed to be a very low-profile ceremony. But, though Natasha's plan had been to keep the marriage a secret, somehow certain sectors of the media became aware of the event. Besides a few reporters and cameramen, only a girlfriend of Natasha and my mate Gabriel attended.

Being a Saturday, Florin couldn't make it, as he had to go to the markets. I thanked him in my mind for that. But otherwise, though I thought I'd never have the guts to face Florin again, now I had no choice. He was … well, he was like a sort of a son to me. And Marin, my daughter-in-law.

A few days after Natasha and I got married, she lined up a project officer job for me, with the Federal Department of Environment. It was a *green job*. The Department actually employed hundred of similar useless bludgers and its official title was about half-a-page long.

'It must sound important and complex,' Natasha had explained, but I wasn't impressed.

To me, all that fuss about the challenges facing us and future generations on the subject of global warming and climate change was a lot of crap.

I had to be honest and tell Natasha of my convictions, I thought. I said my heart was not in that job, because I did not believe in climate change. To me, it was just a monumental lie and an incredible waste of public money.

To my surprise, my new bride replied, 'That's alright – nobody believes in that nonsense anyway.'

'So, why is the subject getting so much attention and publicity?' I asked.

'Because there is easy money in it. The government spends billions on climate change, and when it's free money on offer, there will always be plenty of takers.'

I thought, coming from a *greenie*, it was about the only thing that made perfect sense.

EPILOGUE

Having married an Australian woman, my permanent residence status in the country was no longer an issue. Even so, it was part of the process that I had to get out of the country and wait for the official reply from the Immigration Department in an overseas location.

With all expenses paid by Natasha, I temporarily departed to Fiji. Was I embarrassed, being maintained by a woman? Well, maybe I was, a little bit, but to me, it was déjà vu. Natasha also paid a few grand to that council ranger whom I thumped in Liverpool as an out-of-court settlement.

Miraculously, I was never summoned to the court to face the pending drink driving and speeding charges. Most likely, it was an administrative bungle within the Police Department, which accidentally, put me in the clear with the law.

Before I left for Fiji, I popped in one afternoon at Helen's to pick up my things. Rhonda was there as well. Seeing me, both women were a little nostalgic. In her usual ironic style, Helen confessed she was sorry for not being a little older; otherwise she might have had a chance of becoming Mrs Toma …

As for Rhonda, she seemed puzzled and also a little regretful. I guess she couldn't work out why I'd told her that weird story about my murdering Florin. Strangely enough, Rhonda didn't mention anything about her BMW, which I'd nicked from her garage and used for my private purposes. I'll take it back to her, one day, I said in my mind.

Another day, I also saw Solveig. She'd registered her expression of interest in a number of vacancies at the Sydney's major public hospitals, she said. She'd made a life-changing decision and was determined to start working in her field as a medical practitioner. If she was lucky enough to escape a jail sentence.

Solveig told me that Kate had been released on bail pending her trial. Her lawyers were confident that, considering the circumstances, there was a good chance Kate would escape without a conviction. It meant that all those sordid details of what happened between Diego, Kate and Solveig would become public. Diego's threat of making the media aware of that story had materialised even after his death. I wondered how Doctor Morales would react to that.

According to Solveig, the police hadn't made any progress with catching Kate's kidnappers. Obviously, one of them was actually dead; another was Solveig herself. Alberto fled to Italy and Remy had gone to the Philippines, on an extended vacation.

With Kate refusing to help the police, pretending she'd been mostly sedated and couldn't remember anything, there was a very slim chance the mystery would be unravelled any time soon.

And lastly, with Katarina, my mate Gabriel told me she'd

married the week after I did. Not that she was in love; she'd done it to obtain permanent residence. It sounded familiar.

I left for Fiji in August and came back in October. That same Wednesday when I returned to Australian soil, the Queen Elizabeth the Second of England and Prince Philip, Duke of Edinburgh, landed at the Canberra Airport to start their eleven-day official visit. Her Majesty had never been so close to me before. I mean, in space.

There was a lot of fuss to welcome the royal couple at Canberra Airport, which I watched on television. I also listened to Helen, who was broadcasting live on the radio.

I noted the governor general looked pretty much like royalty herself. But not quite so Julia Lizard, who was also present, together with her consort barber. I actually confused our PM with one of the queen's domestic workers.

'Look, Her Majesty is shaking hands with the PM and they are exchanging pleasantries,' Helen was saying. 'Now, our first bloke is touching the Queen's gloves and the sleeves of her dress with his lips, while the PM lows at the Prince, in an emotional display of profound respect and admiration. Did I say Julia *lows* at the Prince? My apologies – I meant to say she *bows* to the Prince. And listen, it sounds like the first barber is promoting his services to the Queen. *I can do a haircut for you for only twelve dollars this week, if you have a pension card,* he's saying. And look … there is more. *We also have the full Brazilian on special, right to the end of the month,* the barber added. Wow! That's too much for me. It certainly makes my day,' Helen concluded.

I switched the radio off and shook my head, reflecting. I've had, in the past few years, the privilege to mix with some remarkable women. And the misfortune to meet a couple of deadly ones. Somehow, I managed to end up unscathed; but only by chance. Or, by divine intervention. I have to be more careful from now on. You never know with women.